Praise for

Stealing My Heart

I think having a book with a subject matter of stealing and the proceeds from the purchases going toward stopping illegal e-Book downloads is a bit of irony which I find to be immensely entertaining. I would consider this a great purchase just for that reason alone but add sexy man on man love and stories you will enjoy and I can safely say this is one book you will not regret getting! ~ *Coffee Time Romance Reviews*

STEALING MY HEART ANTHOLOGY

STOLEN MEMORIES
CAROL LYNNE

STEALING RAIN
D.J. MANLY AND A.J. LLEWELLYN

HOTWIRED HEART
JAIME SAMMS

THE MAGIC THIEVES
SERENA YATES

STEALING MICHAEL
JAMBREA JO JONES

DRAGON'S EYE
STEPHANI HECHT

Stealing My Heart Anthology
ISBN # 978-0-85715-068-4
Stolen Memories ©Copyright Carol Lynne 2010
Stealing Rain ©Copyright D.J. Manly and A.J. Llewellyn 2010
Hotwired Heart ©Copyright Jaime Samms 2010
The Magic Thieves ©Copyright Serena Yates 2010
Stealing Michael ©Copyright Jambrea Jo Jones 2010
Dragon's Eye ©Copyright Stephani Hecht 2010
Cover Art Natalie Winters ©Copyright 2010
Cover photography Tom Nelson
Cover Model Adam Killian
Interior text design by Claire Siemaszkiewicz
Total-E-Bound Publishing

Foreword:

First of all, we'd like to thank you for your purchase of this anthology. The proceeds will go towards the purchase of advertisement against the illegal downloading of copyrighted materials, specifically, electronic books.

Writing is a craft which demands a great deal from its practitioner. It is often a painstaking effort carried out in solitude.

Authors don't count their hours, like in other kinds of labour, for if we calculated our salary per hour, we'd probably fall into a depression, but even that would never be enough to make us stop writing.

Writers have a compulsion to write. We are artists, like any painter or sculptor, we need to create.

When someone reads a book and enjoys it, they probably don't think much about the process, and they're not supposed to. The best books are those that appear as if they wrote themselves.

But they don't.

There is a living, breathing person behind that book. And that person needs to eat and pay their bills, as unglamorous as that may sound.

Each time someone illegally downloads a copyrighted book, they affect an author's salary. That means the author, readers love to read so much, that author who takes them away from their everyday lives and gives them those moments just to escape, may be struggling financially. Illegal downloading meant that the author's work is being stolen, passed from reader to reader without the author ever seeing a cent of royalties from those downloads.

I've heard all the arguments for illegal downloading; including everything on the internet is there for the taking, and it should be free to use. But that's just not true. The internet is a marketplace. It's the place you can go to purchase what you want. You may have it delivered directly to your doorstep, like something off eBay; or delivered to your personal computer, like a book or a software program. If something is offered for free, it's free. But if something wears a price tag, it means it's for sale, like any book in a physical bookstore. It also means that there are people expecting to receive payment for that book: the publisher who keeps the website where the books are stored, the editor who makes the copy clean, the artist who contributes to the cover, and the author who created the work.

How many times have you passed along a paperback you have purchased? We all do it, without giving it a thought. But there is a difference between lending your novel to your mother, and downloading copies of an eBook for free to post it online so that countless others can download it as well, sometimes thousands of people within days.

Some argue that maybe illegal downloaders can't afford to buy a book, or they represent the ones who wouldn't buy an eBook anyway. I figure if a person has enough money for a computer, and the internet, that person can afford to pay for an eBook. And it's not at all fair to the readers that take money out of their pocket and pay for their books. Should we reward those who steal a book by letting them get away with it, while penalizing those readers who are honest and respect authors? If you knew that you could shoplift in one store and get away with it, would it make sense to shop at the store across the street where you had to pay? If we don't take a stand against illegal downloading of eBooks, there will not be any new books published to download, illegal or otherwise. eBook publishing is a business. It's not a charity.

Electronic books are the future. A great many of us writing in the industry today started writing eBooks when people scoffed at the idea. No one would buy these books! Well, people aren't laughing anymore. Even the major book publishers are now investing in the eBook industry. Big name writers are jumping on the bandwagon. Ebooks are profitable, environmentally responsible, and economical for the reader. And the industry will continue to grow. eBook sales are already surpassing print sales. Laws will become stricter, and eventually illegal downloading will be more difficult to accomplish. It has already started. People have been fined, closed down, and cut off from the internet for copyright theft.

Illegal downloading sites are now scrambling their files, naming them different things, making it difficult for authors to find their books and demand they be taken down. If you need assurance that these people are doing something illegal, their actions to hide their activity speaks volumes.

If you as a reader truly love an author, if you get enjoyment from that author's work, and look forward to the next book, then fight illegal downloading wherever you see it. If a writer isn't making enough money to pay the bills, they will have to take on more unrelated work. That unrelated work takes the writer away from their craft, which means the author you love so much may no longer have enough time to do what you want them to do; write.

I hope you enjoy this anthology. It is a labour of love, and of hope. We hope that readers respect writers enough to keep them writing. Unlike illegal downloaders, we're not asking for anything for free, we're only asking for what we're due.

Thank you.
D.J. Manly (on behalf of Authors Against Copyright Theft)

STOLEN MEMORIES

Carol Lynne

Prologue

"One, two, buckle my shoe. Three, four, better shut the door..." Aden stopped singing as a man dressed all in black stood over him.

"What're you doing on my land?"

Aden swallowed around his fear. His mom had told him hundreds of times to keep to his side of the fence, but like any nine-year-old, Aden hadn't listened. He wanted to know why he never saw his mysterious neighbour enjoying the garden during the daytime. He'd seen Victor DePasse wandering around at night from his bedroom window several times.

"They buried my mom," was all Aden could think to say.

A sad expression crossed the big man's handsome face. "I know. I'm sorry." Aden nodded. He felt the tears burn his eyes as he tried to hold them back. "They're taking me away in the morning, but I don't want to go."

"Who's taking you away?"

"My uncle and his wife. They said they're going to sell my grandfather's house, so I have to go with them." Aden wiped his eyes. "I don't like them very much."

Victor knelt and pulled Aden into his arms. Aden went rigid. He wasn't used to people hugging him. His mom had been sick for too many years to do more than lay in bed.

Tucked against the man's chest, Aden felt safe for the first time in years. "Can I ask you something?"

"Yes," Victor answered.

"How come you don't enjoy your garden during the day? The flowers are so pretty, but you can't really see them in the dark."

Victor chuckled. "I'm allergic to the sun."

Aden's jaw dropped as he stepped back to look into the man's black eyes. "I've never heard of someone being allergic to the sun."

"It's rare, but it happens."

He felt the strangest urge to soothe the kind man. "I'm sorry," Aden whispered. He placed his small hands on either side of Victor's face and kissed his nose. "That's what grandpa used to do when I felt sad. 'Course that was before he died."

Victor grinned. "You've lost a lot of people you love, haven't you?"

Aden nodded. "I guess it's better not to let people get close, huh?"

Victor sighed and glanced away. "It's the reason I'm alone."

"You've lost people?" Aden asked.

"Too many people."

"If I didn't have to move away, I'd be your friend."

Victor ruffled Aden's hair. "We can still be friends."

Aden shook his head. "I have to move to Phoenix. There's too much sunlight there for you."

Chuckling, Victor stood and looked towards Aden's house. "What if I buy your grandfather's house? Then when you're ready, you can come back to claim it."

Aden tried to figure out how old he'd have to be before he could buy a house. "I'd have to finish high school first."

"Yes, and go to college."

Aden bit his lip. "Gosh, that's a long time away. I'm only in the fourth grade."

"Doesn't matter. When you're ready to come home, the house will be waiting."

Aden heard his uncle calling his name. "Oh, shoot. I'm in trouble now."

Victor bent over and placed a kiss on top of Aden's head. "You'd better go before he finds out you're over here. I know they've told you to stay away from me."

Aden shook his head. With the innocence of a single childhood meeting on his side, he smiled up at Victor. "It's because they don't know you like I do."

"If only you really did know me," Victor said in a wistful tone as Aden ran back through the small break in the fence.

Chapter One

Aden Brousseau stared at the laptop screen in front of him. *Why would he do it?* Aden couldn't take his eyes off Josh's screen name, *writersmaster3*. How many times had he complained about someone pirating his books? He lifted his glasses to his forehead and scrubbed at his tired eyes.

The one person in the world who supposedly loved him had sabotaged his livelihood. Why?

The front door opened, and Aden closed his laptop. "The pirates are at it again," he announced, resettling his glasses.

Josh tossed his keys onto the table and tore off his tie. "Not tonight, Aden. I'm too damn tired to listen to this shit. I've told you a million times you were wasting your time. I'm more than capable of supporting you."

"I like making my own money. Sure, it's not much, but at least I contribute what I can."

Josh groaned and crossed the room to the bar. "Did you make dinner?"

"No. I was working."

Josh slammed the heavy bottle of Scotch onto the bar after pouring half a highball glass full of the shit. Aden hated it when Josh drank, and his lover knew it.

"This little hobby of yours is getting out of hand. It's time to stop."

"No." Aden set his laptop on the coffee table and stood to face his lover.

Josh took a big gulp of his drink and turned around. "What did you say?"

"I said no. I'm sorry about dinner, but I won't quit writing just because it's not on the table."

Josh turned back around and continued with his drink. Aden could tell by the rigid set of his partner's spine he was in for a long night. Josh would continue to drink until he was drunk, at which time he'd begin taking it out on Aden.

He shrugged off the uneasy feeling. Getting the shit beat out of him was nothing new. How many times had he believed the promises? If he'd had anywhere else to go, he would've been gone a long time ago.

"I finally hacked into that torrent site I've been working on," he informed Josh.

Josh said nothing but refilled his glass.

"Guess who's uploading my books for every Tom, Dick and Harry to steal?"

When Josh still didn't acknowledge him, Aden continued to push. If he was going to get hit, he'd rather Josh did it while he was still sober. "You fucker! Why'd you do it?"

Josh whirled around and threw the heavy crystal glass at Aden, hitting him in the forehead. Aden blinked several times as he slid to the floor.

* * * *

Aden opened his eyes, surprised to find himself in a heavily draped four poster bed. He sat up, wincing as pain exploded in his head.

"Take it easy," a deep voice soothed.

Aden tried to adjust his eyes to the darkened room. "Where am I?"

"You've been hurt. I brought you here to keep you safe."

"My laptop!" Aden shouted. He may not know where the hell he was but, as a writer, it didn't matter as long as his laptop was safe.

"Relax. It's on the dresser," the man replied.

There was something familiar about the man's voice, but Aden still couldn't see his face. "Do I know you?"

A wistful sigh escaped the man. "You used to. We met when you were just a boy, before your uncle took you away."

"Victor?" he gasped. How many times had he thought of the mysterious neighbour? The man had played the part of lover in so many of his dreams, Aden had convinced himself that's all he'd ever been, a dream.

A dim light beside the bed was switched on and the man of his fantasies came into view. "So you do remember."

Aden tried to nod, but the pain stopped him. "I thought I'd imagined you." He lifted his hand to the thick gauze bandage on his forehead. "How did I get here?"

"The details don't matter. The important thing is that I got you away from the monster you were living with." Using the gentlest of touches, Victor removed Aden's hand from the bandage.

Aden slumped back to the mattress, feeling dizzy. He didn't understand what was happening. The last thing he remembered was fighting with Josh. "He threw a glass at me," Aden mumbled.

"Yes."

"It must've knocked me out."

"Yes."

Aden's mind was trying like hell to connect the dots. "Did someone call you?"

Victor didn't answer right away. "In a manner of speaking, yes."

"So where am I?"

"In my home," Victor replied.

"I'm sorry, but I don't know where that is. I had an accident when I was younger and most of my memories were lost."

"North of Baton Rouge."

Aden's jaw dropped. How was it possible that he'd blacked out in Houston, only to wake in Baton Rouge? "How long have I been out?"

Victor sat on the edge of the bed and carefully brushed Aden's shaggy blond hair back from his face. "I gave you something to sleep. You've been here for almost twenty-four hours."

Aden brought his hand up and pinched the bridge of his nose. He didn't understand what was happening. He should be freaking out at the prospect of a near-stranger drugging him. *So why do I feel safe instead of scared?*

"Sleep," Victor soothed, running his hand down to cup Aden's cheek. "There will be time for questions later."

"Will you be here when I wake up?"

Victor glanced over his shoulder at the window. "I sleep during the day, but I'll stay with you until the sun begins to rise."

A memory from his childhood popped into his head. "There's something about the sun." Aden bit his bottom lip, trying to pull the memory from the depths of his brain. "What is it about the sun that you don't like?"

"I'm allergic to the sun. It's the reason I sleep during the day."

Aden smiled and covered Victor's hand with his own. It was such a simple thing to remember, but he felt he'd made great strides. "Do you have any aspirin?"

Victor nodded and reached towards the bedside table. He held out a glass and two tablets.

"I usually take three," Aden said as he sat up to pop the pills into his mouth.

"You're far too small for three. It's not good for you," Victor admonished.

As Aden washed the pills down with a gulp of water, he glanced down at himself. He knew he was considered small for a man at only five-six, but no matter how hard he tried, he couldn't seem to gain weight. He wondered what Victor thought of him. *Does he think I'm a wimp for letting Josh beat on me?*

"No," Victor said, cutting into his thoughts. "I think you were confused and lonely. That's my fault. I should have come to you before. I'm sorry."

Aden stared into the black eyes of his rescuer. "How did you…"

Victor cut him off with a gentle kiss. Aden opened for the tongue he so desperately needed, but Victor pulled back.

"That is precisely the reason I didn't come to you before."

Aden suddenly felt like a fool. "I'm sorry. I guess someone like you wouldn't go for a geek like me."

Victor shook his head and ran his hand down Aden's chest, to skim across his nipples. "Never doubt that you're desirable, my young friend."

The touch to his pebbled nubs had Aden's cock hard almost instantly. The man he'd spent years dreaming about was actually touching him, and he wanted more. He reached out and trapped Victor's hand against his chest.

"Why don't you want me?" he asked.

Victor pulled his hand out from under Aden's. "Because I'm not the man you think I am."

Without another word, Victor stood and walked to a chair in the corner of the room. "Sleep. I'll watch over you as long as I can."

Hurt and confused, Aden rolled to his side to hide his tears from Victor. As he silently cried himself to sleep, he tried to remember his mother's words spoken so long ago. There was something about Victor that he needed to remember.

* * * *

Victor gripped the arms of the chair. It took everything in him not to go to Aden. How many years had he visited the man in his dreams? It was one of the gifts that came with being immortal.

The mistake he'd made years earlier played on his mind. What would Aden think if he knew Victor had erased portions of his past memories?

Soon he heard the soft snore that signalled the man was asleep. Victor rose, and slipped out to the balcony. He took a deep breath and lifted his face to the moon. "Grant me power to survive another day."

When he opened his eyes, he was in a familiar location, outside *Grandy's Bar* in New Orleans. He pushed open the door to the usual lot of lonely men. Grandy's had become one of his favourite feeding spots, and the bartender was one of his kind. The men didn't want more than a quick fuck in the back room, and they seemed to welcome his bite when the time was right.

Usually, Victor was fairly picky about the men he fed on, but he was in a hurry to get back to Aden. He grabbed the hand of a man sitting at the bar and started to lead him towards the back.

Victor wasn't at all surprised when the man didn't offer a protest. He hadn't roamed the earth for five hundred and sixty-seven years and not figured out he was hot.

As soon as they reached the darkened room, Victor found an available space, and turned the man to face the wall. He ran his hands down the man's torso to knead his cock. There were times he wished he could bypass the seduction and get right to what he needed, but he knew it would raise too many suspicions.

However, when he lowered his jeans enough to pull out his cock, he found the normally rigid shaft had no interest in the man. *Shit.* The thought of Aden asleep in a warm bed waiting for him, helped a little, but not enough.

Victor gave an inner shrug and wrapped his hand around the donor's erection. Perhaps giving the man pleasure while taking what he needed would be enough.

Once the man started thrusting into his fist, Victor leaned against him and bit into his neck. The blood that pumped from the drunk's artery was filling, but not what he wanted. He shook off the thought and fed until the man bucked several times and covered Victor's hand with warmth.

He quickly licked the bite to seal the wound and backed away. For the first time in hundreds of years, he was disgusted by the act of feeding. As he wiped his mouth and walked away, he couldn't help thinking he was somehow cheating on Aden.

Preposterous!

With a nod to the bartender, Victor strode out of the club. He found a dark corner and closed his eyes once again. "Thank you for feeding me another night," he whispered.

When he opened his eyes, he was back on Aden's balcony. The faint smell of the bar and the donor clung to him. He stripped where he stood and tossed the offending garments over the rail to the green grass below, knowing his staff would take care of them.

Entering Aden's room, he was surprised to see his charge staring straight at him.

"You're awake."

Aden nodded and turned on the lamp. The soft glow washed Victor's nude body in a soft amber light.

"Where'd you go?" Aden asked.

Shit. "I was enjoying the garden from the balcony."

Aden sucked his bottom lip into his mouth as his eyes seemed to devour Victor's nudity. "Naked?"

Victor felt his cock begin to fill at the apparent interest Aden paid it. It was too soon to tell Aden the truth, but he knew he needed to come up with a plausible excuse for his missing clothing.

He sat on the edge of the mattress. "I enjoy the night air on my body."

Aden's gaze raked Victor's groin like a physical touch. "I bet the air is pretty happy about that. I know I'd be."

With his cock hard and beginning to drip, Victor groaned. "You shouldn't say things like that. You barely know me."

Aden surprised him by flipping back the covers to expose his own body, and although much thinner than Victor's cock, Aden's shaft was just as hard. "That's the thing I can't stop thinking about. Why do you seem so familiar to me? Even your body is the exact replica of the man in my dreams."

Victor was shocked. Aden wasn't supposed to remember the many nights he'd visited him in his subconscious. He needed to speak to Dante. "I have some business I need to attend to before the sun rises. Will you be okay if I leave you? In the morning, one of the staff will bring you clothes. Feel free to roam about the estate while I rest."

"Why do I make you uncomfortable?" Aden asked, covering his nude body.

He'd already told Aden too many lies for one evening. "Because I want you, but I know it isn't time."

Aden blinked, his eyebrows drawing together. "Is it because of Josh?"

The hurt and shame in Aden's expression drew Victor towards him. He cupped the side of Aden's bruised face and shook his head, "Nothing you've ever done would be enough to keep me away from you. It's me."

"You? But you saved me."

Victor bent and kissed the ruby lips of the younger man. If only he could tell him the truth of what he'd done.

When Aden's mouth opened for him, Victor delved inside. Aden's thin arm wrapped around Victor's neck and pulled him closer as his other hand began to fondle Victor's balls.

A soft growl emitted from his throat as the force of their erotic tongue duel caused Aden's lip to split. The wash of Aden's sweet blood on his tongue threatened every ounce of Victor's control. He quickly laved the small nick and pulled away.

"I can't do this. Not yet." He removed Aden's hand from his cock and kissed the palm before settling it on the slender man's stomach.

"When?" Aden asked.

Victor stared down at the gorgeous blond. "Soon, I hope. I wasn't yet prepared to bring you here. If your lover hadn't injured you, and I hadn't finally heard your cry for help…"

"I didn't love him," Aden cut in.

"I know."

"You never told me how you rescued me, or how you knew I needed help."

"Later. First I must attend to my business. There will be plenty of time to talk."

Victor left the room before he confessed his past sins. He needed his best friend's advice. "Dante!" he yelled as he entered his chamber.

"Well, well, well," Dante's smooth voice said from behind him.

Victor quickly grabbed a robe and put it on. "I need your help."

"I can see that. Who's left my friend hard and wanting?"

Victor waved off Dante's one-track mind. "Aden's here."

Dante's brows shot up. "Seriously? Do I get to see him?"

"Not yet. It'll be a while before he's ready for the likes of you, my friend."

With his black curls falling rakishly in his eyes, Dante dramatically fell into a chair, legs sprawled. "You wound me," he said, clutching his chest.

Victor rolled his eyes. He didn't have the time or patience for his friend's theatrics. "I want him."

Dante nodded. "That's been obvious for several years. Tell me something new."

"I can't take him until he knows the truth about what I am and what I've done."

Dante shook his head. "Not wise."

"I can't continue to lie to him," Victor tried to argue.

Dante shrugged. "So tell him."

Victor began to pace around the room. How did you tell someone you killed their last remaining relatives and then wiped the memory from their mind? Maybe if he stuck with the number one problem at hand. "I guess I could tell him I'm a vampire. Perhaps that would be enough for now."

Dante sighed and got to his feet. "It's not that big of a deal, Victor. Vampire rumours have been circulating for decades."

Victor nodded. "Okay. I think I can do that."

Dante laughed as he pulled Victor into his arms. "You're so cute this way."

"What way?"

"Nervous. I've never seen the big bad Victor DePasse nervous about anything." Dante gave him a quick kiss. "You really do love him."

Victor opened his mouth to deny his friend's statement, but couldn't. Somewhere along the way, Victor's feelings had changed from protectiveness to love, and he knew it.

Chapter Two

Aden woke with a pounding headache. He reached to the bedside table and shook three pain relievers from the bottle. Remembering Victor's admonishment from the previous evening, he put one back and popped the other two in his mouth. After washing them down with a gulp of water, he sunk back into his pillow.

As he stared up at the canopy, he began to wonder what Victor had done to Josh. Was Josh even there when Victor came? No matter how hard he tried, Aden couldn't bring himself to care what had happened to his ex-lover.

Once his headache eased, Aden sat up slowly and waited for the dizziness to pass. At least some of his memories had started to return. Not the missing years after his mother's death, but the time spent living next door to Victor. His stomach began to growl like crazy, but he needed to shower and find something to wear first.

He entered the bathroom and turned on the water before looking at himself in the mirror. With a wince, he peeled back the tape holding the piece of gauze in place. To say he was surprised at the nasty-looking cut would be an understatement. It was one more thing to worry about. He re-secured the tape and stepped into the shower, adjusting the spray nozzle.

As he washed his hair, he paid particular attention to the failing bandage. He would have to find a way to ask Victor about his wound when he awoke.

After drying off, Aden wrapped the towel around his waist and entered the bedroom. He was surprised to see not only the bed made, but a change of clothes laid out for him.

He grinned as he picked up a pair of underwear. Aden couldn't remember the last time someone actually bought his underwear for him. He had to give Victor props though because they were the brand and style he usually wore, but the material was a lot different from his customary white cotton.

The low-rise underwear fit like a glove. Aden chuckled as he looked at himself in the floor-length mirror. "Talk about false advertising," he mumbled. The transparent fabric made his cock appear much bigger than it really was and his ass looked absolutely amazing.

Shaking his head, he turned away from the mirror and picked up the jeans. Now those were nothing like his normal, comfortable pants. "I don't know about this, Victor."

He pulled on the skinny low-rise jeans and zipped the fly. A quick glance at himself had his jaw dropping. *Fuck. I look like I weigh all of about a hundred pounds. Tinkerbell could kick my ass.*

Josh used to nag him incessantly about his poor eating habits. He was always trying to get Aden to drink those nasty protein shakes. Aden had always refused, but looking at his reflection, he began to reconsider.

The tight, white V-neck T-shirt didn't help any, and Aden went in search of food. From the looks of him, he needed a lot of it.

As soon as he stepped out into the hall, a tall man appeared. Aden's hand went to his chest. "Shit. You scared me."

"Sorry, sir. Master DePasse asked me to make sure you could find your way around when you were ready."

"Thank you…"

"Benton, sir." The man gave a slight bow.

"Thank you, Benton. Can you show me the way to the kitchen so I can whip up something to eat?"

"Your breakfast has already been started, sir. I informed the new cook as soon as I heard the shower."

"Please call me Aden." As he started to follow Benton, he began to wonder. "You said new cook?"

"Yes. Emmanuel just arrived."

"Arrived from where?" he asked, holding his head as he made his way down the sweeping staircase.

"I wouldn't know, sir. Master DePasse must have summoned him before retiring for the day."

Aden decided not to make an issue of the 'sir' thing. Evidently, Benton was one of those fancy butlers like Aden had seen on television. He wondered if finding a cook was the business Victor said he needed to take care of.

"It really wasn't necessary. I'm actually a pretty good cook."

Instead of leading Aden into the kitchen, Benton showed him to the formal dining room. "I'll inform Emmanuel that you're ready for your breakfast."

Aden shifted from foot to foot. "I can eat in the kitchen. Seems like a waste to sit in here by myself."

Benton managed a slight grin. "This room hasn't been used in…years. Indulge me. Please."

Aden shrugged and took a seat. "Do you know if there's coffee?"

"Yes, sir. Emmanuel brought all of your favourite foods with him."

Aden chuckled. "Why am I not surprised."

* * * *

At twilight, Victor went in search of Aden. He took the stairs two at a time and went straight out to the garden. The closer he got to his love, the heavier the feeling in his heart.

He found Aden sitting on a stone bench gazing across the expansive lawn towards his old house. *Aahhh, so that's what has you so down.*

"I knew I'd find you out here," he greeted, taking a seat beside Aden.

"I remember that house," Aden mumbled without looking away from it.

"As well you should. You spent the first ten years of your life there."

Aden said nothing for several moments.

"Would you like to go over?" Victor asked.

For the first time since Victor had sat down, Aden looked at him. "So you did buy it?"

Victor nodded. "I told you I would."

"I thought maybe it was part of my dream." Aden glanced back at the house. "I don't think I'm ready yet, but someday."

Victor nodded in understanding. He knew the house held memories of the young man's mother and grandfather. It made him feel even guiltier for his past actions.

"Did you have a nice rest?" Aden asked, bringing Victor out of his despair.

"Yes. Thank you. Did you find something to keep you busy while I slept?"

Aden shrugged. "I slept most of the day. I knew you'd be up, and decided to try to get on your schedule, figured it'd be easier in the long run."

The long run? The simple statement improved Victor's mood immediately. Perhaps he wasn't the only one who felt something. "I need to talk to you about my schedule."

Victor turned to face Aden, straddling the bench. "There are things about me…"

"You're a vampire," Aden cut in.

To say Victor was shocked would be an understatement. "How do you know that?"

Aden shrugged. "I think I've always known. I heard my mom whispering to my grandfather when I was little. I pretended I hadn't heard. She must've told me at least once a day to stay to my own side of the fence."

Aden's chin lowered and Victor watched as a single tear dropped onto his shirt. "That's why I came over that night. I knew I was going away…"

Aden's head sprang up and he gazed into Victor's eyes. "That's the last thing I remember until I woke up in the hospital when I was a teenager. The doctors told me it was possible my memories could come back, but so far they haven't. Do you know what happened to me?" Victor's throat seized with the need to tell Aden the truth. He reached out and pulled Aden into his lap, holding the man possibly for the last time.

"Victor?" Aden asked, his face buried against Victor's neck.

"I erased your memories from that time," he finally confessed. "Please don't ask me why. Maybe someday I'll be able to explain it, but I'm not ready to give you up yet."

Aden pulled back. "Did you do it to hurt me?"

Victor shook his head. "No. I'd never do anything to hurt you."

Aden seemed to study Victor for several moments before nodding. "I can wait."

Victor felt like a huge weight had been lifted from his shoulders. He may not have told Aden the full story, but he'd confessed as much as he could at the moment. As he began to nuzzle the soft skin below Aden's ear, a thought occurred to him.

"Why aren't you afraid of me?"

Aden adjusted himself to straddle Victor's lap, his legs dangling from the end of the bench. "I don't know. You were nice to me that night a long time ago. I guess you've never given me a reason to be afraid."

Aden licked his way up Victor's throat to his lips. "Are you going to suck my blood?"

Victor was at a loss. He knew the subject would come up, but he wasn't expecting it so soon. "No."

Aden began to pepper kisses along Victor's face. "But you need it to live, right? So, do you get it from the people who work here?"

"No. From others I meet." Victor couldn't help running his hands down Aden's lithe body to cup his ass.

Aden pulled back and narrowed his eyes. "Other men?"

Victor glanced away and nodded. "I've little choice in the matter. The only way to feed unnoticed, is by giving the donor pleasure."

Aden tilted his head, exposing his neck. "Feed from me."

Victor couldn't help but to lick his lips at the temptation in front of him. He even went as far as to lean down and smell the soft skin. "I can't."

Aden's back stiffened. "Why? I'm not good enough?"

Given Aden's history, the question didn't surprise Victor. "Because I'm not allowed."

Victor watched the conflicting emotions cross Aden's face before the man he loved finally spoke. "Why?"

Victor closed his eyes. "You continue to ask questions that I'm not prepared to answer."

Aden put his hands on his hips. "And I've already told you I can wait on most of them. But I think I have a right to know why you need to go fuck other men in order to feed, but aren't *allowed* to feed from me."

Victor felt an unseen hand land on his shoulder. *May I tell him?*

"*It is time,*" Valerianus' voice sounded in Victor's head.

Victor refocused on Aden. "Did your mother or grandfather ever mention your father?"

Aden visibly shuddered. "Please don't tell me you're my father."

Victor chuckled and shook his head. "I don't have that kind of power. Vampires, as a rule, aren't given viable sperm."

"As a rule? What're you saying? Do you know who my father is?"

Victor nodded. "He is the Creator."

Aden's jaw dropped. "God?"

"No. Just as man was created in God's image, vampires were created in Valerianus' image."

"I'm a vampire?" Aden asked, a chuckle in his voice.

Victor shook his head. "You are so much more than a mere vampire. You are the son of a god."

Aden doubled over with laughter. "Yeah, like I'm going to believe that."

"I'm sorry, but it's true."

Aden held his arms out to the side. "Look at me. Do I look like a fucking god?"

Victor bit back his affirmative response.

Sobering, Aden blew out a breath and ran his fingers through his shaggy blond hair. "Why don't I have powers? And why would my father allow Josh to do all those things to me?"

Finally a question he didn't have the answers for. "I don't know. You'll have to ask him. Your grandfather was gifted the estate so that I could watch over you."

"Well you did a bang up job." Aden spun around and started walking towards the house. He suddenly stopped and turned back. "Why didn't my father protect my mother?"

"She wasn't a vampire. He had no powers that could save her."

"Did he love her?"

Victor could tell by the wistful sound of his love's voice he needed to believe Valerianus did. Victor knew it was more of a business arrangement than a love affair, but he wouldn't be the one to break Aden's heart. "You'll have to ask him. I'm not allowed to discuss Valerianus' business unless given permission."

Aden stomped over to stand toe to toe with Victor. "Will you take me to him?"

"I cannot. When he's ready to answer your questions, he'll summon you." Victor tried to wrap his arms around Aden, but the smaller man pulled away.

"I need to think." Aden turned and walked away.

"So that's the big bad secret you've been holding," Dante said, stepping out of the shadows.

"Not now," Victor growled.

"He's hot, I'll give you that, but why would you put yourself in the position to piss off Valerianus? I mean, it's not like he's known for having a loving heart."

Victor's gaze went to the second floor window. "You can't always predict who you're going to fall in love with."

Dante sighed and shook his head. "So instead you'll spend the rest of your life loving one man while fucking a host of others. Sounds like a recipe for disaster if you ask me."

"Well I didn't ask you," Victor barked. He knew his feeding requirements were going to be a problem. The last thing he needed was Dante pointing out the obvious. He loved his old friend, but Dante had never come close to falling in love.

An idea suddenly hit him. "Will you do me a favour?"

Dante shrugged. "You've been nothing but snappy, why should I?"

"Because we've been friends for over four hundred years?"

"Yeah, there is that," Dante replied with a grin. "What do you need?"

"To feed."

Laughing, Dante's hands moved up to cover his neck. "Pick something else."

"Not from you, you crusty old bastard. I thought maybe you could fuck them, and I could suck them."

Dante grinned and lowered his hands to cup his balls. "You need my dick in other words?"

"Precisely." Victor knew fucking two men in one night wouldn't be an issue for his friend, hell, Dante usually did at least that many in a night anyway.

"We'd better get going then. I'm not as young as I used to be."

Victor thought of Aden. "Let me run up and talk to him for a few moments first, okay?"

"In the name of Valerianus, please don't ever let me fall in love." Dante made a shooing motion with his hands. "Go take care of your man."

"Thanks," Victor replied. He walked over to stand below the balcony and jumped, landing solidly outside the open door.

"Aden? May I speak with you?" he asked.

"Shit. Don't sneak up on me like that," Aden yelled. He heard the young man blow his nose before he answered. "Come in."

Victor stepped into the room. He wanted to pull the smaller man into his arms, but from Aden's body language, he knew it wouldn't be welcomed.

"I think I've figured out a way to feed without the fucking."

Aden shook his head. "I don't care."

The reply felt like a slap across the face. "Very well," he said with a bow as he turned to leave.

As he readied himself to jump from the balcony, he heard Aden call his name. Victor glanced over his shoulder.

"I'm sorry," Aden said, wrapping his arms around Victor's waist. "I do care. I'm just confused."

Victor turned in Aden's arms and embraced his love. "I don't want to do anything to hurt you, but I have to feed. Without it, I'll begin to look my age."

Aden's dark green eyes stared up at him. "How old are you?"

Victor grinned. "Five hundred and sixty-seven, but I have a creation day next month."

"Creation day? Does that mean the day you were turned into a vampire?"

Victor silently cursed Hollywood. "No. Vampires were never human. I was born this way."

"So you had a mother?"

Victor shrugged. "Of sorts. I was birthed by a female vampire." He didn't know how to explain the complexities of his species. "Valerianus has a selection of females that he uses, but not often. I think our numbers are kept low so as not to draw attention."

Aden's eyes rounded. "Valerianus is your father, too? So we're like…brothers?"

Victor smiled and leant down to place a soft kiss on Aden's forehead. "Only in the way that all humans are related to their God."

"So why me? Why did Valerianus choose to have me with a mortal woman?"

"I don't know, love."

Aden buried his face against Victor's chest. "So tell me how you're going to feed without fucking."

"My best friend, Dante, is going to administer the pleasure as I take what I need from the donor."

"I bet you probably think I'm pretty lame for being jealous, huh?"

Victor ran his hands down Aden's back to cup his ass. "No more than I would be if our positions were reversed. The thought of you bedding another man..."

He shook his head to dispel the vision of someone other than himself fucking Aden. "May I come to you upon my return?"

Aden ran his hands over Victor's chest, rubbing at the hardening nipples. "Will you finally give me what I begged for earlier?"

The way Victor's cock was filling with blood, he started to wonder whether he needed to feed at all. "And more."

He covered Aden's mouth and swept his tongue throughout the interior. When Aden began to suck on his tongue, Victor moaned and picked his soon-to-be lover off the ground.

Aden's legs wrapped around Victor's waist as their kiss became a carnal experience unlike anything he'd ever experienced. "Need you," Victor groaned, wishing away their clothing.

Aden glanced down at his nudity and whistled. "That's a useful tool."

Spreading Aden's cheeks, Victor rubbed the crown of his cock over Aden's puckered hole. "So's this one. Ready to find out just how useful it can be?"

"Do we need stuff?" Aden asked, grinding his cock against Victor.

Victor shook his head, using the pre-cum dripping down the length of his cock to lube Aden's hole. After a few swirls of his own brand of magical lube, Aden was ready to receive his dick.

"Tell me if I hurt you." Victor removed his fingers and slowly began to feed his cock into Aden's hungry ass.

The walls of Aden's ass gripped Victor's cock like none other before. It was if Aden's body was created to house Victor's cock. He wondered briefly why he'd been the one chosen to watch over the small man. Was it one of Valerianus' sick jokes?

Aden moaned as Victor ground his way in to the hilt. He gazed into the younger man's eyes and smiled. The emotion in Aden's eyes was plain to see. It seemed Victor wasn't the only one feeling the strong connection between them.

He held onto Aden's ass as he began to pump in and out of his lover's heated hole. Aden's hands gripped Victor's shoulders as he began to move. Victor chuckled. "Am I not going fast enough?"

Aden's cheeks pinked. "Sorry."

Knowing his own strength was far superior, Victor picked up his pace, lifting Aden up and down on his cock. "Better?"

Aden moaned, his back bowing. Victor had never seen a more beautiful sight than Aden in the throes of ecstasy. He tried to imagine his lover spread out in his bed of black and red satin. Victor knew it was a cliché, but he also knew how sexy it felt to slide around naked on satin.

Without warning, warmth splashed across Victor's stomach as Aden cried out his release. The incredible squeeze of Aden's body on his cock, combined with the red flush working its way up Aden's torso sent Victor's own lust spiralling out of control. He slammed in as deep as he could and filled his lover with his seed.

He continued to manipulate the tight ass cradled in his hands until he felt the undeniable itch of his lengthening incisors.

Victor pulled away, his control threatened. "I need to go," he whispered.

Aden's eyes rounded as the physical change in Victor's appearance. He nodded as he reached out to touch one of Victor's fangs. The razor sharp point sliced through the pad of Aden's index finger before Victor could warn him.

Aden pulled his finger back and stared at the blood. With a wicked gleam in his eyes, he held the injured area to Victor's closed lips. As the crimson nectar began to run down Aden's finger, Victor's mouth watered.

He warred with himself for several moments before lapping at the dark rivulets pooling at the base. Aden moaned and pushed his index finger into Victor's mouth. The taste of Aden's blood exploded on Victor's tongue as he suckled the sweet liquid. It was unlike anything he'd ever tasted.

After a few swallows, he allowed his fangs to drop once more and sealed the cut with another swipe of his tongue.

"You know that'll probably get me into trouble." He grinned as the last of Aden's blood clung to his taste buds. "But it was worth it."

Aden shook his head. "You didn't bite me. I'll protect you," Aden said before puffing up his chest and flexing his arms.

"Although the show was hotter than fuck, I'm getting antsy down here," Dante called from the garden. "So unless you're going to invite me up…"

Aden peered over Victor's shoulder. "Who's that?"

"Dante." He knew the lure of Dante's good looks, and gave Aden's ass a squeeze when he stared too long. "Don't get any ideas. You're mine, and Dante's quite happy being single."

"At least you shouldn't have trouble finding someone to feed on. I bet that guy never gets turned down."

"And you think I do?"

Aden brushed Victor's long black hair over his shoulders and kissed him. "No," he answered in a solemn tone. "That's what worries me the most."

Victor brushed a kiss across Aden's lips. "For the first time in my life I'm in love. Even an old man like me isn't stupid enough to risk that."

"You've never been in love?"

Victor shook his head. "I spent years worrying about it. Wondering if Valerianus had forgotten to give me a soul, but then I found you."

Aden's dark blond brows drew together. "When did you fall in love with me? When I was a kid?"

"No!" He thought about the tortuous years he'd been forced to go without protecting Aden, until he'd found a way. "I learned to come to you in your dreams."

Aden's green eyes rounded. "For real? You mean all those times…"

Victor cut Aden off with a quick kiss. "Shhhh, it's our secret."

Aden nodded. "Got it. So no telling Daddy Dearest."

Victor chuckled at the thought of Valerianus being referred to in such a way. He would love to see the look on the Creator's face when he had his first meeting with Aden.

"Are you coming or not!" Dante yelled.

Victor rolled his eyes. "I'd better go, but I'll be back as soon as I can."

"Be safe," Aden said, untangling himself from Victor's waist.

"I will be. I've got something to look forward to when I get home."

Chapter Three

Victor was surprised to find himself standing outside an Art Deco apartment building in Miami. "Miami? Seriously?"

Dante shrugged. "I've got a regular guy here. I thought it'd be the fastest way to get you back to your man."

Victor reached out and grabbed Dante's forearm before he could go any further. "You have a guy?"

Dante gave Victor's hand a swat before smoothing the wrinkles from the sleeve of his white silk shirt. "Not *my* guy. *A* guy."

"Does he *know* about you?" Victor emphasised the word. Why hadn't he ever heard of this man? He wondered what else his friend had been keeping from him.

Dante grinned. "Yeah. He caught me in the act once, and has been reaming my ass ever since."

Although not nearly as big as Victor, Dante had never been a bottom as far as he knew. "This a new development?"

"What? Letting Saul fuck me?" Dante shrugged. "He's good."

Victor shook his head and gestured to the front door. "After you."

By the time they arrived on the third floor, Victor's nerves were kicking in. He hoped he could get through the feeding without being tempted to join his one-time lover and Saul.

Dante knocked on the door. After a few short moments, the door swung open and Victor almost swallowed his tongue. The man was not only huge, but wore an unbuttoned cops' uniform shirt. The display of muscles was quite impressive, as was the dark bronzed skin covered in short black hair.

"Papi!" Dante cried and launched himself into Saul's strong arms.

With his arms full of horny Dante, Saul gestured Victor in with a nod. Victor shut the door and leaned against it as the two men rubbed and kissed. *This should go quicker than I'd hoped.*

Dante finally came up for air and turned towards Victor. "Papi, this is my best friend, Victor. Victor, Saul."

Saul released Dante's ass and held out his hand. After a quick shake, the hand was right back squeezing and rubbing on Dante. "You bring someone else for us to play with?"

Dante licked a path down Saul's neck before shaking his head. "Victor finds himself in love and unable to feed without betraying his partner. I was wondering if you'd let him bite you if I promised to let you fuck my brains out?"

Saul's deep voice vibrated Victor's chest as he chuckled. "We both know I'm gonna be fucking that sweet ass of yours regardless of what I say, right?"

Dante giggled and nodded. Victor was struck dumb. In four hundred plus years, he'd never heard anything come out of Dante's mouth that remotely sounded like a giggle.

Dante pushed the shirt off Saul's muscled shoulders before leaning in to take a swipe of the man's nipple. Saul threaded his fingers through Dante's black curls and held him in place until Dante took the hint and attached his mouth to the pebbled nub.

Crap. Foreplay. Victor glanced at his watch as Saul began to unfasten Dante's jeans. Once loosened, Saul spit on his fingers. His hand disappeared down the back of Dante's pants as Saul grinned at Victor. His friend's moans gave Victor hope he'd be home with Aden within the hour.

"Yeah, take my fingers, bitch."

Although he'd never been spoken to in such a way, Saul's deep voice sent chills up Victor's spine. He prayed they'd get on with it before his cock erupted in his jeans. Victor was saved when Saul abruptly removed his hand and yanked Dante's jeans down to his ankles.

"Off," Saul ordered.

Victor stood shocked as Dante immediately followed Saul's command, and bent over the back of the beige, non-descript sofa. Dante had always fought for dominance when he and Victor were lovers. There wasn't a single thing, other than the fine ass on display, that remotely resembled his old friend.

"Hurry, Papi," Dante begged.

With his jeans lowered to mid-thigh, Saul bent over and spat on Dante's hole. "You ready for this big daddy cock, baby?"

"Please." Dante hiked one leg up to rest beside his torso on the back of the couch.

Holding his massive cock by the root, Saul stepped up and gently pushed the head just inside Dante's hole. Victor was once again surprised by the dynamic between the two men. With a rather loving hand threading through Dante's hair, Saul bent and placed a kiss to Dante's spine. "Okay?"

Dante nodded and Saul surged forward in a single thrust, driving his dick deep until Victor heard the slap of the man's balls against Dante's ass. *Damn.*

He waited until Saul had set a steady rhythm before stepping to the side of the fucking men. Without missing a stroke, Saul tilted his head to the side, exposing his throat to Victor's bite.

With a nod of thanks, Victor leaned in and sunk his incisors cleanly through Saul's skin, to his external carotid artery. The blood burst into Victor's mouth, coating his tongue before running down his throat. He could definitely see why Dante was so taken with the gorgeous Latin man's blood.

Only allowing himself to feed for a few moments, Victor sealed the wound and stepped back, wiping his mouth. From the way the two men were still going at it, Victor assumed Saul would also be feeding Dante before the night was over.

"Thank you," he whispered in Saul's ear.

"See you in a few days," Saul grunted, slamming into Dante's ass.

Victor slapped Dante's hip before disappearing from the room. When he opened his eyes, he was standing in his bathroom. He quickly disrobed and turned on the shower. Although he hadn't had sex, he wanted to go to his lover's bed as fresh as possible.

A silhouette standing beside the sink caught his attention. "Aden?"

Perfectly, sublimely nude, Aden opened the shower door. "Expecting someone else?"

Victor reached out and ran a hand down Aden's torso to the short bush of blond hair surrounding his cock. With his other hand, he removed the bandage from his lover's forehead.

He pulled Aden into the shower and leaned down to lick the three inch cut. Within a matter of moments, the cut was closed and on its way to being fully healed.

"Why didn't you do that last night?" Aden asked.

Victor gazed into those dark green pools with spiked lashes and melted. "I wasn't sure how I would've explained it to you. You knew Josh hit you with the glass. Don't you think you might've questioned it?"

Aden grinned. "Actually, I questioned myself when I woke up as to whether or not you were a vampire because you didn't heal me."

With Aden's forehead taken care of, Victor squirted shower gel into his hand and began to roam the lithe body in front of him. "Did you write at all today?"

Aden stopped in the act of pouring soap into his own hand. "You know about that?"

Victor chuckled. He leaned down and brushed a kiss across Aden's plump lips. "Of course. I've read every book you've written."

Aden lowered his head, resting it against Victor's chest. "Thanks. I don't think you'll ever understand what that means to me."

Victor tilted Aden's chin back up. "You're good." He could see the insecurities in Aden's eyes. It was obvious Aden's relationship with Josh had damaged more than just his body.

As much as he'd like to take Aden in the shower, he knew the man needed something special this time around. "Why don't we dry off and take a blanket outside to the garden."

Aden grinned. "I like that idea."

"Just don't let me fall asleep out there."

Aden's expression suddenly looked worried. "We can stay inside. I don't want to do anything that'll put you at risk."

"Don't worry. I've got a built-in alarm clock that's never failed me." Victor tried to wash Aden's body without over stimulating certain areas. He couldn't help but take notice of the way Aden's stance widened as Victor began to soap up his cock and balls.

"I think my ass needs a good, deep scrub as well," Aden moaned.

Victor shook his head as he transferred his soapy hands to Aden's ass. "I'm trying to be good, but you're not making it easy."

Aden rubbed against Victor's erection and sighed. "Horizontal is overrated."

Victor could very well imagine fucking Aden standing up again. The possibilities were endless when you didn't need to worry about a soft spot to lie. He reached up and turned the shower head to the side enough that it wasn't pounding down on them, before pouring more soap into his hand.

As he began to tease Aden's puckered hole, he took a page out of Saul's book of seduction. "You want me to fuck you, baby?"

Aden nodded, lifting one foot to rest on the narrow tiled ledge. "As many times as you've reamed my ass in my dreams, I'd think you'd be tired of me by now."

Aden's body relaxed and Victor's finger slipped inside. "Never." Victor couldn't wait to feel the warm walls of Aden's ass surrounding his cock again.

After a few minutes of finger-play, Victor lifted Aden off the tiled floor. As if they'd been doing it for years, Aden kissed him as he wrapped his legs around Victor's torso.

"Fuck me," Aden begged after pulling out of the kiss.

With a hand on each cheek, Victor opened Aden's ass to receive his cock. As if on cue, Aden reached back and pressed the crown of Victor's shaft against his waiting hole.

Aden moaned as he slowly impaled himself. The squeeze of Aden's body was even better the second time. *Fuck.* He'd never last. Already the desire to bury his fangs in his lover's neck threatened to overwhelm him.

Once fully seated, Victor held Aden in place as he began to saw in and out of the hot sheath. "So good," he groaned.

Aden leaned in for a kiss, but Victor shook his head, flashing his lover his extended incisors. "Sorry. It's not safe."

Where he expected a disappointed expression, Aden smiled. Victor wanted to ask what the smile was for, but he was too far immersed in fucking his lover to speak. He turned to brace Aden's back against the wall as his thrusts became harder.

Several times he heard Aden's head thud against the tile, but the smaller man continued to encourage Victor with his pleas. "Harder. Yeah. Fuck. Right there. Yes!"

Victor felt the splash of Aden's cum as his lover's body tightened around his cock. As soon as Aden's muscles relaxed, Victor slammed in as far as he could, and ground his hips in a figure eight as he erupted.

Spent, Victor rested his forehead against Aden's shoulder. He could hear and smell the blood pumping through his lover's veins. *Give me strength.* He continued to pray to Valerianus until his teeth returned to their non-feeding state. *Thank you.*

With his breathing under control, Victor set Aden back on his feet before readjusting the shower spray. When Aden started to sink towards the floor, Victor quickly caught him with an arm around his waist.

"I've got you." He reached for the soap again and began to wash his lover clean. He knew it was imperative to get an audience with Valerianus.

The need to feed from his lover was too great. It didn't matter to Victor that he'd been able to control himself a few minutes earlier. He knew he wouldn't always be able to talk himself down from his desires. The deeper his feelings became, the greater the need for Aden's blood.

"I'm sleepy," Aden mumbled around a yawn.

Victor turned off the water and opened the shower door. With his arm still wrapped around Aden, he dried them both before carrying Aden to his bed.

After settling his lover under the covers, Victor bent and kissed those lips he couldn't resist. "Sleep. I'll be back in a few hours."

Aden struggled to open his eyes. "Where're you going?"

"Downstairs. I need to take care of some business."

"Can I sleep with you?" Aden asked, starting to drift.

"Yes. I'll pull the drapes on the windows and around the bed, so unless you have a problem with claustrophobia, I'd love to sleep with you in my arms."

Aden smiled and snuggled his head into the pillow. Within moments, his lover was sound asleep. Victor walked over to the closet and pulled out his rarely used suit. He dressed with care before leaving his chamber.

A quick glance at the clock in his study, informed him he had several hours before he needed to be back. He closed his eyes and concentrated on Valerianus' palace. After the fluttering feeling passed through him, he opened his eyes to find himself right where he'd wanted to be.

Victor straightened his red silk tie and stepped up to the desk. "I need to speak with the Creator," he informed Ursula, Valerianus' long-time secretary.

Ursula's blonde eyebrow shot up. "Without an appointment?"

Victor expected the question, so he was prepared. "It's about Aden."

Ursula bit her lip, and glanced over the appointment calendar in front of her. "He's in a meeting with Allisis."

Victor grinned. Valerianus had enjoyed a love/hate relationship with the were Creator for as long as Victor had been alive. He wondered if the two men would ever get their shit together. "You mean he's busy fucking."

Ursula blushed. "Let's just say that I doubt he'd appreciate an interruption."

"Do you mind if I wait? It's important."

Ursula shrugged. "Suit yourself, but there's no way of telling how long their…meeting will last."

Victor took a seat outside of Valerianus' door and made himself comfortable.

After forty minutes, the door burst open as an angry Allisis stormed out. Victor watched the tall blond stalk his way across the large room to the hall. With a smile on his face, Victor glanced over to Ursula and winked.

She hid her grin behind her hand as she disappeared into Valerianus' chamber. Despite the reputation they'd received from folklore and bad Hollywood movies, vampires were merely a separate and distinct race of man. They had souls, a heartbeat and needed air to breathe. Sure they couldn't go out in the daylight, but he hadn't been lying to Aden when he said it was more of an allergy issue. No going up in a puff of smoke if he stepped into the light, but he would get a nasty burn.

The one thing Hollywood did get right was his need to feed on the blood of others. Without the rejuvenating fluid, he would begin to grow weak rapidly. It didn't mean he wasn't able to eat regular food, but it did nothing to sustain his body, therefore, he'd always found it a rather pointless activity.

"Valerianus will see you, but he said to warn you he isn't in a good mood," Ursula informed Victor, closing the chamber door.

"What else is new," he mumbled under his breath.

He knocked on Valerianus' door and waited.

"Come in," the gravely voice called out.

With a deep breath to calm his nerves, Victor stepped inside Valerianus' inner sanctum. The room was huge, as was the Creator. Valerianus sat on the raised throne in the centre of the room. For being older than dirt, Valerianus didn't look a day over forty. His beauty was unparalleled and he knew it.

"What do you want, Victor?"

Victor took that as permission to approach. He knelt in front of the Creator with his head bowed. "I need to speak with you about Aden."

"Trouble?" Valerianus asked, shifting in his chair.

Victor swallowed around the lump in his throat. He knew what he was about to say could very well seal his fate, but it was a necessary conversation. "I'm in love with him, Master."

"Yes. I know."

Victor dared to look up at Valerianus. "I can't continue to feed from others."

"Why?"

"Because it causes Aden pain to know how I must feed. I can't continue to hurt him."

"That is your choice. Not mine."

Victor glanced back down at the floor. "Are you saying you don't care that your son is in pain?"

"Emotional pain isn't the same as physical pain. Aden will survive. He was not created to feed you. He is a leader, not a donor."

Victor closed his eyes and rested his fisted hand against his forehead. He didn't know if he'd ever been angrier at Valerianus. He knew one wrong word and he could kiss any hope of a future with Aden goodbye.

"I love him. Treating him like a donor never entered my mind."

"Good. Then you have a choice to make. Either continue to feed from others or starve yourself. It really is as simple as that."

Simple? Victor was being forced into the situation of either betraying the man he loved or starving himself to death. He knew he could continue feeding like he had earlier that evening, but following Dante around every night wasn't what he wanted for the rest of his life.

Victor knew he had one last piece of business before leaving. He gazed at his creator. "Aden would like to meet you."

"In time," Valerianus answered with a dismissive flick of his hand.

Victor got to his feet and turned towards the door. With his hand on the knob, he spoke. "For the first time in my long life, I'm ashamed to be a vampire."

Chapter Four

Aden opened the heavy curtains that surrounded Victor's bed. Since returning from his meeting with Valerianus, his lover had become beyond depressed, only feeding a couple of times a week.

"It's almost eight. Are you planning to stay in bed all night?" Aden asked as he crawled onto the bed.

Victor opened his eyes and pulled Aden into his arms. "I'm tired."

"You're weak," Aden argued.

"That, too," Victor grinned.

"Dante's here. He said he'd take you out." Aden hated the thought of Victor being with another man, but he hated the thought of his vampire dying even more.

Victor shook his head. "I was just out."

"It's been five days, love. You can't continue like this."

"I just can't do it. I know what it does to you every time I leave." Victor gazed into Aden's eyes. "When I come home from feeding, I feel dirty. For the first time in my life, the price I have to pay for blood isn't worth it."

Aden brushed several strands of Victor's long, black hair off his face. "It's time for both of us to get over our hang-ups. I know it's just about getting what you need to survive when you give pleasure to a donor. I've come to terms with that. Now it's your turn. You need to separate your physical needs from your guilt."

Victor shook his head again. "It's still cheating."

"No it's not. I understand that now." Aden snuggled against Victor's chest.

"It is. I understand that now," Victor countered before placing a kiss on top of Aden's head.

Before Aden could argue, he heard the unmistakable sound of Victor's deep snore. He glanced up to find his lover asleep yet again. "What are you doing to yourself?" he whispered.

He knew he couldn't stand by and watch the man he loved die. After giving Victor another kiss, Aden crawled out of bed. He went to the closet and chose one of the more conservative outfits Victor had bought him and dressed quickly.

Aden found Dante in the garden. *Perfect.* "I need you to do me a favour."

Dante glanced up from the rose he was pulling apart petal by petal. "Where's Victor?"

Aden shook his head. "He's refusing to eat. I left him sleeping in his bed."

"I'll go talk to him. He has to eat."

"He won't. That's why I need you to take me to

Valerianus."

Dante started to laugh. "You're as crazy as Victor. You don't just pop in on Valerianus. He's eaten people for less."

"Then he'll just have to eat me, because if he doesn't see me, Victor's gonna die."

Dante tossed the rose to the ground. "I'll get you there, but that's as far as I go. I happen to like all my parts right where they are."

Aden nodded. "I'm ready when you are."

Dante grabbed Aden and in a split second they stood in a depressing room with stone walls. The air was too warm, almost stifling. A musty scent hung in the aging structure. *Creepy.*

Dante pointed to a woman at a massive desk. "That's Ursula. She's the only one who can get you in to see Valerianus." Dante turned and started to walk off.

"Wait! Where are you going?" Aden asked, reaching for Dante.

"Don't worry. I'll be around to pick up the pieces when Valerianus' is finished with you."

Aden narrowed his eyes at the good-looking vampire. "Why aren't you helping? I thought Victor was your best friend?"

"We all have our place in this long life we were given. Mine isn't to play martyr."

"Evidently it's not to play the part of best friend either," Aden mumbled as he crossed to the big desk.

Ursula glanced up from her work when he cleared his throat. One blonde eyebrow rose in question. "Yes?"

"My name is Aden Brousseau. I'm here to see Valerianus."

He shifted under the woman's scrutiny. He realised he didn't exactly look like the son of a god, but he wasn't about to back down.

Ursula glanced around the empty room. "Who brought you here?"

"Doesn't matter. I'm here, and I'd like to speak with my father." *Go me.* Aden silently patted himself on the back for his steady voice.

Ursula sighed and rose from her chair. "I'm surrounded by idiots with death wishes." She went to the large door to the side of her desk. "Wait here."

Aden spent the time trying to calm his nerves. He'd known plenty of bullies and the worst thing you could do was show them fear. Despite knowing Valerianus was his father, Aden had no feelings for the Creator. Actually, he'd begun to despise the man who had implanted his mother with his seed. How many times had Valerianus allowed Josh to beat him without doing something about it? And for what? What did his father gain by seeing him hurt and used?

The door opened and Ursula gestured towards Aden. "He only has a few moments, so make it quick."

Quick? His first meeting with his father and he was supposed to hurry? Aden didn't think so. With an attitude to rival any pissed off teenager, Aden stormed into the large room.

The sheer beauty of the man seated on the magnificently carved throne took his breath. Aden almost fell to his knees but quickly remembered the reason for his visit. He decided to come right out with it, hoping to throw Valerianus off guard.

"Victor's dying and it's your fault," he accused, hands fisted at his sides.

One of Valerianus' perfectly shaped eyebrows rose. "Is that any way to greet your father?"

"You're not my father. A father cares about his son. Fucking my mom doesn't give you the right to call yourself by that name."

Valerianus' eyes narrowed. "Do you have any idea what I've done to men who've dared to speak to me in such a manner?"

Aden shrugged. In his bones, he knew not to show the Creator fear. "It's the truth, and even you can't deny that."

Valerianus' expression softened as the corner of his lip twitched. "I've sent one of my favoured creations to watch over you. How can you say I don't care?"

"Favoured creations? Then why are you allowing Victor to starve to death?"

"I have no control on whether or not Victor chooses to feed. I only stated he couldn't feed from you. Your blood isn't meant for that, and until you fully embrace what you are, you'll never be enough for him."

"Who I am?"

With a bored expression on his face, Valerianus motioned for Aden. "Come closer, my son."

Like a moth to a flame, Aden did as instructed. He was surprised when Valerianus pulled him into a kiss. Despite the Creator's strength, Aden managed to pull back. "What're you doing? You're my father!"

Valerianus sighed. "Yes, and I'm also Victor's father." Valerianus cupped Aden's cheek. "You need to forget what the humans taught you. The morals they live by aren't possible in our world, a world you belong to, Aden.

You're one of us, and until you start acting like it, there will be no future for you and Victor."

"How can I embrace my vampire side when I don't feel like a vampire?" Aden gazed into the ebony eyes of his father, trying desperately to understand.

Valerianus reached down and ran a hand across Aden's hardened cock. "Your body knows to respond to my touch. It is the way of things. Let your mind free itself of the restraints the humans have put on you and you will open yourself to your other half."

"Is it all about sex?" Aden asked. He was ashamed of his body's betrayal at the hands of the Creator, but he couldn't deny the electricity that fired his veins at Valerianus' touch.

"Hmmm," Valerianus hummed as he continued to knead Aden's cock through his jeans. "Sex is the expression of life. Through it, vampires have been kept alive for centuries. We embrace what the humans give us and in return, we give them pleasures of the flesh."

Aden pulled back, brushing away his father's hand. Whether he could rethink his views on sex was to be seen, but he doubted he'd ever welcome it from his father. "Are you saying I need to share Victor's body with humans in order to become a vampire?"

Valerianus chuckled. "You're already a vampire. But until you acknowledge it, you'll always be trapped in the human way of thinking."

Aden bit his lip as he tried to imagine sharing his lover with another. "I'll try to become what you ask. That's all I can do."

"Dig deep within your memories, my son. You are keeping things from yourself that will ease the way not only for you, but for Victor."

"Does this have something to do with the gaps in my memory?" Aden asked.

"Yes. Victor did something for you that he's never forgiven himself for. I think he's been punished long enough. It's up to you to set him free of his guilt."

Before Aden could say another word, he was once again standing in Victor's bedroom. "Fuck!"

Aden pinched the bridge of his nose. He glanced towards the heavy drapes that separated him from his lover and began to undress. His head was filled with more questions than when he'd left.

Parting the curtain, Aden lifted the blanket and slid between the slick sheets. He curled around Victor, deep in thought. He knew the two of them needed to talk. Maybe if he listened to Victor, it would spur his own memories.

Aden ran his hand down Victor's muscled torso to the short cropping of black pubic hair. He buried his fingers in the thick tufts and idly circled his lover's flaccid shaft.

He remembered leaving Louisiana with his aunt and uncle. He also remembered how much he'd hated Phoenix. The abuse had started right away.

He was so deep in thought, he wasn't aware Victor was awake until his lover thrust his groin against Aden's hand. Tilting his head, he gazed into Victor's dark eyes. "I went to see Valerianus."

Victor's body stiffened. "He summoned you?"

Aden shook his head. "I made Dante take me to him."

Victor shot straight up and tossed the covers aside. "I'll kill him," he growled.

Aden dove for Victor, managing to wrap his arms around him before he got too far from the bed. "I made him."

Victor spun around and grabbed Aden by the arms, giving him a shake. "Do you have a death wish?"

"No, but evidently you do," Aden countered. "I went to beg my father to let you feed from me."

"And?"

"He said it wasn't possible for you to live on my blood alone." Aden shrugged. "He also said I needed to embrace my vampire side."

Aden felt Victor's grip tighten. "I'm sorry."

Victor's grip on Aden's arms fell away as he collapsed onto the bed. Aden ran his fingers through Victor's sleep tussled hair. "He told me I needed to release my human sexual hang-ups."

Victor shifted uncomfortably on the bed, refusing to look at Aden.

"Victor?" Aden straddled Victor's hips and lay down. "We need to start being honest with each other."

"You're right," Victor finally replied.

Aden swallowed around the lump in his throat. "There's nothing you can tell me that will drive me away from you."

Victor shook his head. "That's not what I'm afraid of."

Aden placed a kiss in the centre of Victor's chest. "Then what is it?"

"It's about your aunt and uncle."

Aden sat up and stared down at his lover. He knew he'd left Louisiana with his mother's brother and his wife, but there was a four year gap in his memories after that. "What happened?"

Victor pushed himself into a sitting position and wrapped his arms around Aden. "I could feel your sadness, but I convinced myself it was the loss of your mother and your home. One day your rage woke me from my slumber. I couldn't go to you until after the sunset, and by then it was too late."

Aden opened his mouth several times before the words finally spilled from him. "What did I do?"

"They'd been abusing you, and I didn't pick up on it."

"And?" Aden prodded.

For several moments, Victor said nothing. Finally, in a voice Aden could barely hear, he heard his lover whisper, "And you drained them."

"No!" Aden screamed, trying to push his way out of Victor's arms. It couldn't be true. What game was his lover playing?

"I failed you. I was supposed to teach you what you needed to know, but you weren't supposed to have the power until your eighteenth birthday. The pain and anger you were experiencing must've sped up the process. By the time I reached you, you were inconsolable. I didn't know what to do, so I cleaned up the mess and..." Victor's voice trailed off.

"You erased my memory," Aden finished.

"Yes. Valerianus was so mad at what I'd done that he punished me by cutting me off from your thoughts until that night at Josh's."

Things began to make sense to Aden. He'd wondered how his father and Victor could let him suffer at the hands of his ex-lover. "I wonder why I didn't drain Josh?"

Victor shook his head. "I don't know. Maybe you would have, given the right circumstance, or maybe it was because at the time you didn't remember anything about vampires."

Aden touched the tip of his tongue to his teeth. "Why don't I have fangs?"

Victor grinned. "You do, you just haven't learned how to call them down. After you've done it a few times it'll become natural."

"Will I need blood to survive?" he asked.

"I don't think so. Despite the Creator being your father, your mother was human. It's the same reason the sun doesn't seem to affect you."

"Valerianus touched me," he admitted.

Victor nodded. "Don't worry. It's a game he plays, but he'd never follow through. Allisis would kill him."

"Allisis?"

"His lover, tormentor. Allisis is the were Creator."

"So, Valerianus is gay?"

Victor grinned again. "Once again you're thinking in human terms of sexuality. In our world, gender isn't a factor in who you love or who you fuck. You know the old saying, 'Do what makes you feel good.' Well, where do you think that term came from?"

Aden was beginning to understand vampire views on sex were completely different than what he'd grown up with. He wondered if he'd ever be as free with his body and Victor's as would be required for them to be together.

"Will you do me a favour?" Aden asked after several moments of silence.

"Anything, love."

"Feed," Aden begged. "Show me what it's like?"

"Did someone call me?" a smooth voice said from behind him.

Aden spun around and came face to face with Dante.

Victor sighed and shook his head at his friend. "Aden's nowhere near ready for you, Dante."

Dante's gaze zeroed in on Aden's half-hard cock. "Are you sure about that?"

Aden quickly covered himself, once again ashamed of the way his body reacted. He squared his shoulders and looked Dante in the eyes. "Will you feed him?"

Dante shook his head. "I can't give him enough of what he needs, just like you can't, but I know someone who can."

Aden glanced at Victor.

"Are we talking about your big Latin cop?" Victor asked.

"Of course. He's the only one I can bring here. Now, if you'd rather do it in the back of a bar, let me know, and I'm sure I can arrange something," Dante said with a smirk on his face.

"Will you stay?" Victor asked.

Aden nodded. He wasn't sure if he was ready to watch his lover pleasure another man, but he knew it was necessary for Victor's survival.

"Bring him if you can," Victor told Dante.

A quick glance at the clock made Aden worry. "It's almost midnight. Will you have time?"

Dante chuckled. "It's not romance, kid, it's fucking and sucking."

"Dante," Victor growled.

Dante shrugged. "I'm going to stop somewhere on the way to feed since I imagine my Papi will be low by the time the two of you are through with him."

"Papi?" Aden asked, looking from Dante to Victor.

"I'll explain later," Victor replied, caressing Aden's bare ass.

Chapter Five

Once alone with Aden, Victor began to worry. He laid his lover on the bed and curled himself around the smaller man. "Are you sure about this?"

Aden threaded his fingers through Victor's hair. "It might take me a few times to get the hang of it, but I know I've got a lot of relearning to do. It's not that I don't enjoy sex, I guess I've always just thought it should be between two people who care about each other."

Victor nodded. He knew the human views on multiple partners. It had never been a concern to Victor until Aden had come back into his life. He ran his hand down Aden's chest to wrap around his growing cock. "I won't do anything you don't want me to do. Nothing is worth risking you."

Aden thrust against Victor's hand. "You won't lose me."

Victor hoped that was true. He'd seen Dante and Saul in action on more than one occasion, but had never actively participated in anything but feeding. He wasn't averse to the idea of fucking someone else, but Saul didn't look like the type of man who'd bottom for anyone, and he wasn't sure his ass was ready for a cock the size of Dante's big Papi's.

The more he rubbed Aden's cock, the more his lover writhed in his arms. Victor decided it might be easier for Aden to let himself go if he was kept on edge. He slowed his strokes and kissed his man. "I love you."

"Love you," Aden answered back. "I'd do anything for you."

Victor smiled and rolled away enough to tap Aden's hip. "Hands and knees. I want to taste you."

Victor had no plans to fuck Aden until Dante returned, but he wanted to get his lover ready. He leaned in and spread Aden's ass cheeks. He ran his tongue from Aden's balls to the top of his crack, stopping to pay extra attention to the sweet little pucker.

"Oh, fuck," Aden moaned, thrusting his ass against Victor's face.

"No coming," Victor warned between licks.

He felt the ridges under his tongue soften before loosening enough for Victor to penetrate his perfect ass with the tip. He tasted his lover, while introducing as much saliva as possible into the gorgeous hole.

"Oh, oh," Aden continued to moan.

Victor pulled his tongue from Aden's ass and climbed off the bed.

"Where're you going?" Aden asked.

With a grin, Victor opened a small box on top of his dresser and withdrew three silicone cock rings. Carrying the soft objects back to bed, he knelt beside his lover. "Turn over, babe."

Aden flopped to his back and Victor held one of the rings out. "These will help maintain your erection."

Aden flushed and nodded. "Josh used cock rings all the time, but his were usually made of leather."

Victor rolled his eyes. "Leather is for show-offs. These do a better job and are a hell of a lot more comfortable."

Aden reached down and began to stroke his cock. "Do I wear all three?"

Victor shook his head, replacing Aden's hand with his own. "You could, but I thought I'd slip one on myself this time."

Aden's tongue snaked out to lick his bottom lip before sucking the plump bit of pink between his teeth as Victor secured the silicone ring around the base of his cock.

Victor adjusted the second ring and sat back on his heels. "Now don't that look pretty," he said, giving Aden's cock a playful slap.

"It sure as hell does," Dante said, appearing at the edge of the bed with his arm wrapped around Saul.

Still dressed, Saul started to reach for Aden's cock. Victor held up a hand. "Tell me what you want, babe."

Aden's gaze travelled between the three men looming over him. Victor could tell by the slight flare of his lover's nostrils that he was still turned on. He decided to help Aden along, by keeping his mind occupied.

Victor sank his index finger deep into Aden's ass. As expected, the younger man moaned.

"Can we join you?" Dante asked.

Victor stared down at Aden. "It's up to you."

Aden surprised him by reaching out to cup Dante's heavy sac.

"Fuck!" Dante howled, lifting a leg onto the bed.

"You like that?" Victor asked, adding two more fingers to Aden's ass. "Dante's got a pretty cock, doesn't he?"

Aden nodded as he moved his hand to encircle Dante's dripping shaft. "Have you fucked Dante?" Aden asked Victor.

He gazed down at Aden, unsure of how to answer. "Thousands of times."

Aden shifted, driving Victor's fingers in deeper. "Can I watch?"

Victor tried to read Aden's facial expressions. Fucking Dante wasn't a problem, but the hesitant look in Aden's eyes was. "I don't know that I'll ever do it again," Victor whispered. "We'll take things a step at a time."

The corner of Aden's mouth turned up in a smile. He gestured towards Saul. "Would you like to get undressed? Victor needs to feed."

Victor chuckled. Despite his hesitations, Aden still knew what needed to be done. Saul wasted no time shedding his clothes. He walked up behind Victor and pressed his erection against Victor's ass.

Victor half-turned and pulled Saul into a kiss. The taste of the big cop could become very addictive. He briefly wondered if Saul and Dante were going to become regulars in his and Aden's bed.

He broke the kiss and glanced at Dante. "Kiss him," he instructed his friend.

With his fingers still in Aden's ass, Victor returned his attention to Saul. "If you need to fuck someone, it'll have to be Dante."

Saul scraped his teeth across Victor's jaw. "What about your lover, can I fuck him?"

He didn't know how to answer. He knew the way he felt about fucking someone other than Aden, but he knew he couldn't speak for his lover. Aden had only recently learned of his vampire blood. He may fully embrace the vampire views on sexual pleasure being part of the process of feeding, but it was a decision Aden would have to make on his own.

"He's not ready, but maybe someday, if he wants it." Victor ran his free hand down Saul's chest to his cock. "Nice," he commented, massaging the crown with his thumb.

"Dante seems to like it," Saul returned with a chuckle.

Victor once again thrust his tongue deep into Saul's mouth, lapping at the hot stud. He wondered if Saul was the one to ask about safe men to bring home with them. He pulled out of the kiss and stared into Saul's big brown eyes. "Are there others who know about your arrangement with Dante?"

"A few," Saul answered, chasing Victor's mouth with his tongue.

"Are they interested?" Victor asked.

"Maybe. Why, you needing, baby? I can give you everything you need."

Damn this fucker's hot. "You can't feed me and Dante every night. I'll need a few more people I can trust to bring into my home."

Victor surrendered his tongue to Saul's passion. He felt another hand on his thigh and glanced down without breaking the kiss. Aden smiled up at him. No longer content to simply kneel on the bed, Dante was wrapped around Victor's lover with his mouth attached to one of Aden's nipples.

"You doing okay?" Victor asked, coming out of his kiss.

"The two of you look sexy together," Aden said.

Removing his fingers from Aden's ass, Victor released Saul's cock and pulled the bigger man onto the bed. He positioned Saul between Dante and Aden before sitting his ass on the man's cock. He may not allow Saul to fuck him, but he could certainly give him something warm to rub against.

Victor began to move his ass back and forth as Aden rolled to his side to give Saul a kiss. Watching his lover's tongue lick and suck at the big Latin's mouth had Victor glad he was wearing a cock ring.

"Fuck that's sexy," he groaned. He scooted back on Saul's thighs enough to reach out and move Aden's hand to Saul's big man meat.

Aden needed no further prompting as he began to stroke the shaft in his hand. He felt a hand on his ass and gazed down at Dante. The warm smile on his best friend's face warmed Victor. He smiled back with a slight nod of his head. It felt right being with these men, and it seemed they all knew it.

Dante gestured to Saul's groin. "He likes me to bite him down there."

Worried that Aden might not approve, Victor looked down at his lover. Aden was still engaged in a major tongue battle with Saul, but from the way he was pumping Saul's cock, Victor knew a bite wouldn't piss him off.

Repositioning to his stomach, Victor insinuated himself between Saul's spread thighs. He decided to test the waters first and licked up the base of Saul's cock and Aden's hand.

Aden glanced down and locked gazes with Victor. A subtle nod and the removal of Aden's hand, and Victor knew he'd been given permission.

As he bathed the cock in his hand, he watched as Saul lifted Aden's slight frame and positioned Aden's ass on his face. Victor couldn't help but chuckle as Aden's eyes went wide at the first lick of the cop's tongue.

Dante decided to get into the act by engulfing Aden's cock just as Victor swallowed as much as he could of Saul's. The various moans of pleasure turned Victor on even more. He couldn't remember sex ever being this good.

After sliding his mouth up and down Saul's cock several times, Victor began fondling and sucking Saul's hairy sac as he prepared to feed. From the sounds above him, Victor guessed Saul's head was in the right place to give him the blood he was desperately in need of.

Letting his fangs drop, Victor sliced cleanly into one of the plump veins on the upper inside of Saul's thigh. He heard a slight hiss from Saul, but his donor's body remained relaxed as Victor began to feed.

With every swallow, he felt his body becoming more energised. He'd gone too long without the life-saving nourishment, and he knew it. Continuing to drink, Victor wrapped a hand around Saul's big cock and began to stroke him once more.

He heard Dante gasp and glanced up to see Aden sucking from his old friend's neck. The occasion was so monumental for his lover, that Victor decided he'd had enough and quickly sealed Saul's wounds.

Moving closer to Aden, Victor ran a hand down his lover's spine as he continued to drink. He'd known Aden's talents would reveal themselves when he gave himself over to his vampire lineage, he just didn't know it would happen so soon. The swiftness of the turn boded well for their ongoing relationship.

Knowing his lover wouldn't get what he needed from Dante anyway, he allowed Aden to drink a few more moments before bending down to kiss his temple. "That's enough, my love. Seal the wound with a swipe of your tongue."

Aden did as instructed before breaking away from Dante's neck. His eyes were still fully dilated when he looked at Victor. "I can't believe I did that."

Victor pulled Aden into his arms and kissed him, tasting the familiar essence of his best friend. "You feel okay?"

Aden nodded. "Like I could rule the world," he joked.

Victor chuckled. "Let's not get ahead of ourselves."

The four men repositioned with Aden and Dante in the centre of the bed in a traditional sixty-nine position. Victor watched as Aden devoured Dante's cock, taking the full length down his throat.

Victor glanced up and met Saul's heated gaze. "Our men are gorgeous together."

"They certainly are." Saul leant over the moaning, slurping bodies of their lovers and kissed Victor.

Victor sucked on Saul's tongue as he lifted one of Aden's legs. He broke the kiss and grinned at the sexy cop. "Let me watch you fuck Dante."

Saul pressed against Dante's back, fitting his cock into Dante's waiting ass. "He likes it hard," Saul said, looking down Dante's body to where Aden's lips were still wrapped around Dante's cock.

"Start slow and let Aden adjust. I could tell him, but I don't think he'd hear me right now," Victor chuckled. Aden was definitely lost to the outside world as he made love to the crown of Dante's shaft.

Victor pressed the head of his cock to Aden's stretched ass and eased his way inside. Like he'd told Saul to do, Victor started easing his way in and out of Aden's body slowly. Dante's hand landed on Victor's hip, scraping the flesh with short nails. With Dante aware of his surroundings, Victor's pace increased.

Aden began to whimper as Victor fucked him with force. On each thrust, Victor watched as Aden's cock drove deep into Dante's throat. Victor wondered if Aden had ever enjoyed the dual pleasures two lovers could bring.

Victor wished he could see more of Saul's cock disappearing in and out of Dante's hole, but he knew there would be plenty of opportunities to watch the big man fuck his friend.

Aden pulled his mouth from Dante's cock and gasped. "Please. I need to come."

With a loving nip to Aden's shoulder, Victor reached down and tapped Dante on the cheek. "Will you remove Aden's ring?"

Without taking his mouth from Aden's cock, Dante began to do as asked. The moment the binding was worked up the length of Aden's shaft, he began to fill Dante's mouth.

Victor groaned and fucked his lover even harder. Dante made eye contact as he sucked the seed from Aden's cock. "Damn that's hot."

"Uuhhh," Dante growled as he apparently joined Aden in climax. The rich scent of cum filled the air as Aden's orgasm seemed to set off both Dante and Saul.

Victor wrapped his arm tighter around Aden's waist and buried his face in his lover's neck. He scraped the soft flesh with his fangs and lapped at the small drops of blood. The smell of Aden's blood mixed with the hands of all three men roaming his body had Victor pumping Aden's ass full of his cum with the cock ring still in place.

With each spurt, Victor was amazed. Apparently even the ring was no match for the sexual powers of the men in his bed.

Epilogue

At his computer, Aden pulled up a brand new pirate site that had just been launched. He shook his head as he saw the number of illegal downloads. "Are you fucking kidding me?"

What was even worse than the downloads was the attitude of those stealing from him. For some fucked up reason, they thought they had a right to take money out of his pocket. He let out a loud frustrated groan.

"Something wrong, love?" Victor asked, coming up behind him to kiss Aden's neck.

Aden pointed towards his computer screen. "Leeches are after my books again. Can I drain them? Pretty please?"

Victor chuckled. "Why do you let these people upset you so much?" Victor asked, picking Aden up into his arms. Victor sat in the vacated chair and arranged Aden on his lap.

"Because I know if I don't let it upset me, I might as well give up writing. Hell, as it is, there are more people stealing my books than paying for them. Doing absolutely nothing is to let them win."

"So, do something about it."

Aden sighed. As exasperated as he was with the thieves, it was nice to have a partner who supported his anger. "I'm trying, but in order to get the books down you have to jump through hoops and then they put the damn things right back up the next day. I'd much rather just drain them."

"I'll see what I can come up with. I know a few people that might enjoy such an activity, but I'm not one of them," Victor mused.

"I don't know why, you didn't seem to have any problem taking care of Josh."

Victor's expression turned serious. "Yes, perhaps I could start paying them visits as I did Josh."

Aden grinned and circled Victor's exposed nipple with his finger. He loved it when his lover got all protective. Josh had made the mistake of phoning Aden's cell phone one too many times. He still didn't know what Victor had done, but he'd assured Aden, Josh was still alive. Although he did grin when he said his ex-tormenter would be forever afraid of things that went bump in the night.

He pinched Victor's protruding nub between his thumb and forefinger and delighted in the hiss he received in return. Aden parted the black leather vest and touched the tip of his tongue to Victor's other nipple.

"You're looking awfully sexy. Are we going somewhere?" Once he'd sampled Dante's blood, Aden had easily slipped into the vampire way of thinking. No longer did he get jealous of Victor when he gave pleasure to others in order to feed. Of course it helped that Victor never did it without an equally horny Aden by his side.

"No. We're having a dinner party, or had you forgotten?"

Aden chuckled at the term. "In other words, we're having Saul over for dinner."

"Yes, and he's bringing a few friends with him." Victor ran his hand down Aden's chest to the silk pyjama pants he'd taken to wearing around the house.

Aden moaned as Victor's touch began to produce a large amount of pre-cum. He glanced down and smiled at the large wet spot forming on the front of his pants. Aden had been giving a lot of thought to his changed views on sex.

Although they'd discovered Aden's blood was enough to sustain Victor between real feedings, his lover needed what only Saul and the others could provide. He no longer retained his human's way of thinking when it came to sex. It had taken countless visits to convince dear old dad to allow Victor to feed from him, but the practicality of doing it full-time just wasn't there.

"If you want to make love to them, I'll understand," he finally said.

Victor's hand stilled. "No. You're the only one I'll ever make love to."

"Okay, then if you want to fuck them, I'll understand," Aden amended.

Victor shook his head. "I don't want to. I'll admit, I've found certain pleasures in Saul and Dante's bodies, but yours is the only one I have a desire to be inside of."

Aden scratched his head. He thought he had a grip on the vampire sex issue, but now he wasn't so sure. "I don't consider it cheating anymore. I know that you need it in order to feed."

With a hand on his cheek, Victor leaned in and kissed him. "While you've been busy trying to accommodate your vampire half, I've done a good deal of thinking. Bringing pleasure to my donors is one thing, but I feel it would be a betrayal of my love for you to fuck anyone else. Are you unhappy with the way things are?"

"No. I'll admit I take pleasure in our evenings with Saul and Dante, but it's the time we spend alone that I enjoy the most."

Victor's hand pushed under the elastic band of Aden's pants. "Good. Then we're in agreement."

Aden moaned as Victor's hand encircled his cock. He decided to show his lover one of the special powers he'd learned in the previous hours. Aden leant back, giving Victor more room to play and closed his eyes.

He concentrated on sucking Victor's cock.

"Fuck!" Victor groaned, thrusting up against Aden's ass. "What the hell was that?"

"A new talent. You like?"

"I more than like. Do it again."

Aden closed his eyes once more and imagined fingering his lover's asshole as he sucked him.

"Damn. That's the best thing you've learned so far," Victor moaned.

Aden smiled, pleased with himself. He loved giving Victor pleasure. "We'll have to experiment with it. I'm not sure how close you have to be for it to work."

Victor waved a hand and suddenly they were both naked.

"I thought we were having company?" Aden asked with a chuckle. He turned and straddled Victor's lap.

"We are, but I think I'd like to experiment a bit with this new power first."

"Yeah? What did you have in mind?"

"How about we fuck each other? Me with my cock and you with your mind."

Aden nodded enthusiastically as Victor made sure he'd properly stretched himself. It had become Aden's custom to take care of preparations soon after getting out of bed. With their combined sexual appetites, it seemed much easier to always be ready.

As Aden slowly sank down on Victor's cock, he concentrated on the feeling and transferred it to his lover.

"Oh, yeah, baby, that's it, right there." Victor began to thrust in and out of Aden's ass. "I can't wait to see what power you'll discover next."

Aden rested his head against Victor's shoulder as the bigger man held him up enough to drive in deep. He grinned, knowing Victor felt everything he did. No matter what happened in the years to come, Victor was his and Aden knew nothing would ever change that.

STEALING RAIN

D.J. Manly and A.J. Llewellyn

Dedication

A.J. and D.J. would like to dedicate this to all our readers who have spent their hard-earned dollars on our books. Thank you! We love you!

Chapter One

Drew leaned back against the counter, and placed the heels of his hands on the metallic surface. He planted his legs comfortably apart, allowing his head to fall back as he closed his eyes. He tried to concentrate on what Will was doing to his cock, swirling his tongue slowly around the circumference, and then licking the length of his shaft from his balls to the head.

Okay...maybe he needed a mood shift. After all, a cold sterile ancillary control pod wasn't exactly a walking wet dream. *Who am I kidding? I'm always ready for head, always in the mood.* Reaching out one long arm, his dark brown hair fell over his eyes as he reached for the panel of buttons. One of the perks of being Commander was this nifty contraption that redecorated in seconds.

Snap. Will's blue eyes flew open and he surveyed the altered state of the control room with a mixture of awe and pleasure. It looked like a pirate's galleon.

"You like?" Drew stroked the strong, muscled face still going to work on him. Will moaned, pulling back on the cock in his mouth and plunging back down again.

Drew grinned. Pirates. Everybody loved pirates. *Dang.* Not working. The blue-eyed blond on his knees gripped his hips, holding him closer and Drew grunted. It felt good...but he was too distracted. Will was making sounds which indicated that he was thoroughly enjoying his efforts. *Dammit.* He was hard as hell, but Will was not bringing him any closer. He needed to free his mind, but there was too much going on in his head. He didn't understand why in hell they couldn't find it. Pagnotella was a top notch navigator. She had always located her target. But for some damnable reason, they'd been going around in circles for the last three days.

Will came off his cock just as Drew was thinking of redecorating in French provincial. "Drew?"

Drew's dark eyes snapped opened.

Will was sitting back on his heels. "Is there something I'm not doing? You usually enjoy this."

Drew scowled, reaching down to pull up his pants. "Forget it. I thought it would help me relax. Bad timing, I guess. How's Pagnotella doing with her recalibration?"

"I don't know," Will sighed and got up off his knees, wiping his mouth. "You want me to go check?"

"Yeah, and I need to know how many gallons we have on board. The Lukinites have an order in for thirty, and we haven't even delivered what we promised to Mars yet."

"Aren't we making a stop on Devon?"

"No. They've decided not to sell to us anymore. I think they're trying to go solo. They have no idea what in hell they're getting into. The Feds will be onto them soon enough. Anyway, most likely we'll have to go back to the reservoir on Diamond Crest for a pit stop before delivery."

Will looked apprehensive. "I hate going there, especially this time of year. Those caves are so volatile."

"That's what we're paid for, to go where others fear to tread. Now, go do what I asked you to. I've got a communication to do." He grinned. "And my cock's gonna want a rematch with that beautiful mouth...and...ah...maybe that hot ass, so don't go far."

Will's beautiful mouth twitched into an involuntary grin and he disappeared through the automatic sliding door without another word.

Drew threw himself into his chair and flipped on the giant screen in front of him. He pressed the keyboard on his desk. Immediately, Lukins' minister of the environment appeared. The Lukins looked much the same as Earthlings did, except for their ears, which were a little bigger and rather square. "Jamus," Drew said, "how are you, my good friend?"

"Don't good friend me, you black hearted scoundrel. Where's my shipment? You already got your money. I paid you in advance. You probably lost it all gambling."

"Now, now, Jamus, no need for that. I can see you're still sore over that last poker game. I won, fair and square."

"Sure, tell it to your mother, you bastard."

"I almost regret bringing you those old Pirate movies from the twentieth century. I think you've been taking them too seriously."

"If I don't get my shipment, Lacour, I'm going to take it out in trade." He leered at him through the screen. "You know I've always fancied that ass of yours. You might be one cold hearted son of a bitch, but you're gorgeous as sin."

"Ah, Jamus," Drew batted his eyes at him, "I didn't know you cared." He wasn't letting that creep anywhere near his ass.

"Very funny, Lacour. But, I'll be damned," he pointed his finger, "if I'm going to get hung out and dried without at least getting one good shag in first. It will give me something to dream about when I'm rotting away in prison."

"No one is going to prison. You'll get your shipment. It just might take a little longer this time. The supply is drying up. I do have a contract with middle earth. I can't just abandon my own people."

"Screw you, Drew. You have no loyalty to anyone but yourself. Don't give me that shit. You got a week. If not, your ass is mine, honey." His face disappeared from the screen.

Drew knew they were down by at least one hundred gallons. They had to find that planet. He stood up and headed to the main control room. Pagnotella was hard at work, staring into the computer screen.

If Drew had been attracted to women, Pagnotella might have just been his type. Valencian by birth, she'd been ashamed of her earth-bound Italian accent, but now that everything to do with that planet was fashionable again, she perused antique pasta books and joked about meatballs. A former veterinarian, now that animals were virtually extinct, she'd formed an unnatural interest in leeches, the only animals to survive the interplanetary loss of water.

She had a steely reserve that he knew hid a volcanic sexual appetite. She was just like him.

"You rang?" She arched a brow at an enormous, fat leech twirling around her pinky finger, leaving a small trail of blood. He didn't want to think about how the critter had turned quite so...bloated, and he focused instead on Pagnotella's liquid brown eyes and pouty lips. She smelled of flowers, a soft, sweet fragrance. He wondered if the scent would intensify when she was making love. He shook his head...man, he was way too horny.

She glanced at Will who was making some calculations on a magnetic sheet.

"What?" Drew barked. "Someone tell me something."

On the screen, planets floated in a dark blanket of yellow stars...they were far from anywhere and they had to keep moving.

Pagnotella kept her eyes on her course, dropping her strange pet into a glass dish. "I'm sure I'm missing something."

"That's a given," Drew growled.

Will glanced in his direction. "We're at six thousand two."

Drew sighed deeply. "That's lower than I thought. Damn, we're screwed. We need to find this place, and fast."

"Are you sure this Shangri La of yours really exists?" Pagnotella looked at Drew for the first time. She was the only one who'd ever dared speak to him like that.

"It's exists, and we better damn well find it, or we're screwed. Keep working."

"Screwed," Will huffed. "That'll be the day."

"Are you sure you didn't dream it?" Pagnotella asked.

"No," he snapped, "I didn't dream it."

"Then how in the hell do you know there's a frozen lake on this place? There are no bloody lakes left anywhere practically, except for the artificial ones." Pagnotella pushed away from her computer, rubbing her eyes. She stood up, all five feet of her, and looked up at him.

Drew towered over her, at six foot three, but Pagnotella held her own, her gaze never wavering from his. "I don't need a history lesson."

"Sometimes I think you do need a history lesson," she accused. "Damn it, Lacour, we've been going around in circles looking for this place. Tell me where you learned about it?"

Drew walked over to the window of his ship and looked out into the inky atmosphere of space. He already knew what she was going to say if he told her the truth. He turned and looked at her. Will had come closer, also wanting an answer. "I won it in a poker game."

"You won it in a…" Pagnotella's mouth fell open. "Come again?"

He smirked. "Given I haven't been able to come at all…" He couldn't resist.

Will lowered his head, hiding a smile.

"Spare me," she held up a hand. "Now, explain this shit to me. I'm looking for a frozen lake, on a planet I can't locate, because you won it in a poker game. I don't understand. Is this like the time you screwed that alien on Topsmall Island for…?"

"No," he said. "Look, I won a game and the loser had no money. I was livid. He was scared. He said he had something better for me than money. He knew where I could find a frozen lake."

"And you believed this shit?" Pagnotella threw up her hand. "He snowed you, buddy."

"Were you loaded?" Will smirked.

"No. I was sober. And I believe him."

"Yeah, well if he knew this for sure," Pagnotella demanded, "why in hell didn't he go there himself?"

"He didn't have a ship. And—"

"And?" Pagnotella put a hand on her hip.

"The place is guarded, I think."

"So this is an inhabited planet?" Will enquired.

He shrugged. "I guess so. Something about the city being cloaked but look, if we can find that frozen lake, we can transform the ice to water and…"

"I think this guy sold you a load of crap," Pagnotella shook her head.

"Well, you better hope not," Drew said, "'cause if he did, I'm going to be Jamus' cuddle bunny—"

Will snorted. "He'll be sorry."

Drew turned on him, his eyes narrowed. "Yeah, and God knows what he's going to do with you."

Will's eyes widened. "I don't like the sound of that." He paused. "Or do I?"

For a long moment, the only sound that could be heard was the incessant hum of the starboard's sleek engine.

"Get back to work," Drew finally barked. "And I'll try and buy us some more time."

When Trace Delano walked into the surveillance room, he stopped all the computer traffic. His ex French Canadian boyfriend would have said, *Un ange passe,* an angel passed, his mother's charming way of describing a long stretch of awkward silence. Trace was a compelling presence. He was human, but a gifted one. His six foot, muscular frame was accented by jet black hair, green eyes, acute hearing, sharp vision and extra-sensory abilities that set him apart from other men thanks to having died and crossed back again.

One of his men, a tall, wiry Australian by the name of Tor Yanbo, pointed to the radar. Trace stood there for a few minutes studying the tiny blinking light on the screen. He sucked in some air. "We have trouble," he said. He turned to one of the other officers. "Any luck finding out who that ship belongs to?"

"It's Drew Lacour's ship, sir," the officer replied. "I'd bet my life on it."

Trace looked down at him. *Speak of the ex French Canadian.* "I don't want bets, I want facts. We've managed to throw that ship off course several times, what happened? How did it get this close?"

Tor gave him a helpless look.

It didn't surprise him. Drew was one determined son of a bitch, and he usually got what he wanted. "I want the first defence squad armed and ready. If it's Lacour and his band of pirates, they won't stop until they get what they came for."

"Sir?"

Trace didn't realise Tor was talking to him until he felt him touch his sleeve.

Trace gave himself a mental shake. "What is it, Tor?"

"Do I give the order to shoot on sight?"

The question lingered in the air. The other members of the security team waited for his response. Shoot on sight? Shoot Drew? No. He couldn't let them shoot Drew. He cleared his throat. "Take them alive. There's no reason to hurt anyone unless they fire first."

"Yes, sir," Tor nodded.

Trace quickly left the control room, walking past people without speaking. When he got to his office, he slipped inside and locked the door with a sigh of relief. He didn't want to have to answer any more questions. He was sure the security team found his response to be curious. He pressed his thumbs to his eye sockets. What the hell was he going to do with Drew? To give the order to take hostile invaders alive was risky at best. But he had his reasons, reasons he certainly couldn't discuss with his team.

Drew. There was no way he could give any order which might put his life in danger. Drew had been his passport to the living...and was now a sad part of his past. He allowed the anger to seep into his pores. *One last time, Delano,* he warned himself. Trace got up and paced the room. He knew with each step he took he shouldn't even be here. When he was eleven, he had contracted a rare, but treatable form of Myelocytic Leukemia. His parents, who'd been part of a religious cult that didn't believe in medical intervention of any kind, sat back and prayed as he wasted away to nothing. Miraculously, he survived thanks to a lightning storm and now he was part of the living, albeit a distinct, separate race unto himself.

He didn't feel that way when he met Drew. He felt like he'd found his heartbeat again...it was truly that. His heart beat in a different way when he was around Drew.

"You're a big softie," Drew had whispered to him one night, the first time they kissed. He remembered exactly where they were. On the steps of the old tower of their military college. In the months to come, it was the only place they could fuck in private. That's where they had been, Trace imbedded in Drew's ass the very last time it rained on earth and the rainfall, like hot warm tears from a broken-hearted woman had drawn them closer.

"It won't be the last time I fuck you in the rain," Trace had whispered into Drew's mouth as Drew threw his head back to capture the earth's tears on his tongue. Trace never thought anything would come between them. They'd fought side by side in a multitude of interplanetary battles, and fucked each other's brains out...his Drew. And now, he was headed for this very planet, and somehow Trace knew that it was only a matter of time until they met again. How long had it been now...over seven years? After his stint with the military, Drew had gotten out.

Trace quickened his maddening stride back and forth. It had been the last time they'd fucked in the rain. *Dammit.* Drew went solo, and started his own contracting business. At first, he worked for the Confederation, playing within the rules. Now he sold water to the highest bidder, and not all of them were allies.

When Drew told him he was leaving the military, Trace was devastated. He couldn't understand why. Drew was one of the most promising recruits they'd ever had. Drew went out and bought a ship, state of the art, and the night before he left, he invited Trace to go with him. "We'll be partners," he'd said. "Come on Trace, come with me. I don't want to do this without you. Help me find more rain."

Trace came from a long line of distinguished military officers. His family would have been devastated if he'd left the military to run off with Drew. He had been too young to follow his heart then, too young to stand up to his family. He'd turned Drew down, accused him of being a dreamer, of not thinking things through. He hadn't realised at that time that he was crazy in love with Drew. After Drew left, everything had fallen apart. He couldn't eat or sleep. He quickly fell out of love with the military. Eventually, he too left the military to start his own security firm. He didn't care where his job took him, as long as it was a distraction from the ache Drew had left deep inside of him.

God, there was a time when he could think of nothing else but him, couldn't wait to rip off his clothes, touch his skin, kiss that incredibly hot mouth of his. Trace sank down into his chair, remembering the first time he'd ever set eyes on Drew Lacour. He walked into the classroom at military college that first day, and it was as if the sun itself had suddenly entered the room. Everyone loved Drew. He stood six foot three, solid muscle, gorgeous, unruly black hair that was totally against regulation. He wore those military fatigues so damn well.

They clung to that sensational ass of his, framing it, like a God damned work of art. The professor hated him, of course. He was cocky as hell, and totally without respect, making jokes that had all the students cracking up at the most inopportune moments. Trace was sure they would have booted his ass out if he hadn't been the best in all the physical endurance tests. The others all loved him, not only because he was entertaining but because he took time out to help the others, prop up the weaker students who struggled with the rigorous physical requirements.

Trace could still see those wide, dark eyes of his filled with humour and sensuous

mystery, as if he alone had the answer to some wonderful question. He had a crooked kind of grin which emphasised his square jaw which never seemed to get shaved to the sergeant's specifications. He was Drew, beautiful and seemingly unattainable.

Drew paid very little attention to him at first. He'd nod, say hello. Sometimes, he'd ask to borrow a pencil or explain the homework. Every time he came close to him,

Trace's heart hammered in his chest like a drill. He was intoxicated by him.

One evening, a few months into their training, when Trace was in the locker room, Drew surprised him by walking in. Trace kind of froze up. He knew they were alone for the first time.

"Hey," Drew had said casually, knocking Trace's hat off as he walked by.

Trace reached down to pick up the hat with a shy smile. "Hey yourself, big shot." He glanced at him. "What did you do that for?"

Drew was leaning against his locker nearby, grinning at him. "I just wanted to see you bend over, that's all."

"Ha, ha," he said, "very funny." He might have blushed. "What are you doing here, this late at night? You got permission to go into town, didn't you?"

"Yeah."

"I, ah…thought you were going with the other guys?"

He shrugged. "I was going to, until I found out you were grounded."

"I'm not grounded, I…"

Drew came closer. "Yes, you are. And I know why."

Trace didn't say anything. He could scarcely breathe.

"When the Serge asked who it was who stopped to help Nedermere through the mountain hike this morning, you refused to answer. You knew it was me who carried his pack." Drew met Trace's gaze. "Why didn't you squeal? The Serge threatened to take away your pass if you didn't tell him who did it."

He shrugged. "I don't know."

That was the night they ended up on the tower stairs, when Drew reached out to touch his cheek, Trace melted.

He closed his eyes now, remembering. "I dare say you like me a little bit," Drew had said softly.

Trace's eyes opened. It was all playing before him as if it had just happened. He could recite his own dialogue, his excruciating pain. "I..." he began. "I..."

"I...I...what?" Drew asked him, cocking his head, meeting his gaze.

When Trace didn't answer, Drew motioned to him with his finger. "Come on," he said.

Trace's eyes widened. "Where?"

"I know a place." He reached for his hand.

Trace linked his fingers with him. *Heaven.* It was heaven just to hold his hand.

Drew led Trace back down into the kitchen, now closed for the night. In times to come, it also served as a source of privacy, but for him, the nights on the stairs were what he kept close. He remembered walking through the dark as if he were a cat, never bumping into anything. "You've done this before," Trace said rather than asked.

"It's a great place," Drew said, his voice low and sultry.

It sent a shiver up Trace's spine.

Suddenly they were in the kitchen. In front of them was a long, stainless steel table. Drew released his hand and opened the refrigerator. "What...?" Trace began.

"Take your clothes off," he said. "I'm going to drive you wild."

"Drew, I..." Trace glanced around, "I don't know about this. What if...?"

"We won't be disturbed here, don't worry." He turned around, a tray of artificial ice cubes in his hand. "Come on, baby, get 'em off. I want to see paradise." He paused for a second. "I'm not wrong; you do want me, don't you?"

"Oh…ah, yes," Trace nodded. There was no question of that. "It's just that this is the kitchen and…"

"Sweetie, I'm a bad boy, and that's just what you like about me." He grinned. "Turns you on, doesn't it?" He lifted an eyebrow, and set down the tray. "The thought that we might get caught," he began to unzip his fatigues, "makes me hard as hell."

Trace gazed at the bulge in his pants, watching intently as that zipper slid down, his tongue coming out to wet his lips. *Baby.* Suddenly, it wouldn't have mattered if they were in the sergeant's office, he wanted to touch him. He wanted to taste every inch of his hard cock, and there were abundant inches to taste.

When Drew noticed that Trace hadn't made a move to remove his clothes, he laughed. "Hey, I'm standing here butt naked and you haven't even…"

Trace reached out and grabbed him. He could no longer resist. He pulled Drew into his arms and kissed him the way he'd been dreaming of since the first moment he'd set eyes on him. Slow, deep, and passionate, the kiss went on and on until finally, they broke apart, Drew making some crack about needing to come up for air.

Trace could still see him, his chest heaving, dark eyes filled with need. Drew helped him take off his clothes and pressed him down on that stainless steel table. He'd looked up into those eyes as Drew moved up over his body. He showed him one of the artificial ice cubes. "They don't drip like the real ones," he said, "but they can chill or stiffen just the same." He smiled, licked his lips. It was the most erotic thing Trace had ever seen. Drew moved the cube over Trace's lips slowly then to his chin, trailing it down his throat to his chest. When Drew touched it to Trace's nipple, a shiver ran up his spine. His nipple stiffened, tingling as the frozen ice glazed it over and over again. Drew glanced down at his handiwork, laving Trace's nipple with his tongue then moving the frozen cube over it again. "You have amazing nipples," he said, trailing the cube across to the other nipple. Trace could feel Drew's hard cock graze his inner thigh. He swallowed, grunting as Drew's fingers tweaked his frozen nipple while stimulating the other.

"Um, it's so cold."

"Yeah, and you're so hot," Drew groaned, lowering his mouth to Trace's. The frozen cube escaped Drew's fingers, falling off the table onto the floor.

Trace wrapped his legs around Drew's narrow waist, smoothing his hands down over those incredible biceps of his, and thinking that just maybe, this was heaven.

Even now he could feel Drew's hard cock moving inside of him. No man since Drew had been able to reduce him to a quivering mass of need like that, touching places deep within his soul he didn't know existed until Drew brought him to life. He would have done anything for Drew's touch, had done anything for it. And now, after all this time, after tearing himself away, he'd look into those eyes again.

Chapter Two

There was a voice calling to him now, a fist banging on the door. Trace sat up in his chair, his cock hard. "Damn it. Damn you, Drew," he said aloud, propelling himself out of the chair. *I'm not going to let you do this to me again.* He tore open the door, and barked, "What?"

Tor looked taken aback for a moment.

Trace softened his voice, as he ran a hand over his face. "Sorry. What is it?"

"Lacour's ship has found us, sir. He's set up his equipment on the South side of the planet. He and his crew have been spotted. They're wearing all atmosphere gear."

"Well, that's one thing I can say for Drew, he was always prepared."

"Sir?"

Trace shook his head. "Never mind. How many?"

"We've seen three, including Lacour. We've surrounded the ship. We're confiscating the drilling equipment."

Trace nodded, his gut fighting with some invisible enemy.

"We have Drew Lacour on the teleprompter. He's demanding to talk to someone in charge." Tor winced. "He's pissed."

Trace actually smiled. "Is he now? Tell the men to hold their positions, to await orders from me. I'll deal with Mr. Lacour in here, privately."

"Yes, sir, frequency six," Tor said.

Trace nodded, and closed the door. He walked over to his desk and sat. He hesitated a second then switched on his screen. "Captain Lacour," he said, swallowing hard.

Drew was standing in front of his command station, long dark hair hanging down, shading part of his face. He was holding his all atmosphere head gear. His eyes widened as he looked into the screen. "Trace?"

"Yes. It's me. How are you, Captain Lacour?"

"Captain Lacour, is it? Okay. What in hell are you doing on this God forsaken planet?"

"I'm heading up the security force."

"Then, you're the one! What in hell's the meaning of confiscating my God damned equipment?"

"You have no authorisation to get water here, Captain." God, the years had been more than generous. Trace would have never thought it possible but Drew was even more gorgeous than back at military school. His mind flew back to Drew catching raindrops in his mouth. Looking at Drew was like seeing a mirage of a pool of cool water. Impossibly blue. Impossibly beautiful. He could hardly breathe looking at him.

"We weren't sure if this planet was even inhabited," he growled. "Shit, the average temperature is enough to fry someone alive. Is there really a civilisation under the surface?"

"Yes. And the frozen water is linked to its survival. We've developed a technique to keep the lake isolated from the surrounding environmental heat, only ultilising that heat to melt the water for common usage, as needed."

"Fascinating, but you know the rules."

"Rules?" Trace laughed harshly. "You're citing rules now? That's a laugh. Last time I heard, you no longer even work for the Confederation. You're a rogue, Drew, a pirate, selling a precious dwindling resource to the highest bidder. I'm afraid that you and your crew are now our prisoners."

"Prisoners? Fuck you, Trace. I came here for water, and I intend to leave with some. Unless you have a paper signed by the Confederation stating that the lake is someone's personal property, it's open season."

Trace's heart began to beat heavy in his chest. He'd forgotten how determined Drew could be. "Come on, be reasonable. You are three, four at the most? I've got a security force of over five hundred soldiers, not to mention a back up military force of three thousand. You don't stand a chance."

"Well, I always said I'd go out fighting, or fucking." He grinned. "You remember the last part, don't you baby?"

Trace flushed. "You're pissing me off now, Lacour." *Help me find more rain,* he'd said. Did Drew even remember that?

He threw back his head and laughed. "Bring it on. Give me your best shot." His face faded in front of Trace's eyes.

Trace slammed his fist on the desk. He sprang up out of his seat and tore out of his office. The people at the command centre looked up expectedly as he stormed in. "Destroy his equipment," he bellowed, "blow it up. *Now!* Then send twenty men onto that ship. Take them into custody, and bring Lacour to me, alive."

"What in hell are we doing, Drew?" Will demanded. "Are you nuts? You're going to get us killed."

Drew didn't answer. His attention was captured by the commando of soldiers heading to his drilling machine. "No," he shouted, heading for the exit to the ship, "don't you dare touch my…"

Pagnotella pulled him back. "You can't go out there like that," she fought to hold onto him. "Will, help me."

Will jumped in front of the door. "Drew!"

Drew lifted the head gear and struggled to put it back on.

Pagnotella screamed. "There's too many of them! We'll…"

Suddenly, a loud explosion rocked the ship. Drew tore off the head gear again and raced over to the monitor. He slammed his fist down on the control panel, smashing the glass. "No, no, no. Those bloody…"

Will sighed. "We're screwed."

Suddenly, a loud blast blew in the ship's side entrance. Drew picked up his weapon. Will pressed Drew's arm down to his side as at least five heavily armed soldiers filed in, screaming, "Lower your weapons, and get on the floor, hands behind your heads."

Pagnotella and Will obeyed. Drew clutched the weapon in his hand, standing there defiantly, calculating how many he could possibly get before they got him. Pagnotella reached up and tugged on Drew's sleeve.

"Do it," she hissed at him. "We can't win this."

"I'd sure as hell like to try."

One of the soldiers walked over to him, his gun pointed directly to Will's head. "Do it or he gets it," he said. "We have orders to take you alive, but the other two..." He smirked.

Drew dropped the weapon and got to his knees.

"Nice," the soldier said softly, "very nice, Captain. Take the other two out," he yelled, holding his gun steadily on Drew. "I'll take care of this one."

When the ship was empty, Drew looked up at him. He was young, attractive enough, a little cocky.

"So, you're Drew Lacour," he drawled.

"Seems my reputation precedes me. And you are?" Drew lifted an eyebrow.

"Tor Yarbo. You can call me Sergeant Yarbo."

"I'd like to say that I'm pleased to meet you but under the circumstances — is there a reason why you're standing there staring at me?"

"It seems you have a history with my commander. It's the only reason you're still alive."

"You really don't like me. Um. I assume you do like Trace."

"He's a good man. If we had time, I'd make you take off your clothes."

Drew narrowed his eyes. "Ah, well, I really don't know what to say to that, Sergeant."

"I like to know my competition. With that suit on, you don't look like much."

"Thanks."

"My gun could go off by accident."

Drew met his gaze. "Yes. It could. But I don't think Trace would be very happy about that."

"Whatever you had with him back in school is finished. Is that clear?"

"If you say so."

"If I had my way, you'd be dead. Get up." He backed away, the gun steady on him. "Move it. The commander wants to see you."

"Where is my crew?" Drew got to his feet.

"You have no right to ask anything. Just move." Yarbo poked him with the butt of the gun. He picked up his head gear and threw it at him. "Put it on."

Drew fitted it down over his head. "Why don't you need one?"

"We are immune."

Drew didn't understand how that was possible but he decided to save his questions for Trace. Yarbo pushed him outside and Drew walked on the spongy sand-like ground, his gaze on the frozen lake nearby, and on what was left of his equipment. His blood boiled. He'd never raise enough funds to buy another drilling rig.

"Stop," Yarbo said. "Step onto the platform."

"What platform?" Drew asked, looking around.

Yarbo pulled him a few feet to the left. He lifted his communication device. "Interrogation room," he said.

Suddenly, they began to descend into the ground, concrete all around them. A steel door slid open and they were in a room, surrounded by glass. Yarbo gave him the most sinister smile. "Now," he said, "take them off."

Drew stumbled forward as Yarbo gave him a shove. Another glass encasement moved around him. He was trapped. He pulled off the head gear which suddenly felt stifling and blinked. A strong, glaring light glowed down on him. A mechanical arm appeared and snatched up the head gear, pulling it up and out of the encasement.

"Now the suit," Yarbo insisted, his arms akimbo.

Drew unzipped the atmosphere protection jumpsuit and watched with fascination as the mechanical arm dipped down again and removed it from the cell. He looked out at Yarbo, an eyebrow lifted. "I want to see Trace."

"It's Commander Delano to you."

"Fine, whatever, get him."

"Take off your clothes."

"Dream on," Drew glared at him. "If you want me to stand here bare assed naked, you're going to come in here and take them off yourself, or die trying."

"And it might well be worth dying for," a voice suddenly said.

Drew moved his head sharply to the left to see Trace standing on the other side of the cell.

"Leave us, Sergeant," Trace said, never removing his eyes from Drew.

"Yes, Sir," he said, disappearing.

"Quite the little set up you got here, Trace. I really dig that mechanical arm. Does it do anything else?"

Trace laughed a little. "Actually, yes, but that's for later."

"Where is my crew?"

"Safe, in custody. You're lucky you didn't get them killed."

"They know the risks."

"I apologise for Tor. He's a little gung ho."

"He's in love with you."

"I doubt that."

"He was desperate to see me naked, size me up, so to speak."

Trace found it easier to be angry than to be…sweet. He liked seeing the flicker of doubt, the glimmer of fear in Drew's eyes. It still wasn't enough to make up for the lost years. The irregular heart beat. He took a breath. "I'm afraid to tell you that he was just following procedure. I'm afraid you will have to…ah…take your clothes off."

"All of them?"

Trace nodded.

Drew began to undo his shirt, the confidence back now. "You don't get many visitors I guess."

"We have to make sure you don't have any concealed weapons."

"Deep cavity search as well?" Drew smirked. "Do you handle that personally, Trace?"

Trace looked above, Drew following his gaze. "Oh shit," he mouthed.

"I'm told it's relatively painless."

"*Relatively?*"

"The pants?"

"Patience lover," he grinned. "I'm getting around to it. You know I'm a man who doesn't like to rush these things."

"I have no time for this," Trace snapped.

Drew glanced at him. "You used to. You've changed."

"So have you. You used to have some respect." *You could make love for hours and still beg me to fuck you again.*

"Yeah, only thing was, I had to choose sides, and sometimes they weren't the right sides." Drew unzipped his pants. "You blew up my equipment, Trace. Do you know what that stuff was worth?"

"You should have known that one day it was going to happen. I've heard about some of your ah...adventures."

Drew stepped out of the pants and tossed them aside. He looked up.

"It's waiting for the underwear."

"Right. And you? Are you waiting, too?" Trace was growing impatient. He felt Drew watching him. He knew, thanks to his collision with fate that Drew was thinking: *Your mouth always tightens like that when you're pissed off.*

Trace was furious now that in spite of everything, no rain, no contact...the invisible thread connecting them was still there. It would have thrilled him under other circumstances. Now he yearned to punish the man who'd left him.

"Maybe I should give you to Yarbo, or the men to play with."

"So you can watch?"

"I could have you executed."

"You're going to execute me for touching a nerve?" He laughed slightly, slipping his fingers into the waistband of his white briefs. "If it wasn't for that mechanical thing, I might have a hard on. You know, I used to really get off stripping for you."

"You don't seem to realise the seriousness of this, Drew," Trace snapped. "You are trespassing on..." He stopped.

"Damn you, Drew," his voice was shaky. Once, they'd swum in the last natural lake. Its water was like deepest, darkest India ink. He'd forgotten about that lake. He remembered holding Drew in his arms and the long, drowsy kisses they'd shared. Trace reared his brain from the memory, his mouth falling open, drowning in the past...

"You set yourself up for this."

Drew shook his head. He was staring at Trace and all the pretence...all the bravado fell away. Trace knew and Drew knew it, that Drew didn't want to have to use his body against Trace, but he would if that's all he had. He was a gambler, after all. "You still want me? It can be arranged. Actually, I prefer you to...does it have a name?" He looked above.

There was silence. Trace turned his back. "You will stay there until someone comes for you." His voice was icy cold.

Trace started to walk away and heard the sound of that metal contraption descending over Drew. He heard Drew sigh. "Oh well, guess it's just you and me, honey. And to think, I don't even know your name."

Trace turned the corner of the corridor and pressed his back against the wall, his eyes closed. He reached down and pressed a hand discreetly against his erection. He had failed his own damn test. He'd told himself that watching Drew strip down wouldn't affect him in the same way as it used to. Ha! Who in hell was he trying to fool? He certainly didn't fool Drew. And what in the world had gotten into Tor? Sure, they'd fucked a few times but it was never serious. He liked Tor, but he really didn't feel much more than a deep fondness for him.

He sighed, trying to get himself together, stir the trembling deep inside. Then he smiled a little. He heard a loud yelp. The machine was doing its job. "Revenge is sweet," he said softly, laughing a little. It wouldn't do any permanent damage but Drew might have some difficulty sitting down for a few days.

When he arrived back at the command station, he had a message from the commission. He sat down at his desk and listened to it a second time. "Commander, we need to talk," the voice said. "This latest invasion is serious. Lacour must be interrogated. How many others know about the frozen lake? There might be more on the way here now as we speak. This is the biggest security breach we've ever faced. Report?"

Trace picked up the communicator and dialled the security code for the Commissions Office. "The prisoner is undergoing a body search as we speak. I will interrogate him later today."

A voice replied. "We understand you know the Captain."

"Ah, we were at military school together."

"We hope this will not bias your judgement."

"Of course not."

"We will be waiting for your call."

Trace put down the device.

A few minutes later, Tor came in. He shut and locked the door. "Trace?"

He only called him Trace when they were in bed. Trace's cock twitched automatically. An image of Drew naked flashed in his brain.

Tor moved around behind him and began to rub his shoulders. "I know this is stressful for you, seeing Drew again after all these years. You need to relax."

"Um," he replied. He licked his lips, rubbed his palms down his thighs. "Yes. Go on, it feels good."

"You told me you were in love with him once, remember?"

Tor's hands moved down his shoulders to his chest. He began to undo his shirt.

"It was a long time ago."

"But you're hard, Trace." Tor's lips brushed his ear then swirled his chair around. "He makes you hard, the thought of him."

Trace sucked in some breath as Tor reached for the zipper on his pants. Tor got on his knees in front of him, pulling down the zipper. "I want to watch you together."

Trace shuddered when Tor began to stroke his cock. He leant forward and swiped his tongue across the head. "You need to prove to me it's only lust."

He tried to grasp what Tor was saying, but he was close to the edge, Drew's naked body still taunting his thoughts. "What are you...ah...God," he grunted. A couple more firm strokes from Tor's hand, and he came with a satisfied grunt. Tor began licking the cum from the head of his cock.

Trace tried to bring his breathing back to normal. When he'd recovered, he gently pushed Tor's head back. "Stop," he said. "Tell me what you just said?"

Tor smiled at him, running his hands over Trace's thighs. "I want to see you with Drew Lacour, fucking."

"That's out of the question," Trace snapped. "Lacour is a prisoner, and..."

Tor stood up. "The commission doesn't know you and Lacour had a thing. They only know you were at military school together. If they find out, you won't have control over the situation anymore. Lacour will be executed."

Trace stood up, hastily doing up his pants. "What in fuck are you saying, Tor?"

He backed away, put up his hand. "You need to understand, Trace. I won't compete with Drew Lacour. I may have your body, but I need to be sure that Drew no longer has your heart. I know that he can make you hard. Remember all those nights we talked about him? Do you think it was because I really wanted to go down memory lane with you? Hell, Trace, I wanted to fuck you. You were so hot and horny after talking about that prick. He's your aphrodisiac. Without him, you'd be no good to me. I'll make sure Lacour makes it out of here alive, on two conditions, he's going to have to do what we say with your cooperation, and I will have to be convinced that all you feel for Drew is lust."

"I can't believe this. All of this is totally against regulations, Tor. We can't rape the prisoner."

"There will be no rape involved, Trace, and we both know that. From what you told me about Drew, he won't fight too much." Tor gave him a meaningful look. "He's there now, naked, helpless. And you still want him. You can insist on an isolated ten day interrogation. The Commission will sanction it, and you know it. You can request my assistance at any time, day or night."

"It's over between Drew and me, Tor. Why can't you just accept that?"

"Because I see the way you look at him. If it's only lust, I can deal with that. But I'm not convinced."

"Even if I wanted to, I…" Trace threw up his hands.

"There's no harm in it, Trace. He wants you as much as you want him."

"He doesn't like to be ordered about."

"Haven't you ever wanted to have your way with him, dominate him sexually?"

"I..." Trace swallowed. They'd played at that, some very light restraints, but it was voluntary. Drew wasn't his prisoner. "I could report you for this. How dare you blackmail me, Tor?"

"All's fair in love and war. And I dare because I can. Think about it. You have twenty-four hours before I go to the commission and tell them how well you really do know Drew Lacour."

Trace sunk down into his chair. He would have never believed that Tor could do such a thing. If the Commission found out that he and Drew had had an intimate relationship, they would take Drew completely out of his hands, perhaps put Tor in control. Tor wouldn't hesitate to have Drew executed. He couldn't allow that.

He stood up and walked down the corridor, back to the interrogation cell. A bunk had been placed in the cell, along with a portable waste unit. Drew lay on the bunk, his hands tucked under his head, gloriously naked.

"So, are you going to stand there gawking at me all day, or did you come to say something?"

Trace shifted his gaze away from his gorgeous cock to his chest. Not better. He bit his lip when he looked at his face. How was he going to do this? Drew would fight him all the way. "I want you to listen to me. I'm trying to save your life."

Drew sat up. "Now you care?"

"What? What does that mean?"

"I thought you gave up on me years ago."

"I...you left me, remember?" The words sounded bitter suddenly.

"I asked you to come with me. You refused. You loved the military more than me." There was no humour in Drew's voice. That was rare.

"It's in the past."

"Not for me."

Trace was taken aback. He'd always felt like the rejected one, the one left behind. But Drew spoke as if it was him. "You decided to leave, damn you. Don't you blame me!"

"You chose your family. You couldn't stand up to them. Even after they were willing to just let you to die." Drew stood up.

Trace didn't reply. He couldn't argue that. He cleared his throat. "Stop talking. That was then. This is now. You are in deep shit, Drew Lacour. Your life is entirely in my hands right now." He didn't mention Tor. "There are those who think you should be executed."

"I want to plead for the lives of my crew members," he said. "They were only following orders, my orders. I take complete responsibility for my actions."

That was his Drew, his hero. He hadn't changed. No worry for his own life, only those he loved. "I will see what I can do."

"It's me they want."

"Yes. And I need to know what you know."

"About what?"

"How many other people know about the frozen lake?"

"Hell, I don't know. And I don't give a shit."

"We need to know whether others will follow."

"I work alone. You know that. I'm not about to share the wealth with anyone. If others follow me here, they didn't hear it from me."

"How did you know about this place?"

"I won it in a poker game."

"Seriously," Trace persisted, his gaze gravitating back to him. God, he was so beautiful. Tor's idea was beginning to have real appeal.

"I won it in a poker game. The guy couldn't pay in money, so he paid in information."

"Who was it?"

"Who was who?"

"You know who, Drew. Don't fuck around. Who was the poker player?"

"I don't know. We weren't on first name basis."

"Where was he from?"

"I don't remember."

"You're lying."

Drew shrugged, turning and walking back to the bunk, giving Trace a good look at that luscious ass of his. Trace's mouth began to water. *Mercy, Lord.* He turned his back. "I'm recommending a total, intensive, interrogation."

"I think I had one of those already," he sat down on the bunk again and actually gave him one of those crooked grins of his. "I'm not sure who enjoyed it more, me or it."

"This is different. We'll be alone. And you'll be under my control, totally. And if you want to live, Drew," Trace met his gaze, "you'll cooperate."

Drew narrowed his eyes. "Meaning?"

"You'll do everything I tell you to do. And you'll answer my questions or face the consequences."

"God, you're so sexy when you're domineering, Trace." He laughed, but Trace saw the flash of concern in his eyes.

"Someone will be coming for you," Trace said, prepared to walk away.

"Trace," Drew said suddenly.

Trace paused but he didn't turn around.

"Do you remember those imitation ice cubes?"

Trace squared his jaw. "Yeah."

"You used to enjoy it when I'd…"

"Yeah, your point?"

"Be careful you haven't turned into one."

"Fuck you, Drew."

Chapter Three

A few hours later, four soldiers came for him. They dragged him along a long, dark corridor and down a flight of stairs. He was hauled past several locked doors and then pushed into a room which looked more like a sexual torture chamber than an interrogation room. It was cold in there. He could hear the water trickling through the walls. "Get on the bed," one of the soldiers directed.

"Are my crew down here?" he asked, as another soldier pushed him onto the bed.

"Never mind. Put your hands over your head and spread your legs."

He didn't really have much of a chance to comply. One soldier chained his right wrist to the headboard and the other repeated the same with his left. At the same time, his ankles were being attached. Then they left him, locking the door behind them. He looked up to see a camera peering down at him, no mechanical arm this time, which was a relief.

He closed his eyes. He felt as if he was in some kind of a nightmare. He had no idea what had happened to Pagnotella or Will. He'd been stripped naked since the moment he'd arrived and kept in a glass case like an animal, and now, he felt as if he were the star in some kinky porn film. Not to mention Trace.

God, it had been tough to see him again. He'd been so much in love with Trace at one time. And he thought Trace loved him just as much. But, when push came to shove, Trace chose his career over him, and left him high and dry. Drew had vowed never to fall in love like that again. And he never had.

And Trace had changed. He seemed hard, bitter even. It was true, they were in opposite camps right now, but treating him like this seemed a little extreme. These people were making far too much of this. Okay, so he came to take water, water they didn't want taken but they'd destroyed his livelihood. What more did they want? Execution seemed a little far-fetched. And now, this, handcuffed to the bed.

When the door opened a little while later, Drew opened his eyes, realising that he must have dozed off. He grunted, trying to stretch. The muscles of his inner thighs felt sore and his wrists hurt. He blinked when a strong white light came on overhead. Trace and that crazy sergeant stood there. The Tor guy had his hand on Trace's shoulder. He propelled him forward. This was weird. "Have you been demoted?" He asked Trace, trying to sound serious but it came out sarcastic.

"No," Trace said. His gaze moved over him. "God, you're beautiful."

"Is this a new interrogation technique? If it is, it's interesting."

"Shut up," Tor said.

He went to strike Drew, but Trace put up a hand and blocked him. "No."

"Now, that's more like it," Drew muttered.

Tor glared at him. "You are our prisoner. Remember that. You will do as we say."

Drew looked at Trace. His expression was unreadable. His gaze returned to Tor, who was removing his shirt. "What the fuck?"

"I'm trying to save your life," Trace said. "So for once, just do as you're told, okay?"

Drew's eyes returned to Tor, who was taking off his pants. "You're not touching me, cretin," Drew growled. He shifted his gaze to Trace. "You, neither."

"Don't worry," Tor said. "For now, I'm only here to observe. And you, Drew, you're a big boy, not a silly little virgin. Take it like a man, and enjoy. It's better than the alternative. Trace," he licked his lips, "get your clothes off, and get started. I can't stay here with you all night."

Trace could no longer hear anything Tor said. He didn't even care that he was in the room. He ripped off his shirt without unbuttoning and yanked at the zipper on his pants.

Drew had been sputtering off a string of curses a few minutes before but now he was quiet, those beautiful dark eyes looking at him. Trace left his clothes behind on the floor and moved to the bed. He sat down beside Drew, laid a hand on his calf, swallowed, told himself not to fall apart. *Play the part. Don't show any emotion.* He lowered his lips to Drew's thigh and moved his hand up his other leg.

"Have you lost your mind?" Drew struggled. "Trace."

Trace raised his head. "Listen," he said, meeting his gaze, already drunk on his nearness. "You are here. You're my prisoner to do with what I choose. You want to live, you'll be a good boy, and do what I want you to. You used to like me to touch you."

"Yes," he said, nodding. "But you were a different man then."

"A coward, apparently, who couldn't act on what he wanted," Trace said, moving closer and leaning forward to kiss his lips.

Drew moved his head to avert his kiss.

That hurt. "Fine, if that's the way you want to play it." He reached out and grabbed his face between his hands, forcing his mouth on his.

Again, Drew resisted him, trying to pull away. He wasn't going to make it easy.

Trace's fingers grazed Drew's cock. He remembered almost instinctively what used to drive him crazy. He tried not to let his eyes close. He pushed back a moan as he let his tongue trail down over the hard marbled chest to his groin. He inhaled his scent for a moment, pressing his lips against his cock. *Oh God yes, yes. Drew. My beautiful Drew.* His heart sang. He wanted to cry out with joy. But Tor was there, close, watching his every move. He lifted his head, took Drew's cock in his hand, stroking it with determination, while Drew seethed at him.

"Come on, Lacour," Trace told him with a smirk, "get it up for me. I need a nice, stiff cock."

"You need a good kick in the ass," came the reply, as he tried to shrink away from him.

Trace laughed falsely. "You're getting hard. I guess you like it rough. I plan to ride that gorgeous dick of yours."

Drew gave him an incredulous look. "Who in the hell are you?"

The stroking was doing its job.

Drew lost his bravado suddenly and let his body relax, his cock fully erect. Beautiful. He was absolutely breathtaking, his body now slick with sweat, his face strained with need. Trace straddled him, kissed his chin, his throat, brought his tongue down to lap at his nipples, now forming stiff peaks in response. He laved each nipple with gusto, revelling in the taste of him as he reached down to fondle his cock again. "Drew," he groaned, trailing his tongue down to his navel, licking his inner thigh, suckling his balls.

"I want to prepare you," Tor said from behind.

Tor's voice startled him for a moment. He'd almost forgotten he was in the room. Some cold lube hit his anus. He licked his lips, anticipating the feel of Drew's cock moving in and out of him. Tor inserted a finger in his ass, moving it in and out as Trace laved the underside of Drew's cock.

"He's got a big cock," Tor said. "You need to be ready."

"I'm ready," Trace growled, pushing Tor's hand away. He positioned himself on top of Drew, seizing his cock, which earned him a hiss from between Drew's teeth. He met Drew's gaze. "I want you. Give it to me, all of it. Tonight, it's mine, to use exactly the way I want to. Understand?"

Drew gasped as Trace bore down on his cock, guiding it deeper and deeper up inside him. When he could take no more, he began to move, using his knees and the muscles of his thighs to move on and off of Drew's cock. His pace varied between frenzy and a slow sensuous fucking that would have made angels cry. He came in a way he hadn't come in years, stroking his own cock, and watching his spray spread over Drew's belly and chest. Drew came soon after, his hips bucking with a force that practically knocked Trace off the bed.

Tor's hand reached out and steadied him. When Trace glanced at him, he noticed that he was already half dressed. "I'm leaving. I got to go on shift. Do what you want. Have fun." He kissed him on the forehead and headed to the door.

Trace wasn't quite in the world. He sat there on the edge of the bed, breathing hard, the reality of what had just happened finally sinking in. He reached out and laid his hand on Drew's thigh but he couldn't look at him.

"You still love me," Drew said suddenly.

Trace looked at him sharply. "Don't be ridiculous."

"I can feel it. I felt it when I was inside you." Drew's voice was calm, serene. "Why are you doing this? What's going on with you and that fool, Tor? I don't get it."

Trace stood up and clicked off the main light. The room was suddenly bathed in semi darkness. "He's not a fool. He's my...I love him."

"You're a liar."

"You know Drew," Trace shook his head. "You might stop being arrogant for a minute and--"

"It's not arrogance. I'm not an idiot. I could feel it in your touch. You touch me like a man in love. What did you mean earlier about saving my life?"

Trace began to dress. "I'm in charge. I ask the questions. Now, you're going to tell me about that man in the poker game." He paused, looked at him.

"I told you, I don't remember." He glanced at him defiantly.

"Why are you protecting him?"

"Because his life is as valuable as mine."

Trace felt his heart melt. He wanted to touch him, to say, *oh Drew, my Drew*, but he couldn't. "So, thanks for the fuck," he said coldly. "It was okay. Not your best."

"Kind of difficult," Drew replied, his voice equally icy, "with the restraints."

"Yeah, well, when I come back, we'll see if you can still suck cock."

"Aren't you afraid I might bite it off?"

"You won't, if you want to see your crew again."

"You fucker."

Trace shrugged with a bravado he didn't feel. "I'll be back. Don't miss me too much." He headed for the door, trying to block out the host of obscenities Drew hurled at him. When he had closed and locked the door, he hurried down the corridor, brushing away the tears that rolled down his cheeks.

It was all coming back to him. All the pain, the pleasure...he couldn't cope. Why had he done this? It was crazy. What had he proven? He still loved Drew and Drew loved him. But it was stupid, pointless. He wandered down the corridor and felt the blast of cool air. Water. It was all he could think about. There was a time when he and Drew revelled in it, loved in it...before everything went wrong. He turned south, nodding to the guards outside the captive Will's cell. He placed his hand on the override plate and the door clicked open.

He could smell the man's fear, stepping forward to find him cowering on a bunk, blood trickling from his lower lip.

Trace frowned. "Who hit you?" He stepped closer. Somebody had given the guy quite a beating. Will was shivering and Drew saw the dilated pupils. His entire system was in danger of shutting down. "Don't be afraid. I won't let anyone else hurt you. I know we don't know each other but if you'd just talk to me..."

"I do know you," he said weakly through half closed eyes. "You and Trace were at military school together."

"Did he...ah...speak of me?"

"Only when he was drunk."

Trace stiffened. "Oh. Look. If you care anything about your own life and the lives of your..."

"I'll do anything to protect Drew." He half rose off the cot, his voice going up an octave.

Another sucker hopelessly in love. "Relax. Save your strength."

"I don't know anything. Drew would never tell us anything he thought might make us vulnerable. He took all the risks. Don't hurt him, please. Take me instead."

Trace swallowed. "Rest now." He knew that if Will had any information, he would have told him. He would have done anything to save Drew.

As Trace left the cell, he wondered if Drew and Will were lovers. Of course they were.

Drew dreamt of rain. It was warm and enveloping. He gulped it as it quenched him totally. *You are so beautiful.* The voice filled his head at the same time as the warm liquid trickled down his throat. He was impaled by a thick, insistent cock, caught and held in the throes of its need. He thrust his hips upwards, the rain hitting his face, splattering his chest, running in rivers down his belly and over his erection, mingling with its creamy spray. *"Um, you're all wet."* Hands moved down over his flesh. He sighed, closed his eyes, the greedy cock inside of him pulsing with satisfaction. *"I'll love you forever, Drew. I loved you from the moment I saw you. Baby. Baby. Let me lick off the rain...please...please..."*

Drew's eyes snapped open, sensing he wasn't alone. He blinked in the harsh light of the room. Tor Yarbo stood there, a sneer on his face. God, how he would like to wipe that sneer off his face. If he could break these restraints, he would.

"Must have been some dream," Yarbo commented, crossing his arms.

"What do you want?" Drew gave him a hostile look.

"No worries. I didn't come for that. Trace is all that I want. He just needs to come to his senses."

Drew laughed. "Oh."

"Don't get all cocky with me, Lacour. You really do think you're something, don't you?"

"I don't have to, because apparently you do."

"No. But Trace does. It seems he hasn't lost his obsession with you. So, I have two choices. I can kill you now. That would actually be a good choice. You'd be permanently unavailable. And the counsel would let Trace off the hook for not giving the order to kill you on sight."

"Trace is in trouble?"

Tor Yabo shook his head. "Always the hero. Did you hear what I said?"

"Yeah, you want to kill me. Big news flash. But you won't. So, I'm not worried."

"I could kill Will, your cock sucking lackey. Is he good at it? Maybe I'll try him out."

"Don't you touch him."

"Too late for that, I'm afraid."

"If you've hurt him, I'll…"

"You'll what, stud?"

Drew swore under his breath, pushing against the constraints. "What do you want from me?"

"You'll do anything to save your crew?"

"Of course I will."

"Convince Trace you have no feelings for him anymore?"

"I never said differently."

"But you do…have feelings for him still?"

"None of your fucking business."

"I want you to disappear, Lacour. And I can make that happen. I can get you out of here, discreetly. Make it look like an escape."

"You're one devious son of bitch. You'd betray everything to get rid of me? Killing me might be easier."

"No," he shook his head. "Trace would never forgive me for that, I'm afraid."

"Oh, so," Drew laughed softly, "he'd never let you into his bed again, is that it?"

"Don't you laugh at me, you smug son of a bitch," he raised his voice, came forward, and glared down at him.

Drew met his eyes without flinching.

"Just because you look like some kind of Greek God, bad boy, just because you got a..." He raked his eyes over him. "I could cut it off."

"Yes, you could," Drew said between clenched teeth. "But then you'd have to kill me, because if you didn't, I'd come after you, and I'd kill you ever so slowly, Yarbo. I'd make it hurt."

Tor flinched, took a step back suddenly.

Drew smiled faintly at his victory.

"Think about what I said." Tor pointed at him. "I'll get you, the woman, and your cock sucker out of here, on a military craft, no one will know until it's all over. All you got to do is tell Trace you feel nothing for him, and never come back here again."

"And if I refuse?"

"I'll kill Will, and that alien woman. And I'll throw both you and Trace to the wolves. You'll die together."

"You'd sacrifice the man you're supposed to love?"

"Rather than let you have him? In a heartbeat."

"I don't think that's love."

"And what is love?"

"Trace pretending he doesn't feel anything anymore to save my ass and me letting you get us out of here, so that I save his."

He shrugged. "If you say so. I'll arrange it."

"How do I know I can trust you?"

"You don't. Just know this, if you're out of the way, I'll be the one Trace turns to for comfort. He'll be mine. I protect what belongs to me."

Drew considered his words, swallowed hard. "Do it."

Tor saluted him. "Nice knowing you, Captain."

Drew closed his eyes at the same time as the door closed. This was insane. Time hadn't diminished the feelings he'd had for Trace. If anything, they were even more intense, urgent. Earlier when Trace had touched him, Drew knew he'd been trying so hard to appear detached, too damn hard. But his mouth trembled when he kissed him, and his hands shook like a drunk who was in desperate need of a drink. It wasn't just ordinary lust. When Trace came, his entire body roared with its release, as if the sky had opened up and embraced him, drenching him in its moisture. Trace loved him still. And damn it, Drew loved him back. And that was why he had to do all he could to save him.

Less than a half hour, Trace found himself in front of the commission, being asked questions he had no answers for. "You do know the rogue leader of this craft, don't you?"

"We were at military school together."

"Friends?"

"I wouldn't say that."

"Are you sure your judgement is not affected?"

Trace shielded his eyes from the harsh light which hit him in the face and shook his head. "I've put him into intensive interrogation, sir. He will talk."

"Very well. If he doesn't, start eliminating the crew."

Trace sucked in a breath. He nodded. "Yes, Sir."

He was dismissed. He walked out of the room quickly, almost running down the corridor. He had to get Drew to tell him something, anything, so that they could stall for time. He pushed the security code and watched the door slide open. He pressed it again and waited for it to slam shut behind him. Drew lay there, watching him quietly as he approached the bed. "Back for more already?"

"Drew, I'm—sorry."

"Sorry for what?"

"What happened, this. All this. Look, baby," he said, sinking down onto the side of the bed. Drew's dark eyes looked back at him, his expression sombre. "We need to work together. If you give me some information, anything about that poker player, I can…"

"I told you, I don't know anything. And don't call me baby."

Trace sighed. "Fine. Be like that. You know that I still…Drew, I love you."

"Well, that's your problem," he replied. "I don't love you. In fact, what we had was a long time ago. It's over."

Trace felt something break inside him. "You're a liar," he said, barely able to get the words out. "I don't believe you."

He shrugged.

Trace stood up, turned away. He blinked away the tears that threatened, chastising himself silently. *Don't be a damn fool.* He swallowed the sadness and turned it to anger. He whirled back around and glared down at him. "So, you have no feelings left for me. Fine. Then I guess I shouldn't feel guilty about taking what I want. After all," he continued harshly, taking off his clothes, "you're nothing but a fine piece of well hung meat, beautiful, cold and deadly, a pirate, a criminal and a cock sucking thief." Clothes discarded, he crawled naked up over his legs and his torso, roughly pushing Drew's head back, Trace straddled his neck and forced his jaw wide open. He positioned his cock over the opening and leered down at him. "Now, go to work, lowlife, and if you do my cock any damage, be assured, I'll kill you."

The sensation of his cock slipping into the velvet lining of Drew's throat was overwhelming. The tough bravado quickly drained out of him and as Drew expertly sucked his cock, his eyes closed, giving all indication that he was enjoying the job, Trace's head fell back and he began to moan involuntarily. Damn, he'd almost forgotten how good Drew was at that. Almost. He heard whimpering. He realised it was coming from him. He reached his hands down and planted them in Drew's hair. "Baby, baby, oh baby, yes, yes, yessssssssssssss."

His body moved backwards, a jet stream of cum spraying across Drew's chest and down his belly. He sat back between his open thighs, his eyes closed, savouring, recovering.

Drew was quiet when Trace finally looked at him again. Their gazes met. Trace moved his hand up over Drew's thigh to his cock. He was hard, gloriously so, beautifully erect and his for the taking. "I want you," he whispered, leaning forward and swirling his tongue over the head of his dick.

"I can't very well refuse," he said softly.

"You want me too," Trace met his eyes.

"Don't make too much out of it. Lust isn't love."

"No. But at least it's something." He moved his cheek against his cock then took it into his mouth.

Drew's hips rose off the mattress, driving his cock deeper into Trace's eager mouth.

Trace's mouth came off his shaft with a smacking sound. He licked his lips. "I want your cock inside of me. I want you to come inside me." He crawled up over his hips and seized Drew's cock, guiding it up in between his ass cheeks. He spread his knees, opening to him, closing his eyes and holding his breath as he impaled himself with Drew's thickness. "Oh yeah," he breathed, "Yeah." It was his to control. Drew was his for this moment. He had no intention of wasting it. He took it deeper still then began to move off of it, then plunge back down, faster, straining, needed, crying out. He used Drew's cock, rode it exactly the way he wanted, the way he needed it.

Drew's cum flooded up inside of him, his deep grunt of satisfaction and perfect sighs driving Trace to another orgasm. How he loved those sighs, how he loved him. Two tears fell, silently from his eyes, down his cheeks. "I wish I could hate you," he said, stroking the final drops of cum from his own cock and rubbing it over Drew's broad, well muscled chest. He massaged his nipples with the cream for a second, then dipped down to lick the stiffened, glistening peaks, his own cock moving against one of Drew's inner thighs. "You are a beautiful man," he whispered, taking one of his nipples between his teeth and teasing it, nibbling there. "I'm not finished with you tonight."

"So I gathered," he replied, moaning a little as Trace reached down with his hand to fondle his balls.

"It's time I fucked you, don't you think?" Trace fondled his cock carelessly with his hand, pulling at his nipple with the other. It was having the desired effect.

Drew groaned and lifted his ass off the bed.

"What do you want, big boy?" Trace teased, pulling at his nipple again. "Beautiful. I should film you, naked, submissive, willing. No one would believe it." He moved down, kissing his chest, his stomach, burying his face in his groin for a moment and licking his cock, his balls, his inner thighs. Then he inserted one finger up inside of him, deep, without warning, enjoying his grunt of surprise, perhaps initial discomfort. He began to fuck him with the finger, sitting back, watching his face, enjoying the beautiful view. With his thighs spread like this and his knees slightly bent, his hands tied securely over his head, his chest glistening with sweat and his nipples, two, delectable stiff peaks, he was a sight to behold. Trace's cock was already hard and ready again. "I can't wait to be inside your ass, but not like this."

Drew moaned softly as Trace withdrew his finger. He jumped off the bed, searched his pants for the keys to the restraints and undid Drew's ankles. Drew watched him, an eyebrow raised. "You must really want a fuck."

Trace glanced up at him, crawling on the bed again and lifting Drew's legs over his shoulders. "Why'd you say that?"

Suddenly, Drew's legs twisted around Trace's neck, tight.

"You've forgotten your training sweetie, you don't remember? I can break your neck like this."

Trace felt his air being closed off. He struggled, clutching at Drew's legs, but he couldn't move them.

"That's what happens when you think with your cock," Drew laughed. That was the last thing Trace heard before the darkness.

It wasn't long before Tor burst into the room. He froze for a moment surveying the scene of Trace lying with this head on Drew's upper thigh. Drew had to say that he thoroughly enjoyed the expression on that bastard's face, a mix of rage and extreme jealousy. "What the hell?"

Drew cocked his head. "I suggest you undo my wrists and put your little plan into motion."

"What did you do to him?" He demanded, rushing over and taking Trace's pulse.

"It's what he did to me, and I'm sure you're not interested in the details. He's fine. He's just out for a while. Okay, I'm ready, get me out of here."

Tor stood back, took a breath. "It will take at least an hour. I need to enact the shield so no one sees the ship leave. Can you handle a 23A1delta6?"

"I can drive anything. Get my crew."

"I'll just take Trace back to..."

"You won't be taking Trace anywhere. He's coming with me."

Tor folded his arms across his chest and laughed. "No way."

"Ever heard the expression, if you love something, set it free?"

"Ever heard the word, no?"

Drew laughed. "Not too often."

"Um, I can imagine, but you're hearing it now. It defeats my purpose, doesn't it? I'm letting you leave so that..."

"Yes, I know, so that you can lick Trace's wounds, heal his broken heart, drive home to him what a rogue bastard I am...but there's one flaw in your plan, after I'm gone, who do you think they'll blame for my escape? Who'll they punish?"

"If he goes with you, I'll..."

Drew put up his hand. "I'll honour our agreement. You have my word."

"You'll make him believe you don't care for him?"

"If I have to beat the crap out of him, but if you want him to stay alive, he has to go with us. I'll take him home. You can find him there." Drew looked away. It was the only way. He might be a rogue. He might have stretched a few rules, and had a memory lapse or two when it came to integrity, but he was a man of his word. If he had to break Trace's heart, send him back to this prick to keep him alive, he'd do it. He couldn't stand the thought of something happening to Trace. Even if they weren't together, there was peace in knowing he was living and breathing somewhere. It didn't matter anyway, there'd never be anyone else for him but Trace, his drink of water, his life.

"You got quiet there, Captain, second thoughts?"

"Trust me or not, but make your damn choice."

"I could just leave you here, report what you've done. You'd be killed immediately."

"And Trace would hate you."

Tor swore under his breath.

"You want to own, possess him, fuck that sweet ass of his every night, then let me take him out of here, protect him. He'll lose his job but he'll find something else. Or he can just come back and say I kidnapped him, took him hostage."

"Um, that might work. Okay, I'll prepare."

"Hey, ah…the hands? I need clothes too."

"Right, okay." Tore came over and undid his wrists.

It took everything he had not to put his fist through Tor's face, but he couldn't, not if he wanted to get everyone out of here. Instead, he gave him a forced grin. "Get the clothes. Get my crew."

Chapter Four

It was the motion which roused him, a high hurling sound, and then the sensation of movement, fast, reckless. His teeth rattled in his head for a moment. He went to reach out but found he couldn't. His hands were tied behind his back. He swore, struggled with the ropes. He was sitting on the floor in a dark compartment. There was something in his mouth. He tried to call for help but he was only able to utter a muffled sound. His throat hurt. Then he remembered. Drew.

A light flicked on overhead. He blinked. Drew stood there, dressed in some blue pants which looked a little too big on him, and a white shirt which wasn't his style at all. "Hello Trace, comfy?"

Trace glared at him.

Drew laughed. He walked over and leant down, removing the gag from his mouth.

"What in the...?"

"You're my hostage," he shrugged.

"Where are we?"

"On a ship, courtesy of your employers."

"You commandeered a ship?"

"Well, I wasn't just going to lay there and die, or let you fuck me to death, whichever came first. And I really had to take a wicked piss."

"How? How did you...?"

"You look furious."

"Drew. You almost killed me. You..."

Drew grinned. "No honey. If I'd have wanted to kill you, you'd be dead."

"Who undid your cuffs?"

"You're just full of questions, now aren't you?" He folded his arms across his chest and cocked his head.

"Drew!"

"Um?"

"How did you..."

"Captain," a male voice called out suddenly, "we're running into a lot of turbulence."

"I'm coming, Will," he called back.

"Um, wonder how many times you said those words," Trace grumbled.

"I'll never tell," he winked and disappeared from the cabin.

Trace made several attempts to struggle to his feet. With his hands still tied, he made it from the cabin to the control room. Pagnotella was at the controls, Will co-piloting. Drew was peering at the screen over the woman's shoulders. "It's like nothing I've ever seen before," he muttered.

"Yes, and thick," Pagnotella pointed out.

"Go slowly, but keep moving, put the craft into downshift eight. That should keep her steady and alert us to any new navigational problems."

"Okay," she said. "Sounds sane."

"Why, thank you, woman," he teased, looking up as he spotted Trace.

Pagnotella sniggered.

Will glanced at Drew. "Should the hostage be walking around?"

"It's not like I can escape," Trace sneered, coming closer to the screen. He too studied. "Unusual," he said to Drew, "a little frightening."

"Exciting," Drew countered.

Trace hid a smile. That was Drew. Fear was foreign to him. Suddenly, Drew reached over and grabbed his arm. He pulled him forward. For a second, Trace's pulse raced, he thought he was going to kiss him. Instead, he whirled him around and untied his hands.

"That's not a good idea," Will protested.

Drew ignored him.

Trace glanced at him, noticing how battered his face still looked. "I'm sorry about the beating. I would have never authorised that."

Will just looked away.

Drew looked at him suddenly. "Come with me. We need to talk."

"Yes, we damn well do. I want answers."

"You're not in control here," Drew told him, eyeing him. "I give the orders."

Trace groaned as he followed Drew down the corridor to the room at the end of the hall. He rubbed his neck. It was bruised, and beginning to hurt like hell.

Drew looked at him. "It will be all right in few days. Close the door."

Trace sucked in some breath. Alone, with Drew. It was painful, especially since Drew told him he no longer felt anything for him. "So, what do you want to talk about? You want to tell me again how you don't feel anything for me?"

Drew lowered his head, sighed. "No. I've already said what I needed to on that subject. I want to let you know that there's no need for you to worry about your job. We took you hostage. You didn't have a choice and…"

"Do you honestly think I care about my job, or that I could possibly go back there? It doesn't matter how it happened. It showed incompetence on my part, and they were already questioning my judgement where you were concerned."

"Did you tell them that we were lovers?"

"No. But they probably all ready know. So, how did you do it?"

"Tor."

"Tor? Not exactly your greatest ally."

"I threatened to kill you if he didn't help us escape." He paused. "He…ah…loves you."

Trace narrowed his eyes, observing how Drew suddenly turned his back. "I don't love him. And it's not love really. It's more about possession with him and…"

"I'll take you home," he said abruptly. "As soon as it's safe then you can go back to Tor, or…"

"I don't love Tor. I love you." There was no point lying, in trying to deny it.

Silence.

Trace swallowed. "Well," he managed, "I'll try to stay out of your way until…" He stopped, the words stuck in his throat. "And Will?"

"Will is my friend."

"He wants more, much more. He wants to touch you, to make love to you, to kiss that hot, sweet mouth of yours and…"

"Trace!" Drew snapped, turning around.

"I…I'm sorry," he shook himself. It was as if he had no control. Did he want him to beg, fall to his knees and plead for his touch? He would have if he'd thought it would do any good. Drew looked miles away suddenly even though he was standing right in front of him.

"I have to get back to the controls. Feel free to make your way around the ship."

"Where do I sleep?" He met his gaze. The question hung in the air between them.

"We'll talk about that later," Drew said, brushing by him.

It was Will who showed him a bunk in a dark corner of the ship. He threw a blanket and a pillow at him. "Don't make trouble," he barked.

Trace did his best to sleep but to no avail. Finally, he got up and wandered along the long corridor to the control room. It was empty, except for Drew, who sat there in front of the controls, with his face in his hands. He looked up when he heard the sound behind him.

"Can't sleep?"

Trace shook his head. "Your watch?"

"Yep."

"Can I sit with you?"

Drew looked at him for a second then shrugged.

After a few minutes, Trace said softly, "So, who was the gambler?"

"Huh?"

"The gambler who gave you the tip?"

"There wasn't any."

Trace leant back in the seat and laughed. "You made it up?"

"Yep."

"Why?"

He turned in his seat, arms akimbo and grinned. "My crew would have fought me on it if I'd told them the truth. I would have never gotten them to go there."

"So, what was the truth?"

"I had a dream."

"A dream?"

He leant forward. "I dreamt of a frozen lake. I dreamt of you."

Trace met his gaze. His throat ached. "I see."

He leant back again, all of a sudden far away again. There was silence. "Now what?"

"I don't know. I have this ship but my equipment is gone. And this craft isn't exactly equipped for water excavation."

"Back to the military?"

Drew laughed. "No way."

"You could always be a rent boy. You got the body for it."

Drew grinned. "Too old."

Trace reached across and touched his hands. He searched his face, his gaze falling on his mouth. "Oh no, not at all." He grabbed his hair and pulled, surprised when Drew didn't balk. Their lips met hungrily, Drew returning kiss after kiss.

Trace fumbled for the zipper on Drew's pants, whipping it down and struggling to get his hand inside. He sighed into Drew's mouth when his anxious fingers found his cock. His lips went to Drew's throat, pulled his T-shirt up and over his neck, throwing it aside. He pressed his shoulders back to the chair, licked his nipples, his chest, his stomach, squeezing and massaging his cock until it sprang up and out, brushing Trace's lips. "Tell me again how you don't love me, Drew?" He wet his lips and sucked the length of Drew's scrotum.

Drew reared back in the chair. "Lust is lust," he grunted.

"God damn right," Trace growled, taking Drew's cock into his mouth and swallowing it half way.

Drew's hand landed in his hair. "It doesn't mean..." he moaned.

Trace took him deeper into his throat, his hands tightening on Drew's calves. Drew's cum filled his mouth. Drew shouted. Trace released his cock from his mouth and held it for a second, pressing his lips to it just before Drew shrunk away from him, wheeling back in his chair.

Trace sat back watching him silently, waiting while Drew's chest heaved then finally quieted. "Does Will do that to you?"

"Trace, look," Drew threatened, "I don't want to..." He paused. "What's that?"

"What's what?" Trace blinked.

"That. Listen." Drew turned to the control panel, hastily doing up his pants.

Trace sat up, took notice.

"Hear it?"

"Yeah. It's like a tock, tock, tock."

"It's like," he looked at Trace, his mouth open, "Trace, it's rain."

Trace's mouth opened now too, his gaze riveted to Drew. "Rain?" He could scarcely breathe.

"That's what that was on the radar. It was a storm." He fiddled with a few dials, brought up a mapping device.

Trace came closer to him, leaning over his shoulder. "Where are we?"

Suddenly, the rain was pounding the craft sliding down the window in front of their eyes.

"We're approaching earth," Drew said. "Trace," he turned to him, "do you know what this means? Baby? Do you know what...?"

"Yes. It means the climate changes are altering, normalising again and..."

Drew stood up. He grabbed Trace and squeezed him tight. He laughed like a banshee, twirling him around. "We found the rain, Trace. We found the rain!"

They were kissing wildly when Will and Pagnotella came out. Drew hastily released him and put some distance between them. "Will, Tella," Drew gushed, "it's raining. Can you believe it?"

Everyone celebrated for a few seconds then Will demanded to know when they were planning to 'dump the hostage'.

"Soon," Drew said, and left the room.

Trace followed.

"Not now, Trace," Drew muttered, pretending to be busy looking at something on a computer screen.

"We found rain? Are you still going to pretend we...?"

"I'll take you home. I guess I'll have to find a new job."

"Drew?"

"Don't, Trace," he groaned. *Damn, he'd given his word. Even if it was to that scumbag, Tor.* "Look, I'll take you home and then in a while, maybe if I come back and you're still around, I'll..."

"You're blubbering." Trace was grinning at him which meant he wasn't buying it. "Why?"

"I told Tor I'd..."

"Aha. An honour thing. But you can lie to your crew about a gambler."

"Never mind that. That was money, plus..." He paused. "Damn, I'm in a lot of shit in many places. I haven't delivered on my...there might be a price on my head, not to mention my ass."

"Your ass is mine," Trace said meaningfully. He raked his eyes over him. "Speaking of which, get them off."

"What?"

"Your clothes, buck ass naked, now. We're landing this thing."

"You're crazy."

"Yep. Crazy in love with you, Captain. Now, tell that navigator of yours, and while you're at it, tell that little cabin boy you will be no longer in need of his services." Trace pressed the speaker on the wall. "Talk." He began to undo his pants again.

Drew had never seen him like this. He liked it. He liked it a lot. "Ah," he grinned at Trace as Trace took his cock out of his pants and began stroking it, "Tella, please find a place to land."

"Why?" came the reply.

"Because ah...yeah...well..." He licked his lips, trying to keep it out of his voice, the pleasure that was building. "Don't ask, just do it."

"And Will," Trace insisted, nibbling his ear as he continued to make love to his cock.

"Will, I'm ah...oh...ah...Will...you ah...need to find a m...m...an."

Trace pulled his hand away and pushed him against the wall. "I think he got that." He kissed his chest, teased his nipples, tormented his cock just enough to keep it hard and ready.

"Oh, you're going to get it," Drew laughed, a glint in his dark eyes.

"I'm counting on it."

The craft landed with a thud. They both laughed. "Disgruntled crew?" Trace teased, pulling Drew to the exit by his erection.

"Ah...oh yeah..." he managed.

When the door opened, they stepped out, both of them suddenly saturated with the warm rain. Trace tore off his clothes and danced around in it until Drew grabbed him from behind and put him down to the soft ground. Drew bit Trace's shoulder then drove into him.

Trace grunted in satisfaction, shouting Drew's name out as Drew pounded into his ass there in the downpour.

Finally collapsing on the wet earth, they rolled together, kissing deeply, whispering words of love...words of forever. Above them, the inky sky glittered with a multitude of stars.

Chapter Five

A few months later, Drew and Trace bought a brand new ship equipped with huge water transport containers. They were now the sole licensees to transport rain water to dozens of planets, allowed to move freely across the universe in spite of being under government control.

Landed for the night on Planet Devon, Trace stirred in his bunk, waiting for Drew to return from signing the required documents with the Devonian government. The space beside him was cool and for a moment, he felt a flutter of panic. No, it wasn't a dream. Drew was back in his life and they were finally together. They were a team. Trace found himself smiling. They were lovers, where they had always been meant to be. And they'd found rain.

He glanced at the clock on the wall. Drew would be back soon, grumpy for lack of sleep and stressed from dealing with the dense red fog that had greeted them with the coming of a spectral storm.

Trace thought about how he would greet Drew. He glanced down and saw his cock was waking up. Just thinking about Drew got him hard. He recalled their long wet kiss goodbye. He'd been tired, and Drew had told him to get some rest, that he'd deal with the paperwork.

"I promise to give you an amazing night in the sheets when you get back," he'd told Drew.

"Hmmm…I'm holding you to that promise."

Trace heard the door click open and raced towards it. Drew stepped inside the entrance, grinning when he saw his man naked, wearing nothing but a big, hard cock. He kissed Trace, his fingers closing over the shaft.

"This is a nice way to greet your man, baby." They shared a long kiss that sent sparks through Trace's body, until Drew broke away.

"Something smells good." He sniffed appreciatively and Trace started stripping the sweater and jeans from his lover's body.

In the bedroom, Drew took off his boots and Trace pushed him to the bed. Not hard! Hmm! This was a job for Super Bad Boy Lover. Drew lay on his back across the bed, smiling as Trace began kissing and licking him. Trace started to worry. He didn't want to think Drew wasn't in the mood for love because in his experience, Drew was *always* in the mood for love, but in reality, his big head was someplace else, playing havoc with his…er…little head.

Trace looked up at Drew who gazed unblinking at him. "What happened at the meeting?"

Drew shrugged. "Same old…same old." He swept a hand across his eyes. "Same shit, different planetary orbit."

Trace lit a candle in a glass jar by the bed. "Pink lotus. It's a massage candle."

"Massage candle, eh?" Drew watched as Trace stroked his legs upward, making the blood rush straight to his private treasure trove: Drew's cock, balls and ass. He saw desire swim into Drew's eyes as the scent of the candle grew stronger.

"I like those matches," Drew said, his voice hoarse. They were black with white tips, quite sexy...but the thing Trace couldn't wait to try was the brush. He dipped it into the pooling oil that was at the surface of the burning candle. He started with Drew's feet.

"Oh, God, that's good," Drew moaned as Trace brushed along his feet, up his ankles towards his legs. He lay the brush down, following the path of the oil with his hands. Drew loved it. Trace gave him a great massage, repeating his pattern of brushing warm oil onto him and massaging his skin. Drew's cock started to harden. It looked in urgent need of care, but Trace waited, difficult as it was for Drew to really crave the cock to mouth resuscitation. He started thrashing around on the bed when Trace ran his fingertips up Drew's sides. Drew was trying to shove his cock in Trace's mouth.

"For me?" Trace whispered and Drew nodded eagerly as Trace tongued the leaking head. His hand moved to Drew's ass and his legs opened willingly. Trace dipped the brush into the oil again and Drew whined.

"No, don't stop."

Trace brought him to a fast and furious climax, using the brush on Drew's ass hole as he licked and sucked his cock. Drew came so hard, Trace thought he would never stop. He lay the brush down and licked the cream he had not been able to swallow fast enough from Drew's ball sac. He loved those balls of Drew's. He could let his tongue play *who's your daddy* with them all day long. His honey humped his face as Trace dipped the brush in the warm oil once more, this time streaking a determined path across his belly.

"Fuck, Trace," he murmured, suddenly reaching for his face. "You sure you want to transport water with me? It's not very exciting."

"You're the rogue, remember, not me? I don't need that kind of excitement." Trace rubbed the oil into his lover's belly in a clockwork motion all the way up his diaphragm. He was waking up Drew's central nervous system and every cell in his body was on red alert.

"Me neither, not anymore, not now that I have this…shit…fuck me!" Drew shrieked as Trace worked the oil into his skin. Pink lotus, Trace was told was a major aphrodisiac.

"Open your legs, bitch," he said in Drew's ear and Drew's legs widened in happy response. Trace dipped the brush into the oil and placed it right on Drew's ass hole again and the man went crazy. Trace's mouth and tongue followed all the crazy brushstrokes and Drew's breathing became laboured.

"I need to come, I want to come," he moaned, looking up as two of Trace's fingers worked into Drew's warm, open ass. Working the brush along his butt cheeks as his ravenous mouth sucked on Drew's ass hole and cock was too much for Drew who thrashed around on the bunk. Trace's fingers went straight into his ass…the hottest, tightest, naughtiest place in the world…Trace's own private paradise. He reached Drew's prostate, stroking rhythmically. The convulsions from it sucked Trace's hand to his lover's ass and he bent his head and sucked on Drew's thighs and cock with abandon. Drew grabbed Trace's hand, holding it to his ass — as if Trace would ever take it away! He loved how Drew did that. Drew came in a blaze of Asian-induced heat and now he wanted to fuck.

"God help me...I have no idea what's wrong with me."

Trace knew. The pink lotus was working its magic on him. Now that he thought of it, the instructions had said, *you only need a small amount*...ooops. Drew was panting with desire. *Oh, yeah.* Trace instantly got on all fours. Drew got behind him, like a rutting dog in heat and Trace's head dropped to the bed. Drew knew Trace loved to get fucked this way, to feel Drew bearing down on him, owning him, dominating him. Drew's fingers went for the oil and he stroked it once, twice, across Trace's ass hole.

"Stop teasing me and fuck me," Trace snapped.

"I can't believe I'm still hard," Drew said. "What did you do to me, babe?" He cut right into him and they both cried out. Trace loved the way Drew fucked him, his fingers reaching for Trace's nipples, stroking his cock, reaching everywhere he could. Trace closed his legs because he wanted Drew inside him harder and deeper. Drew grasped his hips, slamming into him. It felt incredible. Trace never wanted Drew to come because he did not want him to stop fucking him. He thrust his bottom back into Drew, meeting him each time he took that cock from Trace then planted it right back into him. He rotated his ass the way he had been taught by a male hula dancer many years ago and Drew started to gasp.

Trace knew Drew was going to come again and Drew took his cock out, pausing for a moment before giving it to him again in one delicious stroke.

"Don't stop fucking me, Drew. Don't come. I need your cock in me." But Drew was too far gone. He went right back into his man and he came, his cock spewing and pulsing like Trace's own special pink lotus deep inside him. He remained inside Trace, his balls slapping at his ass.

"I am never, ever going to stop fucking you," he said against Trace's ear. "Don't you know I own your ass?"

Trace grinned. That was quite all right with him.

HOTWIRED HEART

Jaime Samms

Dedication

To all the fans who support our work. Thank you,
from the bottom of my heart.

Chapter One

"Time me!"

Gig sighed. "Now? Marky, we all know you're fast." He shifted his weight to one foot with a quick glance around the deserted car park. "Just hurry up and hotwire the damn thing."

"Get your watch out, Gig." Marky plied his magic on the car, and by the time Gig looked up from setting his watch, the passenger door swung open. Marky grinned at him from his usurped place behind the wheel. "Get in, slowpoke!"

Gig made a face, slipped into the car, and closed the door. "This is nice!" His long, slim fingers caressed the dash, slid under the visor and along the arm rest.

Marky shivered, watching the gentle touch. "Ready?" He gunned the engine, streaking out into traffic before Gig could tell him not to drive like a maniac, or make any more loving gestures over the interior.

Mercedes safely inserted into the flow of traffic, Marky glanced over at Gig. "Record time, yeah?"

"Isn't it always?" Gig's words fogged the window.

"Oh, c'mon, sexy." Marky slapped Gig's thigh, his hand lingering until Gig brushed it away. He moved it back to the wheel, focused on the traffic as Gig fiddled at the glove compartment, which proved to be locked, and flipped the visor down.

"What's this?" He pulled a slim, silvery wrist wrap out of the visor pocket. "Says Joe…Picone and…something…holographic. Not enough light." He slapped the band on Marky's wrist and it snapped into place.

"What is it?"

"Club pass, maybe." Gig shrugged, sighed. "Marky."

Marky's hands began to ache from his grip on the wheel. "What?"

"This is all we know how to do."

"We have a plan."

"Had." When they'd been together, he didn't bother to add. His body language, tight against the passenger door, said it all.

Marky pulled into an alley, parked in a cross-hatching of shadows under a fire escape and killed the engine. Gig had his fingers curled around the door handle, ready to bolt.

"Wait."

"What?"

Marky leant over and peered out of Gig's window.

"What?" Gig said again.

"We're early." Marky glanced back out the back window. "There should be people on the corner."

"Hustlers." Gig snorted. "Someone you were planning on meeting?"

Marky frowned. Once. It had happened once. "Point is," he snarled, "there's no one there." He turned to Gig, pointed to the door. "Get out. Go down the alley, I'll take the street. Anyone says anything to you, run." Marky grinned but it was strained this time, and the strain showed on Gig's face, too. "We'll meet at the usual place."

"You said it would be okay!"

"And it will be. Just do what I say, and it will be fine."

"This job was supposed—"

"Gig!" Gig jumped, and the hand that had been gripping the door handle in a tight fist jerked. "The longer we sit here... Please. Get out and walk away."

Gig nodded, slipped out into the shadows, and headed for the street. Marky cursed, but shouting after him would be too dangerous. Gig was almost around the corner, out of sight when the *pop* sounded. Marky froze half way out of the door. He'd heard that before. It didn't sound right this time, either, didn't sound big enough or loud enough, but it was enough. He turned his head in time to see Gig hit the ground.

He ducked. The gear shift jammed into his gut, mercifully distracting him from the bile. He had seconds, maybe, to get the hell out. Straining up, he fumbled with the glove box. Surely someone who drove a car like this kept something useful in there like a gun or something. For a second, it didn't budge. The lock rattled. Stealthy, booted feet approached from the direction Gig had gone down. Not cops. He'd worried about cops, not thugs. He should have anticipated this.

Curling his fingers under the right edge of the glove box door gave him enough purchase to yank. The lock gave with a snap, showering parking tickets down on him.

"Fuck." He backed out the door.

Staying low in the shadows, he made it to the building and shimmied down behind a reeking grease bin. In a moment, the car started, the door slammed, and the tires squealed away down the street. The distant sound of sirens explained why the shooter took off without looking for him. Took off in *his* prize; his and Gig's.

"Gig." Marky whispered. Leaning back against the spalling brick, he had to fight to keep down his lunch. "I'm so sorry." He peered out from his hiding place. Sirens approached, but he had to know. Darting along the base of the building, it was obvious before he reached the body. It was too still, too empty, the way it lay there, crumpled and unforgiving. Red lights flashed off the slabs of windows across the street, and he was out of time.

"Trust me." He muttered as he stalked away, leaving his friend behind in a pool of blood. "It'll be okay. I told him it would be okay. Fuck!"

A dark car swerved around a corner, moving towards him, and he stopped. Something glimmered out the passenger window. For a split second, he stared. That was Drag's most recent acquisition. Drag 'took care of' things in the Greenback ranks. Marky dove for the subway entrance, almost rolling down the stairs. The car squealed by overhead in a spray of bullets and broken store windows. Nothing to do now but get on the subway, head away from the disaster, from everything.

* * * *

At the far end of the line from his life, he emerged. The streets were cleaner here, the lights less orange. Or maybe that was his perception. Trees hung over the walk, though fall had likely turned them from green to something more flaming and picturesque. It was hard to tell under the flashing neon closed signs. An iron fence delineated a park, with flower beds and close cropped grass stretching like carpet between. Even in the city's excuse for the park, it looked nice. Welcoming.

But Gig was still dead, and Marky had lost the Mercedes. He'd lost everything. He'd promised to get them out. To leave this shit behind. This hadn't been the plan. Everything they'd saved was back at the Hole, and he couldn't go back. Reality slowly made its way past his shock. He couldn't go back. Gig was dead because Marky had talked him into leaving the Greenbacks. He'd be dead too, if he hadn't run.

Past the park the streets came alive with night crowds. Not the skulking, hunch-shouldered punks he'd recognise in his own end of town, but peacock proud men in all their clubbing finery. After a few blocks, the distinct shortage of women who actually were women sorted itself out in his head. He could pass for one of these people with a bit of scrub and polish. He was one of these people under the gang colours and armour.

There had to be a coffee shop or fast food place somewhere he could clean himself up. A small corner shop, probably a deli by day, but more of a drop-in-for-coffee hangout between club stops this time of night, cast a gold square of light onto the sidewalk. Inside, a narrow door, accessed between booths on the right and high tables and stools on the left, lead to a tiny white room with a urinal, a sink and a half-length mirror in an ornate frame painted with metallic, electric blue paint.

A bit of foam soap and warm water, a gel packet from the vending machine on the wall, transformed his gangland scruff to grunge chic. His dark hair was just the right length to spike nicely; a good look for his long slim face and big brown eyes. The holes in the knees of his jeans were going to have to be a fashion statement, but he could ditch the ragged sweater under his leather jacket in favour of the tight red tee beneath that showed off lean muscles and a flat stomach. There was nothing he could do to make himself taller, but sometimes small and inconspicuous was a plus. The last thing to go was the green bandana around his wrist. He shoved it far under the crumpled paper towel in the trash can and swallowed the jagged lump in his throat. So much for family.

Satisfied with the look, he emerged reasonably in control of his emotions, until heads turned to study him. A dark scowl brooded just behind his unease. He managed to hold it back, stuffing his hands into his hip pockets instead and shuffling to the counter. Defensiveness wouldn't fly with this crowd, already barriered against the outside world by their rainbow flags and fairy-lighted bar balconies. He opted for brooding as he pulled out the stool and sat.

The last of his coins barely covered the cup of steaming coffee the past-middle-aged clerk interrupted an animated conversation to push across the counter at him. Marky dropped the remaining quarters into the tip jar and curled his fingers around the warm paper. After a moment, the clerk clunked a plate down in front of him with a bran muffin and a packet of butter on it. Marky looked up into a neutral expression on a slightly weathered face.

"It's stale," the man informed him, then turned back to his conversation.

That wasn't an exaggeration. But it was food, and more packets of butter were forthcoming when Marky had scraped out the last bit from the first one. He'd got most of it down before the crash came and his hands started to shake. He gave the plate a little shove away and wrapped cold fingers around the warm paper cup. The clerk's buddy had left by then, and the man came over to stand opposite Marky.

"You're not selling anything, are you?" the guy asked; practiced question, practiced motions. He cleared the plate away and refilled Marky's cup.

Marky shook his head.

"Good. There might be places for that, but it ain't in this neighbourhood. You understand?"

Marky nodded.

The man held out a hand. "Peter."

Marky looked at the worn palm and ragged cuticles, looked up into Peter's face and gave a little nod. His hands remained where they were around his mug. "Joe."

Peter's head tilted. "If you want. Joe." He dropped his hand to the cloth on the counter and dragged it in slow figure eights over the green-flecked yellow melamine. "You won't be the first to wander into this neighbourhood looking for a safe place to be. There's safe places." He nodded to a rack on the wall near the door that held pamphlets and business cards, and a rainbow poster with an address on it.

"That's Dean's place. He'll sort you out."

Marky nodded and stood. "Thanks for the coffee and the muffin."

Peter nodded. "You want breakfast, I've got floors need sweeping and trash needs hauling around here."

Marky stopped at the door and turned. "You don't even know me."

"Know that look in your eyes, kid. The look of nothing left. Seen it in the mirror enough times."

Marky nodded. "Thanks." He doubted the guy had any idea. Bells over the door tinkled softly as it closed behind him.

* * * *

A few blocks later, with the wind picking up, driving fallen leaves ahead of him down the sidewalk, he began to regret ditching the old sweater. Men hurried past in both directions, carrying laughter and complaints along with them. They travelled in groups, club sweat drying and chilling on too much exposed flesh, persuading them along to the next door, the next adventure. As Marky dropped his empty cup in the trash, the silver wrist band caught the neon of club lights, and he snapped it open. Inside, the address of a club promised shelter of a sort. If he had the map in his head the right way round, it should be just around the corner, towards the more posh end of the neighbourhood. He slapped it back in place and headed in that direction.

Even from the outside, the place was slick, smooth, popular, if the line-up of shivering, shuffling patrons was any indication. The bouncers at the door frowned at him, but he flashed his band and they unclipped the rope to let him pass. Dubious looks followed him inside.

At the inner door, he watched the guy ahead of him stick his hand with its arm band inside a scanner. The woman at the desk looked at her computer monitor, nodded, and waved him on. Marky took his turn. She glanced up at him, back at the monitor, and he tensed, but she just smiled.

"Nice haircut. Suits you. Enjoy."

Inside the club proper, Marky had time to be impressed. A place with that much black lacquered wood, purple glimmer and chrome could easily look like it was trying too hard. He wasn't sure how tasteful had been pulled off, but somehow, it had. Gay bars had never really been his thing, and just looking around the room reminded him why. He wouldn't be allowed to just stand around and not spend money in a place like this.

Across the room, a tall blond eyed the door, watched everyone who came in, and he watched Marky now. At a distance, no one should look that good. Marky swallowed, nodded slightly, and edged his way past the entrance. He felt the intense gaze follow and shivers cascaded down his spine.

Since he didn't have any money, the next thing to do was to find a likely prospect he could induce into spending money, but not have to put out for. He considered and dismissed approaching the blond. Something about the man's stance marked him as other. Attractive, compelling, even, but far out of Marky's range.

He crept carefully closer to the shining hardwood dance floor, less than interested in going out there, but sensing this was how things worked here. Dance your little heart out, and someone would pick you up and make your body sing. The obviousness was more than a little creepy.

"You look lost." A deep voice and a hand on Marky's elbow startled him into yanking away and spinning on the balls of his feet. For a split, heart-thudding moment, he expected to see the blond standing there. The excitement dissipated at the sight of a tall, muscular, olive skinned man instead.

"Thank you, no." His heart hammered up again, slamming his pulse in his throat, and he backed away. The man who'd addressed him, dark eyed, dark haired, wasn't hard to look at, but something in his deep eyes warned Marky. He backed up another step.

"Let me buy you a drink before you say no." He smiled, his lips curling up and deepening a dimple on his left cheek. Nothing in the suggestive glint of his eyes changed. He closed a hand around Marky's elbow again and turned him towards a dark, curtained booth.

"Listen, I…" The man's smile faltered, and a bouncer stepped forward. Marky nodded him away. He'd sit and have a drink with this guy. Better that than spend any more time wandering in the cold than he had to. One drink wouldn't kill him.

"Thanks." He managed a tight quirk of lips as he slid into the booth.

The guy retreated towards the bar, his fingers trailing down over the back of Marky's hand. "Wait here. I won't be long."

Marky should have left. But the prospect of catching the eye of one of the much less desirable onlookers did not appeal. The way their hungry gazes raked over gyrating bodies on the dance floor made him wary. If gay bars weren't his thing, fetish bars were even less so, and he was quickly cluing in that there was more than garden variety courting going on here. Nothing said he had to leave with this guy.

Outside the booth, the music picked up, bass rhythms thumped, and through a chink in the curtain, the blond fixed him with a look that made his pulse beat faster.

Marky bit his lip, looked away. The curtain shifted, blocking his view of the dancers and the man. A tall glass with a paper umbrella appeared. His benefactor gripped his fingers as he shuffled up beside him and pulled the curtains most of the way closed again. "I thought for sure you'd be gone." Only two tea lights on the table brightened the space, but it was enough to illuminate the dimpled smile. He indicated Marky's frosted glass. "Long Island. Thought it'd be safe enough."

"Sure." With its three ounces of liquor. Perfectly safe. Marky took a small sip and winced. Not three. The bartender was definitely not his friend. He set the glass down and leant back against the booth's plush purple cushions.

"So. I'm Jason."

"Joe," Marky said, to the plush pillows on the other side of the booth.

A protracted silence filled the cramped space. Jason leaned close. "Haven't seen you in here before, have I?" His hand landed on Marky's thigh, too distant from his knee to be comfortable, and Marky jerked. Though there was nowhere to pull away to, Jason's fingers tightened, holding him in place.

"No." Marky pressed his shoulder to the wall of the booth, searching Jason for hidden whips or cuffs. A glittering chain dangled from his belt, but that was it. He regarded Marky coolly from beneath thick lashes.

"What do you like, Joe?"

"Like?" Marky twisted the glass around and around on the table, unable to control his racing heart or twisting nerves.

"Unsure?" A wide grin replaced the calculating expression and Jason moved closer. "I can give you a few choices." He was so close. The alcohol on his breath, mingling with the scent of mint, churned Marky's stomach. He turned his head away. Jason settled for his neck, proceeding to lick and suck his way down to Marky's collar bone. The abruptness of it warred with Marky's acknowledgement that the man had a very talented mouth. He shuddered.

It might have seemed an invitation, because Jason's hand moved up Marky's thigh, his fingers tucking into the crease between his leg and his cock, growing rapidly against his better judgement. Jason's lips travelled back up along Marky's throat and over his jaw. Marky twisted awkwardly to avoid meeting lip to lip. Jason just continued on along his jaw until he was sucking Marky's earlobe into his mouth and between his teeth.

"Shit…" Marky moaned, and Jason shifted, pressing him back against the wall and cupping his big hand over Marky's groin.

Too much…too fast… and *not here.* All raced through Marky's brain, but somehow didn't make it to his lips. His heart pounded, and his breath came in little gasps of something approaching fear.

Jason didn't seem to hear it that way. He kneaded Marky through his jeans, cutting off the supply of thought to Marky's brain as his free hand slid up under the red T-shirt to play with a nipple.

"Fuck…"

"Here?" Jason's lips curled against Marky's neck. "Now?" He paused in his hard rubbing against Marky's dick to adjust himself, something like greed in his dark eyes.

"No!" Marky squirmed, but Jason's hand had already moved, worming down inside the back of his jeans. "St— o—ugh." The friction against his hard cock ground the word into nothing, and he rocked, trying to ease pressure that came too close to pain. It only gave Jason better access. The feel of a calloused hand on his ass sent a mewl of real fear past his lips.

Not because he'd never done this before, but this was fast and demanding; assuming too much. He put a hand on Jason's chest to push him away. Like shoving against a brick wall. Jason just chuckled against his temple and popped open the button on the front of his jeans, allowing his hand to slide a little further down Marky's backside. His other ran along the back of Marky's head, tangling in the gelled spikes. When he started pushing Marky's head down towards his own crotch, fear won out over lust, and Marky shoved back hard.

"Oh, it's like that, is it?" Jason's grip tightened and forced Marky to lower his head or lose a lot of hair. It gave Jason just the right angle to slide his fingers between the cheeks of Marky's ass, far too close to an intimacy Marky seriously didn't want.

He squirmed, and his scalp burned. No one heard his shouts above the raging music. Heart thudding, he swung, and Jason had him pinned against the wall in a heartbeat, wrists tight in one hand and the other holding Marky's head against the wall by the jaw. "Easy. I wasn't looking for a fight, Baby." He thumbed the wrist band on Marky's arm. "You're wearing the wrong colour for this action, but if it's what you want…"

Marky could hardly protest with Jason's hand holding his mouth closed. He couldn't punch with his wrists captured. He kicked. Left a boot-sized bruise on Jason's thigh, and got his head cracked lightly against the wall for his efforts. Not enough to really hurt. Just enough to remind him it could hurt and he couldn't do much about it.

"I thought I was up for something lighter tonight," Jason leered at him, "but you're too much." This time, his mouth closed over Marky's, hard and demanding, smothering the last bit of desire Marky might have felt and propelling him into sheer panic. He kicked again, aiming higher than Jason's thigh this time, and it earned him just enough freedom to squirm the rest of the way loose. There was no way out but over the table, and he took it, batting the curtain aside as he went. His still-full drink sprayed ahead of him just before the glass shattered on the floor. He landed almost on all fours, and was half way to his feet when Jason's strong hand closed over his upper arm.

"Before you make any more of a scene, if it's force you want, we can take this into the back. Come on."

"I don't want force!" Marky yanked, completely ineffectual against the big man. "I don't want you! Let go!" Heads started to turn and his plan of inconspicuously passing a few hours in the stolen warmth didn't look so good under the scrutiny. Behind Jason, the blond moved towards them, a concerned look on his handsome face.

Jason pulled him close and leant down to whisper furiously in his ear. "You're a piece of work."

Over his shoulder, the blond caught his eye, the only one who seemed to care what was happening. Then Jason was spinning him, propelling him towards the back of the bar, and he was on his own again in a nightmare of misunderstanding nothing he said was going to clear up.

They'd made it to the entrance of one dark, semi-private back room when a big man, black shirt stretched across thick chest and arms, barred their way. Marky wilted with relief.

"Everything all right?" His bass voice rumbled under the music and Marky had to read his lips to understand his words.

"Yes." Jason began to pull Marky behind him.

"No!" Marky hauled against Jason's grip. "Not all right."

Cool fingers closed over both his wrist and Jason's hand. Marky looked up into eyes green enough to shine through even the flashing disco lights. The blond regarded him cooly, and his insides flipped. Obviously someone important, his presence straightened Jason's shoulders, and changed his expression, from confident and greedy, to wary.

The bouncer nodded to him. "Trouble, Mr Leibow." He jerked his head towards them, and Marky wasn't sure which one of them he meant.

Mr. Leibow nodded and focused a dangerous glare on Marky's captor. "Jason, isn't it?" The voice belonging to the eyes and the hair was just as cool, just as intense as the rest of him. He looked Jason in the eye, both of them staring at one another over Marky's head. "Jason Power?"

Jason nodded, his fingers tightening under the blond's.

"Joss says trouble. He knows trouble when he sees it." Every line of the man's stance warned of danger. It set Marky's blood racing the way just his scrutiny leeched a bit of colour from Jason's face.

"If there was a problem, Mr. Leibow," Jason shifted his feet, but didn't relinquish his grip. "I'm sure he would have used the safe word." Jason's fingers tightened again, enough to bruise. "He didn't."

Leibow's gaze moved back to Marky. One eyebrow went up.

Marky flushed, caught somewhere between fear and fascination. His hands began to shake. "I don't..."

The other eyebrow went up. "You don't know it?" Now Leibow picked up Marky's limp hand and indicated the wrist band. "You don't get one of these without knowing the rules." He turned to Jason. "And you don't get to keep it without respecting the rules." He held out his hand, long fingers spread and waiting.

"But I didn't break any rules!" Marky winced under the pressure of Jason's grip pulling him back again, as though he might hide his indiscretion. Marky resisted the tug, only to earn himself a glare, and a sharp, painful twist from Jason.

"Rule number one." Leibow pointed to Jason's hand and the red marks around Marky's arm. "Listen to your sub. He hasn't said a word to you. I can tell looking at him he's terrified."

The bouncer stepped up and uncurled Jason's wristband, a shimmering blue strap, and replaced it with a black one. "Last chance, Mr. Power."

"Black?" Jason frowned at his new band.

"Meaning you are under scrutiny. You don't so much as breathe in the general direction of anyone who isn't on my staff." Leibow fixed a steady gaze on him. "And if any of my boys speak one word of concern, you never step foot in my place again. Understood?"

Jason nodded, fury kindling in his eyes, and exiting the fingers still clamped painfully around Marky's arm.

Marky winced, bending slightly, over the pain.

"Simon!"

A pale young man, shorter even than Marky, stepped forward, his short hair gelled up to show off tattoos curling up the back of his neck. His hair was coloured to carry a bird's rainbow design from skin to its feathered conclusion in the spikes. A line of silver rings tinkled along his ear as he moved. "Yes, Sir?"

"You'll take care of Jason? He needs a bit of stress relief." Leibow tapped Jason's white-knuckled grip and he let go of Marky, sending him away with a shove. Marky stumbled back rubbing his throbbing wrist.

Simon grinned, ignored Jason's pique, and reached to unclip the chain from Jason's belt. He hooked it onto a ring in his own collar. "Sure thing, Boss." He lead Jason off, though in a few steps, Jason took over the lead and Simon fell a step behind, hands behind his back and his head down.

"You're letting him stay?" Marky glared at Leibow. "He—" Thinking about it reminded him his fly was still hanging open, and he clutched it closed, flushing heat sliding up into his cheeks.

"Better he's here, learning from experienced subs, than out there really hurting someone." Leibow waited for Marky to fumble his buttons closed again, then moved forward to straighten out his jacket collar. Marky shivered as cool fingers brushed his skin. "Come with me."

The heat in Marky's cheeks flared, slithered down to coil in his gut. He nodded, unsure why Leibow's proximity somehow didn't inspire the fear Jason's had. "Where are we going?"

The bouncer tilted his head, narrowed his eyes, and Marky swallowed, covered his stolen wrist band with his other hand, and nodded.

Chapter Two

They headed across the dance floor. Leibow slipped through the spinning crowd with smiles and touches that should have been inappropriate, but were given him as his due. Not a few envious looks glided over Marky as he followed. The motion of the bodies and the bass thump mesmerised him. Swaying hips and liquid smiles distracted his attention, and he almost missed the flash of familiar green until he was practically on top of it. The glimpse froze him in place. Someone slammed into him from behind, and an annoyed shout turned heads in his direction. Marky lunged, deeper into the twists and turns of the dancing, searching for blond hair. The man with the green wrapped around his wrist tossed a glance around, then went back to chatting with another bouncer who caught Marky's eye then cooly looked past him and away.

Marky's frantic flight brought him face first into Leibow's back, and he grunted. Leibow shot a questioning look over his shoulder, and Marky pointed, stretched up on his toes to talk into Leibow's ear. "How did he get in here? He can't see me. If... He'll..." Marky was already turning back, itching to put distance between himself and the gang member who should not have been able to find him here. Where he would go once the bouncer pointed him out, he wasn't sure. Even across the crowded room, he knew the bulge in the back of the guy's jacket, knew what it meant that he was here.

Leibow yanked him back around, though, pulling him through the crowd, around the corner of the glass DJ booth, and hustling him up a narrow set of metal steps camouflaged against the dark-painted brick wall. At the top, a small room looked out over the club through plates of glass. Leibow took up a place against the wall, hands in his pockets, where he could watch almost the entire bar and dance area.

"So." He peered at Marky, hovering at the top of the stairs, just inside the doorway. "Who's the thug?"

Marky moved forward to see down into the milling throng of bodies, but Leibow motioned him back. "It isn't one way. If he looks up, he'll see you. Who is he?" he pulled out a pack of smokes and lit one.

Marky didn't need more of a look than he'd already had to identify the intruder, though. "His name is Drag." He frowned. "Actually, I think his name is Jose. He's not a nice man."

"He has a big gun."

"How did he get it in here? Don't you have security?" Marky's voice rose toward hysteria.

Leibow's eyes flicked around the bar. Men in black shirts seemed to have emerged from the brick work. No corner, no exit from the main room, no inch of the club Drag could get to brought him more than five feet from one of them. If he even looked like he meant to draw his weapon, they'd drop him before he got it out.

"Sometimes," Leibow puffed on his smoke, voice a low drawl, "it's better to let them in and watch them up close, see what they want." His green gaze turned to Marky. "This one wants you?"

"I—" Marky glanced back down at Drag's tense back. "Maybe. Probably."

"Why?"

"It's a long story."

Leibow dashed out his half-smoked cigarette and his hands disappeared back into the pockets of his loose trousers, stretching the fabric across his ass in a way that tugged at Marky's attention. He moved across the room to stand over him, depriving Marky of the view. Maybe it was his broad shoulders, or the way he smelled of spice under the bar sweat and stale beer. His proximity played havoc with Marky's pulse, and it took a moment to get his thoughts back on track.

Leibow's eyes glittered and he studied Marky. "Seems to me you can tell me, or take your chances with him."

Marky nodded and stammered out the highlights of his evening around his flaring libido. His attention kept wandering to the glimpse of skin at Leibow's collar, and the tiny white line marring otherwise smooth skin.

"You missed the part about how you pissed them off in the first place," Leibow said, when he'd reached the halting, unpleasant end of his tale. "Why'd they kill your friend? Why kill one of their own?"

"We wanted out. I didn't think they knew. I thought I was careful enough."

"Did you not read the fine print? You don't leave."

"I thought...they'd never know. Not till we were long gone." Marky closed his eyes. The image of Gig's body limp on the pavement, of the street light glinting from the dark pool around him, cooled every other thought. Even this handsome man's body heat, so close he could feel it, wasn't enough to distract him from that failure.

"So this last job." Leibow's voice mellowed. "You stole Joe Picone's car and identity, and came here. To do what?"

"Escape," Marky breathed.

Leibow sighed. "Escape." He brushed a bit of nothing from Marky's shoulder, and his hand lingered. "Where did you think you and your boyfriend were going to go? Did you think there was a place in this city they wouldn't find you?"

"He wasn't my boyfriend." *Not anymore.* "I don't know what he was going to do after. I wasn't planning on staying. We should have left yesterday, but there was this job. He said we had to do it, had to distract them with this one last, great car. Said it would be a parting gift, so they'd let us go. He knew where it was, when to nab it..." Marky's fingers tightened into balls of tension. His own voice dropped, dulled. "He knew every little thing. He set me up."

Leibow squeezed his shoulder. "And they killed him for that betrayal. They used him to get to you, and they killed him."

"I don't... Why would he?" Once more, his gut tightened, this time, anger tying the knots.

Leibow tilted his head. "How should I know? He was your lover."

"He—" Marky brushed off the hand and Leibow's brows drew together. Sinking, huddling down against the wall, Marky wrapped his arms around his churning stomach. "He just wanted to stay," He whispered. "I thought we wanted more, but he wanted that life. He just... Fuck." He dropped his head, fingers gripping his short spiked hair. "Fuck!"

"All this changes is that he brought his own death on himself," Leibow pointed out. "Not your fault." He crouched, and his firm grip was back on Marky's shoulder. "They're still hunting you. What are you going to do about that?"

"I don't know." Marky chewed on his lip, stared at the brown Berber between his boots. Standing risked upsetting his guts enough to spill all over the carpet.

Leibow sighed again, stood, and after a bit of shuffling and clicking, the smell of cigarette smoke drifted down and Leibow retreated to his desk to lean on it. "While 'I don't know' is a possible response, it isn't the best one. The seat of your pants approach hasn't really worked very well for you so far."

Marky lifted his head slightly, plucking at his wilting spikes.

"Tell you what." Leibow sauntered back. Marky watched his leather shoes pad across the carpet to stop inches from his own boots. He couldn't make himself look up. "You've had a long, difficult day. I'll give you this one for free. Get up."

Finally, Marky met his eye. "This one what?" His heart tripped at the intensity of Leibow's gaze.

"I'll think for you. Come on." He held out a hand. "Get you someplace safe, you can clean up, and we'll figure it out from there."

Marky reached up and took his hand. Heat rushed through him, but he didn't attempt to stand. "Why?"

"Because a guy should only get kicked in the gut so many times in one day, and one of those times happened on my watch. Jason should never have treated you like that, and someone here should have prevented it. Now get your ass in gear."

Marky leveraged himself to his feet and for a moment, with cigarette smoke swirling around them and the din of the bar pounding up through the souls of his feet, it was easy to imagine nothing else existed but the hand in his and the man in front of him. His breath came at last in a little gasp that only teased his lungs and propelled his heart into overdrive.

"Yeah." Leibow huffed out a strange little sound. "I see why Power found it so hard to keep his hands to himself." He stepped away, took his hand back, and sucked on the cigarette. "Let's go." The heat of his hand on Marky's back burned its way right through leather and cotton to get to skin, as it propelled him to the door. The sensation raced up his spine and spread over his cheeks. His body responded, resisting the little push, leaning back into the touch. It had nothing to do with his head, and he was fairly certain he hadn't imagined Leibow's hitched breath as Marky finally got his feet to obey his will and move him forward.

* * * *

They hurried him down and out a narrow door at the foot of the office stairs, through the DJ booth, which got him a speculative look from the DJ, and out another door into a private parking garage behind the building. There, Leibow shuffled him into one of the nicest cars he'd ever seen, disappointingly from the passenger seat, and whisked him away through the dwindling lights of the downtown core.

Leibow didn't speak as they left the nightlife and the rainbow garlands of flags behind to glide through the quieter streets of an expensive neighbourhood. As the dark expanses between houses grew, Marky squirmed. "Where are we?"

"Where Greenbacks don't go." Leibow looked over at him. "Don't worry. You're perfectly safe." Which didn't explain the glint in his eye every time he glanced over, or the cold sweat trickling down under Marky's waistband.

"Look, Mr. Leibow —"

"Rolly."

"Rolly. I appreciate everything you've done. You can just let me out —"

"Here?" He snorted. "You'll be arrested within the hour, back downtown, and if they even let you go, your Greenback buddies will be five ways putting you in a dumpster before you can turn around and get your ass back to the neighbourhood."

Marky let out a rough laugh. "That what they're calling Pride Alley these days?"

Rolly clucked his tongue. "Mock if you want. Then make me believe you don't want a bit of that security. You know what they say about safety in numbers. You could fit in there. Where people will actually protect you because they like you, not because you can hotwire a fancy ride." He glanced in the rear view mirror, made a lane change, and shot Marky a quick look. "I'm not after trying to tell you how to live your life. You were already looking for a way out. I'm just saying."

"You're suggesting I bring my shit into your neighbourhood. Into Peter's deli, into this Dean guy's shelter?" He snorted and turned away to stare out into the dark. "That isn't how things work where I come from."

"No. Where you come from, lovers turn on each other like rabid dogs. That's better." Rolly had pulled off the road and the car purred up a long, canted drive, crunching over tracks of glowing white gravel as it neared the house. He hammered it into park and twisted in his seat to face Marky. "I'm not forcing anything on you. Just..." he shook his head. "Make up your own mind." He exited the car in a flurry of long blond waves and disapproval. The door slammed, and by the time Marky was out too, he was hunched over a new cigarette, protecting the small flame of his lighter with his cupped hand and the curve of his shoulder.

"Look," Marky leant on the roof of the car. "I'm just trying to be practical here."

"You're assuming," Rolly muttered, flicking his lighter again as the wind blew the flame away. Finally, he got the thing lit and turned to Marky. "No one has ever had it as rough as you. No one can possibly understand. Bullshit." He shook his head and turned towards the house. "Whatever. Get the fuck off my car."

Marky glared at his back, but he did shuffle away from the car. "Hey."

Rolly slowed, but didn't stop.

"Lei—Mr. Leibow."

Rolly stopped, drew on his cigarette.

"I…" Marky shoved his hands into his pockets and ground the toe of his boots against the white stones of the drive. "I don't have anywhere to go."

"No shit." Rolly's shoulders rose and fell. "You going to tell me your real name?"

"Marky."

"Come on, then, Marky. Shower. Sleep. Things'll look better in the morning."

"Right." Marky kept the scepticism quiet, though, and hustled to catch up.

* * * *

Well lit and spacious, walls painted cheerful colours, and the floor a massive heat sink of stone, the inside of Leibow's home wasn't at all what he expected. The furniture was simple, wood and leather and comfortable-looking. Marky had expected something more flashy, less…homey.

Rolly opened the front hall closet and hung up his coat. Like any normal, rational, and not horrifically wealthy person might, he turned to Marky, empty hanger in his hand, and waited. Marky pulled his security leather closer around himself. Rolly shrugged.

"Suit yourself." He put the hanger away and closed the door again. "I have a few calls to make. Upstairs and to your right, at the end of the hall. You should find everything you need in the bathroom."

"And then what?"

Rolly watched him for a minute, speculating, stretching the silence into the space bordering Marky's fear. "And then I'll be up."

"Oh." Marky took a deep breath. "Okay."

Rolly was already walking away, cell phone at his ear, and clear voice calling down the hall for someone named Hal. Marky cold have walked out the door. There was no one to stop him leaving. There was no one for him to go to if he did. He headed up the stairs. Below, he caught Rolly watching him, phone in mid air, call going ignored, and his gaze... He didn't look away when Marky noticed his interest, and once again, Marky's heart hammered against his ribs. He smiled a tight smile and dashed up the remaining steps, out of sight.

In the bathroom doorway, he stopped, panting hard from unexpected tension. It took him long moments to focus on his surroundings. Like the rest of the house, the bathroom decor was simple, functional and attractive, and upon closer inspection, expensive.

"Who says money breeds poor taste?" he asked the potted plants. He debated filling the tub, but the last thing he wanted, given the way Rolly had looked at him just now, was for his benefactor to walk in on him wearing nothing but a mound of bubbles.

He turned to the shower, stripped and stepped under the hot, soothing spray. The echoing drum of water on the shower wall cocooned him for a few minutes from the outside, and all he had were his own tangled feelings of failure and probably misplaced desire. The thought of Rolly's hot gaze on him sent sizzling reaction racing up his spine, and his fists clenched. He had to force himself to picture Gig's body, remind himself why he was here, how badly he'd screwed up, and for a moment, it worked. The heat turned to chill, and a fit of uncontrolled shaking left him leaning hard on the wall. He might have huddled there a lot longer if someone hadn't knocked on the door.

A distinctly female voice called through to let him know she'd be taking his clothes to clean. He scrambled to turn the water off and find a towel.

"No! Wait!" But by the time he emerged, the woman was gone, and so were his clothes. Even his jacket. Another discreet knock, and he hardly had the towel secured around his waist before Rolly slipped inside.

"It's settled." He leant against the vanity, long legs relaxed, ankles crossed. His gaze travelled up from Marky's feet to linger over his damp chest before finally making it to his face. His chest rose and fell in heavy breaths, though his voice remained steady. "Dean has a room for you, and Peter a job, though the room won't be free for a couple of days and Peter can't pay you right now. He'll feed you, though, and if you do some yard work for Dean, and a bit of cleaning, he's willing to wave rent for a while."

"Uh." Marky clutched at the twist of his towel, shifted his weight from one slippery foot to the other. The water dribbling and tickling down his legs accentuated how little covered him. Leibow's avid gaze didn't disguise the man's interest in what was under the covering, either, and heat rose up Marky's neck. Living arrangements were the last thing on his mind right that second. Rolly's gaze drifted down again, and Marky ran a self-conscious hand over his chest. His fingers brushed the scar over his ribs, making it tingle.

"Where'd you get that?"

"I—" Marky looked down at the long, pale line marring his skin. "Knife. Bad decision. I don't...really want to..."

Rolly nodded. "I have a few reminders of bad decisions myself." He stood and a few steps brought him close enough Marky could make out one of those reminders just peeking up from his shirt, hugging the curve of his collar bone.

Marky almost reached to touch it, but resisted. The aborted gesture didn't slip past Rolly's notice, because he smiled, touched Marky's elbow with his fingers. "Go ahead."

"Is this your price?" Marky's voice caught roughly on the uncertainty clogging his throat. "A hot shower and clean clothes for a few personal privileges? What do I have to do to get a meal?" He licked his lips suggestively, but a lump of unpleasant emotions sat like lead in the pit of his stomach.

"Asking nicely and saying please usually works," Rolly snapped. But he didn't back off. His fingers drifted from Marky's elbow, up his arm, along his collar bone to rest lightly under his chin. Marky shivered at the trickle of goose bumps that followed. "Can I help it if I react predictably typically when faced with a half naked, very attractive man dripping on my bathroom floor?"

"You just walked in," Marky breathed, his head lifting at the ever-so-slight pressure of Rolly's fingers under his chin.

"I knocked." Rolly leant close. "Kick me out."

"Can't." Marky gasped away a bit of Rolly's breath as the blond's lips closed over his, his tongue slipping into Marky's half open, obviously not protesting mouth. The slick heat was grounded in the same gentle persuasion that pulled Marky a little closer, tipped his head back a little more, drew him irrevocably into Rolly's space and held him there. His own fingers cemented the connection by tightening into fists in the front of Rolly's shirt. In the steamy aftermath of his shower, he barely noticed his towel slip away. It was Rolly's hand caressing the curve of his ass that brought him abruptly out of the spell.

"Hey!" He drew away, but Rolly still had a hand cupping his face, and one curled around his butt.

He looked down at Marky and smiled. "Stop?"

Marky shook, an all over body shudder at the realisation he was completely naked in front of this powerful man, in his home, and essentially helpless.

"Just say the word, Marky."

"What word?"

Rolly smiled. "Piccadilly, jabberwocky. Pick one."

"A safe word?" Rather than helping him feel safer, the idea he might need one made him sweat. He swallowed hard.

Rolly took a deep breath and stepped back, releasing him. "I'll have someone bring you something to wear. Hal's made sandwiches. Kitchen's at the bottom of the stairs. Turn right and you're there." He gripped the door handle, white knuckles showing his tension, but Marky put a hand on his forearm.

"Wait." His voice shook, and maybe his hand did a little, too, but something about the man's willingness to walk away made him brave. "Kensington."

"What about it?"

"It's a word, isn't it?"

Rolly turned back to study him. "This isn't something you just do because you feel you have to."

"I know. You aren't making me." Marky moved forward this time, leaving the towel to soak up the water he'd dripped. "My decision."

"A complete stranger?" Rolly raised the eyebrow again, and Marky gave in to the urge to run a finger along the tawny strip of arched hairs.

"What? You think stealing cars is the only thing I've ever done for a few bucks? Being hungry motivates a person to do things he might not normally do."

"I'm not going to pay you for sleeping with me. I'll feed you anyway."

"I don't want your money."

"Then what are you after?"

"Nothing." Marky moved again, invading Rolly's personal space. "I've had a rough day. Maybe I just want a little something less traumatic to finish it off." It was as good a reason he could come up with to explain his undeniable attraction.

"You didn't want what Jason Power offered."

"Yeah." Marky backed off. "I didn't want him forcing himself on me." He held up his arm to show off the finger-sized bruises already clearly visible against pale skin. "Still don't want that shit."

Rolly nodded. "Kensington. It'll work." He leant close and kissed Marky, brief, first on the lips, then on both eyelids. "Keep them closed."

Marky nodded, heart skipping in anticipation.

Rolly pressed his lips against Marky's ear next. "Wait here."

Again, Marky nodded his breath too short to actually manage a vocal answer. He listened to Rolly's footsteps dwindle down the hallway, heard the distant sound of a drawer opening, and then, for a moment, nothing. He was just about to investigate when Rolly was there, touching his arm, his presence curling around Marky like the last of the heavy, humid bathroom air.

"Turn around, Marky."

"Can I open my eyes yet?"

"Not yet." Rolly guided Marky in a slow spin until he had his back to the taller man. Strong fingers lifted one wrist once Marky had stopped shuffling, and curled something around it. The faint jangle of metal and a bit of tugging gave Marky enough information to know he'd just been cuffed. He ran his fingers over the band of leather, soft, supple and studded with three thick, cool metal rings. He shifted weight from one foot to the other.

"Okay?" Rolly had moved in front of him to caressed his cheek, cup it, and lift Marky's face, brushing a soft kiss across lips parted and panted as his lungs made an attempt to keep up to his racing heart.

Marky nodded and held up the other wrist. He hadn't felt such a rush of fear and excitement since his first grand theft auto. His hand bumped against Rolly's chest and he spread his fingers to lay his palm against the warmth. Under the pressure of his touch, Rolly's heart rate almost matched his own.

"Can I have the other one?" If he hadn't actually been touching him, Marky might have missed the slight gasp, but he felt it, the quick rise and fall of Rolly's chest against his palm, and smiled. "Please?"

Rolly obliged, quickly fastening the other cuff in place and drawing Marky's hands behind his back. He clipped them together, and Marky shifted, a little tug telling him he really was bound. This time, the fear overshadowed the excitement, but Rolly drew his hands together until the cuffs touched. A clatter and metallic ring accompanied something hitting the floor. Marky looked down to see an open, 'c' shaped ring lying between his feet.

"You see?" Rolly picked it up and showed it to him. "Just an illusion. Nothing you can't get out of." He moved back to stand behind Marky and wait. After a second's thought,

Marky put his hands behind his back again. Rolly secured them and leaned close. The cool studs on the buttons of his shirt pressed against Marky's shower-warmed skin. "Good boy," he whispered, lips against the shell of Marky's ear.

Marky shivered, surprised by the thrill of accomplishment and pleasure the words drew from him. He followed Rolly from the room, only belatedly realising anyone might see him naked and bound as he trailed the blond down the hallway. Heat had sparkled right up to his hair line by the time the bedroom door closed behind them, and Rolly's smile was wide when he saw.

"Obedient, and shy. Very sweet." For a moment, Marky wasn't sure the words were praise, then Rolly was drawing him towards another kiss, a hand on the back of his head guiding him into it. Rolly's tongue slid against his, weakened his knees and sent heat straight to his dick. He decided the simple act of doing what Rolly wanted so far proved to be well worth the pay off.

Chapter Three

Foreplay, Marky soon realised, was an art form he obviously had never learned properly. Tricks usually didn't want it, and Gig...well, Gig had liked the quick, fake anonymity of the back seat of the cars they nabbed. Rolly seemed to know all the right places to touch; over his belly, that made him shiver. Where to linger; along the inside of his thighs, and over his nipples; and where to ghost over and leave just the faintest sensation of a promise on Marky's skin. Feather-light fingers brushed the soft skin inside his joints, flickering away so fast he barely had time to gasp his pleasure before they moved on again.

The frustration of not being able to touch his partner left him squirming and reaching for every sensation. Rolly meted out his contact in maddening brief, but tantalising, doses.

"You don't have your hands." Rolly licked up along his neck, nibbled on his ear. "Use your voice. Tell me what you want."

"Mmm." Marky squeezed his eyes shut and tilted his head to get those teeth back.

"Say it." Rolly dashed his tongue just behind Marky's ear and blew on the damp spot.

Marky whimpered. How was he supposed to admit that? He ground his teeth in frustration, against his own need, and his inability to admit it.

"Desperate, yet?"

The whimper this time sounded too close to a sob, and Marky thought seriously about freeing himself.

"Do it," Rolly taunted. "Free yourself and fuck me. You know you want to."

"No." Because, truthfully, he didn't. He wanted more of what Rolly was doing to him, and he was too ashamed to admit it.

"You like my teeth?"

Marky nodded.

"You want them on your skin?" Rolly trailed a finger down the side of his neck, along his collar bone. "You're going to have to learn to say it."

Marky squirmed towards the simple touch. "Yes." His breath caught, and he stared up at the man torturing him.

"You want my little tooth shaped bruises all over your body?" Rolly stroked a hand over Marky's cock.

Marky nodded, biting his lip. "Yes."

"Imagine them running down the side of your cock." He simulated the sensation with a light rake of his fingernails.

Marky groaned, clenched his teeth even as his hips arched up all on their own. "Do it."

Rolly grinned. "Ask nice."

Marky snarled, lunged up from his back, but Leibow easily knocked him back down and pinned him, lowered his head to play with a nipple. "Suck me...?" Marky managed between gasps. "Your mouth. Your teeth..."

Rolly glanced up, that infernal eyebrow lifted.

"Please." Marky sank back onto the bed, his arms trapped under him, his breath heaving. "God, please. Do something!"

Rolly kissed and nibbled his way across Marky's chest.

"Gah! More." Marky's fingers dug into the mattress below him as the man's mouth closed once again over his nipple, to suck it up gently between his teeth. Marky gasped, a shocked little sound, when Rolly actually bit down. Not hard, just enough to elicit a sting and draw the squeak from Marky. Carefully, he licked the sting away and looked up.

"Oh, don't worry. I've got so much more in store for you."

Marky shuddered at the guarantee underlying the words. "Promise?"

Rolly stood. He'd undressed himself earlier, and now he canted a hip and stroked himself, long, slow motions that gathered all Marky's frayed nerves and splintered thoughts to that one point. "Absolutly. Sit up." He gravitated forward, until the musk of his arousal surrounded Marky and the glimmer of moisture on the tip of his cock prompted him to lick his lips. "You want a taste?"

Marky nodded, instinct prompting his reply, but Rolly kept his distance just far enough to make it impossible for Marky to lick away that tantalising drop without leaning forward for it, looking desperate to have the other man's cock in his mouth. So hard to admit he needed it that bad.

"It's okay." Rolly stroked his fingers through Marky's hair. "Take it. Lick me." He didn't move, though, and Marky's desire to taste, to do what Rolly wanted, finally overcame his self consciousness at showing this weakness. He leant forward, lips parting, and Rolly swayed to meet him.

Marky had forgotten. The sensation of a cock gliding over his tongue, bumping against the back of his throat He hadn't done it in so long. Until this moment, he didn't even know he'd missed it. He moaned around Rolly's cock, lying heavy and full in his mouth, and let his eyes drift closed. He'd been good at this once. Gig had hated the sensation, but Rolly ruffled his hair and encouraged him.

"So...good," he whispered, his voice rough, breaking over the words. "Go ahead."

Marky concentrated, focusing his effort on giving Rolly the same pleasure he'd received. Rolly's hands in his hair kept him grounded, guiding him and lending a sense of security, even with his own hands still trapped. It was easy to get into it, to accept all the little sensations that reminded him how much he loved this part; listening to his partner moan and encourage him as he sucked, the sharp intake of Rolly's breath when he pulled back and slipped his tongue around the tip. He especially loved the soft strokes of fingers along his scalp, the hand curling, warm and secure around the back of his head, and the pressure of it holding him still for a moment while Rolly pushed into the back of his throat and groaned.

"Fuck, Marky." Rolly's hand slid down around his cheek. "Marky, stop." Rolly pulled back, slowly removing himself, a bit at a time, from Marky's mouth. "Stop." He crouched, lowering himself to Marky's seated level, one hand still stroking through his hair, the other caressing his check. "Lie down. On your stomach."

Marky swallowed hard. "You're going to fuck me."

"I'd like to."

Marky tugged on the bindings. Knowing he could free himself didn't quite make him feel any less vulnerable. "I can't." He dropped his gaze. "Not tied. Please."

"It's okay." Rolly didn't even make him free himself. He reached behind Marky and slipped the hook free of the rings. "I still want you." His hand went back to sifting through Marky's hair, then rested, warm and reassuring, on the side of his face.

Marky nodded, pulling him down to the bed and spreading his legs.

Like everything else so far, this Rolly did with a firm, gentle hand. It didn't matter that Marky hadn't bottomed for a good long while. Rolly had released his hands, giving Marky the freedom to touch him, but he still used his not inconsiderable strength to hold Marky's legs wide. The exposure brought a hot blush back to Marky's cheeks, and he resisted the hold.

"Shh." Rolly caressed his chest, his stomach, trailed fingers down his inner thigh. "Stick with me, and before long, you'll be trained to hold them open yourself."

"Trained?" Marky's eyes went wide and his breath caught.

Rolly only smiled and leaned down to kiss his stomach. "Don't worry. I'm only going to do what you want." He leaned over Marky, one hand still holding his thighs apart. "Do you want me to fuck you?"

Marky nodded, reached up and touched Rolly's hair. "Yeah."

Rolly took his time preparing Marky with long fingers perfect for teasing, stretching and playing with him until he was beyond ready for the real thing.

"Please!" He grabbed for Rolly's hips, tried to draw him closer, even lifted his ass off the mattress to bring them together. It only pushed him further onto those cruelly inadequate fingers and he moaned.

"Please what?" Rolly crooked his fingers inside Marky and grinned.

"Fuck." Marky's head dropped back, his hips came up further. He gave up what was left of his dignity. "Now. I want your cock in me. Fuck me already!"

Rolly chuckled, drew his fingers free, gripped Marky's hips and settled between his legs, cock laying heavy alongside his own. "Now?"

"Now!"

The sting was inevitable. Rolly eased into Marky's body, hands steadying him through the discomfort. "Take your time. I'm not going anywhere." He bent for a kiss, and the warm distraction, Rolly's tongue gently prying for entry, eased Marky past the moment of pain. When he started to move, the sensation of ribs and knobs sliding past his nerves ripped through Marky like a tidal wave.

"Oh, shit. You got the good condoms…"

"Of course." Rolly lifted himself up a bit, caressed the side of Marky's face. "The best." He caught Marky's gaze. "I never settle for anything less than the best."

"Oh." He blinked up at Rolly. "I'm just a Greenback."

"You're much more than *just* anything, I think," Rolly said, moving again, ever faster, harder, until he'd pushed Marky past thought to an almost embarrassingly quick orgasm. If Rolly noticed, or cared, he didn't utter a word.

His own climax came quietly, but the grip of his arms around Marky was tight.

"Nothing but the best," Rolly whispered in his ear after a few minutes. "I'm going to get us a cloth. Wait here."

He did, though he was shivering a little by the time Rolly came back. The warm cloth was nice against his skin, and the feel of Rolly's body when he lay back down even nicer. Marky turned his back to Rolly, and stared at the wall. He didn't pull away, though. It was comfortable in that field of warmth, and after a few minutes, when his companion turned and curled around him, he slowly relaxed into the curve of his body. He fell asleep to the sensation of Rolly's fingers stroking through his hair.

* * * *

He woke up to blinding sun in his eyes, and rolled over.

"Wha—" He shifted again, to find his arms lifted above his head, strapped to the headboard. "Hey!" His rattling and shouting brought a huge man to the door. "Who are you?" Instinctively, Marky curled his knees up, glad the sheets still covered him.

"Hal." Hal leaned in the door, arms tucked across his chest. "Who are you?"

"Undo me."

"Can't."

"Yes you can! Untie me!"

"Boss said you had no manners." Hal turned to go.

"Please!" Marky yelled after him. "Please. Please will you untie me?"

Hal turned back, his gaze steady, if maybe a little sympathetic. "Sorry, man. Not part of my instructions." He left the door part way open when he left though.

"For god's sake! I have to piss! Hal!"

After a minute, the door opened again. "You aren't going to piss all over my bed are you?"

"Rolly! Let me go!"

"Don't panic." Rolly settled on the edge of the bed and reached above Marky to lay his hand over Marky's wrist, just under the cuff. "Kiss first."

Marky squirmed. "Untie me first. Why…"

Rolly didn't let him finish the question, though, leaning down and kissing him, sliding his expert tongue along his lower lip.

Marky moaned. He couldn't deny the sensation growing in his gut, but still. He tugged at his hands, rattling the metal against the bed frame. He had to turn his head away to gather enough breath, enough composure to think. "Please. Rolly, untie me." There wasn't much breath behind the words, though, and he glanced back, worried Rolly wouldn't understand he really did want to be free.

A smile creased Rolly's face. "I wasn't going to keep you as my sex slave." His eyes twinkled. "Unless you wanted me to." But he did reach over to undo the clip holding Marky to the bed.

Marky slithered out from under him, clutching the covers around his waist. "Then why'd you do that?"

"I had to go out. I needed you to be here when I got back, and I didn't want to put that on Hal. Honestly, I tried to get back before you even woke up."

"You can't just do that to a person!"

"That's what Hal said."

"Well Hal was right!"

"Yes." Rolly nodded. "Hal was right. I'm sorry."

"You're—you should be." Marky twisted his wrist, rubbed at the skin under the cuff.

"You want to take those off?"

Marky sat on the other side of the bed. "Why did you need me to be here when you got back?"

"To be sure you were safe."

"You couldn't just ask me to stay?"

"I told you." Rolly shuffled across the bed dropped a hand on his shoulder and kneaded softly. "I had to be somewhere. I worried you might leave before I got back."

"You could have just asked," Marky said. "Nicely. And said please."

Rolly kissed his shoulder. "And you would have stayed?"

Marky rubbed at the cuffs again. Nodded. "I would have stayed." He turned and caught the grin that crossed Rolly's face. The look, unguarded and happy, prevented Marky from pointing out he had nowhere to go until Dean's room for him was free.

* * * *

The days passed too quickly. Marky might have spent more of that time than was healthy in Rolly's bed, but he had no place else to be. Even cuffed and often bound, he had never felt safer. He couldn't stay forever, though, and that's why he gulped with surprise and remained silent when Rolly suggested it.

"Say something." Rolly was lying on top of him, chest to chest, with his chin resting on his hand on Marky's breastbone. He reached up and wiped a bit of sweat off Marky's temple. "I shouldn't have asked." He rolled off Marky to flop on his back on the bed.

"It isn't that I don't want to." Marky sat up, pulled the sheet into his lap and smoothed the edge of it between his fingers. "I…" He sighed. "I just can't."

"Why? You have everything you need here."

"Everything I want," Marky corrected, and turned his gaze to Rolly. "It would be easy. Stay here and let you take care of everything, make all my problems go away. And it's tempting, believe me." He shifted, leaning on his arm and running his fingers over the scars on Rolly's chest. "But it wouldn't solve anything. I'd be staying because I'm too afraid to face what I've done. Where I came from." He smiled softly. "This creature you've captured, this isn't me. It's a fun fantasy, but it isn't…my life. I need to have a life. One I didn't screw up or run away from."

Rolly pulled away from his touch to sit on the edge of the bed with his back to Marky. "So you're leaving."

"Not leaving." Marky crawled across to him and draped his arms over Rolly's shoulders. "Standing on my own two feet. You deserve something more than a bimbo in your bed, and I don't want that life. I'm better than that."

"That isn't how I think of you."

"Not now. Not yet. But you will, if this is all I ever do."

Rolly wrapped his fingers around Marky's wrists, covering the cuffs he only took off now when he was showering. "Where will you go?"

"Dean's shelter and Peter's deli to start. I'm not above a helping hand, but I won't be kept."

A deep breath and a sigh accompanied Rolly's nod, and he twisted around to face Marky. "You'll come back?"

Marky grinned. "I am not leaving you, Roland Leibow. I'm finding myself."

Rolly nodded again, and pressed a kiss to Marky's brow, crawled up on the bed with him, and pushed him onto his back. "One more for the road, yeah?"

Marky grinned and stretched his arms above his head. "Just one?"

One of Rolly's hands slid up Marky's arm and he fingered the cuff at his wrist. "What's this now? Again with the restraints?" He had a serious glint in his eye, and Marky shivered. "Tell you what, Marky." He kissed him, as he curled his fingers around Marky's wrist. "I'll tie you up and take care of you, but you have to trust me."

"I do." Marky smiled at him, though a bit of a tremor ran through the expression.

"I'm going to secure you to the bed, and this time, you're going to let me fuck you while you're still bound." Rolly's fingers caressed his cheek, his neck, travelled over his collar bone. He straddled Marky, his hard cock dripping onto Marky's stomach. "Are you ready?"

Marky shifted his hips under Rolly and nodded. "I'm ready." He gripped the headboard in two fists and took a deep breath. Once he was secured to the bed, he was trapped and at Rolly's mercy. It would be easy for Rolly to keep him here. The breath let out in a long sigh, and Marky wiggled his legs free and spread them.

Rolly smiled down on him, caressed his face again. "Good boy." He secured Marky's cuffs to the bed, and spent a few minutes in soothing attention, kissing and stroking his fingers through Marky's hair. "This is going to be quick, okay? But it'll be good. I want you just to relax."

Marky could only concentrate on breathing. Rolly's touch was nice, comforting, but not completely distracting from the anxiety of being tied down and taken, even if he was crazy about the man who was doing it. He closed his eyes and focused on Rolly's lips, making their way across his jaw to his ear where he paused to whisper.

"Fingers first." He shifted to the side, lifted one of Marky's legs to his shoulder and pushed slicked fingers into Marky's opening. "Okay?"

Marky nodded, then sighed as Rolly stroked across his prostate. "Good. Do that—"

Rolly did.

"—again." He rocked his hips again, enjoying the now familiar sensation of Rolly's preparations. His cock hardened as Rolly caressed him inside and gazed down on his face, clearly enjoying his task.

"You like me watching, don't you?" Rolly asked.

Marky could hardly deny it as his erection lifted off his belly and his breath came faster with the every thrust of Rolly's fingers.

"God, you have a good 'Fuck me' face." Rolly leaned down and kissed him, a hard, possessive claim on his mouth that stole any response he might have made.

The kiss proved distracting enough for Rolly to pull his fingers free and position himself to take Marky without Marky tensing up again. The breech was fast and as possessive as the kiss. Rolly grunted with the effort, but stilled to allow Marky to adjust before he began to move. As he'd promised it would be, it was quick. His hard thrusts hit home sending shots of pleasure up Marky's spine. More than once, he tried to grab Rolly's shoulders, but the cuffs aborted the movement, and brought home how utterly he had surrendered to this man. And he liked it. Every thrust accentuated how much he liked it. Before he was ready, his body tightened, his balls contracted, and he cried out, his release spurting in a warm flood across his abdomen. Rolly came a moment later, his face buried in the crook of Marky's shoulder.

And Mark couldn't hold him as he shuddered through it. He could only turn his head and kiss Rolly's hair, wrap his legs around him, whisper his name until the blond head finally lifted.

"You were right," Marky whispered as green eyes looked into his. "Short, but very, very good."

"And you're still going to go." It wasn't a question, and Marky had to give him points for that.

"Yeah. I'm still going to go."

This time, when Rolly kissed him, the possessiveness was underlaid with something more intense, more tangible, even if Marky couldn't put a name to it. The effect lingered with him long after Rolly had released him and he'd showered and dressed.

Chapter Four

After only three days, it should not have been that hard to walk out the door. It wasn't like he was never coming back. He'd see Rolly the next night, but something fundamental had changed. Marky was not Mr. Leibow's creature any more, despite the cuffs, and the feel of Rolly's hard fuck still tingling about his backside. He was on his own like he'd never been, not when he'd had parents to love him, or fellow gang members to rely on. The cab waiting on the white stretch of gravel was taking him to something new and a lot scarier than being cuffed to a bed and fucked.

"You're sure about this?"

Marky pressed close to Rolly, tucked his cheek against Rolly's neck. "No." For a minute, he stood there, Rolly's arm around him, and his heart pounding. It shouldn't be so hard. He'd spent years on the street looking after himself. This was nothing compared to that. He had a safe place to live, a guaranteed meal a day, and a lover who wanted to help. The cab horn blew a sharp reminder that he'd already made his decision. He pulled himself away and smiled. "But yeah. I'm sure."

Rolly pulled a cell phone out of his pocket and handed it to Marky. "Just in case."

Marky looked at the cell resting on Rolly's palm and picked up the new duffle bag at his feet, with it's contents, new clothes Rolly had insisted on buying for him. All he had left that Rolly hadn't given him was the familiar leather jacket, a heavy comfort on his back. "You've given me enough."

"Take it."

Marky nodded and pocketed the phone. "Thanks." He backed down one step. "Don't worry. I'll see you tomorrow night. At the club."

"I'll be there." Rolly stood on the front step, hands in his pockets, until the cab rounded the curve in the drive. Marky knew, because he glanced back at that last minute, and Rolly raised a hand to wave.

Dean's shelter was a huge brownstone set back from the street with a waist-high iron fence across the front yard. A messy, slightly overgrown garden graced the lawn and most of the walk leading up to the door. A series of pots with wilting petunias marched up the steps beside him. A young man in a James Dean denim look opened the front door when he rang the bell, but left the screen closed.

"Who're you?"

Marky swallowed, but before he could answer, a middle-aged man wheeled up behind him.

"Scott. Manners." The wheelchair-bound man smiled. "Marky?"

Marky nodded. "I'm looking for Dean? Roland Leibow sent me."

"I'm Dean." He backed his chair away from the door and nodded at Scott, who flipped open the lock and walked away.

Marky opened the door and stepped inside. The interior looked just as it should; lots of craftsman style wood and high, detailed stained glass windows letting in light filtered to a golden hue. Evidence of many young men lay everywhere; sports magazines, sweaters, empty water bottles, and a pizza box of crumbs on the coffee table. Still, it was a lot better than the Hole.

"Good to meet you, Marky. Roland mentioned you needed a place to stay, and one of the guys just found himself a nice place on Riverside, so we had a room. Welcome."

"Thanks." Marky stood awkwardly, gripping the handles of his duffle.

"Your room's upstairs." Dean rolled, not to the stairs, but around the bottom step and into the hallway. "We had the dumbwaiter modified..." Dean wheeled himself onto the large, re-enforced platform and motioned Marky on beside him. He was quiet as he pushed the button and the lift brought them up to the second floor. They passed down the hall to the east end, and Dean motioned to the door on the left. "Small, but should do you."

Marky stepped into his new home. A single bed, a dresser in the corner, and a tiny wardrobe were all the furniture that fit in the room. A large window showed a view of a back yard sorely in need of a good trim, more gardens overflowing their confines, and an empty fountain. Behind him, Dean sighed.

"Sorry about the view. Paul used to…" His abrupt pause made Marky turn. "Sorry. My partner. Paul. He took care of the yard work. He got sick." Dean shrugged. "It was over pretty quick. In the spring, he was planning out the new landscaping, and by mid-summer…" He shrugged again. "Make yourself at home. Peter's not expecting you until tomorrow. Come on down and find me once you're settled. We'll see what we can work out about those gardens."

"I don't know anything about—" But Dean was already wheeling away down the hall, and Marky was left with heavy silence and messy view.

* * * *

"It's fairly straightforward this time of year," Rolly said, sitting back in his office chair. Marky sat across from him nursing a hot coffee and watching the dancing. "Dead head everything. If it isn't green, cut it down. Of course, that doesn't apply to shrubs."

"How do you know this?" Marky's gaze shifted to Rolly, and for a moment, he was caught up in the way the lights played behind him, giving him a shifting, rainbow halo. He snorted at the appropriateness.

"What's so funny about me working in a garden centre? Paid my first three semesters of college I'll have you know."

"No. Not that. Nothing's funny. Sorry. Deadhead. Got it. I can do that." He was quiet a while, fingers of one hand turning one of the rings on the cuff of the other. "So." He leant forward. "Dean and Paul. What's that about?"

Rolly sighed and dropped his feet from where they rested on the desk. "Twenty years is what that was about.

Twenty years of shit and aggravation, and they never once stopped loving each other. Paul hated the idea of the shelter at first. Thought it would be too dangerous, and maybe he was right. One kid," Rolly shook his head, "couldn't let anything go. Brought his past and his fucked up life to their doorstep, and Dean got a bullet through his gut trying to protect the idiot. Never walked again. And if that's not shitty enough, Paul got HIV from a messed up blood transfusion so Dean wouldn't bleed to death. Fucking shared everything, the two of them. Five years in, and both of them with a life sentence because they cared too much. Dean says he's fine, but he's not. Too thin, too tired." Rolly rubbed at the bridge of his nose. "You get to know the signs after a while. And I don't think he cares any more. Not since Paul..."

Marky rose, put his mug down and knelt in front of Rolly's chair. "It'll get better. He's still mourning. Once the place starts looking decent again, it'll get better."

"Maybe." Rolly kissed Marky's knuckles. "How was work? How's Peter?"

Marky smiled. "A slave driver."

"He's a huge proponent of hard work. Idle hands and all that."

"He's a good guy. God, he can cook!" Marky patted his stomach. "And pushy. I think I've put on five pounds already."

"In a week?" Rolly laughed and pulled Marky up into his lap. "You need some meat on these bones." His smile shone up at Marky, though. "It's good. This is good, yeah? You're happy?"

Marky nodded. "I am." He caressed Rolly's face and leant down to kiss him. "I know they're all about helping me get back on my feet, but it goes both ways. They need me. I like that feeling."

"I need you too." Rolly took Marky's hand that he was holding, and pushed it down between them, to the growing erection in his pants.

"That's an entirely different kind of need," Marky teased.

"One you are uniquely positioned to satisfy." Rolly stood, dumping Marky back onto his feet. "Or will be, in a minute." He snapped off the light. The office went dark, making it near impossible for anyone in the bar to see through the expanse of window above. "Bend over, Baby." Rolly pressed the back of Marky's neck until he was leaning over the desk.

"Someone might—"

"See me fucking you?" Rolly reached around, undid Marky's jeans, and yanked them down. "So?"

"So..." Marky's breath caught as his cock sprang free and slapped against his belly. Rolly didn't waste any time lubing and getting his fingers up Marky's ass. "So...fuck." He dropped his head and reached for his cock and the leather ring surrounding its base.

"Uh, uh." Rolly slapped his hand away. "I told you to wear it. I didn't tell you to take it off. Wait for it." He did stroke Marky a few times, though, good, firm strokes that made him moan. "So what if someone did walk in and find us with my cock up your ass?" Rolly asked, his voice a raw rumble that crawled up Marky's spine and raised the hair on the back of his neck.

"So," Marky's voice hitched, his breath caught as Rolly slid into him. "They'd know I was yours." Rolly's cock ran over Marky's prostate, drove into him, deep and satisfying, and he gasped. The next few minutes narrowed to Rolly's greedy pleasure as he thrust into Marky, intent on getting himself to the edge of release. It worked for Marky, too, driving him to beg. "God, please, Rolly."

"Not yet." Rolly leant forward and clamped Marky's hands to the desk with his own. "Say it again. With conviction."

"I'm yours," Marky whispered, breath too short to allow anything more.

Rolly licked at his ear. "Louder."

"Yours." Marky found his voice, the need to come, the need to please his lover overriding everything. "I belong to you. Please. I wanna come."

Rolly chuckled, a soft, loving sound that wrapped around Marky, just as his arm did, as he unfastened the cock ring. The invitation to finish was not even off his lips before Marky's orgasm thundered through him, leaving black spots and limp satisfaction in its wake. Rolly was still holding him tight in the wake of his own release as Marky blinked his vision clear.

"God...good," Marky muttered, voice wavering, and arms shaking to hold him up.

Rolly held him close, stroked in and out a few more times with his softening cock, before pulling out with a happy sigh. He kissed Marky softly between the shoulder blades. "You so own me," he whispered, pressing his cheek to the soft cotton of his T-shirt.

Marky felt his lips move again, but the din from the bar, and his own pulse still hammering in his ears drowned out the actual words. He straightened up and turned in Rolly's embrace to ask what he'd said.

Rolly held out the cock ring to him with a smile. "Clean up quick, now. We have dinner reservations."

Marky grinned. "Yes, Sir." He took the bit of leather, shuffled to the bathroom to rinse himself off. He was just fastening the ring back in place when Rolly came in behind him. He turned, jeans still around his knees and the narrow band of black surrounding his cock and balls. The hungry look in Rolly's eyes was deeply gratifying.

"You're so beautiful." Rolly ran a finger along his cock. It twitched lethargically. "Not uncomfortable, is it?"

Marky shook his head. "It feels good." He grinned. "Can't forget it's there when I have to ask your permission to pee."

"You don't have to—"

"I don't mind, or I wouldn't." Marky touched his cheek. "You've never made me do anything I didn't want to do. Now are you finished ogling? Can I put my pants back on?"

Rolly grinned and nodded. "For now."

"Promises, promises," Marky muttered, though it made his heart skip a beat, because it was a promise. One he could count on, and that was a nice feeling to get used to.

Chapter Five

There were a lot of things Marky was finding it easy to get used to. Peter's cooking, for one, and Dean's easy, giving nature, though the sadness underlying it worried him. He was beginning to enjoy the fact he no longer had to look over his shoulder for cops, or rival gangs, or the sudden appearance of one of his own, finally come to exact the price of leaving. Under the right conditions, some days, he almost could believe this was his life, something he could keep, maybe even something that could make up for the past, if he played it right.

So when the bright green bandana hanging out a back pocket of a man sitting at Peter's deli bar caught his eye one day, the cold shiver that ran through him was a nasty reminder that he'd been living on borrowed time.

Peter glanced up when he entered, face grim, eyes shadowed. Marky stopped. He knew that 'not-in-my-place' look in Peter's eyes, and nodded.

"Skate."

The man at the bar turned. Blue eyes, so much like his brother Gig's, glimmered at him. "Marky."

Marky held the door open and motioned outside. "Come on."

Skate picked up his board from where it leant on the counter and followed Marky outside.

"What do you want, Skate?"

"Nothing, man." Skate thumped his shoulder. "Just to see how an old pal's doing."

"I'm fine. You've seen. You can go." Marky ran a hand through his hair, backed his way toward Pete's Deli.

"Hmm." Skate dropped his board on the sidewalk. "You know Drag is seriously pissed at you."

"Why? 'Cause I didn't let him shoot me? Poor baby. He'll just have to get over it."

"Right." Skate smirked. "He just gets over shit like that. Dayton's ridin' his ass to find you."

Marky frowned. "Obviously, he knows where I am. What's stopping him?"

"Shit. What kind of friend do you think I am? I know where you are. Doesn't mean they do."

"Not yet."

"I ain't about to tell them, Marky."

"Why wouldn't you? I got your little brother killed."

"He got himself killed, Marky. You think I don't know that?" Skate focused on the ground again. "You an' me, we're still okay. I mean, I know you left, but," Skate straightened, flipped his board up into his hand and met Marky's gaze. "The Greenbacks aren't perfect. I know that. I'm in and I got no way out. Not like you. I just..." He nodded as if he'd decided something. "I had my little brother to worry about, right? To make sure he didn't do this same stupid shit I did. Only no one ever listens to me. Gig sure as fuck didn't. Look what it got him. I thought he...you... I know you tried. I appreciate that, so I'm not going to tell anyone where you are. I just thought you should know Drag's been poking around, and someone needs to do something about that, cause you know he'll go through whoever he has to to get to you. Hell, asshole shot Gig, he'll shoot anyone." His scowl momentarily covered the sadness in his eyes, and Marky didn't envy him his position. "You got a life here. I ain't gonna let him take that away from you. I know what it's like to have someone to protect and not be able to. All I'm sayin'. This time, I'm gonna do right."

"Skate?"

"I gotta go." He hopped on his board and pushed himself away down the street without a backward glance.

"Skate! Be careful!"

"Later, Marky!" Skate waved back over his shoulder once then he was gone around the corner. Marky stood watching the empty street for a long minute, half expecting to hear the pop of a gunshot. The street remained quiet, though, and eventually he went back inside.

"So?" Peter eyed him from across the counter, but Marky merely shook his head.

"So nothing. Just an old friend come by to say hi."

"That's it?" Peter frowned at him.

"And warn me." He slumped into the seat opposite Peter. "But there's nothing to warn me about I didn't already know, so why'd he come?"

"You should call Rolly."

"And tell him what? It's nothing, Peter. Just an old friend who wanted to make things right... Shit." Marky spun off his stool for the door, turned and held out his hand. "I need your car."

"I don't know, Marky."

"Please. God, please lend me your car." When Peter still looked doubtful, Marky snarled. "Just give me the keys. I'll take it with or without them."

"That's grand theft auto."

"Skate's going after Drag. He'll get himself killed if I don't stop him. Peter, please."

"Call Rolly." But he did reach for the keys and toss them over the counter to Marky. "You be careful!"

Marky only heard the shout through the door as he sped around to Peter's old Buick and slammed inside. A cloud of old candy wrappers and dust trailed him down the street as he sped away, tires smoking around the corner.

He did call Rolly, after his calls to Skate went straight to voice mail. After the police. After there was nothing his lover could do to stop him, because he was already there, and witness to Skate pressing the gun barrel to Drag's temple.

"Skate!" He skidded the car to a stop across the street from the Hole, and got out. "Skate don't!"

"Why not? He shot Gig. He'll kill you if I give him the chance."

"This isn't going to make any of it better."

"You should listen to him, asshole," Drag shouted at Marky. "He's right. He lets me go, you're a dead man!"

"You're not a killer, Skate." Marky was almost across the street, almost within reach. "You're not like him."

"This is the only way to survive."

"No it isn't."

Drag snorted. "Just find yourself a sugar daddy, Skate. Like Marky." His lip curled up in a dark sneer. "Someone to fuck you so hard you just don't have to think any more."

Marky didn't think before he swung. The crack of his fist against Drag's face came almost as much a surprise to him as to the big enforcer. Drag toppled, arms flailing to protect his face from the pavement. Skate stepped back, the gun wavered, then Drag was heaving himself up, pointing at Marky. He heard a popping sound, and suddenly, the street exploded in sound; sirens and screeching tires, gunshots, shouting, and spinning lights, and Marky reeled back from it onto his ass then his back. He stared up at the swirling beams of blue and red chasing each other across the sky.

"Skate?" He struggled up, saw one body sprawled across the pavement, and panicked, but then Skate was being lowered gently to the edge of the sidewalk by a cop, and paramedics were turning over Drag's limp form. He shifted and tried to get up, to the agonizing realisation moving was going to be an issue.

"Shit." He glanced over at one of the paramedics and pointed to his leg. "Is that all mine?" He touched the sticky mess covering his jeans, and his fingers came away stained dark. "I don't...I think...um..."

"Hey! Someone! He's bleeding." Rolly's voice filtered through all the noise, his strong hands lifted Marky's shoulders, and the smell of him surrounded Marky, blocking out a little of the fear.

"Where'd you come from?"

Rolly peered at him. "You called me, remember?"

"Oh. Yeah."

"After you called everyone else on the planet, which we'll talk about later."

"I...was in a hurry."

"Yeah. Now shut up and let them do their job, yeah?"

Marky nodded, too wrung out to do anything else.

* * * *

"It was loud." Marky shrugged at the cop standing at the end of his hospital bed.

"You don't remember anything else?"

"Sorry, no. I got there, Drag said something..."

"He insulted your boyfriend," the cop supplied. "Your friend Daniel filled us in on that part."

"Daniel? Oh. Skate. Yeah. He was there."

"Mr. Strand, do you remember who shot first?"

"I just..." Marky frowned and shook his head. "I just remember it was loud. It's never been loud before. Just a little pop. Like Gig. Barely a sound, but he was still dead." He looked up at the cop. "There was this small little pop. I remember that. And then..." He shook his head. "Everything got loud. I fell. I heard an explosion, sirens, yelling. And then Rolly was there. I just...that's all I can remember."

"Good enough. We'll let you get some rest, Marky." She patted his foot.

"Mark. Just Mark."

Mark lay back as the cops wandered to the door, and Rolly trailed after them. "So?" Rolly's voice was low, but not so low Mark couldn't hear.

"He says he heard a pop, then an explosion, which suggests," the cop consulted her notes, "that Drag fired first. He had a silencer on his gun. Which supports Daniel's claim of self defence. I don't think there's anything further to investigate here."

"Good enough. I'm taking Marky—Mark home this afternoon, so if there's anything else you need, you can contact us there."

"You've been very helpful, Mr. Leibow."

Home was a nice thought, and Mark said so when Rolly came back from seeing the cops out.

It was an even nicer reality when Rolly opened the front door a few hours later and ushered him inside.

"I'll have to go back to Dean's eventually," Mark reminded him

"Not on your life!" Rolly hurried around to his weak side to support him up the stairs.

Mark whacked his ankle with his crutch to get him out of the way.

"You're staying right here, where you belong. Where I can keep an eye on you." He backed off, though, and let Mark hobble up on his own.

"Whatever happened to asking nicely?"

"Out the window when you went off to catch bullets."

"I had to do something." Mark paused in the doorway to the bedroom and sighed. The big bed looked too comfortable for words, and he tottered over to sit on the edge. He rubbed at his bare wrist, glanced around, and then looked at Rolly. "He needed my help. I almost didn't get there..."

"But you did."

"He still—"

"He protected you. And himself. He did what neither of you could do for Gig. Don't take that away from him."

Mark closed his eyes, but the flashing images of anger and gunfire still lingered behind his lids. His fingers tripped over the bones of his wrist and he sighed.

"Stop that." Rolly batted at his restless fingers. "Is it sore? Did you fall on it or something?"

"What?" Mark glanced down at his wrist. "No. It's fine." He picked up his bag and rooted through it, found what he was looking for, and held them out to Rolly. "Guess I got used to them."

Rolly took the offered cuffs and turned them over in his hands. "You don't have to wear them all the time."

Mark dropped his hands back into his lap. "I won't, if you don't want me to."

"You're the one said you had to go out on your own."

"And find myself." He took one of the cuffs and held it up. "This is part of who I am. I like this part. I like how I am with you. I like knowing you're here, that I can go out and do what I need to do, and come home, and you're here. That's why I need to go back to Dean's. He needs me."

"He needs help, it's true." Rolly caressed Mark's face and smiled. "But it doesn't have to be you. Your friend, Skate?"

Mark nodded.

"He needs a place to stay."

"I don't know how he'd feel about this neighbourhood. It's fine for me, but…"

"What? You think everyone who lives in Pride Alley's gay? He needs a place, something he can fix, and Dean needs the help. And you need a nurse."

"I do not!" Mark grinned at him. "Unless a certain blond I know is applying for the job."

Rolly smiled and crouched in front of him. "No one else better be considered." He took one of Mark's hands and curled the leather cuff around his wrist, buckled it in place. "You're all mine." He kissed Mark's palm and looked up, his green eyes soft. "You scared the shit out of me, you know. Don't ever do that again."

Mark smiled and cupped Rolly's face. "I promise, I will make every effort never to have a gun pointed at me ever again." He leaned close, brushed his lips over Rolly's and moved to whisper in his ear, "I love you too."

Rolly sank forward, onto his knees, and wrapped both arms around Mark. For a few moments, he just hung on, his breathing heavy and ragged. When he backed off to look at Mark, his watery, blinking gaze never wavered. "I'm completely yours. You know that?"

"It works out, then." Mark held out his other wrist and watched as Rolly fastened his cuff in place. The familiar weight, the clank of the metal rings against the buckle made him smile. "It's good to be home."

THE MAGIC THIEVES

Serena Yates

Dedication

To all the honest people who spend some of their hard-earned money on books so that authors can write the stories they need to write.
Thank you!

Chapter One

"It has been said that history is written by the victor. The Scrolls of Vengeance will record all of history – so that none of its lessons are forgotten." ~ *From the opening paragraphs of the Tah'Nutian Scrolls of Vengeance, Tah'Nut, year 0*

"A thief thinks everyone steals." ~ *Edward W. Howe, Late 19th to early 20th Earth centuries ~ From the opening paragraphs of the Terran Scrolls of Vengeance, Earth, year 2015*

Everything changed on the day true magic came to Earth. Humans thought that the inter-dimensional gateway to Tah'Nut was a miracle because it appeared just in time to save them from extinction.

Elryk Muyd'omir knew better.

This wasn't a lucky coincidence, miraculous or otherwise. This was the result of a three-year concerted effort to track him down. He'd refused to work with the Xoh'kas family and had incurred their wrath. Now that the Tah'Nutian Law Forces had located his refuge, he needed to make a decision: accept his punishment or fight.

Elryk stood on the white sands of his favourite beach and stared out over the stillness of the blue-green waves. Not a breath of wind to be felt in the physical world. The magical realm was another matter.

"You're going to leave, aren't you?" Parker Stokes was a good friend, sharing his beach house and keeping Elryk company when his job as a physicist allowed.

"I'm sorry." Elryk saw no other way. Even though the gateway had opened on the other side of the planet, he already sensed its currents reaching out for him. Once they touched him there'd be no escape. And he didn't want to risk Parker's safety.

"You've always said this might happen." Parker smiled, showing the dimples that were so at odds with his normally serious demeanour.

"I can't fight them, not yet." His magic was going to start working again once he linked with the power flowing from the gateway. But he couldn't gain his strength back quickly enough. His magic had been inactive for too long.

"But you will, right?" Parker's green eyes shone with the force of his conviction. "You can't let those Xoh'kas 're-programme' you and make you a mindless zombie."

Elryk had told Parker the whole story after his friend had sworn to never tell another soul. He'd been fascinated that magic existed in another dimension. The physicist in him had unsuccessfully tried to develop an explanation. With the gateway open, Parker was going to study the phenomenon.

"Yes, I'll fight." Elryk snorted. The Law Forces were sure to hand him over to the Xoh'kas. The Rah'loyst procedure would neutralize both his memory and his magic.

Permanently. The ruling Xoh'kas family may have wanted more docile citizens but Elryk shuddered at the thought of losing his personality. *Anything* was better than that.

"Good!" Parker slapped him on the back. His lean frame was deceptive, the man's strength tangible in his touch. "They don't deserve to control your Ruling Assembly."

"I never thought they did." Elryk sighed. "I just wasn't ready to step up and face them three years ago. I'm not a fighter, you know?"

"I know." Parker nodded, his black hair bobbing around his patrician face. "But you can't let them take over Earth. We've got enough problems of our own."

"Right." Elryk grimaced. "You've certainly managed to make life difficult for yourselves. You do realise that magic isn't going to solve everything, don't you?"

"Obviously." Parker grinned. "Science is going to play a role."

Elryk nodded.

"Goodbye my friend." Parker smiled and stepped away.

"Thank you for everything." Elryk turned back towards the ocean.

It was time. He had to return to Tah'Nut to be effective. The gateway was the only way back. Once through it, he'd need some time to recover his magic. Then he'd find a way to escape and fix things.

He took one last breath of the salty ocean air. Mentally reaching out to the currents emanating from the gateway to increase his power, he wove the spell that would transport him straight into the Tah'Nutian Law Forces Commander's temporary office on Earth.

Kaythan Vs'urr looked up from the three-dimensional map of Earth, an irritated frown on his face. Transportation lightning inside an office, even one as hastily built and temporary as his current location, was highly irregular.

The smouldering black eyes that stared back at him belonged to a tall muscular man with long black hair, a classically chiselled face with a high forehead and a strong beardless chin and jaw. His skin was white, almost translucent. His lips were the deep red of winter roses. In short, he was looking at the wanted criminal he'd been sent here to capture. The man—no, wizard—stood in the middle of the room, hands relaxed at his sides, acting as if he'd been invited over for some social occasion.

Kaythan's mouth dropped open.

Elryk was not at all what Kaythan had expected. He'd been warned about the potent wizard, an outlaw of the worst kind, headstrong and evil. He'd prepared himself for any and all tricks the 'traitor' was going to throw at him.

This wizard fit the physical description he'd been given down to the last gorgeous molecule of his perfect body. Kaythan swallowed. Crap. He was going to have to be careful about betraying the undeniable attraction he felt. The pictures had been one thing, but the wizard's physical presence was ten times more powerful. He couldn't reveal his plans before he got them both to safety. Nobody could know about his real reason for taking this assignment until it was too late for them to do anything about it.

What surprised him was the lack of aggression in the wizard's body language. Elryk's whole attitude radiated a peacefulness that touched Kaythan's warrior heart. Not that he could show it. He was being watched just as much as Elryk.

So he closed his mouth and hardened his gaze. He walked up to the wizard, his heavy steps making Elryk wince. But the wizard stood his ground, black eyes undeterred.

"So, wizard, you've come to turn yourself in?" Kaythan's voice sounded gruff even to his own ears.

"Why else would I be here?" Elryk shook his head and sneered. "I'm curious, is this the level of intelligence I can expect during the upcoming interrogations?"

"Not good enough for you?" Good, there was at least some fight in him.

"Hardly a challenge." Elryk shrugged. "Not that I expected anyone of any intellectual ability to be part of this operation."

"Is that so?" Kaythan raised his eyebrows, presenting the right effect for the visual chronicling equipment. "You do realise that showing this sort of disrespect of the Law Forces would get you into trouble even if you were a citizen of hitherto unblemished reputation?"

"You don't say!" Elryk laughed. "I see that nothing has changed. Looks like the Xoh'kas have still got everyone, including the Law Forces, under their thumbs."

"Now, now, there's no need to insult us." Kaythan had difficulty keeping a smile off his face. "You're in enough trouble as it is."

"Would *not* insulting you reduce my predicament?" Elryk snorted. "Don't get me wrong, it's not that I care. I'm just curious."

"Based on your file, I'd wager that nothing can reduce your 'predicament'." He grinned, making sure he seemed appropriately disdainful. "However, there's still plenty of potential for making it worse."

"Really?" Elryk crossed his muscular arms across his broad chest. "Do tell me what can be worse than the painful Ray'loyst procedure which wipes people's personality?"

"You don't want to know." He shuddered, careful to keep a neutral facial expression. He'd seen some of the torture inflicted *before* the deletion of a prisoner's mind. Since the prisoners never remembered any of it after receiving the new 'programming', nobody was ever the wiser.

"Probably not." Elryk nodded, agreeing with him for once. "So, to get back to why I'm here, aren't you going to arrest me and put me into restraints or something?"

Oh, the wizard had no idea. Just thinking of him naked, all tied up, powerless to prevent anything that Kaythan was going to do to him, made him rock hard in his uniform pants. Crap! He couldn't stand here sporting an erection. He was supposed to arrest the wizard and get him back to Tah'Nut. Even if it was to follow his own agenda, he had a job to do here.

"Why, are you going to try and run away after turning yourself in?" He pulled the magic-suppressant handcuffs from his belt and opened them.

"Maybe not right now." Elryk shrugged and held out his hands. "But I might change my mind."

He ignored that last remark as he cuffed the wizard, making sure the device adjusted itself properly and didn't cut off the circulation.

Oh, Elryk had given as good as he got verbally, but Kaythan wasn't really convinced the wizard would fight. He'd fled rather than confront his enemies three years ago, hadn't he? He'd have to get his 'prisoner' out of here and talking if he wanted his plan to succeed.

He needed the most powerful lightning wizard currently alive willing to fight if they were going to have a chance at stopping the magic thieves from doing more damage. Spreading magic abilities to more people was a good thing in principle. But it also meant more and more unqualified people using it, including the elusive magic thieves who didn't care about the damage they did.

He couldn't stand the fact that those thieving vermin were only tracked down and punished when they attacked someone important to the Xoh'kas. Most people accepted that their Ruling Assembly had only 'limited resources' to pursue the thieves and that it was better to 'focus on the big offenders', who stole magic in a major way. You couldn't really control something as intangible as magic, could you?

That sure as hell didn't make it right to let them go on unhindered, though.

Chapter Two

Elryk's head hurt so badly he wanted to scream. He lay on his back on some soft surface. As he was trying to figure out what was going on he found that the pulsing behind his temples was matched by an equally painful ache between his legs. What the hell?

"You're okay." The deep voice made him panic. Who was that? Where was he? What had happened? "Don't worry, you're safe. Just breathe and let your body recover."

That was easy for him to say, whoever he was. Elryk was ready to jump out of his skin as the headache got worse, now accompanied by a tingling itch at the back of his neck. Shit, but that didn't feel right.

"You had a nasty shock when we crossed the gateway to Tah'Nut. I suspect it has something to do with your magic." The voice sounded familiar. It was deep and smooth and made him feel safe. It also intensified the ache between his legs every time the man spoke.

His sense of smell was next to return. The musky scent that assaulted his brain was overwhelming. It was strong, male, with an underlying note of sandalwood and leather. His cock throbbed in response, increasing the pressure in his balls. He moaned.

"Ah, your voice is back." The man chuckled. "That's a good sign."

"What—where ..." Elryk swallowed past the pain in his parched throat, trying to open his eyes. He'd had it with the darkness and the not knowing who the hell was talking to him.

"Easy." The man slid a straw between his dehydrated lips. "Have some water to relieve the pain in your throat."

Elryk sipped the ice cold liquid gratefully, wishing it would reduce the pain in his head and groin as well. No such luck. He decided to try and open his eyes again. When he succeeded, the bright light almost blinded him at first.

He was in a large well-lit room, sunlight streaming in from floor to ceiling windows on his left. Nothing but trees outside and birdsong that was uninterrupted by traffic noise. He wasn't in the capital city Tah'Algor. For some reason he'd expected to be there. The walls and ceiling were light blue, one wooden door leading to a bathroom, the other to a hallway.

The man sitting to his right, one deliciously muscled thigh on the bed, faced him with a hesitant smile. Rugged looking with a square jaw and a straight nose his face exuded strength. The eyes were the deep blue of the ocean right before a storm and the full lips were as red as ripe cranberries. Short dark brown hair and skin the colour of golden olives made Elryk's mouth water. He'd be at least six feet five when standing and the man's broad shoulders and muscular, well trained body made the ache between his legs almost unbearable.

"Kaythan." Elryk's memory came back in a rush. Shit. The Law Forces Commander had gotten to him from the very first moment, making him wish they weren't enemies. He'd felt a longing to be in his arms that had made his knees weak.

"You remember my name." The smile broke through and lit up Kaythan's eyes.

"Uhm, aren't you supposed to hand me over to the Xoh'kas?" Elryk frowned. "You did arrest me back on Earth, didn't you?"

"Do you *want* me to hand you over to those idiots?" Kaythan's eyebrows rose.

"Huh? Are you the same Law Forces Commander who put handcuffs on me and threatened me with 'worse than torture'?" Elryk shook his head to clear it, wincing with the shooting pain that stabbed the back of his eyeballs. "Not that I'm complaining, but are you even allowed to think of them as idiots, never mind say it out loud?"

"I'm not their puppet, I never was," Kaythan grunted, anger briefly clouding his eyes. "Look, this may sound weird, but what I said and did in that office was all an act. I had to make it seem real until I could get you away from the surveillance equipment."

"An act?" Now he'd heard it all. Yet it made hope surge in his heart and increased the pounding between his legs. "It was pretty damned convincing."

"I assure you, I had no choice." Kaythan swallowed. "I've been planning this for a long time, ever since I found out that you refused to become head of the Magic Council.

That made me hope you might become an ally in my plan to defeat the thrice-damned magic thieves. Then, of course, you decided to run and make things very difficult for me."

"*I* made things difficult for *you*?" The man was obviously deluded. "I wasn't about to become the leader of the Magic Council with the Xoh'kas breathing down my neck. Shit, they took my lover hostage to make me do what they wanted. I couldn't give in though, not with their plans for total control. So I tried to negotiate with them, but they wouldn't even listen and killed Zolak in cold blood. I had to flee before rage took over. I didn't want to kill innocent people by unleashing uncontrolled lighting magic on them."

"I know. It wasn't your fault and I'm sorry you had to suffer like that." Kaythan's hand covered his and squeezed his fingers is silent support. The fire between Elryk's legs flared up as Kaythan's eyes widened. That could only mean one thing. "What the fuck?"

Kaythan withdrew his hand and stared at him as though he'd caused the problem. Elryk shrugged, helpless to prevent any of what was about to happen. Not even magic could stop a mating bond from forming.

Kaythan took several deep breaths, trying to calm his insistently throbbing cock the hell down. He'd found the wizard attractive all along but this was absurd.

"What did you do to me?" He almost growled the words.

"I didn't do anything." Elryk closed his eyes. The wizard was even paler than before.

"So what's going on?" He was going to get to the bottom of this.

"I believe we are mates." Elryk swallowed and opened his eyes.

"Mates?" Kaythan almost got up to walk away. "That's not possible. There hasn't been a reported mate bond in at least two hundred years."

"Ever since the Xoh'kas took over." Elryk nodded. "Something they did to the gateway. Nobody ever found out for sure."

"So why is it happening to us now?" Kaythan thought there might be worse things than having the wizard as his mate. If the man—and yes, he was no longer just a wizard—could only stop hating him for being a Law Forces Commander.

"I think it's because we first touched when we went through the gateway. I hadn't gotten full control of my magic back when I went in, so I must have fainted from the sudden power surge." Elryk waited for him to nod before he continued. "When you caught me the touch must have triggered the mate bond since we were still away from Tah'Nut. Whatever the Xoh'kas did to the gateway must only affect people on Tah'Nut itself."

"So what do we do about it?" Surely they didn't have to just—mate.

"We either fight it and die, or we give in and live." Elryk's lips drew into a tight line.

"What? That's our choice? I'm not just going to follow some damned instinct like an animal!" Not that he'd mind fucking the gorgeous wizard but he wanted it to be *his* choice, not the need to follow some primitive impulse.

"I'm sorry you don't like it." Elryk turned his head away.

Was that pain in his eyes? Shit, Kaythan hadn't wanted to hurt him. He just needed time to adjust. It wasn't as if he hadn't found the man attractive even before this mating bond nonsense happened.

"Why did you bring me here?" Elryk turned back, all traces of emotion gone from his eyes and face.

"What?" That wasn't what he'd expected. "You're just dropping this mating thing?"

"Your reaction told me everything I need to know. There's no point in wasting time now that you've made your decision. So I suggest we use what time we have left wisely." Elryk glared at him. "I'm still not sure I can trust you, you being a Law Forces Commander and all. But at least I want to find out what it is you think you can accomplish by taking me to some remote location rather than handing me over to the Xoh'kas."

"What time we have left?" All Kaythan was able to focus on was the other man's well-toned body under the sheet, his black glossy hair surrounding his head like a dark halo on the pillow. He wanted to kiss him.

"Has your brain stopped working already? It's a little early for that." Elryk was definitely impatient.

"My brain is going to stop working?" Actually, he wasn't sure that hadn't happened already with all the blood trapped in his painfully erect cock.

Elryk just raised his eyebrows at him.

"Okay, okay. A friend of mine is a seer." They'd get back to the mating bond issues soon enough. "Arith unearthed new information about the Muyd'Othar when he was looking for ways to stop the magic thieves."

"The Magic Shield?" Elryk's eyes grew big. "But that's just a legend!"

"No, apparently it's real. It's supposed to stop magic being siphoned off. According to Arith, any Great Wizard who knows where to go can find it." Kaythan grinned.

"You're a Great Wizard and he's found out just where to send us."

Chapter Three

It hadn't worked. Elryk couldn't sense the Muyd'Othar even after trying the unusual revealing spell for the third time.

"You must have gotten the directions wrong." He rubbed the persistently tingling itch at the back of his neck. Kaythan was only trained as a Law Forces Commander. How could he be expected to know about magic?

"I certainly didn't." Kaythan frowned. "Maybe your magic isn't back to full strength?"

"Once I entered the gateway it should have returned to normal." Elryk didn't want to consider the alternative. He'd already spent three years without magic abilities.

"If the directions are right and you weren't able to locate the Muyd'Othar, then there's only one other explanation." Kaythan knitted his eyebrows.

"Shit!" Annoyingly Kaythan had come to the same conclusion. "Okay, I'm going to find out. But I'll go outside just in case."

"You need help?" Kaythan got up and stood next to the bed.

Elryk shook his head and sat up. He closed his eyes, trying to will the pain away. When he blinked them back open, Kaythan looked worried.

"I'm fine." It was a lie, but he didn't want to touch Kaythan if the man had such issues about bonding. Touching without—relief would only make it worse.

Elryk got up, so dizzy he almost fainted. He made it to the glass doors leading out onto the balcony and opened one with shaking hands. Stepping outside he took a deep breath. Damp earth, green leaves and the scent of blossoms mingled into a heady perfume almost as good as his favourite ocean aroma. He gripped the railing and closed his eyes, summoning the magic. A simple wind spell would do.

Nothing.

He tried again. The back of his neck was now tingling so hard it was painful.

Still nothing.

"I was right, wasn't I?" Kaythan's voice came from right behind him.

"Yes." Elryk opened his eyes, helpless anger making him lash out, raise his voice. "My magic isn't working and, if the legends are to be believed, it won't return until we've mated. Your negative reaction earlier made it clear that isn't going to happen. So now who's going to stop the magic thieves and the Xoh'kas?"

"Whoa, Elryk. What's wrong?" Kaythan raised his hands and took a step back. "I'm not your enemy here."

"Sorry. But you're not exactly a friend either." Elryk breathed, trying to find his centre. It didn't really matter. Even if Kaythan were his friend, his earlier reaction to a potential mating wasn't promising.

"Hold on. Why do you still think I'm not your friend?" Kaythan frowned. "I brought you here instead of handing you over to the Xoh'kas. I offered my help to fight the magic thieves so we can stop them from stealing the magic needed to balance the Ruling Assembly's activities. I want to help you return the Magic Council to full strength so they can kick out the Xoh'kas."

"You're right, those are the actions of a friend." Elryk sighed and walked back inside to sit on the bed. He felt weak and confused. "I just can't get myself to believe that a Law Forces Commander would give up all his privileges as a Xoh'kas favoured citizen to help a wanted criminal remove their power."

"That's all you see me as, isn't it?" Kaythan's eyes flashed with anger.

"It's really hard to see you as anything else." He wanted to, even more so now that he knew Kaythan was his mate. "But your reaction to us being mates made me feel as though you didn't want anything to do with me on a more personal level."

"I'm sorry I reacted that way. It was mostly surprise that the mating legend is true. And yes, I don't like the thought that I'm being drawn to you by some instinct rather than choice. But I'll be honest with you." Kaythan's stormy blue eyes stared right into Elryk's soul. "I was attracted to you way before we touched and set this mating thing in motion."

"Be-before?" Elryk's heart sped up right along with the pounding in his cock.

"When you first appeared in my office on Earth." Kaythan swallowed. "You made me so hard I thought my pants were going to burst."

"It wasn't just me?" Elryk sagged with relief. Maybe it would all work out.

"No, it wasn't just you." Kaythan sat down on the bed, their thighs almost touching. It made Elryk want to pounce on the man. "Now that I know we're both attracted to each other anyway *and* are supposed to be mates—what's stopping us from doing something about it?"

What indeed?

Kaythan stared into those black eyes that were making him burn with desire beyond even the ache in his balls. Why had he ever thought bonding with Elryk was a bad idea? He was everything he'd ever wanted in a man, physically at least. He didn't know him well enough to judge the rest. But he did know that Elryk was honourable. He hadn't given in to the Xoh'kas' demands to become the token leader of the Magic Council even though they had caught and probably tortured his lover. And when they'd killed him, Elryk had fled into exile rather than endanger innocents' lives.

"So, how do we do this?" Kaythan lifted his hand and caressed Elryk's cheek. A spike of desire made the ache between his legs flare up into pain. "Fuck!"

"Yeah, that'll work." Elryk grinned, but there was tension in the lines around his eyes.

"Not-not what I meant." Kaythan knew touching Elryk made it worse. But he couldn't let go of the warm cheek covered in light stubble that rasped against the palm of his hand. He bent closer, bringing his lips to Elryk's other cheek, brushing the skin. Tah', but the scent of the man drove him crazy. Fresh like an ocean breeze yet musky and definitely male.

"I know." Elryk's breath hitched and he turned his head, brushing his burning lips along Kaythan's. "The Xoh'kas destroyed most of the information about the bonding ritual."

"We'll just do what feels right." Kaythan slid his other arm around Elryk and bent towards his lips. Hot, supple and soft, they made him want more. He used his hand to turn Elryk's head so he'd have a better angle and licked his way inside the other man's mouth. The ache in his balls lessened a little and the relief made him moan as their tongues met. The deeper the kiss went, the better Kaythan felt.

"Skin." Elryk pulled back, gasping, dark eyes glazed with lust. "Please, I need to feel your skin on mine."

Kaythan was beyond words. He pulled back and tore his clothes off. Elryk just sat there, staring at him as he revealed his body. Once he was naked he started on Elryk's clothes, kissing and licking every bit of alabaster skin as he revealed it. When he pulled down the pants and the hard, darkly flushed cock almost jumped at him he nearly came on the spot.

With a last glance at Elryk's blissful gaze he slid one arm under a shoulder and the other one under the knees and bodily lifted his lover into the centre of the bed.

"What?" Elryk actually squealed.

"Need to taste you." Kaythan's voice was rough with need.

He lay down next to Elryk, head towards his feet and licked his lover's wide cock from base to tip. *Yes!* The salty bitter flavour hit his taste buds and made him whimper. That was what he craved. He carefully lifted the engorged organ away from Elryk's flat stomach so he could start licking in earnest. He took the wide head into his mouth and slowly slid down, taking as much of the other man's cock as possible.

Hot lips suddenly surrounded his own glans and he moaned when Elryk reciprocated by taking him all the way down. The man swallowed around his glans before letting him go and Kaythan felt his hips buck. And then they both started bobbing their heads, sucking and licking in a rhythm that drove Kaythan absolutely mad with lust. He slid his arms around Elryk's slim hips and held onto the muscular arse cheeks, encouraging the other man to fuck his mouth in earnest.

Almost choking on the cock moving in and out of his mouth, he felt his own balls tighten as Elryk sucked him with equal force. He wasn't going to last. With a scream that was muffled by the thick organ starting to pulse down his throat, he came in hot spurts of blessed relief. He drank down Elryk's seed, revelling in the soothing flavour as he emptied his balls with a new and exhilarating intensity he never wanted to go without ever again.

He pulled back, trying to catch his breath. Elryk turned around — how did he find the energy? — and crawled into his arms. Kaythan tightened his embrace and held on. For the first time in hours he felt okay, the pain between his legs was gone and the beautiful man who lay trembling in his arms was now his.

"Mhm, that was good." Elryk nuzzled Kaythan's neck, turning his head up for a kiss.

This one was slow, tender and the tingles that moved all the way from the top of his head right down into his balls were good ones. He entwined their legs and pulled Elryk as close to him as possible. This was where he belonged, with his mate.

Long minutes later the other man sighed.

"Guess I should try and see if my magic works now." Elryk lifted his head and focused on the curtains.

Kaythan felt him tremble, then sag against him.

"Nothing." Elryk sounded dejected. "Maybe I've just lost it."

"I don't think so. You are the most powerful lightning wizard born in many generations, aren't you?" Kaythan wanted to fix this for his mate.

"That's what the Ritual of Muyd'pol revealed when they tested me." Elryk snuggled in.

"That means that something else is wrong." Kaythan would bet the damned Xoh'kas had something to do with it. "And we're going to find out what it is."

"How?" Elryk's voice sounded tired.

"I'm sure that Arith can help us figure it out." Kaythan pulled the blankets over them. "Once we've had a nap."

Chapter Four

Elryk tried not to stare at Arith as the ancient wizard led them along a narrow hallway into the back of his house. The wrinkles all over his face and hands were one thing. But the gnarled fingers and bent posture were highly unusual for a seer. The air magic that formed the core of his abilities should have minimised these overt signs of aging.

"Welcome to my sanctuary." Arith grinned and suddenly looked about a hundred years younger. He gestured around the room and Elryk gasped.

Perched atop what felt like a giant tree, the front and both side walls were made of glass, a few leaved branches knocking on the windows on each side. The view across a deep wooded gorge and a distant mountain range was breathtaking. When Elryk turned around the back wall was as rough as a bark-covered tree trunk.

"Quite amazing, isn't it?" Kaythan stepped closer to him, making him feel safe despite the height.

"How did we get here?" He thought they'd walked into a modest farm house after Kaythan had flown them to the seer's home in an undetectable glider.

"That's right, your magic isn't working, so you wouldn't have noticed." Arith sank into a comfortable armchair near the front. It almost swallowed his fragile body. "We passed a few layers of protective and concealing spells. They're necessary to hide this place from the Xoh'kas as well as the magic thieves."

"How did you know my magic isn't working?" Elryk frowned. Arith winked. "Uhm, okay, you're a seer, but even Kaythan and I only found out a few hours ago."

"Sit down." Arith motioned to a couch across from his armchair. "This will take a while."

Elryk took a seat and Kaythan followed, putting a protective arm around his shoulders. The contact reduced the slight pulling sensation in his groin immediately. Tah', but this mate bond would take some getting used to.

"Let me get to the point." Arith ran a hand through his shoulder length white hair. "The formation of the first mate bond in over two hundred years has activated the Muyd'Zel."

"The Magic Key?" Elryk sat up. "That's the second legendary magical object to suddenly reappear from the shrouding mists of history. And how would the formation of a mate bond even be noticed? What in Tah's name is going on?"

"I'm getting to that." Arith shook his head. "You young ones are always so impatient. Right, where was I? Oh, yes. Two hundred years ago, when the Xoh'kas family took over, they had an ally inside the Magic Council, the last

Lightning Grand Master in charge. His name was Rhunnyt Bak'omir."

"That's right." Kaythan nodded. "Elryk is the first lightning wizard in many years to show the potential to advance from Great Wizard to Grand Master level and join the Council."

"That's because for all that time the Xoh'kas have killed all candidates before they made it to the Ritual of Muyd'pol." Arith's eyes flashed with anger. "So the Council has been weak by definition because their leader was a fire, water, earth or air wizard. Only a lightning wizard has parts of all the others types of magic inside him plus his own. That's why he can unite and strengthen the Council members to enable them to effectively check and balance the Ruling Assembly's activities. With the magic thieves now stealing magic on top of this, the Council has been weakened to the point where they are totally ineffective and the Ruling Assembly, under the leadership of the Xoh'kas, is unopposed."

"So how does this link to the Muyd'Zel?" Elryk wiggled in his seat.

"Patience, my son." Arith grinned and leant back in his armchair. "One of the things Rhunnyt did was banish the Muyd'Othar, or Magic Shield, from the real world into the magic realm. This left the Magic Council open to any attacks, further strengthening the Xoh'kas' hold on them. Once Rhunnyt had created the hiding place he was executed by the Xoh'kas. Knowing that the Magic Shield would be needed to restore the power of the Council at some point, a group of 'rebellious' wizards created the Muyd'Zel to enable the right person to find and use the Shield."

"Let me guess—the right person is Elryk?" Kaythan's grip on Elryk's shoulders tightened.

Arith nodded.

"And this will be dangerous." Kaythan growled.

Arith nodded again.

"I'm sure you'll keep me safe." Elryk patted Kaythan's thigh and grinned inwardly at his mate's protectiveness. He could take care of himself, well, once his magic was back, but it was nice to have someone else's support. He'd missed that.

"You bet your sweet little—ahem—on that." Kaythan's yes twinkled wickedly.

Elryk winked at his mate, letting him know he understood and appreciated Kaythan's words. He just saw one major problem, so he turned back to Arith.

"How am I going to retrieve the Muyd'Othar, though, without my magic? It seems to be blocked and I have no idea how to get it back." It *was* rather embarrassing. "We thought it was the mate bond, but that can't be it, can it?

"Well, that *is* part of the problem." Arith frowned. "We can't wait for the bond to solidify, because the Xoh'kas are also trying to find the Shield. If they get to it before you do they will surely destroy it. You have absolutely no time to lose."

"So how do we do this? Sounds rather hopeless to me." Kaythan was obviously still worried about his safety.

"Two things. One is that you have to work together, use both your strengths to overcome the initial disadvantage of no magic." Arith leant forward in his armchair. "But the more important part is that the Muyd'Zel itself will help restore Elryk's magic as you progress. It's been divided into five pieces, one for each type of magic. Obtaining each piece will result in the ability to gain access to the next location as well as strengthen Elryk's magical abilities in the area just conquered."

"And how do I get the first one? Without magic?" Elryk's stomach was rebelling.

"That's where my friend Nysat comes in." Arith grinned. "Like me, he comes from the era before the Xoh'kas. He was one of the wizards involved in creating the Muyd'Zel. He may be a lot younger than me but he's a very powerful earth wizard and has infused that first piece with the ability to awaken that part of your magic inside you. Each of the next pieces will build on that until all of them can fuse and restore you fully."

Arith got up and walked to the back of the room. Close to the door where they'd entered, he bent down and lifted a small wooden box about the size of three hand widths on each side. Its top was green and it felt warm when Arith put it in Elryk's lap.

"This contains the earth magic part of the Key." Arith returned to his seat. "Just be careful when you open it."

"You must be joking." Kaythan stared at Arith. "You're letting Elryk take all the risk?"

Oh, his mate was in a fine mood now. Elryk almost grinned.

"He's not going to die, Kaythan." Arith tilted his head. "But it's good to see that you are so protective of him, even though the bond isn't fully formed. That's a good sign."

"I don't care about any signs." Kaythan had relaxed a little and sounded less aggressive. "I just ca- I just want to make sure he's safe."

"And you will." Arith nodded. "I can see that."

"So I just open this thing and see what happens, right?" Elryk wanted to get to the interesting part.

Arith nodded and Kaythan squeezed his shoulders.

Elryk put his hand on the lid of the little box and closed his eyes. Touch was an important part of earth magic and he wanted to know if he could find out anything before opening the box. The warmth against his legs increased and the box started to hum. The lid snapped open and there was a small egg-shaped crystal inside that shimmered a deep vibrant brown and bright green in turn.

He lifted his hand and pulled it out, feeling waves of earth magic pulsing into him. Kaythan's grip on his shoulder tightened and his mate moaned. The box tumbled to the floor and Elryk folded his hands around the crystal, absorbing all it had to give. Strength flooded the back of his neck, he could smell earth and growing plants, feel soft grass under his feet and hear the soft vibrations of a small earth tremor.

After a while the imagined perceptions faded and he returned to reality. His hands were empty, the crystal was gone.

Elryk turned towards his mate, Kaythan's big blue eyes burning into his, and smiled. He already felt so much stronger, so much more alive, and he'd only absorbed one of the five types of magic. But there was hope now.

When Kaythan bent down to kiss him he forgot everything and gave himself over to the feeling of being wanted. Surely they had some time to enjoy their new mated status?

The earth magic soon started building inside him and he rejoiced. When it didn't stop until it grew into an overwhelming need to move—now—he got worried. And when a rolling rumble surrounded them he almost panicked.

By the time he was able to tear himself away from Kaythan's lips to see what was going on there was a thunderous bang and the comfortable sofa vanished from under them. Instead, they were floating on a flimsy raft in the middle of the wide open ocean.

Chapter Five

"Crap!" Kaythan gasped from the sudden change of environment. He was used to initiating a transport to a new location with the appropriate magical devices. But being transferred without his consent was a new experience and one he found he didn't like.

"I guess water magic is the next one on the list." Elryk gazed around them with wide eyes, took a deep breath and smiled. "I just love the ocean."

"Humph." Kaythan relaxed, detecting no immediate danger. "There's just an awful lot of it around."

Elryk threw his head back and laughed. What a beautiful sound. Kaythan was going to ensure he heard it often.

The water next to one side of their raft started churning, as though it was about to boil. He grabbed Elryk's arm and held onto the edge of the raft with his other hand, trying to stabilise them. Not knowing what creatures lived here he wasn't about to let them take an involuntary swim.

Sea grass bubbled up from the depths. A head followed, making him realise it was hair not grass. A woman's delicate face was revealed, then naked shoulders, the skin as white as Kaythan's but with a bluish hue. Her slender arms floated up, resting at the surface and the splash of a fishtail where her feet should be completed the picture.

"I'm Alwiil, the guardian of the second chamber of the temple of Tah'Muyd." Her voice was melodious but her smile held no real warmth. "What is your business here?"

"We're looking for a piece of the Muyd'Zel." Elryk smiled. "Can you please tell us where it is?"

"That all depends." Alwiil's eyes narrowed.

"On what?" Elryk's smile turned less certain.

"On who sent you." Alwiil's tail vanished. "And on how strong your water magic is."

"Arith the seer sent us." Elryk's shoulders slumped. "And I have no water magic."

"Arith? So he remains among the living." Alwiil nodded. "All right, I'll tell you where you can find the Key. But obtaining it will not be easy if, as you say, you are without water magic."

"Of course not." Kaythan snorted. "These things never are."

Alwiil stared at him as if he was slime that she'd just pulled out from under a rock.

"Kaythan!" Elryk flashed him an angry glance.

"The reason it won't be easy, *warrior*, is your mate's lack of water magic." Alwiil grinned. "The second piece of the Muyd'Zel lies at the bottom of the ocean. Only a very strong water wizard would be able to lift it up from the depths."

"So how can we possibly do it without water magic?" Elryk frowned. "We don't even know where it is."

"You can thank Arith for placing you directly above it. You only need to dive straight down and get it." Alwiil smirked. "However, only one of you can go. The other has to stay on the raft or it will vanish, making it impossible for you to advance to the next chamber. Also, your time is limited because once the diver enters the water, the raft will start to disintegrate."

Kaythan sighed. He knew where this was going.

"So it's a test of our trust in each other as well as of our determination to obtain the Magic Key." Elryk nodded.

"It is indeed." Alwiil turned serious. "Do you accept the challenge?"

Elryk looked at him, the question clear in his eyes.

"I think I should go." Kaythan held up a hand to stop Elryk from protesting right away. "I'm physically stronger with you still recovering from the gateway episode. And you might be able to stop the raft from disintegrating too quickly, giving us more time."

"Huh?" Elryk's eyes widened. "Of course! The raft is made from wood and should be susceptible to earth magic."

Alwiil chortled. Whether in agreement or for a darker reason he really didn't want to know. A dive of unknown length into unfamiliar waters was challenge enough.

"Let's do this." Kaythan took off his boots, vest and tunic, briefly enjoying the interest in Elryk's gaze as it roamed across his bared chest. His belt and pants followed, leaving him in his briefs.

"Are you sure?" Elryk tore his gaze away from Kaythan's crotch with an effort.

"I'm sure." Kaythan cupped his mate's cheek and pressed a brief kiss onto his cool lips. "Hold the raft for me?"

Before he could change his mind, he started taking deep breaths to increase the oxygen level in his blood. When he was ready he smiled at Elryk, filled his lungs with as much air as possible and dove head-first into the freezing water.

Elryk didn't like being left behind. His mate had to risk his life because he hadn't been able to recover his magic. Fuck! He hated feeling so powerless.

And every second that Kaythan remained underwater seemed to last hours. Who knew how deep down that Key was going to be? Would Kaythan be able to see it in the darkness? Was he going to be able to hold his breath long enough, withstand the water pressure? What about sharks and other horrible sea creatures?

"Are you worried yet?" Alwiil's voice and gleeful grin grated on already raw nerves.

"Is that the point of this stupid exercise?" He was ready to yell at her, the universe and anything else that got between him and his mate. Tah', but he wanted Kaythan to be safe.

"It's not an 'exercise'." Alwiil shook her head and pointed at the raft. "It's a test of your ability to trust that your mate will do his part just like he trusts you to do your part. Only if you work together will you succeed."

And with that the vexing mermaid waved at him and vanished into the depths.

Elryk's eyes were fixed on the raft which began to fade at the edges, dissolving as the mermaid had promised. He called up the earth magic within him and tried to coax the wooden logs into growing back for him. It was hard work and when the wood finally reacted he was so relieved that he almost lost his focus.

Sweat soon beaded on his brow and when he noticed first one and then two more shark fins circling the raft, a full-out panic was no longer unlikely. How long had Kaythan been gone? Minutes? And how was he going to make his way back up unto the raft without being eaten by those evil - monsters?

Elryk's heart beat so fast he was about to lose it.

A loud splash right next to him made him jump and he lost his magical hold on the logs. Kaythan was back! Gulping for air and shaking from the exertion, his mate clung to the dissolving raft with the shaking fingers of one hand. In the other he held a shell-shaped urn which was a deep green on the bottom and a swirling blue and white on top.

"Here." Kaythan coughed and took some more deep breaths.

"Come on up." Elryk held out a hand, focusing on keeping at least the logs under Kaythan's hand from vanishing.

"No time." Kaythan shook his head, dislodging rivulets of sea water from his drenched hair. "Get the water magic back, then we can worry about me getting up on the raft."

Not too sure they'd have time to worry he took the urn, eying the sharks carefully. There were at least seven of the great beasts now.

"Don't worry about them." Kaythan brought his now empty second hand up to help him hold on while he regained his breath. "They actually helped me."

"Helped you?" Elryk was distracted from the cool urn for a moment.

"Yeah, they helped push me back up to the surface when I started to run out of air. I don't think I would've made it without their help." Kaythan smiled.

Huh. Would wonders never cease? The sharks *were* giving Kaythan a wide berth, just seemed to be circling them like guard dogs or something.

The creaking logs reminded Elryk that he had a job to do and he sat back, cradling the urn in his hands as if he was holding water. Within seconds the top half of the urn sprang open and revealed a deep blue pearl.

The pearl started glowing and the whole shell-shaped urn dissolved into a bubbling fount of quickly dissolving beauty. The water magic bubbled up from his cupped hands and flowed over the rim to flood his entire being. Water magic poured into him, stroking the back of his neck like waves stroke a beach. It almost swept him away, it was so powerful.

Elryk absorbed all it had to give, smelling salt and brine, feeling warm sand caress his feet and hearing a lake ripple against a rocky shore. Like with the earth magic, after a while the imagined perceptions faded and he returned to reality. His hands were empty and the urn was gone.

From the corner of his eye he saw a huge tidal wave appear on the horizon and he suspected their time in the second chamber was up. He grasped Kaythan's hands and pulled him up onto the raft with him, holding him tightly in his arms.

He barely had time to grab Kaythan's clothes before there was a roar similar to that made by a giant waterfall and the disintegrating raft vanished completely. Just before they were swallowed by the shark filled waters the giant wave enveloped them, lifting them up into the sky. With a final blue flash it was gone.

Elryk sighed. They were now precariously perched on the top of a high rock arch so thin that he was amazed it was able to support their weight.

Chapter Six

Kaythan sensed his mate's unease with the height they'd been deposited at. Elryk hadn't been really comfortable at Arith's place either. He tightened his embrace and bent his head for a kiss to help distract his man.

Scorching heat met Kaythan's lips and Elryk clung to him almost desperately as they caressed each other's tongues. He let his hands roam up and down Elryk's spine, leaving one to stroke his nape when that made the man moan. Elryk had placed his hands flat against Kaythan's shoulder blades and held on. The skin to skin contact reminded him that he was still half naked and he pulled back slowly.

"Probably should get dressed before the next guardian shows up." He grinned into Elryk's widening eyes.

"Good idea." Elryk nodded and looked around while Kaythan slipped his clothes back on. "You know, air magic was never my strong suit. And being as high up as we are now isn't likely to change that."

A mournful squawk, followed by a second louder one made him raise his eyes. Two black vultures were circling above their heads. Their glowing red eyes looked like burning coals, their sharp beaks were the size of daggers. They were at least as large as horses and the powerful whoosh-whoosh of their beating wings fanned foul smelling air towards him that made him retch.

"Do you think they're the guardians of this place?" Kaythan sure hoped not. How were they going to get information from birds?

"If they are, I think we're in trouble." Elryk swallowed.

Just then there was a sound of rock crumbling and when Kaythan peeked down, there were a few fissures in the rock below them. The vultures' squawks got louder.

"Great. Another test with a time limit." Elryk trembled.

"All right, let's consider our options." Kaythan tried to sound calm. "We can try and climb down the arch, we can jump off it, or we can ask the nice birds to carry us down to ground level."

"I think you forgot that we need to find the third part of the Key while we're at it." Elryk went pale as the fissures creaked and widened.

"Good point." Kaythan scratched his head. "Can you try and use your magic to sense where the Key is? I'm not holding my breath for these fellows to tell us."

Elryk raised his eyebrows but nodded and closed his eyes. The rocks didn't stop crumbling and Kaythan was about to say something when Elryk's eyes opened.

"It's over there." Elryk pointed at a rock formation a few hundred feet away. It had the shape of a column and was about half as high as the arch that was now fissuring at an alarming rate. Kaythan wondered who had come up with these hiding places.

"Okay, we're going to have to find a way to fly." Kaythan gripped Elryk's hand before he was able to pull away. "And those birds are our only option."

Elryk nodded and turned to the birds.

"Can you please help us get to that rock formation over there?" Elryk sure sounded pleading enough.

"Finally." The first bird's voice sounded scratchier than a needle on glass. "We were about to give up hope you'd figure it out."

"We weren't allowed to help you until you spoke to us." The second bird came closer, hovering right over Elryk while the first one came to hover over Kaythan. "Now that you have, there's no time to lose."

"The arch is about to collapse." The first bird came closer, the stench almost too much to bear. "Grab onto our feet and we'll fly you where you need to go."

Kaythan was still trying to close his mouth as Elryk grabbed the other bird's feet.

"Don't let me fall." Elryk closed his eyes and the bird took off.

Kaythan grabbed his own bird's feet and followed.

As they approached the rock formation a thundering noise behind them announced the collapse of the giant arch. Kaythan didn't even look back.

Elryk shook so hard he was afraid he was going to lose his grip on the bird. When his own feet finally touched ground he opened his eyes only briefly to make sure he didn't collapse towards the edge of the rock pillar. Then he let go of the bird's talons and crumpled into a relieved heap.

Kaythan's warm arms came around him, lifted him up and cradled him against his muscled chest. Listening to his mate's strong heartbeat calmed him down a little. He opened his eyes and saw smiling deep blue ones gazing back.

"You okay?" Kaythan lifted a hand and caressed his cheek.

"I am now." Elryk took one last deep breath and settled down. "That was the scariest thing I've ever done in my life."

"You did well." Kaythan looked across to the circling birds. "Thank you for your help."

"You are welcome." Both birds replied in unison, then turned and flew away.

"Okay, let's do some air magic." Elryk kissed his mate on the cheek and walked over to the small golden cage with a shimmering feather inside.

He picked up the cage and walked back to his mate. Kaythan opened his arms for him and he sat down in his lap, wiggling a little to make sure he was comfortable.

Kaythan groaned and he grinned. He couldn't wait for all this magic stuff to be sorted so he could finally make love to his mate like he wanted to.

"Only two more types of magic to go after this." Kaythan grumbled and held onto his hips, stopping him from moving. "And then your sweet arse is mine."

"Oh Tah'. That's supposed to help me focus?" Elryk's groin was suddenly tight.

"No, dearling, it's supposed to make you stop wiggling." Kaythan slid a hand behind the back of his neck making him shiver. "If you don't, I may not be able to wait."

"Oh, shit, you make me want." Elryk tilted his head for a kiss. At least he could have one of those, right?

He only pulled back when he ran out of air. He was about to come in his pants, and needed to calm down before it was too late. Kaythan's erection pushed against him from below and that didn't help either.

"Soon." He smiled at his mate whose pupils were dilated with lust. "Soon your arse is going to be mine, just as much as mine's going to be yours."

Kaythan's eyes widened but he didn't say anything. Then a slow grin spread across his face and he nodded.

Okay, back to business.

Elryk opened the little cage and pulled out the feather. It started to vibrate as if stroked by a strong wind and dissolved into a fine mist that hovered in front of his face. The air magic wafted into his nose and made its way into his lungs like a breath of pristine air. It was as quiet and soft as the earth magic had been strong and the water magic had been overwhelming.

He absorbed all it had to give, first feeling a soft breeze against his cheek and then a strong storm against his back. After a short while the imagined sensations faded and he returned to reality. His hands were empty and the mist was gone.

A gigantic tornado approached them faster than any of its kind should be able to move. He slid his arms around Kaythan and held on as his mate returned the favour. The wind buffeted them, pushing them towards the edge of the rock pillar. When they went over the edge Elryk was sure his life was over.

But they didn't fall. Instead they were suddenly surrounded by immense heat. They were inside a cave. It was dark but orange and red flames danced on the surface of a lake of magma to their left. The heat was almost unbearable and sweat ran down his back in little rivulets within a minute.

Chapter Seven

Kaythan shuddered despite the heat. Fire had never been his thing, ever since his parents' house had been burned down by an arsonist when he was three years old. Heat and smoke got to him on a subliminal level and fear coiled tightly in his belly. He fought it back, knowing that he needed to be there for Elryk and whatever trial was next.

A small flame flickered into existence above the lake of magma. It grew larger and then started to approach them. About the size of a large dog by the time it arrived at the lake's rocky edge, it stopped as if it could see them.

"Wow, a fire imp." Elryk's voice was low and respectful. "They're very rare and extremely temperamental, so it makes a perfect guardian for this place."

"This isn't a 'place'." The fire imp's voice hissed and crackled like a real fire. "This is the fourth chamber of the temple of Tah'Muyd and you will show the appropriate respect or suffer the consequences."

"I meant no disrespect." Elryk bowed deeply but remained in Kaythan's lap. It made the heat worse, but Kaythan loved having his mate this close. "We're new to this realm and in dire need of your help."

"Why should I help you?" The fir imp flamed more brightly.

Kaythan almost grinned. It acted like a small animal trying to puff itself up so it looked more dangerous.

"We're trying to stop some truly unscrupulous people from stealing even more magic than they already have." Elryk swallowed and wiped the sweat from his brow. "You may not feel the effects in here yet, but if we don't find a way to prevent them from taking more, the balance on Tah'Nut will be damaged beyond repair. I have lost my magic and need to retrieve it by finding and absorbing the pieces of the Muyd'Zel."

"All right, your cause is worthy." The fire imp's colour changed from a bright orange to a duller red. "However, I do not yet see what's in it for me."

"Why you..." That was as far as Kaythan got before Elryk's elbow made contact with his stomach. "Ouch!"

"Please." Elryk's eyes pleaded with him. "Don't make it angry."

"I didn't mean to." Kaythan hung his head. He'd never been this impulsive. Maybe it was the new mate bond, or maybe he was just getting irritated from sweating buckets. He turned towards the fire imp and bowed from the waist like he'd seen Elryk do. "I am sorry for insulting you."

"You are forgiven." The fire imp turned a bright red. "This time. However, I'm still waiting to hear what's in it for me if I help you."

"What would you like?" Kaythan was happy to see Elryk regard him with approval in his eyes. Much better.

"I'm bored." The fire imp shrank and turned purple. "It's very lonely here."

"And there isn't a whole lot to do." Elryk looked around the rock cavern. It was fairly large, with a few alcoves, but otherwise empty. "So, what would you say if I gave you something to play with?"

"You would do that?" The fire imp grew back to its earlier size and went from purple to red in a heartbeat.

"If you help us — sure." Elryk smiled.

"Yes, yes, I'll help you." The fire flickered wildly. "Please, let me see."

"Okay, hold on. This is only the second time I've used magic in a long time, so it may take a while." Elryk made a move as if to get up.

"Don't go." Kaythan pulled him back, close against his body. He wasn't too happy about all the magma and heat around them.

"You're not worried I'll hurt you if the magic goes wrong?" Elryk wiped more sweat from his face.

"You would never hurt me." Kaythan kissed Elryk's nose. "And nothing will go wrong with your magic. It was fine when you repaired the raft earlier and it'll be fine now. Whatever it is you're planning to do."

"If you're sure…" Elryk smiled when Kaythan nodded. "Okay, here we go."

Elryk stared at one of the alcoves for long moments, then started to move his hands in slow, graceful gestures. He closed his eyes and a deep humming sound poured from his chest. Kaythan kept watching the alcove and blinked when there was a shimmer, then a fog and finally a solid stack of wooden logs. Wow. This magic stuff would never get old.

Elryk sighed and opened his eyes.

"There you go, fire imp." Elryk sagged back against Kaythan's chest. "You can play with the wood as much as you want. Singe it, char it or burn it, it will always return to its current state after you're done."

"Really?" The fire imp perked up and moved towards the stack, completely engulfing it.

Crackling flames licked along the logs, caressing them like a lover's hand at first. Then the wood started turning black and the first wisps of smoke rose towards the ceiling. Finally a sea of flames engulfed the wood until it turned to ashes.

The fire imp moved back, obviously waiting. As soon as it no longer touched the edge of the alcove the stack reappeared, looking like new. Jumping up and down with glee the fire imp moved inside the alcove again and this time hissed at the wood like a flame thrower. The logs went up in flame and were gone within seconds.

"Impressive." The fire imp moved towards them. "That was a worthy gift. So now it is time for me to release the Key to you."

"What do you want me to do?" Elryk seemed exhausted but sat up straight at the fire imp's words.

"The Key is hidden within my body." The fire imp flared brightly as if in pride. "You will need to reach inside me to retrieve it."

"What?" Kaythan held onto Elryk more tightly. That— that thing had just burned a stack of logs to cinders and now it was asking Elryk to put his hand inside what was obviously a very dangerous fire? How was his mate going to survive that without serious injury? And he was expected to just stand by and say nothing?

Elryk smiled when he felt Kaythan's arms tighten around his middle. His mate was worried for him. Not that the gorgeous man needed to be anxious, but it was nice to have someone care again. He hadn't had that since he was about five years old. Tears pooled in his eyes despite the heat and he wiped them away quickly.

This was the wrong time for him to remember how his parents and little sister had died, struck by lightning on a sunny day. Lightning that he had caused because he was playing with his magic and lost control. Sure, the counsellors had explained that it wasn't his fault, that he hadn't been trained and that accidents happened. But that hadn't taken away the guilt for a long time. And the pain still hadn't gone away even almost fifty years later.

"Elryk? What's wrong?" Kaythan's voice pulled him back to the present.

"Nothing." He smiled at his mate. "I'm fine. You don't need to worry. I'll be okay."

"Reaching inside that fire? Are you sure?" Kaythan was shaking.

"Now that I have some of my magic back I can use what I have to protect me." Elryk grinned. "It's a good thing fire came towards the end."

"Oh." Kaythan relaxed a little and tilted his head in thought. "I guess you could use water magic, right?"

"Now you're thinking like a wizard." Elryk nodded. "I'll be using a variation on water magic. The heat inside the fire imp will be so intense that I'll need ice to protect my skin from burning."

Kaythan finally let him go and he walked over to the fire imp. He stopped when he could feel its heat on his face. Focusing on his hands he surrounded them with a layer of magic ice before reaching inside the flame.

Elryk almost pulled back out. The heat was still intense enough to make his hand feel like it was burning. Strengthening the ice magic a little more he took a deep breath and focused on detecting the Key.

He smiled when he felt the tiny flame that was hidden in the very centre of the fire imp's body. He enclosed it inside a fist and pulled out his arm.

Kaythan's eyes widened when Elryk sat back in his lap, the little flame dancing on the upturned palm of his now open hand. It started sparkling and soon covered his entire arm. The fire magic started engulfing Elryk's body, making him feel hot all over. It was wild and untamed, ravenous and almost playful.

He absorbed all it had to give, feeling the heat sink into him, smelling smoke and crumbling ashes under his feet. After a few seconds the imagined sensations faded and he returned to reality. His hands were empty and the little flame was no more.

"Goodbye my friends." The fire imp came closer, but instead of burning heat there was a soothing warmth that lulled them to sleep.

Elryk leaned his head against Kaythan's shoulder and closed his eyes. Kaythan held him close as they drifted off. With a last flare the flame vanished and just before Elryk fell asleep the landscape around them changed. Barren desert surrounded them, a grey wasteland with some dead trees between the rocks and blackened bushes.

Chapter Eight

Kaythan twitched when the crackling tension travelled along his skin. It felt as though someone was trying to shock him awake by using electricity. His eyes flew open. They were supposed to be in the fifth chamber of the temple of Tah'Muyd to obtain the last part of the Key. Instead they'd fallen asleep? Crap!

As his eyes adjusted to the low light levels he recognised a few skeletal remainders of trees, some rocks and a few burned-looking bushes. Dark clouds rolled overhead. Surely the mother of all thunderstorms was about to break. The very air around them felt tense.

Elryk was still asleep, snuggled against him. His breath was shallow and fast and an occasional shudder went through his body. Kaythan carefully shook him awake.

"What? Where?" Elryk sat up with a start, still clinging to Kaythan's arm.

"Shhh, it's okay." Kaythan stroked the back of Elryk's head. "I don't think we're supposed to be sleeping and I have no clue whether we're even in the right place."

Elryk's dark eyes widened as he examined their new environment.

"So I wasn't wrong. Tah', it's bleak enough to depress anyone." Elryk blinked the last remnants of sleep from his eyes. "I thought that's what I saw right before I fell asleep. But it isn't right."

"You mean it shouldn't be like this?" Kaythan itched all over. The first distant lightning bolt lit up the sky. "Or that we're in the wrong place?"

"I don't think we're in the wrong place. I can feel the lightning magic all over my body. But it shouldn't be this barren." Elryk shook his head as his eyes surveyed their environment yet again as if staring at it could make it change. "Lightning is the spark that brings life. It's a positive elemental just like the other four in their own way. The way this chamber looks makes it all about death and destruction. That's just wrong."

"So this tingling and itching is what lightning magic feels like?" While he was relieved that he knew what it was, Kaythan still didn't like the feeling.

"You can feel it too?" Elryk's eyes widened. "Now I *know* something is wrong. Non-wizards aren't supposed to be able to feel magic."

Screeching laughter suddenly surrounded them and the air sizzled with static.

"Clever, clever wizard." The voice sounded like rumbling thunder. "Unfortunately for you this brilliant deduction will not help you obtain the last piece of the Muyd'Zel."

Yep, sounded like another guardian. This one was the most unfriendly yet. He hadn't even shown himself. Another distant flash of lightning briefly brightened the doom.

"So, what *will* help me find the last piece?" Elryk closed his eyes.

"Nothing." The cackling made Kaythan's head hurt. "You are too late. The Xoh'kas made me an offer I couldn't refuse and they've taken the Key to a safe place."

"Shit! I can't believe they managed to get in here." Elryk's eyes flew open. "I guess it's not impossible with the entire Magic Council behind them, but still."

"So how do we make up for the missing bit of the Key?" Kaythan shivered when another thunderous chortle rent the air. He wanted to strangle this guardian.

"I'm not sure what to do." Elryk's shoulders drooped. "Without the missing piece I have no idea how to get my full power back, never mind how to find the Muyd'Othar. And obviously the Xoh'kas are using the Key as a weapon, the way it was never intended to be used. It explains the desolation around us. Everything is out of balance now."

Thunderous laughter and another flash in the distance increased Kaythan's unease.

"That will be fixed soon." The guardian's voice shrieked. "When the thunderstorm gets here it will kill you and your life force will restore the balance. Enjoy the last minutes of your miserable lives. I'm finally leaving this place."

And with that the immediate sense of crackling tension stopped.

"I'm glad he's gone." Kaythan rubbed his arms. "Even if he might be back, I'll take what rest I can. Why is he invisible anyway?"

"Lightning can't be seen, so this guardian apparently doesn't have a visible form either." Elryk's brow furrowed.

"What are you thinking?" Kaythan scanned the darkening sky. "I hope you're about to figure out how to get us away from here. I don't like the look of that thunderstorm one bit."

"Well, I'm just wondering…" Elryk sat up and turned around in Kaythan's arms to make eye contact. "This is a bit of a shot in the dark, but—remember how Arith explained that lightning wizards have a bit of all the other types of magic inside them? And how I would gain my magic back by absorbing all the other types first?"

"Yes…?" Kaythan got hard just from watching Elryk think. It was sexy as hell.

"Well, I've got all the other types back now and have used earth and water magic successfully already." Elryk ran a hand through his tousled hair. "And it's not like I haven't got any lightning magic at all. It's still inside me, it just isn't active."

"Ah, I can see where you're going with this." Kaythan grinned. "You're thinking that you can use the other types of magic to coax the missing one back to life, right?"

"Basically yes. But I don't think that's going to work on its own. If it did, the lightning magic would have already come back and we wouldn't be sitting here anymore. No, I think it'll need an external spark, some extra energy to work." Elryk blushed.

Oh, that was cute. He grinned when he realised what Elryk was thinking. The grin made Elryk's cheeks even darker.

"So you're suggesting…" Kaythan was going to make his mate say it. He decided he liked him even more when he was all flustered.

"I'm suggesting…" Elryk swallowed. "You're going to make me say it, aren't you?"

"Just want to make sure there are no misunderstandings about this, dearling." Kaythan couldn't resist any longer. He cupped his mate's face between his hands and kissed him.

"That's what I mean." Elryk closed his eyes and brought their lips back together.

It made Kaythan forget all about his intention to make Elryk say what he wanted. His mate's body melted against him as they deepened the kiss. He was already hard and, by the feel of it, so was Elryk.

A bright flash and the first rolling of thunder brought him back to reality. They broke apart as Elryk glanced at the approaching thunderstorm. With a quick movement of his hands there was a sheet-covered mattress next to them. Elryk bent down to take off his boots, followed by the rest of his clothes. When he was naked he lay down on the improvised bed and looked at Kaythan expectantly.

Kaythan's eyes were riveted on his mate's gorgeous body. Lightly muscled all over and well toned, Elryk drew Kaythan like no other man ever had. His chest was almost hairless, his large red-brown nipples already erect. His gorgeous cock was hard and lay heavy on his flat belly, the dark red head starting to leak pre-cum when Kaythan kept staring.

Elryk grinned and lifted a hand, crooking his index finger at him in an unmistakable gesture. Kaythan had never shed his clothes so quickly. When he lay down next to his mate he pulled him close so they were skin to skin.

Elryk's arms slid around him in welcome and they kissed like they had never kissed before.

Kaythan tingled from the top of his head to his curling toes from the tongue fucking his mate was giving him. Intense, demanding and unbelievably arousing, Elryk's tongue explored every part of his mouth. The caresses went straight to his swollen cock and his balls started pulling up way too soon.

Kaythan pulled back and looked into Elryk's midnight black eyes. More than passion shone back at him and he swallowed the lump of emotion in his throat.

"I want you to take me, Kaythan." Elryk's voice was deep and husky from desire.

"Tah', what you do to me." Kaythan's hips bucked involuntarily, his arousal almost painful.

"It's totally mutual." Elryk smiled and turned onto his back, pulling Kaythan on top of him, pushing their cocks even more closely together.

Kaythan moaned.

When Elryk slowly spread and lifted his legs Kaythan put his hands next to his mate's shoulders and lifted his hips a little. His cock slid past Elryk's heavy balls and along his opening crack as his mate lifted his hips, resting his lower back on a cushion that had magically appeared out of thin air.

"Cool." Kaythan grinned. Making love to a wizard apparently had its advantages.

Elryk slid his arms around Kaythan's chest, placing his hands on his shoulder blades to pull him down. Open lips and hot breath greeted him when he lowered his head. His cock head touched Elryk's opening and they both moaned.

"Take me." Elryk lifted his hips a little more and pushed up. "I'm ready for you."

With a sigh Kaythan pushed inside the tightest, hottest space his cock had ever been in. It was probably magic lube that made entry so easy. Not that he really cared at this point, it just felt fantastic. Elryk's eyes widened but didn't show any pain as Kaythan kept pushing until he was balls deep inside his mate for the first time.

"Fuck." He wasn't going to last.

"Please!" Elryk nodded and clenched his muscles.

With a deep groan he pulled almost all the way back out before pushing back in. All the air left his lungs in a rush and he thought he was going to fly apart into a million pieces.

"Oh, yes." Elryk panted, trying to pull him closer. "Just like that."

Kaythan moved to his elbows to hold Elryk's face between his hands and started to move. He fused their lips in a kiss, his tongue imitating the thrusts of his lower body. The pressure around his cock was incredible as he pushed inside Elryk's body again and again.

His mate met him thrust for thrust and he could feel his orgasm approach even as he lost his rhythm. Their arousal went higher and higher, the tension palpable in the air as lightning lit up the murky night and thunder rolled overhead.

Finally it was too much. Tingling all over his body he pulled back his head and howled with the power of his orgasm. Spurting his release into Elryk, pulse after pulse, he felt Elryk spray their chests and stomachs with hot sperm in response.

Shaking and still spasming with pleasure he saw a bright flash in Elryk's eyes before his mate closed them and smiled. It seemed they'd been successful on more than one front.

Chapter Nine

Elryk tingled all over. Little sparks were dancing across his skin. He grinned, his eyes still closed. Not only had he just had the best orgasm of his life while his mate's deep blue eyes stared into his soul, his magic was back. Full force, better-than-ever back.

"You okay, dearling?" Kaythan's voice rumbled in his ear as his mate nuzzled his neck and burrowed his face into the sensitive space between his neck and his shoulder.

"More than." Elryk opened his eyes. "I feel like a new wizard."

"Well, you are." Kaythan chuckled and pulled out before turning them onto their sides and pulling him close. "Your magic is definitely new."

"You're right." Elryk slipped a leg between Kaythan's. "It feels different, more alive and powerful."

"It could be the mate bond." Kaythan grinned mischievously and winked.

"It could be." That was entirely possible. The legends did say that mated pairs were always stronger, more resistant than single wizards. Huh.

"I thought I was joking?" Kaythan's eyebrows rose.

"Maybe you were, but I think there may be something to the mate bond myth." Elryk stretched. "I guess we'll find out soon enough."

"We need to get going, I know." Kaythan lifted his head and kissed him much too briefly. Tah', but the man could kiss.

They got dressed the normal way, Elryk wanting to save his magic strength since he didn't know what was coming. He took Kaythan's hand and closed his eyes, focusing on the Muyd'Othar. Using the directions Kaythan had relayed to him before, a clear picture of a room in black and purple rose before his mind's eye. Even though the room seemed empty it was clear that it was where they needed to go.

A bright flash of light later they stood inside the room. A large, cloth-covered pedestal rose from the middle of the room, obviously meant to hold the Magic Shield.

There was only one problem.

The Shield was shattered.

A thousand jagged pieces reflected the light from numerous sconces on the wall, adding a silvery halo to the jumbled mess. That's what the Xoh'kas had used the last piece of the Magic Key for.

Shit.

As he stood there, trying to comprehend the enormity of their loss, he noticed a crackling, hissing presence floating just above the destroyed object.

"You are too late!" The triumphant screech hurt Elryk's head. "You shouldn't be here at all, but you are too late anyway."

"The guardian." Kaythan tensed. "I knew I should have strangled him."

Elryk almost laughed. His mate was such a physical person.

The presence became more real, mist turning into dense fog. Tendrils of the silvery essence of the Shield reached up into the hovering mass to feed it, to make it more real.

Double shit.

The guardian was trying to become corporeal. Elryk quickly focused on the now doughy-looking mass and tried to probe it, but the Shield must have retained some power because it reflected his efforts back at him. Absorbing the spike of energy easily he tried to sever the thing's connection to the Shield's residue instead. Nothing. He couldn't get in.

The writhing mass above the Shield slowly changed to the colour of skin and started to morph into a human body. Legs, arms, torso, a head with long grey hair, and then a black robe covering the body. It stopped moving after having absorbed the last rays from the now only dimly flickering shards of the former Muyd'Othar.

The body floated away from the central pedestal, legs stretching and touching the floor, standing straight before turning around. When the face became visible Elryk gasped.

High forehead, bushy eyebrows and a nose like a hawk's beak sat above a thin mouth that was twisted into a cruel smirk. Black eyes stared at him as the man shook out his hands and stamped his feet a few times.

Elryk would have recognised him anywhere.

Fuck!

Rhunnyt, the last Lightning Grand Master to have run the Magic Council in over two hundred years was back. And he didn't look happy.

"Lost your tongue, little one?" Rhunnyt's voice sounded like shards of glass grating on a hard surface. "The Xoh'kas warned me about you. Guess I should have known better than to believe them after they'd already double-crossed me when they killed me last time. You're not much of a threat to my plans at all, are you?"

"I don't care what the Xoh'kas think about me." Elryk needed a plan. He couldn't let Rhunnyt loose on Tah'Nut again. But how was he going to stop him?

"Then you're even more stupid than I thought." Rhunnyt's evil grin distorted his face into a mask of hatred. "I will squash you like the worthless bug you are and then nothing will stand in the way of me taking over the Magic Council again."

Kaythan stared at the evil wizard in mute disbelief. Not just because he'd rather not have had to deal with him. But how could the Xoh'kas have made him an offer to come back to physical life after they'd decided he was too dangerous for them two hundred years ago? How dumb was that? There was only one advantage to their current situation—the evil being whom they'd met as the guardian now had a neck to wring.

"I can't let you take over the Magic Council." Elryk drew himself up to his full height. "Things are bad enough with the Xoh'kas exploiting and terrorizing the people of Tah'Nut."

"Try and stop me then." Rhunnyt's angry snarl made Elryk flinch.

Kaythan squeezed his mate's hand for moral support. Damn it, he wished he could do more. But he had no magic at all.

"Keep touching me, Kaythan." Elryk's voice was a low whisper. "I need you to ground me as I try and fight this bastard."

"Anything." Kaythan moved behind Elryk and slid his arms around his mate's chest and belly for maximum protection without being in his way.

"Thank you." Elryk had barely murmured the words when the first bolt of lightning flashed across the room.

Elryk raised his arms and made a defensive motion, deflecting the crackling electricity into the wall. Rhunnyt screeched and threw bolt after bolt at them, almost faster than Kaythan could follow with his eyes.

Elryk did what he could, even got the occasional bolt of his own thrown at the evil wizard. For a long while they appeared pretty evenly matched but then Elryk slumped a little. Kaythan tightened his grip and the battle continued. When Rhunnyt started spitting strange sounding words, adding colour to his lightning bolts Kaythan knew something was wrong.

"Shit." Elryk panted with the effort. "Somehow he's using the fragments of the Shield to help him, even though they're almost useless. I have no idea how to stop him."

Cackling in glee, Rhunnyt drew a circle around himself with one of the green bolts and a shimmering energy shield sprang up around him. Elryk's attacks were completely deflected after that and Rhunnyt visibly gained strength.

"I've got you now!" Rhunnyt pulled back, took a deep breath and flung a multicoloured ball of lightning into the air. The colours spread out, coating the walls, ceiling and even the floor in hues of shimmering energy. Another ball of multicoloured lightning formed and was thrown in their direction.

"Fuck!" Elryk panted, sweat running down his temples. "I can't stop that ball of lightning, I can only try and save our lives."

Elryk leant his head back against Kaythan's shoulder and closed his eyes. A wall of wet mud surrounded them and started growing into a dome above their heads. Little flames danced on the walls, helping to deflect the multicoloured lightning bolts from the outside and adding a little light on the inside as the walls around them rose. It all happened almost too quickly for the eye to follow. When the dome was completed there was a loud bang, probably the ball of lightning hitting their protective shell. But nothing more happened. It was suddenly very quiet. The crackling attacks had stopped.

"Enjoy your imprisonment." The grating voice was loud enough to penetrate the layers of mud around them. "It should only last for the next five thousand years or so. Enough time for me to get Tah'Nut into shape."

There was a loud roar and the floor shook. Then there was silence. The evil wizard had apparently left.

"I am so sorry." Elryk shook in his arms. "I've failed utterly. We're stuck in this chamber. There's no way out."

Kaythan turned Elryk around so they were facing each other in the dim light of the little magic flames.

"There is always a way out." He brushed his mate's sweat soaked hair out of his face. "We only have to find it."

Chapter Ten

"I like your optimism." Elryk smiled at Kaythan who hadn't let go of him. "The problem is that Rhunnyt is stronger than I am. So while I was able to protect us from the second ball of lightning killing us, I don't see how we could possibly break through the first ball of lightning that he's used to seal this whole chamber."

"We won't know that until we've tried. " Kaythan pulled him closer for a moment, squeezing him for reassurance. "So, why don't we get out of this earthen igloo you've built for us and have a look around?"

Elryk nodded. He really didn't want to spend the rest of his life in here. And it wouldn't hurt to check their options. Who knew? Maybe the broken pieces of the Muyd'Othar would be good for something.

With a sigh he waved their protective shell back into the magical realm. They were immediately bathed in the eerie glow of the multicoloured ball of lightning that had spread out to seal them in. With Kaythan's words in his ears he tried all five types of magic on it.

"Nothing." Elryk felt so tense he thought he'd burst. "It only reflects my magic back at me. It's as though the lightning acts as a mirror."

"And there's no hole anywhere that you could use as leverage?" Kaythan stood next to the pedestal and examined the chamber with narrowed eyes.

"No, it's solid all around us. It goes underground as well, I've followed it all the way." Elryk stared at the dimly flickering shards on the pedestal. Something about the Magic Shield and its properties was nagging him but he couldn't figure out what.

"Okay, so how do you destroy a mirror?" Kaythan tilted his head in thought.

"Huh?" Elryk looked up from his contemplation. "You do ask the weirdest questions."

"Not weird." Kaythan grinned. "I just don't think like a wizard, I guess."

"Hm, that may actually be the key to getting us out of here." Elryk nodded. "Keep thinking. There's something about that Magic Shield that's bugging me, but I can't figure out what it is exactly."

"All right, so we've got a ball of lightning magic surrounding us which acts like a mirror to other kinds of magic." Kaythan started pacing. "To answer my earlier question, the way to destroy a mirror is to shatter it with physical force. Would that work on this — thing?"

"That's a good idea except we don't have anything here that we could use to throw at it with enough force, right?" Elryk glanced at Kaythan.

"Unless we can use our bodies?" Kaythan looked ready to jump.

"Not a good idea." Elryk shook his head. "We'd be killed on impact."

"Okay, what else have we got?" Kaythan stared at the heap of shards. "What about them? Would it hurt us to touch them?"

"Probably not, they seem pretty much extinguished to me." Elryk wasn't going to risk his mate trying. "Here, let me go first. I can use my magic to protect me."

"Just be careful." Kaythan reached out for him, cupping his jaw before withdrawing.

"Always." Elryk grinned. His mate in protective mode was even sexier than normal.

Elryk turned his attention to the heap of shards, hoping to find one that was a little bigger, maybe with smoother edges. Most of them were either tiny pieces or dull and lifeless. Preparing to pull away quickly if needed, he touched one of the dead-looking ones. Other than a tiny tingle there was nothing.

"Anything?" Kaythan sounded anxious. He stood close enough so Elryk sensed his mate's body heat.

"Just a little tingle, as though it's trying to come back to life." Elryk put it into the upturned palm of his left hand and searched for a second shard. "Maybe it needs company?"

Kaythan laughed but didn't relax his watchful stance.

More tingling, but nothing happened.

"You want me to try it?" Kaythan looked hopeful to be doing something.

"Sure, just pick one up and see what happens." It couldn't hurt to see if a non-magical person had a different effect.

Kaythan picked up a dimly flickering one before Elryk could stop him.

"You were supposed to pick a dull one!" He watched carefully, ready to jump to his mate's rescue.

"Was I?" Kaythan grinned as he watched the little shard flicker in his hand. "But these are prettier. And it's just sitting there, making me itch a little."

Elryk just shook his head.

Kaythan put the first shard on the palm of his right hand, then picked another one and put it right next to it. More flickering ensued, but that was it.

"Something is definitely going on with these." Elryk dry-washed his face with his free hand. "I wonder what would happen if we combined the dull and the flickering ones?"

"Good idea." Kaythan reached out to offer his to Elryk but as soon as their fingers touched a low humming sound came from all four shards and they started to glow with a warm golden radiance that stopped both men in their tracks.

The two shards on Elryk's hand moved closer together and melded into a teardrop-shaped crystal. It immediately started moving towards Elryk's wrist and sank into the skin until only its top half was visible. There was no pain, only a deep sense of happiness.

"What the hell?" Kaythan stared at his own hand where his crystal was behaving in exactly the same way.

Kaythan let go of Elryk's hand to touch the embedded teardrop in his own wrist and the crystals stopped glowing.

"Okay, that's officially weird." Elryk blinked and reached out for Kaythan's hand.

As soon as they touched the crystals started glowing again. Elryk felt an irresistible urge to link hands with Kaythan. His left hand pulsed with it.

"You feel it too?" Kaythan's eyes were wide, shocked. "This thing wants me to link hands with you. It's as if a magnet is drawing my right hand to you."

"Yeah, I can feel it as well." Elryk thought for a moment. "It's a warm feeling though, nice. My magic can't detect anything dangerous."

"You want to give in?" Kaythan smiled. "It feels like my crystal wants its little mate."

"That's exactly it!" Elryk was elated. "It's got something to do with the mate bond. Maybe that's what activated these pieces?"

"Who knows what they can do when we let them work together?" Kaythan's eyes were bright with excitement.

"Only one way to find out." Elryk grinned at Kaythan's surprised laugh when his mate heard his own favourite mantra quoted back at him.

They stood next to each other and let their hands link, fingers entwined. It brought their wrists together and as soon as the two crystals touched the low humming started up and the golden radiance was back. It surrounded their hands in a small pulsing sphere.

"All right, this is interesting. It makes me feel nice, but I wonder what it can do? I'm sure it's not just meant to sit there and make us feel happy, is it?" Kaythan frowned.

"Hardly." Elryk looked at the multicoloured chamber wall. "I wonder whether whatever it is might help us break through that lightning magic?"

"You know the answer to that." Kaythan grinned. "What do you think we need to do?"

"I think we need to focus our thoughts on wanting the Shield to open up for us." Elryk figured it might work just like magic.

"Okay, let's focus away." Kaythan winked at him and turned his attention onto the lightning-covered wall.

"Open for us." Elryk was sure speaking the words would help Kaythan focus. So he kept repeating the simple sentence again and again.

When Kaythan started speaking it with him the small golden sphere started to grow. Kaythan stopped speaking and the sphere shrank back to its original size.

"Okay, got it. Don't stop the focus." Kaythan smiled sheepishly and concentrated on the wall and their words again.

When the golden sphere reached the chamber wall there was a crackle and a hiss, but nothing happened.

"More pressure." Elryk willed himself to help the golden sphere push outward. "Focus on it pushing against the walls."

Kaythan nodded and closed his eyes.

The golden sphere started pulsing until the multicoloured lights vanished with a surprisingly soft plopping sound. They were free!

Chapter Eleven

Kaythan had never been as relieved in his life as when they escaped that chamber. Leaving the broken Muyd'Othar behind had been hard. Those shards might be useful for other bonded mates. The shards were too valuable to fall into the wrong hands. Elryk put a concealing spell on it, but you never knew what prying wizards might be able to find out.

They'd transported back to the safe house in the countryside to get some sleep. He grinned. It wasn't all they'd gotten. Elryk had been too sexy for him to resist. Taking his mate again had made Kaythan realise how much he was beginning to love his wizard. He hadn't said anything, and neither had Elryk. Kaythan had seen his own feelings mirrored in Elryk's eyes though, had felt it in his touch and had almost heard it in his soft sighs and moans.

Tah' — he needed this mess with the Xoh'kas, the magic thieves and now Rhunnyt to be over. All he wanted was a peaceful life with his mate.

Instead, they were getting ready to transport into the Magic Council's meeting chamber where Rhunnyt was probably about to take over. If he hadn't already.

"Ready?" Elryk looked like he was ready to do battle. Well, he had personal reasons enough to want to defeat the assorted evil wizards, politicians and magic thieves.

"Sure, whenever you are." Kaythan smiled and took his mate's right hand with his left. "Ready to make the connection anytime we need it."

"I'm sure that'll be soon." Elryk frowned. "In fact, I think it might be best if we went in there already linked. We don't know what they'll throw at us."

Kaythan nodded and shifted his hand so their wrists and the little crystals inside them connected. The small golden sphere formed instantly, much faster than the first time.

"Hm, this might work better with practice." Elryk stared down at their linked hands. "I really want to know what it is, though. It's amazing because it gives you some magical ability and I can feel your strength and support flow into me."

"Let's just be grateful that it works." Kaythan wanted to get this over with.

"I am." Elryk looked up at him with that brilliant smile of his.

Kaythan bent down and kissed his mate on the mouth.

"Let's go." He pulled back, forcing himself to focus on the upcoming fight rather than his mate's tempting lips.

Elryk closed his eyes, there was a light tingle in their link and they stood inside the Magic Council's meeting chamber. Nine very pale and slightly crumpled wizards in purple robes sat around the round table. The tenth wizard stood, his black robe hung in loose folds, and his grey hair was held back by a black leather strip. Rhunnyt, as expected.

"What—how dare you enter here." The evil wizard's voice was shrill and many of the other wizards cringed.

"We dare with the right of those wanting justice." Elryk stood tall and proud. "You wronged Tah'Nut two hundred years ago by selling out to the Xoh'kas. You're about to do so again by taking over a Magic Council too weak from continuous theft of their power to fight you. We will not allow this."

"You will not allow…" Rhunnyt turned beet red and sputtered with rage. "You have no say here."

"Neither do you." Elryk smiled. "I will ask you once to step back and leave. If you refuse, I will let the golden magic decide for all of us."

The golden magic? Kaythan almost laughed. His mate sure made it sound like he knew what he was talking about. He'd had no idea Elryk was this clever a bluffer.

"Golden magic?" Rhunnyt's laughter was a nauseating mix between a screech and a shriek. "Don't be ridiculous, there is no such thing as golden magic."

"Will you yield and leave the Magic Council never to return?" Elryk stared into the blood red eyes of the evil wizard.

His mate showed no outward sign of weakness but Kaythan felt his hand shake. He gripped Elryk's fingers more tightly and the shaking stopped.

"Never." Rhunnyt lifted his hands, electricity crackling between his bony fingers. "I'll destroy you this time, since I have the entire Magic Council's strength to support me."

Elryk lifted their hands so everyone could see the small golden sphere.

"You have been warned." Elryk's voice was heavy with authority. "We banish you from all worlds and dimensions containing life. Be gone."

The golden sphere expanded quickly as they both repeated 'be gone' under their breaths. The sphere reflected Rhunnyt's bolts of lightning back at him and hit him in the heart. Eyes widening in horror, a black hole in his chest, Rhunnyt made a gurgling sound and sank to his knees before toppling onto his face.

Elryk was shocked at how easy it had turned out to be to defeat Rhunnyt. With his own weapons as it were.

The silence following the battle was deafening.

The nine wizards around the table could have been made of stone, they were so still. It was as if all life had been drained from them. Elryk felt their heartbeats but they were much too slow, as if they were all asleep.

"I think it's time for some healing." Elryk turned towards the table, taking a willing Kaythan with him.

When they lifted their joined hands, the golden sphere, which had returned to its small original size once Rhunnyt was dead, started pulsing and expanding again. It had a slightly red hue this time. Was that due to a link to the healing and cleansing powers of fire magic?

Whatever it was, as the sphere's surface reached each wizard there was a brief flash, a small sigh and the wizard's head dropped onto the table. When it reached the fire wizard who was the current head of the Council he shuddered, his entire body stiffened and he dropped to the floor.

"I guess it was too late to save him." Elryk shrugged. "He's always been too much in line with what the Xoh'kas wanted. Not a real loss, I'm afraid."

Speaking of the Xoh'kas — at that moment the heavy double door to the outside world burst open and a large group of Xoh'kas entered, flanked by armed members of the Law Forces. At the head of the group was the current head of the Xoh'kas family, Trolar.

"What in the divine spirit's name is going on here?" Trolar looked around the chamber, his eyes widening when he discovered the two dead bodies.

"Justice has been served." Elryk lowered their hands but maintained the sphere around the still sleeping wizards. No reason to endanger their lives now that there was hope for a recovery of both their power and their common sense.

"Jus-justice?" Trolar took a step further into the room. "And who are you to be handing out justice? That's the Ruling Assembly's job. And since I'm its head, I get to decide what justice needs to be done."

"You are wrong." Kaythan's voice was quiet but clear. "Handing out justice used to be the Law Force's job. Until the Xoh'kas family disbanded all the judges and took matters into its own hands. This will no longer be tolerated."

"And who are you to be making these pronouncements?" Trolar's face showed his disdain clearly. "A mere Law Forces Commander getting involved in politics. Ridiculous!"

"Actually what he says is true." Elryk smiled. "And it is time your despicable practices of torture, blackmail, and plain exploitation stop."

"And who's going to stop us—exactly?" Trolar sneered. "The two of you? Look at you, a pathetic lawman and a wanted criminal wizard. Holding hands like two children too afraid to stand on their own. Don't make me laugh."

Well, that did it. Nobody insulted his mate.

Elryk nodded at Kaythan and they lifted their linked hands, making the sphere expand beyond the round table and the now snoring wizards.

"May only the just survive the wrath of the golden magic." Elryk had no idea where these words came from but Kaythan spoke the exact same ones simultaneously. It was as if a higher power had decided what to do.

Xoh'kas and Law Force guards alike were scanned by the golden wall as it advanced outward from where Kaythan and he stood in mute amazement. Most of them stiffened and dropped to the floor unmoving. Some of them simply sighed and crumpled as if in slow motion, deep breaths or snores emanating from their chests. A very few remained standing and stared at what was going on.

Elryk had never felt so happy. Everything was going to be all right now. Tah'Nut was being cleansed from the evil that had taken hold so long ago. Whatever the golden magic was, it was doing a long overdue job.

Kaythan turned to him and smiled, making the best promise of all.

Elryk smiled back. He was finally going to have the peace of mind he'd wished for all his life. Better yet, he was going to share it with the best mate in the entire universe.

Chapter Twelve

Kaythan looked at his sleeping mate. He'd awoken a while ago to find Elryk cuddled against his side. Squashed against him, actually. Their legs were entwined, pressing the other man's pelvis against his hip, and an arm was flung possessively across his chest. Elryk's head was buried into the space between Kaythan's neck and his shoulder, the warm breath caressing Kaythan's skin on every exhale. Kaythan grinned. It was as if Elryk had tried to crawl inside him.

It had been a hectic few days since their victory. After the wizards had awoken from their healing sleep they'd unanimously elected Elryk as their new leader. Elryk hadn't wanted to become the High Wizard, but he was the right man to unite them and face the upcoming challenges.

Kaythan snorted. He himself hadn't been very comfortable either once he found out he was to be the new Law Forces High Commander. Being the highest ranked officer left, it was the logical choice. His first order had been dealing with the magic thieves. Legally and on a massive scale they were being traced and arrested all over Tah'Nut, much to the amazement of many ordinary citizens. Talk about a new Age of Justice abounded.

An election to replace the corrupt members of the Ruling Assembly would take place in a few days. Elryk and Kaythan had settled down. They'd moved into the High Wizard's official residence, making the High Commander's residence available as a home for the new judges in training.

It all seemed to be in perfect order and yet Kaythan felt uneasy. Something was missing. Was it just that the last few days had left them too exhausted to make love? Quick hand jobs in the shower had been all they'd managed. He shook his head. No, there was more to it than that.

"What's wrong?" Elryk turned his head slightly to nuzzle Kaythan's neck.

"Sorry, I didn't mean to wake you." He sighed. "I don't know what's bothering me. Everything should be okay and yet I feel like something important is missing."

"Come here." Elryk pulled him onto his side so they were lying front to front.

Nice. His cock started filling, as did Elryk's, pushing up against him. Tah', but he had it bad for this man. Elryk placed an open-mouthed kiss on his lips, tongue moving inside to caress his own. Sweet moans were pushed inside his lungs as Elryk deepened the kiss.

When Elryk pulled back minutes later Kaythan almost voiced his protest.

"Do you trust me?" Those midnight black eyes were wide, his mate's gaze open and loving.

"Of course I trust you. With my life." What sort of a question was that?

"It's just that—something is missing." Elryk blinked, his eyes shining.

"You feel it too?" Kaythan felt his eyebrows rise.

"Yes. I just wasn't sure you did." Elryk sighed. "This mate business is turning out to be more mutual than I expected."

"Well that's good, right?" He was confused now.

"That depends on how far you're willing to go." Elryk swallowed. "I need to make love to you, Kaythan. It's been driving me mad ever since you took me for the first time in the fifth chamber."

"So where's the problem?" Kaythan smiled and relaxed. He knew what was wrong now. Their mate bond wasn't complete. "Don't you know that I'd do anything for you and with you?"

"No, I don't." Elryk dropped his head. "I don't know how willing you are to let me—you know?"

"Elryk, dearling. Look at me." Kaythan used a finger to push Elryk's chin up so he could see his mate's eyes. "I've never wanted it with anyone else. But with you everything is different. I didn't know why I was so uneasy. I had no idea how to fix it. Now that you've mentioned the solution I can *feel* that it's right."

"You can?" Elryk's big eyes brightened.

"Oh, yes." He was more relieved than he could express, so he kissed Elryk instead. It was a deep kiss, claiming and passionate. Their cocks came to full arousal almost at the same time. He moaned and turned onto his back, taking Elryk with him so his mate lay on top of him. He spread his legs and Elryk wiggled until their cocks were aligned comfortably. This was good.

Elryk started kissing and nibbling his way along his jaw, down his neck and across his pecs to a nipple. At the first careful lick Kaythan almost came up off the bed. The feeling was so intense, it sent shivers of desire straight to his cock. When the first nipple had been thoroughly licked, teased and lightly bitten, Elryk moved to the other one. Kaythan was writhing with desire by the time his mate finally moved on, licking a path to his bellybutton and straight down to his pubes.

Taking a deep sniff of his scent, Elryk slid his warm hands along Kaythan's inner thighs and pushed them up and apart. Oh, Tah', he was done for now. Elryk licked and laved his balls, deep sighs of enjoyment making it clear how much he liked this. Kaythan made sure his legs were spread as wide as possible so his mate could get everywhere he wanted.

When Elryk slid his thumbs along Kaythan's thighs, caressing the crease between groin and thigh, Kaythan whimpered. When his mate pushed further inward and exerted light pressure on the sensitive skin just behind Kaythan's balls, he yelped and his hips bucked up of their own accord.

"Perfect." Elryk quickly slid his hands back along his thighs to hold them up and back, exposing Kaythan completely.

At the first tentative lick of Elryk's tongue across the entire length of his crack Kaythan thought he'd come. The pleasure was indescribable. Elryk followed up with more licks until he finally honed in on his hole.

"Fuck!" Kaythan had never felt anything like it.

"We will." Elryk lifted his head and winked at him.

"Please." Kaythan wiggled and pushed towards that tongue as if his life depended on it.

Elryk didn't disappoint him. Licking around the hole in dizzy-making circles and finally pushing his way in, his mate drove him totally crazy with desire. Kaythan swore he was going to do the same to Elryk. Soon. Nobody should go without this sort of pleasure.

"Please." Kaythan was breathing hard, the need for more almost too much to bear. "Please fuck me."

Elryk chuckled and replaced his tongue with a slender finger. His head came up between Kaythan's legs and his mate watched him as the finger went in further. Next thing Kaythan knew, a pleasure so overwhelming that he had to scream with it, raced up his spine. The need to come became almost overwhelming.

"Fuck." Breaths coming in irregular gasps Kaythan bucked and pushed until Elryk hit that spot again. "What. Is. That?"

"Sex magic." Elryk's grin almost split his face.

Kaythan could believe it. When a second finger joined the first in rubbing that magical spot in just the right way he thought he wasn't going to make it.

"Can't. Can't hold it." Kaythan arched his back, his balls rising in readiness for much needed relief.

At the last moment Elryk squeezed the base of his cock and the need to come receded. Just enough to leave him panting for it.

"Not yet." Elryk's eyes were large and glazed with lust. "I want you to wait until I'm inside you."

"Then fuck me." Tah', he needed that beautiful cock inside him. Now. "Please, fuck me."

"With pleasure." Elryk lined up his swollen cock and pushed the head inside.

"Tah'!" Kaythan breathed through the sudden burn. "Tah', that feels good. Give me more."

With a look of intense concentration and rising lust Elryk pushed his entire fat cock inside in one smooth movement. Full. He'd never been this full. He'd also never been more aroused or more in need of release.

Elryk slid his hands to Kaythan's side, holding his hips up at the right angle and keeping his legs spread. Staring into his eyes, his mate began to move. Slow, deep strokes that hit his pleasure spot every time and made him howl with the rising arousal. Then Elryk moved faster and Kaythan started meeting his thrusts, increasing the power of their coupling almost beyond what was bearable.

Finally, still looking deep into his eyes, Elryk pounded him so hard that he couldn't hold back.

"Elryk!" Kaythan's balls rose and his orgasm overwhelmed him. Without a touch to his cock he started coming so hard that his teeth rattled. Spurt after spurt of hot cum coated his chest and abdomen, his hole contracting with each glorious burst of relief.

"Kaythan!" Elryk's response was just as vocal and his mate drove deep one last time before releasing his semen into Kaythan's still clenching channel. Elryk's cock pulsed inside Kaythan, filling him with his love. It was the most amazing feeling to have part of his mate so deep inside him.

"I love you." Kaythan couldn't hold back the words anymore. He knew deep down that it was true and he needed to let Elryk know.

Elryk's eyes widened and his mate collapsed onto his chest, letting Kaythan's legs slide down. Kaythan brought up his arms and held his lover as close as possible while they were trying to catch their breaths.

"I love you too, my mate." Elryk finally lifted his head and Kaythan looked into the black depths that were now filled with love. "I'll love you forever."

"Forever." Kaythan nodded. That might just be enough time to explore the depth of their love. Together.

STEALING
MICHAEL

Jambrea Jo Jones

Dedication

First and always, I need to thank Joy. She helps keep
me sane. I also need to thank my yahoo group,
HeatWave for helping me with tag lines, with a
special shout out to Janis. And to the International
Heat Ladies, thanks for being my sounding board
when I needed it.
To all of you buying this to help stop Copyright
Theft, thank you, thank you, thank you. It is a big
problem that I hope someday won't be an issue.

Chapter One

Robert Mitchell scurried across the leaves littering the cold fall ground behind Thomas Eli's house. The moon hung bright in the sky making it hard for the pale man to hide. He made himself as small as possible and scooped up some dirt, using it to darken his complexion.

It wouldn't do for me to be seen.

His objective was to sneak into the author's house and steal a painting. His mom had seen a spread in a magazine and said the painting was worth a fortune, that it would keep her in her medicine for months.

Robert shivered in the cold. He'd left his coat at home, it wasn't on Mom's list of things to carry. A sound reached his ears and he perked up, tilting his head to the side.

Shit, he isn't supposed to be home. What should I do?

Robert held his breath and concentrated on the sound of shoes clicking on the cement walk. He let the air trapped in his lungs seep out like a tire deflated with a knife.

Thomas' footsteps sounded closer—it had to be Thomas—and then they passed. Robert waited a few minutes before leaving his hiding place. He slithered across the yard until he reached the stairs at Thomas' front door. He stayed close to the ground on the way up. He couldn't give himself away. Maybe he should wait to see if the author would leave the house again. It was a bad idea to go in with Thomas home. His Mom had given him some chloroform she'd swiped, from where he had no idea. Robert knew it was best not to ask questions.

He paused as light flared to life inside, but the door stayed closed. Continuing to the entrance, he patted the bulge in his front pocket for reassurance. The chemical would help him knock Thomas out so he could take the painting. Hopefully the guy wouldn't linger in the front room; the drug was a last ditch effort. He pulled the zip-locked bag from his pocket and opened it, preparing himself for the worst case scenario.

The door beckoned him, the handle mocking him.

He shook his head.

Open the door, Robert.

Mom's voice gave him the courage he needed. Robert closed his eyes, grasped the knob and turned. He pushed the door open and crept into the room.

"Who the fuck are you?"

He shouldn't have seen me. What do I do now?

"I asked you a question. Who are you and what are you doing in my house?"

Robert's mind whirled in confusion at the confrontation. Thomas was not what he pictured, he loomed over Robert. Bigger than he'd expected.

"Uh...I—"

"You need to leave or I'm calling the police."

"I'm sorry, Thomas. I have to do this."

"Who is Thomas?"

That confused Robert further. He couldn't be wrong. *This* had to be Thomas Eli's house. The bewilderment must have shown because the man lowered his voice as if placating a wild animal.

"Are you in the wrong house?"

He jerked out of his trance. "It'll be okay, Thomas. I don't want to hurt you. I just need the painting."

Robert lunged, holding the chloroform drenched rag by his side. He jumped on Thomas and wrapped his legs around the man's waist.

"Wh—what are you doing?" Thomas stumbled backwards. "I'm not Thomas. Michael, my name is Mic—"

Robert shoved the cloth against the author's mouth, holding on as he struggled to throw him off. Screams echoed in his head, but he didn't know if they were his or Thomas'.

Robert pulled away as Thomas fought to retain his footing. When Thomas' back hit the wall and he slid to the ground, Robert jumped, startled at the sound.

Why did the man keep denying who he was? Robert's head started to pound.

What have I done? Robert crumpled to the floor and threw the chloroformed rag away from him. He clutched his head, rocking back and forth.

Pull yourself together!

The sound of his mom's voice in his head sent a shiver of fear down his spine. Robert stopped rocking and crawled over to the body sprawled on the floor. Tentatively, he stretched his arm out and brushed a finger along the man's lips. His cock twitched at the thought of those lips wrapped around it. He was unbelievably sexy. Not at all what Robert had been expecting.

Could he really do this? He wasn't a criminal. Maybe his mom didn't need the money as much as she thought. He could get another job to help out. Robert could leave now and no one would be the wiser.

Mom wouldn't ask if she wasn't needing. And she would be very angry if he came home without the artwork.

He had to think. Robert didn't know when his unexpected captive would awaken and now he feared he didn't have the right house. His plan needed to be altered. He couldn't leave Thomas sitting there while he searched for the painting. What was mom thinking? What had *he* been thinking? Panic raced through his body. His stomach rolled, but he had to do something.

Determined, Robert went to the front door, locked it and started a search. Whoever the guy turned out to be, he would need to be secured before he awakened. He remembered a shed out back from when he'd cased the place. There should be rope or something he could use. At home, he had all the supplies he could want. Not that his mom used them on him anymore.

He walked to the back of the house hoping to find a door to the backyard. After he had the author secure, he'd check for identification. He didn't know what he would do if the unconscious man turned out not to be the author. Did his mom send him here on purpose? To punish him for something? It was time to find out.

* * * *

His head hurt and his mouth was so dry he could drink a lake and it might not help. What the hell had happened?

Michael kept his eyes closed so he could focus his thoughts. He remembered pulling up to the house. He'd walked in and — and — something happened, the thought just out of his reach.

A noise to his left made his eyes open. What he saw startled him. A dirty angel. He blinked, trying to clear his vision, but the young man still stood there. Michael's memory came rushing back. The little fucker had knocked him out with something.

Anger flooded his body. He tried to move, but he couldn't. He managed to glance down, only now noticing the rope tying him to the chair. He struggled with his bonds.

"You won't be able to get free," the angel stated.

"What the fuck is going on?" His voice sounded rough to his own ears. He still couldn't get the taste out of his mouth.

"I'm sorry, Thomas. Mom wants your painting and what she wants, she gets."

"For the last time, who the hell is Thomas?"

Confusion flittered across the angel's face before a calm mask replaced it.

"You're Thomas Eli, the author of my mom's favourite books. She saw the magazine article on you and made a plan. She needs the money or I wouldn't be here."

"Listen, I'm *not* this Thomas fellow. My name is Michael Barrett, I own a bar. I'm *not* a writer. You've got the wrong house. Now let me go and leave and I'll forget this ever happened." He made his tone sound confident and authoritative.

Puzzlement reappeared on the young man's face, and then it morphed into fear before shutting down again.

Good, maybe he could get out of this in one piece. It would be okay if he wasn't tied down, he out-muscled the angel.

"You have to be him. I—I can't go back if…"

"If what? Where can't you go? Talk to me. Let's start with something easy. What's your name?" If he kept his captor calm and reasoned with him, maybe he could get untied.

For the first time he stared into the face of his intruder. He could drown in those crystal blue orbs. A man stood before him, not a kid. He seemed unsure, but older than Michael had first thought.

"Robert M—just Robert."

"That's a good start. Now, how old are you?" Michael knew there were more important questions he should be asking, but he needed to know how old this man-child was.

"I—why does that matter?"

I have no idea, but it does.

"Just trying to figure some things out here, like how I can help you. Talk to me."

"I don't know. This isn't in the plan. Mom was very specific about what I had to do." Fear leaked back in the thief's voice. "Now, I don't know. I saw your driver's licence. I know you're Michael, but, you see, you can't be."

The voice teetered on panic, Michael had to bring him back down.

"Don't worry about that right now. Take a deep breath and tell me how old you are."

"I'm twenty-three. Why are you being so nice to me?"

That was the question of the day and he didn't have the answer.

"I want to help, Robert. I don't want you to get into any trouble. Why were you trying to find Thomas?" That's it, keep him talking.

"I shouldn't be talking to you. If you can help—I, well, Mom said it would be easy to take it and he didn't need it. She has to have that money. She needs it." Robert sighed.

"Do you always do what Mom says?" Michael needed to know more about this woman's control of the man in front of him.

Robert hesitated and Michael wasn't sure if he would answer the question. He waited for a minute trying to think up a new tactic when Robert spoke.

"I have to. I'm all she has," Robert mumbled.

"What did you use to knock me out?" He switched topics in hopes of an honest answer.

"Chloroform." His eyes widened when the answer slipped from his lips. And what beautiful lips they were. So red and ripe, like cherries waiting to be picked.

I've got to stop this. I'm tied to a fucking chair. He is bad news, not someone I can kiss. Can I?

He stopped his internal struggle when Robert spoke again.

"Mom said I should take it in case someone was home." He paused again. "I—I didn't want to hurt anyone, but she wanted that painting. What am I going to do?" The words come out as a whisper.

Robert dropped to the floor, demeanor so forlorn.

"I can help you, if you let me." He wanted to wipe that look off Robert's face, to protect him from this 'mom'. To comfort him somehow.

Fuck, what is wrong with me.

"You'll help me find Thomas' house?" Hope laced with fear tinged Robert's words as he glanced up at him.

"Robert, I think we have more important things to do right now. Let's forget about Thomas and the painting, at least for now."

"I can't. I have to bring it to Mom, but I don't know what to do." Robert sounded stubborn for the first time, but he clutched his knees and started rocking back and forth.

He should be thinking of calling the police, but he only wanted to wrap his arms around Robert. He needed to get rid of these thoughts and feelings. This thief, for that's what he was, had broken into his home.

"Robert, stop rocking and listen to me." He waited until he had Robert's attention. "Good. Come a little closer, that's it. Stealing something is wrong. You know that, right?"

"Stop! Don't talk to me like I'm an idiot, I can't think straight and I'm not a fucking child."

Robert scooted away from him and slammed his fist against a wall. Shit.

"Sorry. You have me at a disadvantage here. I'm tied up and you're the boss. Got it. So, what do we do now, Boss Man?"

"I need to talk to my mom."

"Wait! No. Um…I mean, talk to me a little more. You can come closer you know. It's not like I can hurt you." Michael wiggled his fingers at Robert.

"I don't know. Maybe—"

"Your mom put you up to this, right? Does she have something over you? How is she controlling you? I have a friend who can help you. Talk to me."

He sounded desperate, but he didn't want Robert talking to the person whose idea this was in the first place. He was afraid of what she might say. So far Robert had stayed pretty calm with the exception of his small outburst and he didn't have any weapon that Michael could see. He wanted to keep it that way.

"You're talking too much and I can't think. I need to get out of here."

Robert jumped up from the floor, turned and left the room.

Shit, this can't be good.

"Robert!"

* * * *

The man—Michael—yelled his name, but he ignored it. Robert could barely breathe much less think. Mom always told him what to do. He knew stealing was all kinds of wrong but he hated what happened when he didn't listen to her. His gut clenched just thinking about it. It had been years since the last time she'd beat him and locked him in his room. Once he'd outgrown her, all of that had stopped. But the words she flung at him hurt just as much. And he was all she had left. He couldn't leave her on her own. She was sick. What kind of man would that make him? He wasn't his father.

Michael's voice did something to his insides. Something he'd never felt before. He closed his eyes and Michael's face appeared. He was too handsome for words with his salt and pepper hair and dark brown eyes. Even the scruff on the man's face made his cock ache. The urge to kiss Michael overwhelmed him.

Robert opened his eyes. He couldn't call his mom. Not yet. He had to figure out these thoughts first. To do that, he'd have to talk to Michael. He had no idea where this independent streak was coming from, he'd never stood up to the woman who gave birth to him. Why now? Would Michael really help him or did he say those things just to get Robert to untie him?

Indecision caused him to bite down on his lip. When he tasted blood, he released it and reached up to wipe off his mouth.

He walked back to the room where he'd tied Michael up. "Will you really help me?"

"First you need to untie me."

"I think we should talk a little more first. I can't have you jump me after I untie you. My mom needs me and you could overpower me and turn me in."

"Just who is this woman? Is she really your mom?"

"Yes, she is."

He peeked at Michael and bit his lip again. He hissed at the pain.

"What about your dad?"

"I don't want to talk about him, he isn't part of this equation. You said you could help me, were you lying?"

"I'm just trying to understand why a grown man would be at home and listening when his mom tells him to break into someone's house. Is she blackmailing you? Help me out here."

"No." He didn't know what he should tell Michael. He ran a hand through his hair.

"You're the one who wanted to talk. Tell me more."

"I don't want you to think badly of Mom. She did what she had to do."

"How does she treat you now?"

"Why is this important?"

"I need information, the more the better."

"We get along fine as long as I mind her. I'm all she has."

"I'm sure she tells you that," Michael whispered.

Robert didn't know how to respond. His whole word revolved around his mom. It always had. Was there more to life than what he knew?

"She's going to be upset if I'm not home soon."

"Do you think she'll come searching for you?" Michael sounded worried.

"I was told to call her if I had any problems. I think this is a big problem."

Michael snorted. "I would say so, Boss Man."

"Are you making fun of me?" He couldn't tell.

"No, I'm not, but we have a problem here and until you let me go, I don't think we can fix it. Calling your mom will *not* help this situation. I think it could make it worse, for you."

"Why do you say that?"

Robert had a hard time glancing away from Michael's mouth when he spoke. He liked talking to him. Robert moved closer and sat down next to the chair, just out of reach.

"What do you think she'll tell you to do with me now that we've been talking?"

Robert shrugged. "Tell me to let you go and to find the real Thomas I guess."

"Do you really think she'll let you leave me here when I know what you look like? Think hard, Robert. What will she tell you to do?"

"Shit. I don't want to believe it, but she'd probably tell me to...hurt you," Robert whispered the last two words.

"Yes, Robert, she'll probably tell you to hurt me."

"I don't want to hurt you. Hell, I don't want to be here at all, but she told me she needs the drugs."

"I don't want that either. It would make things tough on you because I have friends who would come to see if I was okay, and if you hurt me, they will find you. Do you understand?"

"I think I've already told you to stop talking to me like I'm a child. I still haven't untied you yet." Robert had to do something he wasn't comfortable with, make his own decision. He was letting his lust, because he couldn't deny it—he wanted to kiss Michael—interfere with what he needed to do. He didn't know this man. He could be saying anything to get away.

"It's your show, Boss Man."

"I should just leave. You said someone would know you're missing, right?"

What would he do about his mom? He couldn't go back to the house without the painting. Fear coursed through his body. Disappointing her was not an option. He always failed her one way or another and this would be one more strike against him.

"Are you okay?"

Michael sounded concerned, but Robert couldn't trust that. Mom did the same thing—sounded like she cared, and then turned on him, spewing forth all kinds of vile words. He would do anything for her. He had to. He had to prove he wouldn't be like his dad. That he would stay. She needed him.

"No, I'm not."

Why did he have this compulsion to pour his soul out to a stranger? Could it be because in his twenty-three years he'd never been as attracted to someone like he was Michael? He made Robert want things he couldn't name.

"Let me help."

Robert gazed into Michael's eyes and made up his mind. He sat up so he could reach the ropes.

"I—I can't get these untied."

Michael hesitated for a moment before speaking, "There's a box cutter in the kitchen. Middle drawer, on the left of the sink."

He gave Michael a swift nod and went to get the tool before he lost his nerve.

Chapter Two

Michael released a breath he hadn't realised he'd been holding. He played a dangerous game putting a weapon in Robert's hands, but if it got him out of the fucking chair, he would consider it worth it. His fingers felt numb, so did his feet.

It didn't take Robert long to come back. He kept his head down and knelt at Michael's feet. When he peered up at him with those blue eyes, an image of Robert with his lips wrapped around his cock flashed through his mind. He had to hold in the moan.

"Did I hurt you?"

The concern in Robert's voice made him jerk his thoughts to the present. The noise must have escaped. While he'd been fantasising, Robert had cut both of his arms free. Now that he was paying attention he could feel the blood racing back to his hands.

"No. I'm okay." He wiggled his fingers to hurry the circulation along. The ropes fell from his ankles and he stood to tower over Robert. He could easily take the slight man down, but something stopped him. Robert wouldn't look at him, backing away until he hit the wall on the opposite end of the room.

"What now?"

Michael had a hard time hearing the whisper.

"I didn't lie. I want to help you, but you have to want the help."

"What do you mean?" Finally, Robert glanced at him.

"Are you hungry? Let's go into the kitchen."

Michael didn't wait for Robert to acknowledge him; he turned and went into the kitchen. He waited for the anger to boil up, but it didn't. He wanted to rage at Robert, but he couldn't.

"Why aren't you calling the police?"

"I'm asking myself the same question."

"At least you're honest." Robert shrugged, pulled out a stool and sat down at the bar in the kitchen.

Michael didn't know what force pushed him towards Robert, but he went with it. He stopped in front of the stool and pulled Robert into his arms and hugged him. Not the smartest thing he'd ever done, but it seemed right.

"I told you, I want to help."

Robert hesitated before wrapping his arms around Michael's waist. There was no awkward manly pat on the back; it was a real hug between two men who'd had a rough night.

"I don't understand."

"Neither do I, Robert. I've learned through the years to go with my gut and it's telling me right now that you never intended to hurt me."

He pulled away and went to the refrigerator to take his mind off how perfect Robert's body fit to his. Certifiable. That had to be it. The men with the 'I love myself' jackets would show up any minute. But he knew deep down there was more to Robert.

"I'm lost." The whispered confession reached Michael's ears.

"What do you mean?" He turned around before reaching for the food.

"This is the first time Mom trusted me to do something like this for her. Of course, I screwed everything up, so maybe that's not a good thing."

Michael didn't say anything. Not yet. He had to let the words sink in. He let it drop, for now.

"Would you like to clean up a little before we eat?"

Robert jerked his head in Michael's direction. "What?"

"You have some dirt on your face and a few leaves in your hair. You know, when I first woke up, I thought of you as my — um — a dirty angel." He allowed himself a small laugh. "Of course, then I remembered you'd knocked me out."

"I'm sorry."

"The bathroom is down the hall. I'll make us a couple of sandwiches."

He turned back to gather what he needed. Not much time had passed when he heard the snick of a door closing. Why did it relieve him that the sound didn't come from the front door?

A few minutes later a noise at the doorway made him glance up. His cock leapt to attention. Robert *was* an angel. His brown hair stuck to his forehead, curls going every which way. It seemed like he'd tried to wet it down, but the curls didn't want to cooperate. His lips were plump and red, and his blue eyes brighter against his pale skin. Michael fought the urge to claim Robert then and there. His hands went into his pocket, drawing Michael's gaze to Robert's crotch. Michael licked his lips and turned away from temptation.

He returned his focus to making sandwiches. Robert brushed past him, but his foot caught on something and Michael turned to catch him before Robert fell on his face. He pulled Robert towards him and couldn't resist. He had to have a taste. Michael nibbled on Robert's bottom lip, his tongue asking for entrance. Robert hesitated, and then opened his mouth. Michael took it slow, caressing Robert's mouth, savouring the flavour of mint. He deepened the kiss when Robert groaned. Wrapping his arms tighter around the other man, Michael ground his cock against Robert. The arms around him tightened. He straightened up, moved the food out of his way, and placed Robert on the counter, never breaking the kiss. Robert's legs wrapped around his hips, cradling him. The two rubbed together, Robert felt so right in his arms. He never wanted to let him go. Michael wanted Robert naked.

As Michael reached to unbutton Robert's pants, the phone rang. He pulled back, both men panted as if they'd ran for miles.

"What the fuck am I doing?" Michael muttered.

Robert whimpered and pulled away, trying to get as far from Michael as fast as he could. "Sorry, sorry, I'm sorry."

It was like a mantra; Robert said the words over and over. Ignoring the phone, he concentrated on Robert.

"Shh, it's okay." He moved slowly, he didn't want to startle Robert. Michael reached for him. He flinched, but let Michael touch his leg. "Come here."

He appeared unsure, but Robert scooted forward to the edge of the counter. Michael wrapped his arms around Robert to and soothed him. He took a moment to caress Robert's back, murmuring nonsense words. It took a few minutes, but Robert finally stopped shaking and relaxed in Michael's arms.

"What happened, Robert? Didn't you like the kiss?"

"I did." He seemed surprised at his answer and flittered his fingers over his lips.

"Then why did you move away?"

"You sounded upset. You're bigger than Mom. I didn't want you to hit me."

A few things clicked in Michael's mind. He kissed Robert on the forehead and helped him off the counter.

"Why don't you go into the living room. I'll be out in a minute with sandwiches."

"You're not angry with me?"

"Not for this Robert. Never for this. Now, go on. I'll be there in a second."

Robert nodded and left. What the fuck was he going to do with his little thief?

Talk, I'm going to talk to him and nothing else. Sure you are, keep telling yourself that and maybe you'll believe it.

He made quick work of the sandwiches and headed for the living room. When he got there, Robert sat curled on the couch.

"I hope turkey is okay. I should have asked if you wanted anything else on it. Sorry."

"I'm not picky," he said quietly.

He sat down beside Robert and put their plates on the coffee table. He turned towards the couch.

"I'm not going to call the police, if that's what you're worried about. But I need you to promise you won't go after that author."

"But Mom—"

"No, we'll figure out your mom situation too, but I can't have you going off and breaking into someone else's home. You're going to get hurt or worse."

"Why do you care? I tried to steal from you, knocked you out, tied you up. I don't understand."

"We keep coming back to this. I don't understand either. Something about you makes me trust you despite that. I think you've led a pretty rough, if sheltered, life. You need to know, I'm not a violent man. I'd never hit another person unless they swung first. I don't go searching for fights and I sure as hell don't punch someone just for kicks."

Michael moved closer to Robert and waited for his response.

"She isn't going to be happy."

Robert bit his lip and twisted his hands together in a worried gesture so Michael had no choice but to pull him closer and hug Robert to his body. He breathed in the scent of the outdoors and underlying smell that was pure Robert. He could get lost in the man.

Michael should control himself, but when Robert whimpered against him all thoughts of stopping flew out of his brain. He nuzzled into Robert's neck and stroked down until his hands cupped Robert's ass and pulled him onto his lap, Robert straddled one of his legs. He kissed his way to Robert's mouth and devoured it, licking and nipping, demanding entrance. He rubbed their jean-clad cocks together, trying for just the right angle for the friction they both needed. Robert began to rock his body against

Michael's leg, the sounds he made going straight to Michael's cock.

Robert pulled away from the kiss enough to start chanting.

"Oh God, oh God. Michael, I'm…oh God."

He shuddered in Michael's arms and he felt warmth against his legs where Robert's cum seeped through his pants.

"I'm sorry, I didn't mean, oh no, I'm sorry."

Robert's words made Michael feel like shit. He'd just taken advantage of Robert.

"Shh, don't apologise. It's okay, I'm the one who's sorry, and I shouldn't have kissed you. I knew it could get out of control."

Neither man said anything. For a while, they held on to each other. If Michael wasn't so in tune to Robert he wouldn't have heard the whispered words.

"I liked it. I—I want more."

Michael sucked in air. *That* he hadn't expected to hear.

"Shit." The expletive slipped out.

"What, did I say something wrong?" Fear crept back into Robert's voice.

"No, but hearing you say those words makes me want to lose control. I want to bury my cock in your ass and show you how good it feels. But we can't."

"You just said you wanted me. Why can't we?"

Michael placed his forehead against Robert's, closed his eyes and got himself under control. Robert may have broken in, but he was an innocent and if Michael was right, abused. He needed to handle the situation with kid gloves if he hoped to have a future with Robert.

Where the hell did that come from?

What kind of future could the two of them have?

Don't you want to find out?

"We need to figure out what we're going to do. First things first, let's go get you cleaned up. I have a robe you might be able to wear."

Robert looked disappointed, but he climbed off Michael's leg.

Leading the way, he took Robert to the bathroom.

Keep your hands to yourself. Clean up, that's it. Then talk.

Plan firm in his mind, he left Robert to get clothes for the two of them.

* * * *

Robert watched Michael walk out of the room. What had just happened? Confusion settled over him. For the first time, he didn't care what his mom might think. Michael made him feel good. Of course, now that his cum had dried in his pants he was uncomfortable, but even that couldn't faze him. He closed his eyes and remembered the heated glances Michael shot his way; he wanted to see more of it. What would it be like to have Michael care for him, to have him love him just for being him?

Michael didn't yell or hit, even when he had every right to. So different from his mom. He couldn't remember a time where she hadn't taken her anger out on him.

He shook himself out of his thoughts. Robert's hands went to his pants. He unfastened them and let them fall to the floor along with his boxer briefs. Stepping out of them, he shed his shirt. He heard a gasp and turned around. Michael had come back with clothes. Should he have gotten into the shower already? Did he do something wrong?

"I had an idea, but I wasn't sure." Michael spoke on a whisper.

"Wasn't sure of what?" Bewilderment coloured his voice.

"That you were beaten. Your mom?"

Michael stepped forward, threw the clothes on the counter and turned him around to trace the lines on his back.

"It's nothing I didn't deserve. She's a single mom and I was a devil of a child."

"I don't care what kind of child you were, no one deserves this. She doesn't still beat you, does she?"

Michael's fingers traced the scars on his back. Robert shivered and his cock responded. He'd never had these kinds of feelings before, and it was a little overwhelming.

"N-no. Not anymore."

"I need to know, why do you stay?"

"My dad left and I'm all that she has. She—she needs me." He finished the sentence on a moan. Michael started kissing the lines on his back.

"You can't stay with her any longer. You know that, right? Not after she had you try to commit a crime," Michael murmured against his skin.

Robert turned around, Michael's lips landed on his chest.

"I don't want to talk about my mom right now."

Michael smiled against him, "What *would* you like to talk about?"

"I—" he hesitated.

The other man stood up and pulled him close, "You can tell me anything. What do you want, Robert?"

"You, I want, um, you. To make me feel like before."

"You liked that did you?"

His face warmed. He had to be blushing. "I've never felt anything like it before." He hid his face in Michael's shoulder.

"There's more to it. Things that will feel even better."

"Show me," he mumbled.

"I don't think you're ready for that, yet."

But he wanted it; in fact, he'd started to crave it. Robert wanted to see Michael naked. He wanted things he couldn't even name. Robert wanted to taste the flesh under his face. He placed a light kiss on Michael's collarbone and let his tongue trace the skin. The other man shuddered against him. Awe washed over him. He had caused this reaction. Him, Robert, Mr. Nobody. His Mom told him every chance she could that he would never amount to anything and it was a good thing he had her.

Enough!

He pushed thoughts of him mom out of his head and concentrated on making Michael feel as good as he'd made Robert feel. He continued to nibble on Michael's neck while unbuttoning his shirt.

"I need this," he whispered, "Please."

Michael let him push his shirt off his shoulders and Robert smiled at the clink of buttons hitting the floor.

Fingers forced his face up. He stared into Michael's eyes and his smile grew at the heat he'd put there.

"Never beg me for this. Take what you need, babe. I'm here."

"I'm not sure, I want—I need…"

"Do what feels right. Nothing you do will be wrong."

Michael pulled him in for a kiss and he sighed against Robert's lips. This is what he wanted, the connection with another human being. He wrapped his arms around Michael and clung to him, losing himself in the kiss. He gasped when Michael lifted him up and took advantage of his position to wrap his legs around Michael, locking his ankles. Michael deepened the kiss and he moaned.

He rubbed his naked body against Michael's jeans. It was time they came off. Each new touch and experience put him closer to the edge. He didn't want to come this way.

"Please." He whispered.

"What do you want, baby?"

"More, I need more."

Michael's hands gripped his ass and gave it a squeeze before letting one hand wander. Robert couldn't believe the sensation caused by Michael's finger circling and playing with his hole. Robert moved his ass up and down. He wanted that finger inside him. He let out a sound of disappointment when Michael released his ass. He slid his body down the other man's until his feet hit the floor.

He let Michael turn him so he faced the mirror above the sink. Robert almost didn't recognise himself. Happiness made his eyes sparkle in a way he'd never seen before. Michael winked at him and he watched as his face turned a bright shade of red. He bowed his head only to have Michael raise it back.

"See how good we are together. Keep looking at me. Don't let your eyes leave mine. I want to watch."

Robert didn't know what to say, he couldn't stop staring even if he wanted to. Michael's finger traced his spine. He whimpered when the fingers left his body, but soon moaned when the mirror showed him Michael's digits enter the man's mouth.

"Please?" he asked again, his gaze never leaving the glass.

Michael nodded and his fingers returned to Robert's body.

"You ready? I need you to relax, okay?"

"Will it hurt?"

"There may be some burn, it's your first time, but we'll get you ready. I'm not going to ram into you. Don't worry, once you relax, you'll love it. I promise."

It was Robert's turn to nod. He wanted this, he needed this.

* * * *

Michael couldn't believe his eyes. His angel's face glowed and the twinkle in Robert's eyes belonged to him. He'd put that there.

Robert kept his gaze on him in the mirror. He eased his finger into his lover's ass searching his face for any sign of pain. When Robert bit his lip and his eyes widened, Michael groaned.

He had to have some lube around here somewhere. Not leaving Robert, he reached around him to search the drawers. Luck was on his side, he held up the lube in triumph. He popped the top and squeezed some on his finger before pushing it deeper into Robert's ass. Michael sighed. He slid in with little resistance. He moved inside the tight warmth and added a second finger.

"You okay?" His gaze never left Robert, but he needed the words.

"Y-yes." Robert panted. "More."

He added more lube, set it down and searched for Robert's gland. He knew he found it when the other man gasped.

"You like that?"

"Yes. God, yes. Again."

He complied with his angel's wish and pegged the gland again before adding another finger. The joy on Robert's face was almost his undoing. He needed inside this man more than he needed to breathe.

"I want inside."

"Hurry, I'm going to come."

"Not yet. Don't come yet."

Michael pulled his fingers away and wrapped them around his own cock and started to enter him.

"Please."

The need in his man's voice almost made him forget.

"Fuck, condom."

He searched the drawer for a prophylactic. He had to have one.

"Why did you stop?"

The question in Robert's eyes caused him to place a kiss on the man's shoulder.

"I need to protect us."

Robert still looked unsure and Michael held up the condom he'd found. He opened it as understanding entered Roberts gaze. He put it on and reached for the lube to coat his dick. He gripped Robert's hip with one hand to hold him steady. He inched his way into Robert's body, never letting his gaze waver from the man in the mirror. When Robert flinched he stopped.

"Don't stop." Robert begged.

"I don't want to hurt you. We have all the time in the world. I won't rush your first time. I want this to be good for you."

Robert nodded. "I'm ready. Please, *move*."

Michael waited until Robert pushed his ass back before moving again. He took his cues from Robert's face. He couldn't hold back, Robert panted, like he couldn't catch his breath. The sound of flesh on flesh echoed in the small room. It felt right, being inside Robert. Like the two were made to fit each other. His hands squeezed Robert's hips as he sped up, pounding into his new lover's ass. Through the glass, he saw Robert's hands flex against the counter. His beautiful dick trapped against the counter.

"Come for me, baby." Michael moved so he could take Robert's cock into his hand. He used the pre-cum glistening on Robert's dick to stop the friction as he matched the tempo of his hand and his cock.

Robert's hips bucked against Michael and pure bliss spread across the man's face. Michael had never seen something so beautiful as Robert cuming for him. He thrust into him one more time before filling the condom.

Sobs racked Robert's body. He didn't want to hurt the smaller man so he slowly pulled out. He disposed of his condom before turning Robert and taking him into his arms. He soothed him the best he could.

"Shh, Robert, it will be okay. Please don't cry, baby. What did I do wrong? Did I hurt you? Please, tell me."

He rubbed his hand up and down Robert's back until the sobbing stopped.

"I'm sorry. I—I don't know why, I—why—I—um. Sorry."

"You can tell me if I hurt you. Don't be afraid. Not of me, never of me. I wouldn't hurt you."

"You should, you know. I deserve it."

He pulled back from Robert. "No one deserves to be hurt. Not on purpose."

"But I hurt you. You should hurt me back."

"Is that why you let me…" Michael trailed off and waved his hands between the two of them. "Because you thought I should hurt you?"

Robert appeared shocked. "No, God no. Everything is so intense with you. I shouldn't even be here. I should have called mom and left."

"Why, so she can hurt you?"

"She doesn't—"

"Never mind, Robert. Forget I said anything. It's been a long night. Will you come to bed with me?"

"What about Mo—"

"I'll protect you," Michael interrupted him. "Are you sure you're okay?"

Robert nodded. Michael took his hand and led his new lover into the shower so they could clean up before they went to bed. He made quick work of the clean up and tugged Robert to his room. Tomorrow would be soon enough to deal with the woman who'd hurt his man. There was no way Robert would be going back with her. Not if he had any say in the matter. His need to protect the smaller man should puzzle him after all Robert had done to him. It couldn't be natural, but he was too tired to fight it. Michael pulled the covers down and ushered Robert between the sheets. His new lover's lids drooping before he even covered him up. Michael slid into the bed and pulled Robert close. He threw the blanket over them and Robert snuggled into his arms.

So innocent.

Michael placed a kiss on Robert's forehead. He drifted to sleep, dreaming of the dark-haired man in his bed.

Chapter Three

Pound, pound, pound.

The noise lifted the fog of sleep.

"Whe — what?"

Michael glanced over at the confused man beside him and blinked as the night before rushed into his head.

"It's only the door, Robert. Stay here, I'll go get it."

He patted Robert's hip before getting out of bed. He grabbed a robe from his closet, but noise from the door was getting louder.

"Just a minute," he shouted over the banging.

He swung open the door to a beautiful woman. Maybe in her forties with long brown hair and bright blue eyes.

"Sorry to bother you so early. I'm Betsy."

"Good morning, Betsy. Is there something I can help you with?"

It couldn't be her. No way would she show up at his door. Of course, after hearing Robert talk about her, it really shouldn't surprise him.

"I'm looking for my son. I think he might have come to this address by mistake."

"Oh, I'm sorry. I haven't seen any kids around here this morning."

"Oh, no sir. He's not a little kid, but I think he might be confused. He's about my height with brown hair and blue eyes. He left the house in search of a friend and I'm afraid I gave him the wrong address. I was hoping you might have seen him."

The woman had to be crazy.

A noise sounded behind him, he turned to see Robert standing in the doorway, fully clothed.

"Robert! Where have you been? I was worried about you."

Robert's face lost all of its colour and he backed away until he hit the wall. The woman, Betsy, forced her way into his home. He stood between her and Robert; no way would he let her get close to his lover.

"So, you're the famous Mom. I suggest you stay right where you are. You're not welcome in my home."

"I'm not sure what—"

"Stop it right there. I know what you did and you won't get away with it." He wouldn't put up with her bullshit.

"I didn't do anything," she started.

"But Mom—"

His lover turned into a little boy before his eyes. The woman had that much power over Robert. It had to be stopped.

"You shut up, boy. I'll deal with you in a minute."

"I don't think so, Betsy. Your days of control are over."
He turned to the man who could mean so much to him.
"Robert, why don't you go to the kitchen and have some
breakfast. Me and your mom have some talking we need to
do."

He waited until Robert left the room before he turned
back to his lover's tormentor. Anger radiated from the
woman.

"Who are you to order my son around? I won't stand for
it. We're leaving."

"Someone is leaving and it won't be Robert. You are
going to forget you ever had a son or I'm going to the
authorities. Attempted theft ring any bells?"

Fear flashed in the woman's eyes, but disappeared before
he could blink. Hatred shone through now.

"You have nothing on me. I came to collect my son.
That's it."

"I won't let you take him out of here. You don't deserve
him."

"This is none of your concern. Robert!"

"This is my concern. You sent Robert out to steal
something, maybe even hurt someone. It isn't my fault you
sent him to the wrong house. How could you do that to
him?" He gave a harsh laugh. "He loves you, you know. I
have no idea how he could love a monster who has done
nothing but beat him down his whole life. He deserves
better."

"Oh, and you're going to give it to him? Who do you
think you are?"

"I'm the person who has family in the police department
and I'm not afraid to use them. One call from me and you
could be in lockup before you can blink. I'm willing to let it
go as long as you leave now. If Robert wants to contact

you, he will. If you don't, I'll make that call. I'll give you a couple seconds, but no more."

"You-you can't do that." For the first time she sounded unsure.

"What, not used to someone standing up for themselves with you? You can't intimidate me. You aren't my mom and I didn't spend years under your thumb. Now are you leaving or do I need to make a call?"

"This isn't the end of—"

"Yes, it is the end. I suggest you lose my address and head home."

"He's a worthless piece of shit. He'll never amount to anything, I don't see why you're wasting your time with him."

"Then you have nothing to lose, do you? Leave." He pointed to the open door.

"He won't stay with you. He'll come running back."

"You just keep telling yourself that. Maybe you'll eventually understand when you're all alone."

He slammed the door in the woman's face as she turned around to say something else.

Michael turned to see Robert peeking out of the doorway.

"I'm sorry you had to hear that, Robert."

"She's right, you know?"

"Right about what?" He walked over and pulled Robert into his arms. Michael snuggled Robert into him, it felt so good.

"I'm useless and not good for anything. I'm still not sure why you're helping me. I should go with her. It isn't too late."

He squeezed Robert closer. "If you really want to go, I won't stop you. I would never try to control you, but I think you and I both know you really don't want to go back. We could have a good thing here."

"How can you tell after only one night?"

He soothed Robert, sliding his hand up and down the man's back. "I can't, not really. But I want to give us time to get to know each other."

"How? I have a crappy job and nowhere to live. I have no real education. It's almost like I don't exist."

"We'll start out slow. I think you might need someone to talk to about your mom and what happened to you. There are agencies out there who can help. Tomorrow, we'll talk to one of my brothers. He's a lawyer. We'll figure it out. We have time. It's all about what you want. What do you want, Robert?"

"I—no one has ever asked me that before. I don't know."

"You can think about it. Do you want me to stop your mom? Do you want to go back to her?"

Robert looked up at him, "No." he said softly. "No." he said again with more conviction. "You've shown me there is more out there and I want that. I want it so bad I can taste it. What did I do to deserve you?"

"I'll be here. I'm not going anywhere. You tell me what you want to do and we'll see about making it happen."

"Right now? Right now I think I just want you."

"Done."

Michael took Robert's lips in a kiss filled with hope.

Two Years later…

"Are you sure about this? We don't have to go if you don't want to." Michael sounded hesitant as he peered at himself in the mirror, adjusting his tie.

Usually his lover was the strong one in the relationship. It felt nice to be the one sure of himself.

"Of course we're going. It's your brother's wedding. I'll be fine."

Robert's therapy had come a long way. Thanks in part to Michael. He could always count on him. He really didn't know what he'd done to deserve him, but he was thankful every day.

"I know you're still not comfortable in crowds, so does Paul."

"It's your family. I promise, I'll be okay."

He stepped up close to his lover and smoothed the suit over his broad shoulders. They hadn't heard from his mom in a long time. That helped, knowing she wasn't as powerful as he thought.

"Good. I want to dance with you."

Michael turned around and Robert went into his arms. The place he felt the safest.

"Sounds good to me. You know I love being in your arms."

"Move in with me."

Robert leant back. "What? Where did that come from?"

"I know we said we'd wait, but I miss you on the nights you stay in your apartment. I want to wake up with you every day."

Robert smiled. He loved Michael more and more. He pulled his mouth to his. Robert's tongue traced his lover's lips, asking for entrance. Michael didn't make him wait long. He loved the way his lover tasted, he could kiss him for days.

He pulled back before things became too heated. "We can't. We have to leave."

"You started it. Is that a yes?"

"I'm ready, if you're sure. I still have a lot of baggage."

"I'm sure. Maybe we should skip the wedding and start packing?"

Robert laughed. "Are you *trying* to get out of this wedding? I thought you wanted to dance with me."

"A horizontal dance might be better." Michael wiggled his eyebrows.

"Michael! We're going to the wedding." Robert chuckled.

"I like hearing you laugh."

"And I like laughing." Robert smiled.

"Okay, let's go."

"Don't sound so excited. Weren't you the one who said we always have time?"

"Me and my big mouth."

Robert's gazed landed on Michael's mouth and he bit his lip. He wanted nothing more than to crawl into his lover.

"Stop looking at me like that or both our suits will be bunched on the floor."

Robert's heartbeat sped up but he shook his head. "Stop trying to distract me. You ready?"

"You sure I can't convince you?" Michael's hands went to his zipper, slowly lowering it and pulling his cock from his slacks. "You know how much I love your lips. Just a little taste?"

Michael smiled and Robert's heart stuttered. He licked his lips and Robert had to sink to his knees on the floor in front of him. Robert's lips wrapped gently around Michael's cock. He'd never get tired of his lover's taste.

A couple of strokes up and down and Robert knew Michael wouldn't last. Robert's hum let Michael know he could fuck Robert's mouth, his own cock so hard he was ready to cum without a touch.

"Shit, Robert, I'm not going to last."

When Robert gripped Michael's hips to control the blow job, he knew he'd leave bruises, but he didn't think Michael would care. A couple more passes of Michael's dick into his mouth and he shot his load. This was the taste Robert had waited for, his lover tasted sweet and Robert swallowed every drop.

He let Michael's cock slip from his lips and wasn't surprised when his lover dropped in front of him for a kiss.

"We need to get going if we aren't going to be late. I need to brush my teeth." Robert gave Michael another kiss and hurried to clean up. Before he got to the door, Michael spoke.

"Wait, what about you? You needing?"

"I'm good. You can take care of me after the wedding." Robert winked and went to get himself under control. He finished in no time and headed back to the living room to the waiting Michael.

"Ready now?"

Michael gave him a smirk and a wink."When you are. Let's go."

Robert shook his head and followed Michael out the door.

They walked out to the car. Michael threw Robert the keys, "You drive."

"Really?" He let excitement creep into his voice.

He'd gotten his licence last year, but didn't have much time to actually drive. His mom had always had control and usually drove him places or made him take a bus or cab. The ability to take himself places felt good. He loved being behind the wheel. It gave him a sense of freedom he only felt when he was with Michael.

"Get us there in one piece."

"Hey!"

They both laughed and got into the vehicle. Michael grabbed for his hand and he entwined their fingers once they were on the road. When they were together, they couldn't keep their hands off of each other.

"Did you remember the present?" Robert inquired.

"Mom and Dad came by earlier and took it out to the hall so we wouldn't have to worry about it."

"I'm sorry I missed them." Robert had come to love Michael's parents almost as much as he loved Michael. He loved going to family functions because it was so normal. If someone had told him two years ago that he would be part of a wonderful family who loved him just for being himself, he wouldn't have believed it. It was like a wonderful dream come true.

"They said to tell you hi and they couldn't wait to see you. It's been a few weeks. We should plan a dinner at the house after you move in."

He smiled and squeezed Michael's hand.

"I'd like that."

It didn't take long for them to reach the church. Robert was a little disappointed that he couldn't drive more. Next week he planned to talk Michael into helping him pick out his own car. He'd finally saved up enough money for something of his own. It helped that Michael let him use the apartment above the bar and had given him a job bartending. He liked it. It forced him to get comfortable with strangers. He still had problems sometimes, but his therapist and Michael helped him on those days.

The ceremony didn't last too long and they were off to party. Robert couldn't wait for his dance with Michael. It was all a blur until he danced in his man's arms. The soft music drifted around them. He laid his cheek on Michael's chest so he could hear his lover's heartbeat. He wanted to capture this moment for his memories.

When the song ended, they walked back to their table hand and hand.

"I don't want this moment to end," Robert whispered.

"Why not?" Michael whispered back.

"It's perfect."

"There will be other perfect moments."

"I know, but I can't help thinking, what if. What if I didn't go to your house that night? What if I had gone back with my mom? I want to treasure every normal moment I can to help erase all the years with her."

Michael brought their joined hands to his lips and brushed his mouth over it. "No more what ifs. They don't matter. Only now does." Michael leant over and kissed him.

All was right in his world. He was ready for their future.

* * * *

Michael thanked all that was holy that the wedding was over. He wanted to get Robert alone. They were finally at a point where things could start to be normal for both of them. The first year, they'd both worried Robert's mom would show up. His family had been wonderful, accepting Robert as one of their own. He loved their giving nature.

"Bye, Paul. Welcome to the family, Beth." Michael gave Beth a kiss on the cheek, Paul a hug, and waved goodbye, tugging Robert out the door.

"What's your hurry?" Robert laughed at him. The sound warmed his heart.

"I need you alone. Dancing wasn't enough."

"You're acting like we haven't seen each other in months. I spent the night last night and I'm staying tonight. Heck, I stay most nights with you."

"Yes, but you just agreed to move in with me so we need to celebrate."

Robert shook his head and gazed out the window giving Michael a minute to take in his angel. He let Robert drive home, he knew how much Robert loved to drive. Every day was like a new adventure with Robert. There was so much to show him. He wondered if he could convince the man to go on a trip with him.

They drove up to the house to see someone standing on the stairs of his house.

"Michael, do you know who that is?"

"No. Why don't you stay in the car and I'll go find out?"

"I'm coming with you."

He didn't argue. They parked the car and walked to the door. Michael kept Robert behind him.

"Good evening. Are you Robert Mitchell?"

"I'm not. Who are you?"

Michael didn't give Robert a chance to speak. Not until they found out who the guy was.

"I'm Detective Daniels. I need to speak to Mr. Mitchell."

Robert came out from behind him, "I'm Robert. What can I do for you?"

"Sir, I'm here to inform you that your mom, Betsy Mitchell, was found dead earlier this evening. When she didn't show up for work for over a week, her boss called the police. We went to her home and found a few disturbing things that led us to believe you could have been involved in a robbery attempt a few years ago."

Robert clutched for his hand, "She—she's dead?"

"Yes, she is."

"I don't know why you're here. Robert hasn't seen her in two years."

"She had a journal talking about a plan to steal a painting and that it went wrong, causing her to lose her son. We just want to tie up some loose ends so we can close this case."

Robert looked at him with fear in his eyes. Something he never wanted to see again. All because of his deranged mom.

"I—I don't—" Robert stuttered.

"How much do you know about Robert's mom?" Michael inquired.

"Only what we found in her home. Not many people knew her."

"Let's go inside." Michael let them into the house. "Detective, please have a seat, Robert and I will be right with you."

They went into the kitchen and he sat Robert on a stool.

"What did she do, Michael?"

"I don't know, but you need to decide what you want to tell the detective." He would support Robert in whatever he chose.

"What do you mean?"

"Do you want to tell him what she did to you?"

"Does it matter now?" Hurt coloured Robert's words.

"Not to me, that is why you need to think about what you want to say."

"Okay, let's go talk to him so we can put her behind us for good."

Michael nodded and the two of them went to the living room.

He sat down, but Robert paced the room. The detective started to talk but Michael put his hand up to stop the officer. He wanted to give his lover time to sort out what he wanted to say.

"Um, I." He stopped and Michael reached for him as he passed the couch to squeeze his hand. Robert stared at him and Michael was able to see the confidence come back into his man's gaze. "My mom abused me for years." It started as a whisper. "She convinced me to steal an item from an author she'd read about in a magazine, but she gave me the wrong address. This address. That night changed my life."

Robert came to his side and settled next to him and took his hand.

The detective's orbs darted between the two. "So you haven't had any contact with her recently?"

"No, sir." Michael spoke for them both.

The detective rose from the chair. "That's all I really need for my report. I might have some follow up for the two of you."

"Before you go, may I ask how she died?" Robert asked hesitantly.

"It appears to be natural causes. We'll let you know after the autopsy what the official findings are." The detective nodded to the two of them and turned to leave.

Michael walked the detective to the door and closed it. He looked to Robert, holding his arms open. Robert rushed into them.

"Thank you," Robert mumbled.

"For what, babe?"

"For saving me. Helping me become the man I should have always been."

"You saved yourself, I just came along for the ride."

They stood that way for a while before Michael took Robert to bed.

"I love you, Michael," Robert said as they removed their clothes.

Michael's heart sped up. "I love you too, Robert. That night changed my life too. I hope you know that. For the better. I was a lonely man until you came into my life."

"Who would have thought a break in would turn into love?" Robert chuckled.

"Not me, but I'm glad you tried to steal from me."

"I'm glad my mom got the address wrong. No more thinking of yesterday, just tomorrows for us from now on."

"I'll agree to that. Now come here. I believe I owe you a little oral attention."

They met in the middle of the bed, a tangle of arms and legs as they kissed each other.

Panting, they both pulled back. "Michael, make love to me."

Michael nudged Robert so they were lying down.

"I'll take care of you, baby." Taking Robert's hands in his he moved them so they could grip the headboard. "Don't move, just feel." Michael whispered against Robert's ear and licked the lobe.

Michael used the tip of his tongue to trace his way to Robert's throat; he scrapped his teeth of his lover's pulse. He'd never get tired of this, of being with Robert. He peppered little kisses until he reached Robert's nipple. Michael tugged and sucked, leaving a pretty red mark. Satisfied, Michael went to the neglected nipple to give it a little attention.

"Michael, please."

Robert wiggled his hips, but Michael ignored him. He wouldn't be rushed. The noises coming from Robert made his cock jump. Michael loved how responsive Robert was. Taking his time he kissed his way down, ignoring Robert's dick and nuzzled his nose in the crisp brown curls. He loved the scent that was Robert.

"Michael. Oh, God. I can't—"

"Shh," he murmured against his lover's flesh.

Michael worked his way down Robert's legs to his feet. He kissed the arches of each before crawling back up Robert's body. He rocked his body, letting their cocks brush against each other, but only for a second. He didn't want to come until he was inside Robert's tight hole and the needy noise coming from Robert had him close to the edge.

"Turn over." He commanded in a gruff voice.

Robert didn't hesitate and flipped to his stomach. Michael put Robert's hands back on the headboard and placed his body so his dick rocked between Robert's ass. God, it felt good, but not yet, he had more tasting to do.

Michael kissed the scars that ran along Robert's back, letting his lover know he loved every part of who he was. When he got to the last one, he hugged Robert to him.

"Now, Michael. Fuck me, now. No more, please. I'm so close."

"Not yet. Not yet. I want to be buried inside you before you come. On your knees. Don't let go of that headboard."

Robert scrambled to obey. Michael caressed the bubble butt in front of him. He reached over Robert to get the lube out of the night stand. He wasn't ready yet, but wanted to be prepared. Once he was inside Robert, it would be over and he wanted to savour his foreplay.

Michael threw the lube down beside him and spread Robert's ass cheeks. He ran his tongue around his lover's sweet rosette. Round and round he licked until he could wiggle his tongue inside, fucking his lover's ass.

"*Michael!*"

Robert had to be close, Michael rose up and reached for the lube. He coated his cock and stretched Robert's ass with a finger.

"Ready?"

"Yes, God yes. Fuck me. Now. Please, oh. Please."

Michael eased his dick into the tight hole.

"I'm not going to last long."

"I don't care. Hard. Please."

Michael stretched over Robert's body to entwine their fingers and slammed home, again and again. Robert hissed and Michael knew he'd hit Robert's gland. He angled his body so every thrust pegged Robert. The body under him shuddered and milked his cock as Robert came. It caused Michael to shake. His control gone along with his rhythm, he was a goner, shooting into Robert.

He rested on Robert's back until he could breathe again and rolled them over, cuddling Robert to his chest, squeezing him tight.

Robert caressed his cheek, brought him down for a kiss and whispered against his lips.

"I love you, Michael."

"I love you, too."

Michael smiled against Robert's mouth, thinking of the future. Robert had managed to steal something that night and it was Michael's heart and he would gladly let him steal it again for the next fifty years.

DRAGON'S EYE

Stephani Hecht

Chapter One

It was cold and snowing the night Duncan Moore snuck into the house to steal his *dragon's eye* back.

He cursed the fact that Michigan had such harsh winters, as he hid behind a large tree and studied the huge, opulent mansion. Too opulent in his opinion, with its long white columns and large drive that circled a fountain, it even had a pair of frigging stone lions. It was one of those houses where the people living in them were trying to give the rest of the world a fuck-you-I'm-better-than-you message. It would have made him hate the bastard who owned it, if Duncan didn't already harbour a deep hatred for the recently deceased man.

Several wet, heavy flakes had fallen on his face and got stuck to his dark lashes, making it hard to case out the place. Not exactly the sexy, stealth missions he'd always dreamed he would be doing when he was growing up as a dragon whelp. Then again, he'd never imagined he'd be such a colossal fuck-up and disappointment to their ruler either. Especially since said ruler was Brian, the big brother he'd always lauded, but never impressed.

He shook off those unpleasant thoughts. If he ever wanted to get back into Brian's good graces then he had to get his damn *dragon's eye* back. Until he did, he would never be free and his dragon would forever be trapped.

The lights to the kitchen snapped off and he knew it was time to make his move. Fail or succeed, this nightmare of a decade was finally ending tonight. Sneaking into the back servant's entrance, because that had been the one he'd always been forced to use, he eased the door shut behind him as he let his eyes get adjusted to the darkness.

Since he was from the ancient race of dragon shifters, it didn't take long and he was soon able to make out the shape and layout of the kitchens to the mansion that he'd lived in for ten years, but had never called home.

The aromas of fresh baked bread, steak and cheese hit his nose, making his stomach growl so loud in protest it was a wonder the noise didn't raise an alarm. That would be his luck, to get this far only to have his gut give him away. He could just see the headlines now: *Thieving Dragon Shifter busted when his grumbling tum-tum gives him away.*

As much fun as that sounded, he hadn't gone this far to blow it now. It was hard though since he hadn't eaten in days and was halfway to starved. He still passed by the food and stole up the back stairs. Since they, like the entrance, were meant for the poor working saps, they were narrow, dank and dark. Several of the wood steps were so rickety he had to walk on the balls of his feet so they didn't creak and give him away.

The sounds of voices and clinking silverware drifted from the main part of the house letting him know the wake was still under way. They were all honouring the deceased, Richard, the sorcerer whom they considered to be the best thing to happen to their society. He was their saviour, their leader and a hero to everyone. To Duncan he'd been a bastard, a viscous killer and his tormentor.

Worst of all, the sorcerer had been his slave master.

Duncan reached the top of the stairs. The object he was seeking now so close it was all he could do not to run down the hall to the room. It was only years of training and discipline that held him back.

Now in the main part of the house, everything around him was rich and classy, from the heavy oak walks to the red, plush carpet that nearly swallowed up his black boots, muffling his footsteps. There were large portraits lining the hallway and despite his haste, Duncan still stopped at one and studied it.

It had been of his master, the sorcerer who was now being mourned by the crowd down below. Even though Duncan knew the man was dead, he still shivered under the hard, penetrating stare of the painting. The artist had captured Richard's appearance perfectly, from his cruel thin smile, long grey hair and light blue eyes. How many times had he looked into that same face right before he was forced to endure yet another punishment? Panic clawed at the insides of Duncan's chest as he stared at the picture, irrational fear making him shake from head to boot.

"You're dead and you don't control me any longer," Duncan whispered to the painting. He pulled the sides of his black leather jacket tighter together, as if to form a protective barrier.

It was stupid to stand there and have this one-sided chat, but he couldn't make himself move forward until he'd proven he could stare down the sorcerer, even if it was just a paint and oil replica of him. After several seconds, Duncan felt some of the fear and anxiety leave his body, the dragon in him came to life for the first time in a decade. Not much, just a little bit of shifting and it let out a long sigh of relief, as if it knew that their suffering was almost over.

It was comforting, that small bit of movement. It let him know that, despite having his *dragon's eye* taken and used against him, he hadn't lost the other half of his heart. His dragon form was buried, yes, but it was there just waiting to be awoken again, after ten long years of being held down.

But to do that he had to get his *dragon's eye* back. Which is why he'd come here. It sure as hell wasn't to stop and gawk at pictures on the wall.

Even through his resolve, Duncan felt his gaze drift to the last painting in the hallway. It was of the sorcerer's son, Trent. Even though they'd met several times over the years, he'd only spoken half a dozen words to Duncan.

For a while he'd though it was because Trent was a rich, snobby nancy. Then Duncan had slowly come to realise that Trent was just as much a slave as he was. Sure Richard didn't hold his life essence like with Duncan, but his hold on his son was just as strong, pinning his son down with hard discipline and a firm controlling hand. He made sure everyone around knew what a disappointment his son was too. Trent was one of those rare individuals who still believe in being honorable and always doing the right thing. To Richard that was a personality fault and he'd done everything he could to break it.

Duncan raised a finger to lightly touch the picture. Where his father was cold and hard, Trent had a warm sensuality that had always intrigued him. With dark brown hair, deep blue eyes and a body that had just the right amount of muscles, he turned heads of both sexes. The most endearing thing about him though, was he didn't realise his appeal and went through life not knowing the affect he had on others.

There was a reserved almost shy aura around him that made Duncan want him all the more. So many times he had to stop himself from reaching out to touch the sorcerer as they passed each other in hallway. To stop himself from seeking out the male, just so he could hear the soft tones of his voice. To accidently brush against him, so he could inhale his warm scent. Duncan shook his head as he brought his hand down. Even if Trent noticed him there could never be anything between them.

Sorcerers and dragons made war not love.

Finally reaching his destination, Duncan found himself frozen in place again. Before him stood the massive black door that led into Richard's private bedroom. His gut clenched at the memories of all the punishments he'd endured in here. Whippings, beatings and being forced to grovel on the ground, begging for forgiveness. To anyone else this would look like just another room. Lavishly decorated, yes. Dangerous and forbidding, no. But then again, they wouldn't have been through what he had.

"Just open the damn door and get what you came here for before you find yourself some other sorcerer's bitch," he growled to himself, he knew it was only a matter of time before some other asshole stumbled upon the *dragon's eye* and realised what it was. He had to get to it first, before he found himself under some other sorcerer's control. The self-pep talk helped and he managed to force himself to open the door.

Despite the fact Richard was dead, his bedroom remained as always. Rich mahogany furniture, deep, red bedding and more of that damn fluffy carpet. Some would call the room tasteful and even comforting, but they would be wrong. Duncan knew better because he'd seen some of the horrors that'd taken place here.

With a slight shake of his head, he pushed those memories to the back of his mind and rushed to the armoire. It stood so large and wide it almost took up the space of an entire wall, but he knew instantly what drawer to go to. At first it seemed like all the others lining one side of the piece of furniture, but when he pulled the clothing out of it and tapped on the back, a hidden compartment opened.

"Bingo!" he whispered, letting a triumphant grin spread out over his face.

For the first time in a decade he felt a small blossom of hope building up in his chest. His hands shook with excitement and a bit of fear too. After all this time of wishing and suffering, he half expected something to block his way to freedom once again. He was just starting to reach in when a voice interrupted him. "I should have known you would come."

Whirling around, hand going to his gun he found himself face-to-face with Trent. With a growl of frustration, Duncan pulled his weapon out and trained it on the man's face. Despite having the barrel of a gun pointing at him, the young sorcerer didn't show any fear, the corners of his mouth curled up into a smile, one dimple making an appearance on his cheek. It made him appear more endearing than usual and Duncan found himself nearly lowering the gun in response. Trent wore dark slacks and a matching dress shirt, showing he'd come from the wake. The clothes fit him nicely, accentuating his thin, yet muscular body.

"How did you manage to sneak up on me?" Duncan demanded. It wasn't easy to get the drop on a dragon shifter since they usually heard or smelled their opponents from several yards away. He'd even heard tales of some ancients who could detect trouble as far away as a mile.

"I transported here," Trent replied, simply.

"Impossible." Duncan tightened his grip on the gun and wondered what kind of game the sorcerer was playing. "Only the strongest of your kind can do that."

"I've been able to transport for years now, ever since I was eighteen." Trent shrugged, still acting like it was no big deal Duncan had a weapon aimed at him.

"Then how come I've never seen you do it?" Duncan challenged. He didn't add how he'd spent a lot of time watching Trent and it wasn't to see what the sorcerer could and couldn't do. From the first day he'd been forced to live at the mansion, he'd longed for Trent.

"Let's just say that my father controlled a lot more individuals than you." A flurry of expressions went over Trent's face; fear, pain and then anger. No sadness or regret, which Duncan would expect from someone who was still wearing all black and supposedly grieving.

"Well, I have to admit that's a pretty neat skill you got there, but you're not going to stop me from getting what I came here for." Duncan waved the gun even though he knew he'd never be able to bring himself to shoot Trent if it came right down to it. Not even if it meant he'd lose what he'd come here for — his very life.

"I'm not here to stop you from taking the *dragon's eye*," Trent said, his eyes growing soft. When Duncan didn't respond, too shocked to speak, the sorcerer continued, "I know what it really is and I don't blame you for wanting it. If someone had taken all my magic and basically my soul along with it, I would be fighting to get it back too."

"If you understand so much then why are you even here?" Duncan croaked. Fear and shock had made his throat suddenly dry.

"I came up to help you find it. That and to say goodbye." A slight flush appeared on his cheeks as he averted his gaze to the ground. "I know as soon as you get the *eye* you'll go back to your kind and I'll never see you again."

Now Duncan knew the punk was playing games. In all the time he'd known Trent, the sorcerer had never looked twice at him. "Just stand there and don't move. Make sure you keep your hands up too and don't even think about using magic," he ordered as he slowly took a step back towards the armoire.

Still facing forward, he twisted one arm behind him and reached inside the hidden compartment. When his fingers found nothing, but empty space, his heart clenched in horror and a cold sweat broke out over his entire body. Desperate now, despite the fact the truth was literally at his fingertips, he continued to blindly search the compartment. Nothing…nothing…nothing!

"Where is it?" he roared, thrusting the gun forward.

"What do you mean?" Trent seemed so genuinely perplexed Duncan almost believed him before reminding himself that all sorcerers were lying bastards.

"The *dragon's eye*, where did you put it?"

"It's in there." Trent gave a slight shake of his head as all the colour drained from his face.

"No, it's not," Duncan bit back around his clenched teeth. His finger caressed the trigger of the gun, but despite his rage he still couldn't bring himself to pull it. Perhaps the years in captivity had made him weak and now, even when he did get his *eye* back, he would be useless. That thought enraged him even more and he let out another roar.

"Calm down," Trent snapped, casting a worried glance over at the door. "Do you want to bring everyone up here? Even though my dad is dead his bodyguards are here and they're still carrying weapons."

"Good, because you're going to be needing them if you don't tell me where the fuck my *dragon's eye* is!" Duncan rushed forward so the gun was inches from Trent's chest.

"I didn't do anything with it, honest. I'd been planning on giving it back to you so why I would I take it?" Trent held his hands up in the *surrender* pose, panic making his eyes so wide they seemed to take up half his face.

"Bullshit!" Duncan spat. "Getting a *dragon's eye* is the biggest prize to all sorcerers. Yet you're going to stand there and tell me that you had these grand plans on handing mine back to me, like it was some great big fucking present wrapped up in a bow?"

"Yes." Trent's voice was sharp with exasperation. "Are you going to believe me or would you rather sit around arguing about this long enough for the guards to discover you?"

"I could just shoot you and then look for it. Cut out the whole arguing factor all together."

"You won't do that." Despite his brave words, Trent eyed up the gun nervously.

"Are you so sure of that?" Duncan challenged, trying his damndest to sound convincing.

"Yes, I am. You may be desperate, but you're still good."

"A sorcerer calling a dragon good. That's rich." Duncan gave a bitter laugh.

"It's true though." Trent looked up, his gaze so earnest it did strange things to Duncan's emotions. The sorcerer swallowed hard before continuing, "I've seen how, even with everything my father put you through, you always remained kind and caring to those around you. I'm unarmed and, unlike my father, I've never done anything to you. So no matter how bad you want your *eye* back, you won't hurt me for it."

"You're just trying to guilt me into lowering my weapon," Duncan scoffed. Sadly enough it worked. With a deep sigh, he dropped his arm and lowered his head in defeat.

"I'm going to look too, just to make sure you didn't miss it," Trent soothed as he slowly edged his way around Duncan. As he went by, their bodies brushed for one second and even though he was at his lowest, Duncan couldn't help but notice how nice it felt. He breathed in deep realising, not for the first time, how Trent had a sensual, unique scent. It was mix of herbs, oils and other plant life that sorcerers used in their spells.

"You're right, it isn't here. Something is seriously fucked up here," Trent said, his brow creasing in confusion.

"Yeah, some thief is running around with my magic and life force. I would say there is a lot fucking wrong with that," Duncan snarled as he ran a hand through his hair in frustration.

"But nobody except you and me should have been able to get through the spell I wove around it." Trent waved his hand over the compartment like he hoped to grab onto the elusive magic that had beaten his shield.

"You were protecting it?" The suspicious part in Duncan wondered if Trent was thinking of using the *dragon's eye* himself. Duncan had seen the guy in action when it came to using his gifts and he was so powerful at times he was scary. With the added magic Trent could get from the *eye*, he could be an even more dominant sorcerer than his father.

"Of course I was. I was going to give it back to you." Trent turned to look at him. Hurt marring his face. "You believe me don't you?"

Before Duncan had a chance to answer, the door flew open with a loud bang. Both men jumped and spun around in time to face half a dozen sorcerers. Duncan's heart dropped as he recognised them all as members of Richard's bodyguard team. Since he knew they would be out for blood, he instantly went on the defensive, raising his gun up.

One of the guards raised his hand, throwing off a magic bolt. It hit Duncan hard in the hand. He let out a cry of pain and felt his fingers go limp. A shock wave went up his arm, like he'd been hit with a brick. The gun slipped from his grip and went flying across the room.

"What in the hell do you think you're doing?" Trent asked the guards. His tone so hard and commanding it reminded Duncan a lot of Richard. He barely suppressed a shudder by reminding himself it was Trent and he'd never shown any signs of being anything like his father.

"Protecting you from this animal," the guard sneered, his lip curling up in repugnance. While sorcerers may covet the magic from dragons like Duncan, they still thought his kind was inferior and one step below dogs.

"Hey asshole, Duncan is in my protection." Trent gave the guard a dour look. "I took him on as my personal guard the day Dad died."

"You don't honestly expect us to believe that, do you?" The guard calmly reached inside his suit coat and pulled out a gun of his own.

"Why shouldn't you?" Trent asked, wearily watching the guard. Alarm bells, whistles and trains started going off in Duncan's head. Suddenly the group of sorcerers were starting to look a lot less like bodyguards and a lot more like assassins. He wanted to grab Trent and shove him behind him protectively, but he resisted knowing if things went down the way he thought they were, he would need all the help he could get.

"I guess it really doesn't matter." The guard shrugged as he raised the gun, the other sorcerers behind him did the same thing. "In fact it makes it so much easier for us to kill you both since you're together in one place."

"Shit!" Trent cursed as he waved his arm in one large circle, at the same time the sorcerers all fired.

Duncan cringed, waiting for the hit, instead he was amazed to see all the bullets freeze in midair. Shocked, he felt his mouth drop open as he gasped. Even though he'd spent a lot of time around magic, he'd never seen anything quite like this. Even the guards were frozen in place, except for their eyes. The pupils raced back and forth in panic and fear. In a different situation, he may have felt sorry for them.

"We need to get out of here," Trent announced, in a hurried manner.

"How long can you keep them like that?"

"Not long, which means we're going to have to travel my way." Trent walked in front of him, so they were facing each other.

"You don't mean—"

Trent cut him off, "That's exactly what I mean. I'm teleporting us out."

Before Duncan could argue, Trent grabbed him by the sides of the face and brought him down into a kiss.

The move stunned Duncan so much that it took him a few seconds to realise one of his greatest fantasies had come true. Trent's lips were on him. Then the sorcerer slid out his tongue and ran it along the seam of Duncan's lips and he really got into it. Using one hand to cup the back of Trent's head he brought him in even closer.

Duncan slanted his mouth over Trent, so he could get at him better and took control of the kiss. The sorcerer fisted his hands into the front of Duncan's shirt and parted his lips in an open invitation. Not needing another, Duncan slid his tongue inside Trent's hot mouth so he could finally find out what the man tasted like. For years he wondered, dreamt what his flavour would be and finally now he got his answer.

Honey and cinnamon. Nice.

His cock swelled as the blood roared in his head. *More.* Now that he had this one taste, he needed more. The bed was just feet away and Duncan's every instinct screamed at him to lead Trent there so he could quench the fire ripping through his body. He didn't even give a damn that they had an audience.

When a bright yellow light surrounded the two of them, at first Duncan thought he was having one of those sappy *stars and moon* moments that was in all those teen movies. Not that he'd ever watched one of those. Honest.

It wasn't until he felt some unseen force grab him around the waist and jerk did he understand that Trent and done just what he'd promised. He'd zapped them the hell out of Dodge.

Chapter Two

Even though Trent fought to keep the transportation smooth, he still lost his grip on Duncan when they popped in front of the safe house. Trent cursed himself for his lack of control, not because the dragon lost his balance and fell due to the not-so-smooth landing, but because the kiss of his lifetime had ended.

It was dark outside and Trent was thankful because it hid the embarrassment he felt burning his cheeks. What in the hell had he been thinking, kissing Duncan like that? He was lucky the dragon hadn't hauled off and hit him for it. Breath hitching in his chest, he cast a wary glance over at the man. There was nothing that said Duncan still might not attack him for getting frisky. Instead the man got up and calmly brushed dirt and leaves off his clothes as he looked around.

"Where are we?" he asked, in a neutral voice. Trent would have given anything at that moment to be able to clearly see his face. To gaze into those eyes that were so dark brown they were almost black. Black like the clothes he wore, he'd no doubt chosen the colour to blend in easier when he'd broke in. Back at the house, Trent had noticed how nice the cargo pants and T-shirt had moulded to the man's huge body. Most dragon shifters were tall and muscular and Duncan was no different.

Trent thought about all the times he'd dreamed of running his fingers through the man's short, raven hair. Of tasting his full lips right before he slowly peeled away his clothes so he could sample the rest of his body. From the moment he'd first seen Duncan there had been no other man who could even begin to compare. Having him so close, but untouchable all these years had been sheer torture to Trent.

"It's a safe house I set up in case I ever needed it." Trent didn't add that he'd bought it a year ago with the express purpose of using it if and when he ever managed to help Duncan escape. Even before his father had died, Trent had been finding a way to get the *dragon's eye* back.

"Why didn't you just zap us inside it?"

"I put anti-teleporting shields around it so nobody, not even me, can pop in." He turned and faced the non-descript ranch-style house, putting his magic feelers out. When he was satisfied that everything was undisturbed, he let out a sigh of relief. At least he had that going for him. He started for the front door, happy when Duncan followed without any coaxing.

"You said you knew what the *dragon's eye* was, but do you really know how it's connected to me?" the dragon asked, cautiously, like he was afraid of revealing too much. Trent tried not to let his distrust hurt too much.

After all if he were in the same situation, he might not be the most trusting either.

"Yes, it's what some would call your dragon soul, but in reality it's much more. It holds your magic, your ability to shift, who you are. Not only that, without it you can never go home because you are considered tainted and a danger to all involved since the sorcerer who has it can find you by simply using a tracing spell."

"It also holds my free will," Duncan growled. "Whoever holds it controls what I can and cannot do. While Richard had it, I was his slave. I had to do whatever he asked of me no matter how vile and terrible it was."

"What would happen if you tried to go against him?" Trent asked his heart breaking at the agony he felt coming from the man.

"I feel pain ripping through my body," Duncan whispered in a haunted voice. "They say some dragons have been driven mad from the agony of it. That's what must have happened to me, because I must be crazy to trust you since you're a sorcerer just like him."

Trent pulled up short, hurt slicing through him like a blade. "I may be a sorcerer but I'm nothing like Richard."

"Why are you helping me? What do you have to gain from all this?" Duncan demanded.

I'm doing it because I've stupidly fallen in love with you. Trent kept that damning confession to himself and instead said, "Because it's the right thing to do. I know you are missing your home, family and friends and I want to help you get back to them." He opened the door and went inside.

"But most sorcerers would jump at the chance to get a dragon's essence. I'm supposed to believe that you're willing to give up all that magic and power just because you're a stand up kind of guy?" Duncan asked, incredulously as he followed Trent inside and closed the door behind them.

"Not all of my kind are power hungry," Trent said as he reached around Duncan to lock the door. The dragon didn't shift to give him room so their bodies brushed together. Trent sucked in a breath and hoped that it wasn't obvious how hard his cock was. It had been that way ever since they'd kissed.

"Yeah, I could tell that when your buddies were trying to kill you," Duncan drawled as he rolled his eyes sarcastically.

"Richard's guards have never been friends." He felt the burn of bitter hatred as he remembered the *fun* the other sorcerers liked to throw at him. Beatings, emotional abuse and sometimes worse. In the beginning he'd used to run to his father for protection only to have Richard push him away and tell him to man up. Much to the head sorcerer's disappointment Trent had never developed a mean streak to match his guards. Lifting his palm, he muttered a protection spell.

"Are you sealing the door?" Duncan asked, turning his head to look at Trent. Since they were standing so close, the move made it so their lips were inches apart. Without meaning to, Trent breathed in deep getting a lungful of Duncan's smoky scent. It wasn't an unpleasant ashy one, but rather like the rich, warm aroma of a blaze coming from a fireplace. This led to thinking about how nice it would be to roll around on a rug, with nothing to warm themselves with but a crackling fire and each other.

Goddess, he really needed to get a frigging grip on his cock and emotions. He was here to help Duncan not continue pining for him. Before tonight the dragon had never said two words to him, let alone noticed he existed. Not once had he even hinted that he might be feeling the same attraction. Although he had seemed pretty into the kiss. Duncan had been doing just as much exploring with his tongue as Trent had.

"What are you going to do now?" Duncan's face grew soft with concern. "I have a feeling those guys aren't going to stop until they kill you and you can pretty much forget about asking any other sorcerer for help since you're associating with a dragon."

"I'll think of something. I always do." Trent licked his lips, still tasting a bit of Duncan on them.

"Stop that," Duncan commanded harshly. His eyes grew dark as his breathing grew harsh. Never had he looked so dangerous or so sexy before.

"Stop what?"

"Looking at me like that." Duncan took a step closer and leant down so his lips were inches from Trent's ear. The dragon exhaled, his breath teasing Trent's sensitive flesh. Nuzzling in even closer, the dragon whispered, "I can smell the desire on you and god help me, even though I know I should run the hell away from you, I can't. I like knowing that you want me as much as I want you. That you're feeling the same need."

"It's always been there," Trent gulped, nerves making his body tingle. "Since the day I first saw you. I just never dared let anyone know before tonight because if Richard knew I cared he would harm you just to spite me."

"You did a good job of hiding it. I had no idea how you felt." Duncan placed the softest of kisses on his neck. Trent let out a low moan as he tilted his head slightly to the side.

"I'll help you get the *eye* back, I swear it," he vowed as he brought his hands up to grip Duncan's hips. The dragon growled in approval as he thrust forward, his hard cock pressing against Trent's stomach. Holy crap, he was huge! Even through the thick layer of his pants, Trent could feel the long thickness of him.

"How are you going to do that?" Duncan gave his neck another kiss.

"If I have some of your blood I can scry for it," Trent panted as he tried to keep his sex addled brain focused. All that kept coming to him was the fact that his very large bed was just down the hallway.

"Will that be hard to do? I've heard of scrying for individuals before but never an object." Duncan put his hand on Trent's chest and started backing him up to the couch.

"Since the *eye* is basically a part of you it won't be too difficult. We'll just have to get a battle plan ready before I do it. A spell like that uses a lot of magic and it will let any sorcerers looking for me know right where I am." Trent grunted in surprise when Duncan gave him a shove, forcing him to sit on the couch. He looked up at the dragon wondering what he was up to. Duncan's face didn't reveal anything as he remained standing, looking bigger than ever as he towered over him.

"I know of a couple old friends I can call for help if you like," Duncan offered as he dropped to his knees in front of the sorcerer.

Trent opened his mouth in shock. Of all this things he'd been expecting this was rock bottom on the list. Then a terrifying thought occurred to him. What if Duncan thought he had to do this in order to get his help? Gods knew he wanted it, but not like this. He leant forward, cupping Duncan's cheeks in his hands.

"You don't need to do this because you feel like you owe me."

"Don't you get it?" Duncan replied, his eyes growing even darker from desire. "I've wanted to do this to you for as long I can remember. I want to suck your cock, not because I feel like I'm repaying you in some way, but because I can't go one moment longer without knowing how you taste — all over. I'm begging you to let me."

Too turned on to speak, he just nodded his head. It wasn't until Duncan had Trent's pants undone and was taking out his cock, did he come to his senses. Reaching a hand out to stay the dragon, he asked, "Shouldn't you call your friends first? In case it takes them a while to get here. Not that I don't want to do this. I do, I really, really do. We just don't have that much time to waste and I would hate for you to have your *eye* taken control of again because we were too busy playing around."

"Don't worry." Duncan gifted his with a lazy smile. "I already contacted them." He pointed a finger to his head. "All dragon shifters share a mental link."

"I guess that would come in handy. Probably a lot cheaper than cell phones too." Trent swallowed, realised that he was coming off as an idiot. Duncan didn't seem to mind though, he leant forward and gave him a brief kiss.

"So we have plenty of time to finally get to know one another. That is if you haven't changed your mind." Duncan gave a pointed glance to Trent's hand, which was still holding the dragon's wrist in a tight grip.

"There is no way in hell I'm going to change my mind." Trent let go and leant back against the couch, getting in a position where he could both be comfortable and still watch the action.

Duncan reached down and wrapped his fingers around Trent's erection. "You're so sexy right now," the dragon observed in a husky whisper. "Your cheeks all flushed and your eyes begging me to fuck you. I used to dream of you gazing down at me that way. It got so bad that I had to jack off in the shower on a daily basis, just so I didn't walk around hard all the time."

"Oh god," Trent moaned. His cock throbbed, clamoring for more attention and he dug his fingers into the cushion on the couch to stop from thrusting his hips up.

Duncan licked a slow lazy path along the tip of Trent's cock, but did no more. "Tell me you want this as much as I do," he demanded.

"You know I do," Trent gasped when the dragon flicked his tongue across him again.

"I need to hear you say it. All of it." Duncan grabbed Trent's balls and gave them a gentle squeeze.

"I want this as much as you do," Trent panted. At this point he'd do anything to get inside Duncan's mouth. Even yell out something he never dared admit before. "It's always been you I've wanted. I've tried to be with other men but I can't because the only one I want to fuck is you."

That seemed to be enough to please Duncan because he wrapped his lips around Trent's cock and took him in. Pleasure shot up Trent's spine as he arched his hips forward, wanting to get every single inch inside the dragon's hot mouth. The man put a strong hand on his leg to stop him from moving. Pulling back, Duncan gave him a hard, sensual glare that seemed to make his eyes glow in the darkness of the room.

"Oh no you don't," Duncan admonished. "This is my show. You just lie back and take it."

"Okay. Sorry." Trent bit his bottom lip. Never had he been so aroused before. The harsh dominance Duncan displayed was exactly what he'd always hoped he'd get from the man.

"I mean it. You're not even allowed to come unless I give you permission."

"Fuck," Trent breathed, almost blowing it and shooting off right then.

"That will come later," Duncan teased, a dark gleam covering over his face. Dipping his head, he took Trent's erection back in his mouth.

Still clutching at the cushions, Trent watched the action through his half-closed eyes. It was so erotic, watching his wet cock slide in and out of Duncan's lips. The dragon would alternate, sucking him hard before pulling back to run his tongue along the length of his shaft. It seemed like it went on for hours, Duncan continuing with his sweet torture, Trent fighting every inch of himself for control.

Finally it became too much and he started to beg, "Please, Duncan. I need to come."

That only made Duncan suck him harder, drawing in so deep, his cheeks hollowed out. It wasn't until he had been driven nearly mad that the dragon's strong voice floated through Trent's head, "*Now! I want to savour the sweet tang of your cum as it covers my tongue and slides down my throat.*"

Trent paused a second, shocked that the bond between the two of them was so strong they were actually sharing thoughts. Then Duncan sucked hard one last time and that threw Trent over the edge. With a loud groan, he released himself inside the dragon's mouth. Even though he was in the throes of the hardest orgasm of his life, he still couldn't tear his gaze away from the sight of Duncan's mouth working as he swallowed. It wasn't until every last drop was gone, that he let Trent's cock slide out from his lips.

Running his tongue over his full lips, Duncan stood up and held his hand out. "Come on, let's go finish this in your bed."

Trent didn't even hesitate for a moment before he reached up and laced his fingers with Duncan's.

Chapter Three

As Trent led the way back to his bedroom, he couldn't calm the hammering beat of his heart. While he wanted this more than anything, a part of him was afraid too. Not that he thought Duncan would hurt him with his massive cock, but that things would never be the same for either one of them again.

A lifetime of living under his father's iron will made it so easy for him to doubt himself. What if he couldn't live up to Duncan's expectations? What if he was a big disappointment? What if he wasn't good enough?

They had reached the edge of the bed and Trent paused, afraid to turn around. Duncan tugged on his hand and pulled him closer. Cupping his chin, he forced Trent to gaze into his eyes. "You will never disappoint me. Not when everything about you is already perfect," the dragon vowed, solemnly.

"You were still in my mind?" Trent asked, a deep burning sensation coming to his cheeks.

"I can't help it. It's like I'm locked into you and can't get out." He fanned his thumb along Trent's bottom lip before adding, "I don't think I want out either."

"I'm not going anywhere," Trent said before he grabbed the front of Duncan's coat and brought him in for a passionate kiss.

The dragon growled low in approval, the noise making a soft rumbling sensation against their lips. It still wasn't enough for him though. Trent wanted to feel Duncan's flesh against him. He yearned to caress, lick and learn every inch of that hard muscular body.

Since he still had his hands fisted in the opening of Duncan's coat, Trent started there. Never breaking off the kiss he slid it from the dragon and tossed it to the side. As soon as the coat hit the floor, Duncan went into a sexual fury, tearing at Trent's clothes. The mood proved contagious and soon they were both pulling and tugging at each other until they were both blessedly naked.

Duncan ran his hand down Trent's chest, leaving behind a heated path.

"I've waited so long for this moment," he said as his gaze drank in the length of Trent's body almost as if he was worshiping it.

"I have too. I still can't believe it's happening." Trent closed his eyes, savouring the dragon's touch.

"Hey," Duncan chuckled, suddenly looking younger. "I just got done giving you the blowjob of your life and you still don't think this is going down?"

"Sorry." Trent felt a flush come to his face. How many times was he going to blush today? "I'm just not used to getting what I want in life."

"Like you said, I'm not going anywhere," Duncan's voice rumbled in Trent's head.

This times they connected minds, it didn't seem odd to Trent anymore. Instead it felt like a gentle slide. Almost as if he'd been missing this all his life and everything was finally clicking into place.

Duncan lowered Trent to the bed and stretched out on top of him. Getting up on his elbows so they could gaze into each other's eyes, the dragon declared, "I don't know what will happen to us tomorrow and I can't make any promises. Even though I want more than anything for this to last forever, all I can guarantee is that we have now."

"It's already more than I'd ever hoped for," Trent replied as he reached up to caress the man's cheek.

Duncan groaned in approval as he swept down and started to kiss Trent, first the lips, then his face, down to his neck, until he travelled even lower. Soon he was back at his cock. This time he only lingered a moment before spreading Trent's legs over his shoulders, opening him up so he was more exposed.

At first Trent tensed. He'd never felt so open and vulnerable, then Duncan lowered his head and started to use his mouth on him and all worries quickly fled his mind. Trent arched his back, crying out in pleasure when he felt the wicked sensation of the dragon's tongue circling his hole. He made slow paths over the sensitive opening, his heated touch awaking nerve endings Trent never knew he possessed. Then Duncan plunged his tongue inside, slowly fucking him. Trent clawed at the sheets as he arched up, a strangled gasp bursting past his lips.

"The sounds you're making are better than any aphrodisiac," Duncan's told him via their new mental bond.

Before Trent could respond, Duncan slid a finger up his ass. Trent arched up again, crying out against the wonderful burning sensation of his body stretching to accommodate the intrusion. Duncan didn't waste time, adding another finger, scissoring them so Trent would be ready to take the width of his cock.

"Please Duncan, fuck me now. I can't wait any longer." Trent shook all over from need.

"Well, aren't you the eager one," Duncan teased, but he did slide his body up so his cock was poised at the entrance of Trent's ass. Moving his hips forward, he slowly slid in, his face a beautiful mask of passion as he closed his eyes with a sigh. Trent let out a choked sob as his walls were stretched almost to the point of pain. Not that he had any complaints, it was an exquisite hurt that he never wanted to end.

"Oh god, you feel so good," Duncan moaned as he started to fuck Trent in slow even strokes.

Trent wanted to answer him but he was too breathless from the wonderful sensation of Duncan's large cock filling him. So instead he let his groans do the talking for him. He gazed up at Duncan, awed marvelling at his strong beauty. His hair was slick with sweat and the sharp lines on his face were even more pronounced, yet he'd never looked sexier. It dawned on Trent that Duncan was trying to go easy on him. A wave of frustration went through him. After waiting so long for this, the last thing Trent wanted was small measures. He wanted to experience every bit of Duncan and his passion.

"Don't hold back on me," Trent gasped. "I want it all."

"I don't want to hurt you," Duncan bit out between clenched teeth.

"Don't worry, I can take all of you."

With a low growl Duncan started to move faster, harder, the sound of slapping flesh filling the room. Trent gripped the dragon's shoulders, his fingers digging into the hard flesh as he silently urged him on. It felt like heaven, finally having the man he lusted after so long, over him. Trent ran his hands down Duncan's back, loving the way the muscles clenched and flexed as he moved.

Even though he'd gotten off not too long ago, his balls soon grew tight to his body as another orgasm built up. After a couple more hard thrusts from Duncan, Trent gave in, hot jets of semen splashing on both their stomachs as he came. He cried out Duncan's name so loud, his voice grew hoarse. Through his sex haze, he could hear Duncan yell as he came too, his cock pulsating in Trent's ass.

After it was over Duncan collapsed on top of him. The man was heavy and his breath rasped in Trent's ear and the cum was starting to dry and stick to their bodies He didn't care though. All that mattered was he'd finally got to know how it was to be with the dragon.

"I am so fucked and not in a good way," Duncan declared in a slightly panicked voice.

Trent tensed up wondering if this was the part where the man realised he'd just made a colossal mistake and now it was time to dump the sorcerer before things got even more complicated.

"That's okay," he said, tensely. Inside his heart was breaking. "We never made any permanent promises to each other, remember?"

"No, it's not that, babe. I swear." Duncan pulled away, retreating to the edge of the bed. Not looking at Trent, he ran hands through his hair as he took in several deep breaths.

"Then what is it?" Trent sat up and wrapped the sheet around his waist. God, this was not how he wanted things to end. He'd been ready for a gentle parting. Even one of those fake *I'll call you in the morning* promises. What he hadn't been ready for was Duncan to act like the whole world was coming to an end because he'd slipped up and fucked a sorcerer.

So caught up in his inner pity party, Trent almost missed the words that came next. The ones that forever changed his life.

"I just realised I love you. I always have." Duncan turned to look at him, his eyes bright with tears. "How am I ever going to be able to give you up when it's time for me to go home?"

* * * *

The early rays of sunlight were just beginning to shine through the windows when Duncan slipped out of the warm bed and the comfort of Trent's arms. While he didn't want the moment to end, he could sense two of his kind approaching the house and it was time to come back to reality.

It sure did bite though.

As soon as he'd connected minds with Trent last night he'd realised how complicated things really were. They had mentally bonded at an intimate level that he'd never experienced before, not even with his dragon brethren. As a kid, he'd heard tales about how destined mates shared a special connection, one that no one else could breach. A once in a lifetime gift that the gods bestowed on a couple who were destined for one another.

He let out a short laugh. How ironic could things get? His mate was not only a sorcerer, but he was also the son of the very man who'd enslaved Duncan for all those years. It couldn't be helped though, his love for Trent combined with their mental link left no doubt in his mind that it was real.

Sliding on his jeans and shirt, he didn't bother with socks as he went to the door. In between bouts of lovemaking last night, Trent had told him that he'd made it so the shield would stay in place if either one of them opened the door from the inside and welcomed someone in.

Duncan could sense the two dragons were on the porch now, waiting to be let in. Since they knew he would already be aware of their presence, they didn't bother to knock. As he reached for the handle, he noticed his hand shook with trepidation. It had been a decade since he'd talked to anyone from back home. Too ashamed of what was happening to him, he hadn't even bothered with a call, email, or even a cheap postcard. For all he knew they could have written him off as a traitor and the pair could be here to execute him, not lend a helping hand.

Still, he had no choice. That was the song of his life and he was getting damn sick of listening to it. Steeling himself for whatever reception he would get, he opened the door. When he saw the two dragons on the other side, he couldn't hide his surprise.

"Nicolas," he breathed, feeling numb with shock. He'd never imagine one of his brothers would be part of the rescue mission.

Nicolas hadn't changed much in the past ten years. He had light brown hair that was collar length in the back, but still managed to fall into his face. While he had on the same type of faded blue jeans he'd always worn, he'd upgraded from rock tees to a long-sleeved button up shirt. The one thing that had changed was his eyes. Once bright blue and dancing with life, they were now dull and almost haunted looking. He just gazed at Duncan, his face cold and giving nothing away.

"Someone has some 'splaining to do," the other dragon sang.

Duncan smiled. He recognised that smartass tone anywhere. Mick.

The youngest of the dragon shifters' fighters serving under Brian, Mick had always been more mouth than brain and it looked like that hadn't changed one bit. Even his appearance was a giant 'fuck you'. From his jet black hair that he had styled into a faux hawk to the long row of earrings marching up the sides of his ears. He also had his lip and one of his eyebrows pierced. He wore baggy black pants and a T-shirt that had a dragon chomping on some poor knight.

For all the punk attitude about him though, Duncan knew it was all an act. He caught the way Mick's intense green-eyed gaze swept inside the house, looking for potential danger. Nor was it lost on him that the young dragon's hand was at his side, right by the holster that held his gun.

"Relax, it's all clear," Duncan told them.

"I'm sorry brother," Nicolas sneered, adding extra venom to the word *brother*, "but we're not about to take your word for that. We could smell a sorcerer in here."

"Trent is on my side. You have nothing to fear here, I swear it to you." Duncan stood aside and gestured with his arm. "Why don't you come in and check for yourselves."

Nicolas ignored the invite where Mick waltzed right in, his mouth already working again. "You'll have to excuse Nic's bad attitude. He's still a little miffed about you dropping off the face of the earth. Funny thing about family is they tend to be clingy like that. Which is why I'm so glad I don't have any."

"You call me Nic again and you won't have to worry about my attitude," Nicolas snarled, but Mick didn't seemed fazed by it. He just kept yammering away.

"So where have you been all this time? Brian and Nicolas looked for you for years before they finally gave up. Most of us thought you were dead, but not your brothers. They kept saying they *sensed* you." Mick made air quotes in the air while he said the last part.

Nicolas finally stepped inside and shut the door behind him. Both he and Mick jumped when they sensed the magical shield locking back into place. Narrowing his eyes suspiciously, Nicolas fixed Duncan with a hard glare.

"You want to tell me exactly what in the fuck is going on?" he snapped. "And you better not leave out one detail."

Duncan paused, not knowing where to start. Under Nicolas' penetrating stare he squirmed a bit, suddenly reminded that he was the baby brother in the family and up until he left, he'd always answered to his brothers. Always did what they said. Always came to them for help.

That was before that one major fuck-up that changed his whole reality.

"You guys hungry?" he asked, hitching a thumb towards the kitchen. "I'm starved and it's a long story. Might as well tell it to you while I'm making breakfast."

"I don't think—" Nicolas started, but Mick was already making a beeline to the kitchen. The dragon sighed, getting the same annoyed glare on his face that he'd directed at Duncan so many times when they'd been growing up together.

"Please." After so many years of being forced to beg, Duncan hated having to do it now, but he would do anything to get Nicolas to listen to him.

"Give me one good reason why I should?"

"Because we're still brothers and that has to count for something," Duncan tried, his gut clenching at the brief look of pain that flashed over his brother's face.

"It obviously doesn't or else you would have never disappeared on us," Nicolas returned between clenched teeth. But he did move forward to the kitchen.

"It's a really long story," Duncan said, as he went into the large, open kitchen and headed for the refrigerator. It was obvious that Trent hadn't redecorated when he moved in. Or at least Duncan hoped he hadn't because then he would have to have a serious talk with his guy about his fetish for apples and roosters. They were everywhere; the border, the curtains even the light switch was in the shape of a giant Macintosh. At least the table looked sturdy, plain and functional as Mick and Nicolas took seats.

"Just start from the beginning and make sure you don't leave anything out." Nicolas crossed his arms over his chest as he stretched his long legs out in front of him.

"My *dragon's eye* got taken." As he delivered that bombshell, Duncan pretended to be searching the inside of the fridge. Anything, not to have to see the looks of disappointment and disgust on the other dragons' faces.

"What? Who?" Nicolas stammered, sounding more shocked than pissed.

"A sorcerer named Richard had it and he used it to control me." Having found eggs and bacon, he finally forced himself to turn around. Instead of looking over at the table though, he instead directed his gaze to the food as he started cooking.

"I've heard of Richard. He's supposed to be pretty badass," Mick said in an awed voice.

"He *was* badass," Duncan corrected as he cracked the eggs into a pan. "The bastard died a few days ago."

"Did you kill him?" Nicolas asked. His tone was hard and didn't let Duncan know one way or the other what he was thinking.

"No, since he still had possession of my *dragon's eye* I wouldn't have been able to give him a paper cut let alone kill him. Believe me, if I could have, the sorcerer would have been dead a long time ago."

Nicolas sprang to his feet, letting out a loud curse as he pushed the chair away. "How in the hell did he get your *dragon's eye* in the first place?"

"One night I was out flying and Richard spotted me. When he challenged me to a fight, I was so young and cocky I didn't even think twice about taking him on. Right as soon as it started, I knew I was in over my head. His magic was so strong...so ancient feeling. I didn't even last five minutes." Duncan swallowed hard, feeling more like the failure than ever.

"Why didn't you come to us for help?" Nicolas started pacing. It was trait of his, to do that whenever he got pissed, scared or upset.

"I couldn't leave his side. Whenever I got more than a mile away from him my body would seize up in pain. The same thing would happen if I ever tried to disobey an order."

"You could have found a way. Called us, sent a message out with someone, contacted us mentally, anything!" Nicolas shouted.

"And tell you what? That I had failed my ruler and people, and now I was some sorcerer's bitch? I know how things work, I would have been seen as ruined and then Brian would have been forced to take action to get rid of my dishonour. I didn't want to put you guys through that," Duncan yelled back.

"Things aren't like when Dad ruled. Brian never would have punished you for something like that."

"No, but he would have made damn sure that I knew how much of a failure I was." Duncan winced as soon as he let those damning words slip through his lips. Nicolas paused mid-pace to give him a look of hurt.

"Do you honestly think he would hold something this big against you?" Nicolas' voice cracked just a bit.

"Let's just say I thought it would be better if you guys never had to know about it," Duncan replied, all the anger draining from his body to be replaced by numb acceptance. It would only be a matter of time now before both Nicolas and Brian kicked his ass to the kerb.

"You stupid fuck." Nicolas crossed the room and captured Duncan in a rib-crushing hug. Still holding on he continued, "We're your brothers and no matter what, we'll always be there for you. You could never disappoint or dishonour us. We love you, you jackass."

Chapter Four

It wasn't until halfway through breakfast that Nicolas asked the question Duncan had been dreading. "So if the sorcerer that had your *dragon eye* is dead, then where is it now?"

Duncan admitted, "I don't know." Taking a deep breath, he told them about what had happened since last night, deliberately glossing over his relationship with Trent. Not that he was ashamed of it. He just didn't know how his brother was going to react to him hooking up with the son of the very sorcerer who had ripped their family apart. Unfortunately, Nicolas was too sharp to let anything slide by his attention.

"So, why would Trent help out a dragon shifter?" he asked, his gaze way too knowing. "There has to be something in it for him."

"He told me he was helping because it was the right thing to do." Duncan shrugged, trying hard to be nonchalant about the whole thing.

"Sure," Mick drawled, "he's just helping you out of the goodness of his heart no other reason. Forget that he's going to become a pariah amongst his kind, that they'll probably bring him up on charges and take all of his possessions as punishment. Good 'ol Trent is helping because, well, gee willikers, it's the right thing to do."

"I see your sarcasm hasn't changed," Duncan deadpanned as he resisted the urge to lunge across the table and wrap his hands around the idiot's throat. Knowing Mick, not even having his air supply impeded would shut him up and he would keep talking away during his strangulation.

"If you want to know my motives then why don't you just ask me?" Trent asked softly as he walked into the room.

As one Mick and Nicolas looked over at the sorcerer. Their gazes travelled over his wrinkled clothing, to his messed up hair and the light stubble burn on his neck. Duncan groaned. It was going to hit the fan for sure now since it didn't take a genius to figure out what he'd been up to the night before and with whom.

"You're fucking Richard's son?" Mick spat out incredulously.

"He has a name, Trent, and what he and I are doing is none of your damn business." Duncan jumped to his feet and moved over to stand in front of Trent, protecting the man in case the others decided to attack.

"Have you lost your mind?" Nicolas asked, glaring viciously at Trent. "For all we know this guy may have been the one who stole your *dragon's eye* and he's just playing around and leading you by the dick."

"Trent would never do that," Duncan defended.

"How do you know that?" Nicolas challenged.

"I know him and that's not how he is." Duncan balled his hands into fists, close to using them.

"Why? Because he's a good lay?" Nicolas cocked his head to the side as he let out a harsh laugh.

"No, because he cares for me and I care him," Duncan admitted. The hell with hiding it anymore, now that the fact that they had been together was out, may as well let the whole cat, whiskers and all, out of the bag.

"Really?" Nicolas' outrage echoed through the kitchen.

"Yes, it's true," Trent added. "There's nothing I wouldn't do for Duncan."

"A dragon and a sorcerer mixing it up. Brian is going to piss kittens over this one." Mick flashed a cocky grin.

"Look, I know you're upset about this," Trent reasoned in a smooth voice, "but we really don't have time for this conversation now. It's only going to be matter of time before whoever did take the *eye* says the spell that will bind Duncan to him. We need to get to it before that happens."

"Fine," Nicolas agreed in clipped tones. "But if I suspect for even one second that you're up to something, I'll take you out so fast you won't even see me coming."

Duncan turned on his brother, a low growl rumbling in the back of his throat. "Don't threaten him."

"It's okay, he's just trying to protect you." Trent put hand on Duncan's arm.

"Let's just get this done and over with." Nicolas sighed and looked at Trent. "Duncan says you can scry for the *eye*?"

"Yes, I just need a few minutes to get set up." He walked out of the room, but not before giving Duncan one last comforting squeeze.

"I hope you're right about this," Nicolas grumbled after he'd left.

* * * *

Trent kneeled in front of his black ceremonial bowl, aware of the penetrating stares of the dragons boring down on him. Trying his best to ignore them, he poured in the purified water and said a few words to bless it.

"What's that for?" the one Duncan had called Mick asked. He leaned in so close that his breath caused ripples across the surface of the water.

"It will help me see where the *eye* is," Trent explained as he tried to keep his annoyance in check.

"How?" Mick reached out to touch the bowl. Right before his finger made contact Nicolas smacked the young dragon on the back of the head to make him stop. Mick stepped away, rubbing the back of his head.

"Why don't you watch and see?" Nicolas ordered. His voice was still as cold as his eyes and Trent could feel the hostility rolling off the dragon. It wouldn't be a far stretch to guess that if it weren't for Duncan he would have attacked Trent long ago

"Right, sorry." Mick shot a chastised grin over to Trent.

Picking up his athame, Trent held it over the water. The blade on the knife was black and it seemed to glow from his magic. While he normally would never use it for cutting flesh, today's spell was different.

"It's time," he said softly to Duncan. The dragon nodded and held his hand out, palm up.

Trent held the knife over the dragon's hand and hesitated, that all-too-familiar feeling of doubt plaguing him. There was so much riding on this and they only had one chance. If he were to fail now, not only would he be letting down the man he loved, but he would be alerting all the other sorcerers of their presence for nothing.

"You can do this. I believe in you," Duncan whispered, brushing a kiss on Trent's cheek.

Trent slowly nodded, warmed from the inside out by his words. While to anyone else it may have seemed just a couple of sentences, to Trent they meant everything. For the first time in his life, someone trusted and supported him. With one flick of his wrist, he made a shallow cut in Duncan's palm. When the dragon hissed in pain, Trent muttered an apology as he tilted Duncan's hand to the side so several drops of blood fell into the water.

"What now?" Nicolas asked. He was still eyeing Trent, with suspicion.

"Now you guys stand back and let me do all the work," Trent replied as he dipped his finger into the bowl and started to stir, counterclockwise.

The blood mixed and swirled within the water making a red whirlpool that continued to move even when he took his finger out. Mumbling the spell under his breath, Trent stared deep into the water and let the magic take him over.

The water shimmered and then black blobs seemed to grow and bubble within before they gradually took on the shapes of objects. A brocade chair, a tall window with heavy curtains on them, a tall shelf lined with leather bound books and then a large, oak desk. Trent sucked in a breath. He knew this place. Had seen it so many times while he was growing up. Hell, he'd played cars on the Oriental rug that took up the centre of the room.

It was the study in his uncle's house.

He sucked in a breath slowly letting it out with a whisper, "Adam."

His uncle suddenly came into sight. His lips pressed in a cruel smile so reminiscent of Richard's that Trent started to shake in fear. The sorcerer even had the same white blond hair and cold eyes. Fuck! This was not good, not only did Adam know he was being watched, but he was somehow managing to confront Trent even though they were miles apart.

"I knew it was only a matter of time before you came sniffing around," Adam sneered, his voice warbling through the magic connection.

"What's going on? Why do you want the *dragon's eye*?" Trent demanded, his chest tight with fear. How would Adam have known where the eye was hidden? Only he, his father and Duncan knew. There was no way Richard would have ever shared that information with his brother either. Not with the way they were both so power hungry and distrustful of each other.

"Oh, this thing?" Richard cocked a brow as he slowly held up the stone. It looked like an uncut emerald and there was a bright, gold streak inside, that spun inside the gem in lazy circles. Trent knew it was Duncan's magic — his dragon — that was trapped inside and he felt a cold rage fill him.

"Give it to me," Trent ordered, trying to match the cool commanding tone his father had used so many times. "As Richard's heir it rightfully belongs to me."

"Now, let's not be coy, boy," Adam clucked his tongue. "We both know that's not the real reason you want this.

You don't think I haven't noticed how much you've been lusting after that dragon."

"Damn you, return it me!" Trent roared.

"You want it so bad? Come and get it." Adam threw up his arm and Trent felt himself being forced out of his trance. The magical blow was so hard that it threw him back into his conscious mind and across the room at the same time. Just before his head slammed into the doorframe, he could hear Duncan's cry of alarm.

Not waiting for anyone to help him, Trent scrambled to his feet and went over to the bowl. Letting out a feral yell, he swept his arm to the side, sending the bowl flying. Water sprayed all over, hitting wall and furniture, but he didn't care. He was too busy fighting the nausea and anger inside him.

Duncan wrapped his arms around him and Trent allowed himself to be pulled to the man's large chest. "What is it, babe? What did you see?"

"My uncle Adam has it." Trent took in several deep breaths, taking in Duncan's warm scent. It helped calm him down some.

"So why are you wigging out so much? Were you guys close or something?" Mick asked.

"Far from it," Trent scoffed as he pulled back so he could look at the other dragons. "He was no more loving than my father."

"So why the big drama party?" Mick gestured the mess on the walls.

"Because he just realised what this was all about," Nicolas said grimly, his jaw clenched in fury. Duncan must have caught on though because he let out a low hiss as his face became a mask of worry.

"Well someone fill in the idiot here. What in the hell is going on?" Mick threw his hands up in disgust.

"It's never really been about the *eye* or Duncan. This whole thing is a trap to draw Trent out," Nicolas growled.

"Why?" Mick cocked his head to the side.

"Because now that Richard is dead Trent has the potential to become the most powerful sorcerer around," Duncan said, his pained gaze looking down at Trent.

Trent turned his head, not being able to face the hurt and anger he might see there. Because of him Duncan might never get his *eye* back. All along it had been his fault that Duncan wasn't already free and back home. The dragon probably despised him now.

"He was the one that sent the guards to shoot me." Trent felt all the pieces fall into place.

"How exactly did your father die?" Nicolas asked.

"There was a fire. Everyone thought it was from a dragon attack." Trent clutched his stomach, feeling sicker with each passing second.

"Damn, are you saying that Adam killed his own brother just to get some power? That's fucked up even for a sorcerer." Mick shook his head.

"And now he's holding *my* brother's magic as bait," Nicolas spat.

"Not for long." Trent straightened up. For the first time ever, instead of letting the anger drag him down, he embraced it. He might not have had the courage to stand up for himself in the past, but for Duncan he would do anything. Even die. Levelling a steady glare at the dragons he said, "Everyone get ready. We leave in ten minutes."

Chapter Five

Since they knew Adam would be on the lookout for dragons flying in from the sky, Trent transported them all to the house, one by one. He saved Duncan for last. As he felt the sorcerer's arms around him, he closed his eyes and breathed in Trent's special scent. Wishing there was some way to put off the oncoming battle.

"As soon as you pop me in there I want you to leave." Duncan ordered, his chest tight with worry.

"I can't, you'll be no match for Adam's magic without me," Trent refused, showing a stubborn streak Duncan had never seen before.

"We can handle it. It's not like we haven't killed off plenty of sorcerers before," Duncan growled, fear making him sound angry.

"You're in this mess because of my family so I'm the one who's going to get you out of it."

Duncan reached down so he could cup Trent's chin, looking into the sorcerer's eyes, he declared, "I would rather be in captivity again than lose you."

Instead of answering him directly, Trent gave a wry smile and said, "I love you so much. I just wanted you to know that."

Before Duncan could respond the sorcerer transported them. They landed in a grove of trees behind a house that was even more garish than Richard's had been. This one had a pair of stone lions and a set of gargoyles. It was large and foreboding, almost like the evil from the sorcerer inside had bled into the architecture.

"This place looks creepy," Mick observed, echoing Duncan's thoughts.

"Agreed," Nicolas nodded. "We all know that they're waiting for us so how do you think we should approach this?"

"We don't have much time." Trent lifted his face into the wind. "I can sense magic building up in there. A lot of it. It could mean Adam has already started the spell."

"So what do you suggest?" Nicolas asked, shocking Duncan by actually asking a sorcerer for advice.

"That you guys stay back here," Trent answered.

Before Duncan could stop him Trent transported out of the grove of trees. He reappeared a second later at the end of the long walkway that led to the front door of the house. Before they had left, Trent had changed into a long, black trench coat and it now billowed slightly in the wind as he stared up at the house. He didn't turn back to look at them, instead keeping his gaze directed to the door as he waited for Adam to come out.

"No!" Duncan roared as he lunged forward. Nicolas tackled him and held him down.

"Let's just give him a second and see where he's going with this," his brother said, as he struggled to hold Duncan.

"He's going to let himself be killed to save me."

"That's his choice. Who am I to deny it?" Nicolas grunted when Duncan elbowed him in the gut.

"He's just not some sorcerer. He's everything to me. I love him," Duncan bellowed. He strained his neck to look up and saw that Trent wasn't there anymore and the front door of the house hung open like some ominous sign.

Digging deep, he found a surge of strength and managed to throw Nicolas off him. Scrambling to his feet, he ran to the house. Behind him he could hear Nicolas yelling, but he didn't even turn around, too intent on finding Trent.

He got to the door and ran through, shouting Trent's name. A couple of guards came charging and just as they were approaching, shots rang out. Both the men dropped, twin expressions of shock on their faces. Stunned himself, Duncan turned and saw Nicolas and Mick behind him, Glocks in their hands.

"What are you waiting for? Go get your sorcerer," Nicolas said.

"Yeah, we'll take care of things out here," Mick added, a cold mask slipping over his usual cocky face.

Nodding his thanks, Duncan took off running. He didn't know how, but some part of him sensed exactly where Trent was. At the end of the hallway a double set of doors were closed. He threw them open and found himself in a study.

Trent and Adam stood on opposite sides of the room facing off. With a growl, Duncan lunged at the older sorcerer. Just as he was within striking distance, Adam threw up a hand and muttered a few words. Duncan found himself frozen in place, unable to move to help, but still able to see the horror unfolding. No matter how hard he tried to fight and struggle, he was hopelessly locked in place.

"I still can't believe you would risk yourself for this," Adam chided as he held the *eye* up.

"Some things are worth dying for," Trent replied in a calm voice.

"So you would actually try to cross swords with me magically all for some dirty dragon?" Adam face twisted in disgust.

"Yeah, I would." Trent nodded slowly as he let his hands hang lose at his sides.

"I have so many other *dragon's eyes* in my collection. It's amazing that this one would hold so much value to me. With it I can finally eliminate all my threats and take hold of leadership of the sorcerers." Adam held the stone aloft and looked thoughtfully into it.

"If you want to get rid of me, fine. We don't have to do battle, Uncle. Just give me the *eye* and I'll leave and never come back," Trent bargained.

"Fine, if that's the way you want it then...here." Adam tossed the *eye* to Trent.

Duncan caught the sly grin on the evil sorcerer's face and knew it was all a trick. He tired to shout of a warning, but his jaws remained locked in place. Trent took his gaze off Adam, intent on catching the *eye* as it sailed towards him. His fingers were just closing around it when the loud rapport of a gunshot echoed through the room.

Duncan screamed in his head, bone-crunching grief going through him as he saw Trent's eyes grow wide in shock. Trent clutched his chest with his empty hand as he fell to his knees. Raising his blue-eyed gaze to Duncan he mouthed a silent apology as blood gushed between his fingers and splattered over the Oriental rug.

"You honestly don't think I would actually just give it to you?" Adam spat. "If I had let you live then I would always have to worry about you coming for me some day. You filthy dragon lover."

With that final insult Adam transported out of the house. As soon as he was gone the force holding Duncan vanished and he could move again. Letting out a cry of despair he ran forward just in time to catch Trent before he collapsed face first into the carpet. Cradling the sorcerer in his arms, Duncan's stomach clenched with despair when he felt the man's blood soaking through his clothes.

"No, no, no," he chanted. Maybe if he said it enough times it would be true. He could hear the sound of footsteps as Nicolas and Mick came in, but Duncan was too caught up in his grief to even look up.

"It's okay. It was worth it," Trent replied weakly as he fumbled around and placed something warm into Duncan's hand.

Duncan didn't have to glance down to see what it was. The surge of power through his body as his magic returned to him let him know it was his *dragon's eye*. A roar rebounded through his head as his dragon form merged back with him, awakening after being tamped down for far too long.

It should have felt exhilarating. He should be celebrating. Instead he found himself weeping as he held Trent close and gently rocked him.

"We can still save him," Nicolas' voice cut into his grieving.

"How?" Duncan asked, tears falling down his face.

"We could have our healers help him. With their magic they may be able to save him."

"Brian would never allow a sorcerer around his people." Duncan shook his head. *Trent can't be dying. Not someone as pure of heart as him. It's not fair that he should die when the crud of the earth like Adam still get to breathe.*

"You let me worry about Brian," Nicolas ordered. "You just fly and get Trent to our house as fast as possible."

The smallest spark of optimism flared inside him. Maybe, just maybe there was hope after all. Still carrying Trent in his arms he ran out of the house and into the front yard. Jumping into the air, he did something he hadn't done in a decade. He shifted into the form of his emerald green dragon.

He was careful to keep his hold on Trent so the man ended up being held gingerly in the claws of the dragon's front feet. Cresting high into the sky, he banked hard to the left and flew as fast as he could. He only hoped he made it in time. Even though the family home was also in Michigan, it was far up north, in the heavily wooded area of the Upper Peninsula and hundreds of miles away.

* * * *

By the time Duncan made it to the large farmhouse that he'd grown up in, Trent was barely breathing. His heartbeat was almost nonexistent and his skin was pasty and cold. Duncan swooped down and landed, shifting at the same time. As he returned to human form, his clothes were still in place and he didn't even fumble once as he shifted his hold on Trent.

Brian stood at the door. A giant hulk of man with dark hair and eyes, he always looked fierce. Today was no different and Duncan only hoped he would be willing to help. Rushing to the top step, Duncan bowed as best he could while still holding Trent.

Keeping his head lowered he spoke in the ancient language of their kind, "Please, lord of mine. I beg that you help he that is mine."

Cursing, Brian replied in English, "Shit, I can't believe I'm doing this, but bring him inside."

* * * *

Trent slowly woke up, the first thing greeting him was sunlight filtering through a window and illuminating a strange room. Moaning, he brought his hand up to scratch his bare chest and touched the puckered skin left from a gunshot wound. *Shot? When did that happen?* How was that possible and why wasn't he still in pain? Suddenly the memories came back in a rush.

He'd got the *eye* back for Duncan, but his uncle had shot him in the process. He also vaguely remembered Duncan being in his dragon form and then there was nothing. So how was he still alive? Scanning his gaze around again, he took in his surroundings.

He was in a bedroom that was small but comfortable looking, with warm coloured walls and neutral wood furniture. There was one window off to the side that was covered in white, gauzy curtains, making the room seem even homier. His gaze finally settled at the foot of the bed and he saw Duncan.

He was sound asleep, his large body crammed into a straight backed chair. Even though his head rested on the bed, the dragon looked uncomfortable. He must have sensed Trent looking at him because he instantly came awake.

"How are you feeling?" Duncan asked, his warm tone full of concern.

"Confused as hell," Trent admitted as he drank in the sight of the dragon. "Where am I?"

"You're in our family home," a deep voice said. For the first time Trent noticed there was a man standing in the corner of the room. How he'd missed him being there was a shocker given how huge the guy was. Tall and broad, he reminded him of Duncan since they both had the same coloured hair and eyes.

"Dragons healed me?" Trent was so shocked his question came out a little high-pitched.

"It was our honour." Brian formally bowed his head.

"It was?" Trent shot an incredulous look over at Duncan who had the nerve to smile at him.

"Yes, it was," Brian continued, his stoic face revealing nothing. "While my brother may have been an idiot to think we would turn our backs on him for one stupid mistake, we still love him. We will never be able to repay our debt to you for helping him find his way back home to us."

"No problem," Trent replied. While he should have been elated that he was alive, a part of his heart was still breaking. He knew that as soon as he got better he would have to leave and then he would never see Duncan again.

"I know we have no right to ask any more of you, but I find that I need your help with something." Brian came closer to the bed.

"What?" Trent asked suspiciously, wondering if the request was going to be that he leave Duncan alone.

"Duncan informed me that your uncle claimed to have more *dragons' eyes*. Do you think it's true?"

"Sure, that would explain how he was powerful enough to murder my father," Trent responded, a little thrown off by the line of questioning.

"Do you think you would be able to track them down?"

Trent sucked in his breath in surprise. That had been the last thing that he thought the shifter leader would ask him. "Yes, it may take some time, but I could do it," Trent replied, honestly.

"Then I was wondering if you would be willing to stay on and help us with that?"

Trent had to stop himself from going slack jawed in shock as hope bloomed in his chest. "Are you serious?"

"I think it might be a good move to have a sorcerer on our side for once." Brian smiled. "It may help even things out for us."

Trent looked at Duncan. The dragon was gazing at him with such love in his eyes and suddenly he realised that they would be able to find their happiness together after all. "Of course, I'll stay," Trent replied, his face spreading into a happy grin.

"I thought you'd say that," Brian chuckled, as he leant over and ruffled Duncan's hair. "I guess we'll put Duncan in charge of watching over you."

"It'll be a tough job, but I think I can handle it," Duncan drawled in that sexy way of his.

Brian rolled his eyes, but there was a smile on his face as he left the room.

Once they were alone, Duncan got up from the chair and sat on the edge of the bed so they were closer together. Bending down, he placed a tender kiss on Trent's lips. "Thank you for getting my *dragon's eye* back. But if you ever do anything like that again, I'll skin you myself," the dragon, the tender expression in his gaze at odds with his words.

"Don't you realise I'd do anything for you? I love you." Trent steeled himself, still expecting the rejection he'd always endured up until now. Instead he got another kiss, this one longer and hotter than before.

"I love you, too." Duncan's fingers slowly trailed up Trent's side, the skin-on-skin contact making him shiver in desire.

"You're just not saying that because I got your *eye* back are you?" Trent asked, only half teasing.

"No, I'm saying it because you're everything to me."

Duncan gave him another kiss, but this time he didn't pull back, going so far as to shift his body so he was stretched out over Trent. With a satisfied sigh, Trent threaded his fingers through Duncan's hair and started to return the passion in earnest. Duncan growled in approval before he plunged his tongue into Trent's mouth.

A whimper slipped past Trent's lips, surprising and embarrassing him. The last thing he wanted was to come off as desperate or needy. Duncan didn't seem to mind though, instead rolling his hips forward so their cocks ground tighter.

Jolts of pleasure shot through Trent. Even though the healers had taken off his pants, Duncan still had his on and Trent, could feel the heat of the man's erection soaking through. It wasn't enough though, he wanted so much more. Eager to feel Duncan's flesh, Trent tugged at the dragon's shirt.

"Off," he grunted, too dumb from need to be more eloquent.

Duncan sat up just enough to take off the shirt. Once he'd tossed it to the side, he got back into position. Trent moaned in appreciation as soon as their bodies rubbed together. Duncan buried his nose in the crook of Trent's neck and inhaled loudly.

"Do you have any idea how fucking good you smell?" he asked before his tongue darted out to lick Trent's throat.

"Not nearly as good as you do," Trent replied with heartfelt honesty as he tilted his head to the side .

Duncan started to suck and nip at Trent's skin, no doubt leaving behind a mark. At the same time Duncan's hand slid in between their bodies, his fingers not stopping until they were at the top of his boxers Duncan slipped his hand in them so he could grab Trent's aching cock. Trent bit his bottom lip so hard he tasted blood, as he fought back a cry of passion.

"Why are you holding back?" Duncan asked, his voice laced with amusement.

"I don't think we need to broadcast what we're doing to your brothers and friends." Trent didn't think the house was that big. If he were to yell, he felt pretty sure they'd hear him.

"Do you honestly think you can last without screaming at least once?" Duncan pulled back so he could gaze down at Trent.

Trent's heart thumped madly in his chest as the saw the desire and smoky promise in the dragon's gaze. The throb in Trent's cock grew more intense. It certainly didn't help matters when Duncan ran his thumb over the tip of Trent's cock. Little traitor that it was, his dick jerked like it was in full agreement with Duncan. A triumphant gleam went through Duncan's eyes as he started to slowly pump his fist up and down Trent's shaft.

"Please, Duncan, I can't take much more of this." Trent jerked his hips up into Duncan's hand. Already his balls were drawn tight to his body and Trent knew he couldn't last much longer.

"Begging already?" Duncan cocked his head to the side, a wicked smile playing on his full lips. "We're just getting started, too. If you're already this close to the edge, I'll have you screaming for sure before I'm done."

A soft cry of disappointment ripped from Trent's throat when Duncan moved his hand. He thrust his hips up in a silent plea, but Duncan ignored it, instead he started to kiss his way down Trent's chest. He stopped long enough to nip and suck on one of Trent's nipples, making his squirm in pleasure.

Trent bit his bottom lip, determined to keep his vow of silence. It was hard though, especially when Duncan gave him another not-so-gentle love bite. It was the sweetest of tortures as Duncan continued to take his time, like there was no rush and they could stay in bed all day if need be.

After one last lick, Duncan started to move lower, his lips raining kisses down Trent's abdomen. When he got to Trent's boxers, Duncan lowered them just enough so he could get at Trent's cock.

Trent bit his lip harder, even though he knew it was coming, he almost lost control and yelled when he felt the hot sensation of Duncan's lips on the tip of his cock. A strangled sob still found its way out, loud, but not so much so that it would carry outside of the room.

To his dismay, Duncan only gave his cock a few licks. Before Trent had a chance to voice his disappointment, though, Duncan got off the bed and started to strip. Tent watched, breath catching in his chest as every inch of Duncan's glorious body was revealed. Just seeing all those hard muscles made the ache in his cock more unbearable and he had to reach down and stroke himself to ease some of the ache.

"Oh no you don't," Duncan tsked. "If you're going to find any pleasure it's going to be from my touch alone."

Trent gasped in frustration, but he obeyed, letting go. As soon as he did, Duncan reached down and slowly peeled off Trent's boxers. As soon as they were off, Duncan tossed them to the side and gazed down, his stare seeming to burn into Trent.

"Turn over," Duncan commanded, his voice harsh with passion.

Confused at the strange order, Trent obeyed, moaning as his cock became trapped between his stomach and the mattress. The urge to rub into it and relieve some of the pressure was strong, but Trent resisted, remembering that Duncan had forbade self-gratification.

Trent tensed as he waited to see what Duncan had planned. The mattress dipped as the dragon climbed back on, his legs on either side of Trent's knees. Giving a low hum of approval, Duncan ran a palm along one side of Trent's ass.

"If you could only see how hot you look right now. All flushed and trembling with need," Duncan observed before he slowly trailed a finger down Trent's crack. When Trent tried to thrust back into his touch, Duncan gave him a light slap on the hip. "You're a greedy little thing. I think I'm going to have fun teaching you some manners."

"Sorry," Trent panted, shocked he could talk at all. "I just need you."

He closed his eyes and forced himself to hold still as Duncan continued to caress his back and ass. It was then he realised Duncan was deliberately driving him to the edge, so he'd lose control. Trent also realised that there was no way he'd be able to keep himself from screaming when Duncan finally did take him.

A smile passed over Trent's lips when he heard the drawer to the bedside table open. It slammed closed and a few seconds later he felt the cool, wet sensation of Duncan's lubed fingers. Duncan took his time, slowly circling Trent's hole before finally sliding one finger in.

"Is this what you wanted?" Duncan asked, as he slowly started to work the digit in and out.

"It's a start," Trent moaned. He tilted his ass up, tucking his knees under him, so he could rock back against Duncan's finger.

"You moved," Duncan admonished as he added another finger. "I should punish you for not listening, but you feel so good right now, I just can't bring myself to do it."

"Can't help myself." Trent moaned as Duncan's finger curled inside him, brushing against his sweet spot. He had to bite the pillow to hold back the cries of pleasure as he fisted his hands in the bedcovers.

When Duncan removed his fingers, Trent nearly sobbed in relief, knowing what was coming next. Sure enough, a few seconds later he felt the hard press of Duncan's cock. Trent scrambled, lifting his ass up even higher, trying to speed things along, but Duncan put a hand on his hip to still him.

"Easy, babe," Duncan cooed.

"Can't. Need you," Trent whimpered, not even able to speak full sentences anymore.

It seemed to be enough for Duncan though, because he finally entered Trent in one hard thrust. That was finally enough to make Trent scream. Even though he tried to muffle it with the pillow, it still rang out loud enough to carry through the whole house.

"Looks like I won," Duncan observed with a wry chuckle.

"Yes, I'll make sure to make you up a nice certificate of achievement later. Now I just want you to fuck me," Trent growled.

Duncan laughed again, but he did have mercy and start to pound into Trent in hard, quick strokes. Trent cried out again, this time not even bothering to stifle it as he braced his arms into the mattress so he didn't fall forward. His cock was leaking, his balls tight and aching as a fine sheen of sweat coated his body. It felt so good, so right and before he knew it he felt himself nearing his limit.

"Please, touch me. I need to come," he begged.

Duncan reached around and fisted Tent's cock. His grip was hard and warm. Trent opened his mouth to thank him, but all that came out was a loud groan. He knew he wasn't going to last long. Not being as jacked up as Duncan had made him with foreplay.

"Need to. Going." Trent stammered, once again reduced to broken declarations.

"Go ahead, come for me," Duncan said.

Trent threw back his head and did just that, his cock pumping as cum washed over his stomach and Duncan's hand.

"Love you so much," Duncan moaned right before he found release too, his cock throbbing against the walls of Trent's ass.

"*Mine.*" Duncan's voice growled in Trent's head.

"Yes, god yes," Trent replied, using the same mental path.

After it was over, they both stayed in position for several moments, catching their breath. Finally Duncan rolled off Trent and laid on his side. He tugged at Trent's waist. Trent got the message, going to his side too, his back to Duncan's chest. When Duncan wrapped his arms around his waist and held him tight, Trent let out a low hum of pleasure.

Trent knew they should get up and take a shower to clean up, but for a moment he was content to just be in the embrace of the man he loved more than life itself. The man who was his soul mate.

"Is it true?' Trent asked, still not ready to believe that everything was finally working out for them. "Do I really get to stay?"

"Yes, babe and now that I got you I'm not going to ever let you go." Duncan gave him another kiss. "I may have my *dragon's eye* back, but you have my heart."

About the Authors

Carol Lynne

An avid reader for years, one day Carol Lynne decided to write her own brand of erotic romance. Carol juggles between being a full-time mother and a full-time writer. These days, you can usually find Carol either cleaning jelly out of the carpet or nestled in her favourite chair writing steamy love scenes.

D.J. Manly

I write not only for my own pleasure, but for the pleasure of my readers. I can't remember a time in my life when I haven't written and told stories. When I'm not writing, I'm dreaming about writing. Eroticism between consenting adults, in all its many forms is the icing on the cake of life but one does not live by sex alone. The story of how two people find love in spite of the odds is what really turns me on.

A.J. Llewellyn

A. J. Llewellyn is the author of over fifty published gay erotic romance novels. He lives in California, but dreams of living in Hawaii. Frequent trips to all the islands, bags of Kona coffee in his fridge and a healthy collection of Hawaiian records keep this writer refueled. A. J. loves male/male erotica, has a passion for all animals (especially the dog, the cat and the turtle). A. J. believes that love is a song best sung out loud.

Jaime Samms

Jaime writes, romance, fantasy, urban fantasy, shifter stories about men, about life, about love. Her work is populated with mostly men, most of whom are into each other, and yes, we do mean into each other. You can find plenty of free reading on her website.

She also reviews for Dark Diva Reviews, mostly the same types of stories, and will happily spout her opinion on the books she reads to her kids, who she home schools. Finally, she's occasionally gainfully employed. She writes for the love it, and hopes to pass on that love to her readers, her kids, and anyone else who comes along.

Serena Yates

I'm a night owl who starts writing when everyone else in my time zone is asleep. I've loved reading all my life and spent most of my childhood with my nose buried in a book. Today I like exploring the different cultures, beliefs, attitudes and preferences that exist on our planet in my stories. My characters have a tendency to want to do their own thing, so I often have to rein them back in. The one thing we all agree on is the desire for a happy ending.

Jambrea Jo Jones

Jambrea wanted to be the youngest romance author published, but life impeded the dreams. She put her writing aside and went to college briefly, then enlisted in the Air Force. After serving in the military, she returned home to Indiana to start her family. A few years later, she discovered yahoo groups and book reviews. There was no turning back. She was bit by the writing bug.

She enjoys spending time with her son when not writing and loves to receive reader feedback. She's addicted to the internet so feel free to email her anytime.

Stephani Hecht

Stephani Hecht is a happily married mother of two. Born and raised in Michigan, she loves all things about the state, from the frigid winters to the Detroit Red Wings hockey team. You can usually find her snuggled up to her laptop, creating her next book.

All of the above authors love to hear from readers. You can find thier contact information, website details and author profile pages at http://www.total-e-bound.com.

Total-E-Bound Publishing

www.total-e-bound.com

Take a look at our exciting range of literagasmic™
erotic romance titles and discover pure quality
at Total-E-Bound.

Printed in Great Britain by
Amazon.co.uk, Ltd.,
Marston Gate.